biography of Vesta Tilley.

sceptre

Sara Maitland

HOME TRUTHS

The lines on p. 66 are by Hilaire Belloc, from *Cautionary Tales from Children*; the lines on p. 113 are by Michelene Wandor, from *Poems for Eve and Lilith* (Random Century, 1990); the lines on p. 114 are from *No Strange Country* by Francis Thompson; 'Suspice', the prayer on p. 120, is traditionally ascribed to St. Ignatius Loyola; the book referred to on p. 187 (*Peasant Consciousness and Guerilla War*) is by Professor Terence Ranger; and the stories on pp. 188–190 are reproduced by courtesy of the members of Class IV B & C of Daramombe Mission School, Zimbabwe and their teacher, Ann Howard.

First published in Great Britain in 1993 by Chatto & Windus Ltd

First published in paperback in 1994 by Hodder and Stoughton, a division of Hodder Headline PLC

A Sceptre paperback

British Library C.I.P.

A CIP catalogue record is available from the British Library

ISBN 0 340 609680

10 9 8 7 6 5 4 3 2

Printed and bound in Great Britain for Hodder and Stoughton, a division of Hodder Headline PLC, 338 Euston Road London NW1 3BH by Cox & Wyman Ltd.

For Ros

and with special thanks to Anni Holmes with whom I climbed Mount Nyangani, Zimbabwe, on 8th February 1990, and came down again safely.

Zvino kana ruoke rwako rworudyi richikugumbura rudimure ururase nokuti zvinotova nane kwauri kuti mutezo wako mumwe chete ufe panokuti muviri wako wose upinde mumoto usinggadzimi

(Matthew 5:30. Shona Bible)

At the foot of Mount Nyangani, the highest mountain in Zimbabwe, there is a green notice board. In letters of gold it carries fourteen instructions for would-be climbers:

1. No lone person to attempt ascent.
2. No child under ten years of age to attempt ascent accompanied or not.
3. Young persons aged between 11 and 17 years must be accompanied by *responsible* adult at ratio of not more than four to one responsible adult.
4. All members of parties to be within sight of each other at all times on the mountain.
5. Follow the track indicated by cairns and painted arrows to beacon and return by same route.
6. Do not leave track to explore as danger of quicksands, concealed crevices and potholes.
7. Do not attempt ascent if low cloud, mist or rain in vicinity.
8. If enveloped in mist whilst on the mountain make immediate descent via indicated track.
9. Ensure you have suitable protective clothing and necessities irrespective of prevailing conditions.
10. If climbers should become lost remain in position make group conspicuous and await search.
11. Do not attempt climb after 1430 hours, minimum time to beacon and return is 3 hours.
12. Always inform a non-climber of return time or inform park officer of departure *and return*.
13. Full costs of searches will be borne by lost persons.
14. No fires, plant picking or litter please.

Joyful Masvingise, only half laughing, had added another:

15. Do not mock, insult or abuse the mountain.

When they climbed Mount Nyangani on 2nd February, the Feast of Candlemass, Clare Kerslake and David Holland managed not to disobey rules 2 and 3. Clare and her family later found themselves forcibly abiding by rule 13. The rest they broke.

Underneath the list of rules, still in gold and heavily underlined the notice reads:

> *These regulations have been made necessary due to recent tragedies. Do not underestimate the potential danger of this mountain.*

Three days later they found Clare, battered, bleeding and with her right hand smashed, nearly twelve miles from the approved route up the mountain.

They never found David at all.

People had disappeared before on Mount Nyangani, had disappeared and never been seen again, dead or alive. It was to these disappearances that the notice referred with its cautious euphemism – 'recent tragedies'.

There are three explanations for these disappearances.

The country is rough, wild, dangerous; there are fissured uncertain rock faces, deep crevasses and cliffs of fall. The mountain is subject to sudden and violent changes in the weather; thick mists emerge from nowhere, blanketing the path, dissolving perspective. Storms crash without warning on the steep rock faces. People are foolish and do not keep to the clearly marked paths; lost in the mists, it is too easy to slip, to stumble, to fall. The best searches cannot guarantee to cover every inch of this terrain. Nor will the wild, the water and the scavengers, leave a body intact and tidy, waiting conveniently for its searchers. Some of the soldiers who searched for David and Clare had once had good reason to rejoice in the complexities of that mountain range: passes through it had been the way out of Rhodesia into Mozambique, to train for the new Chimurenga; and had been the way back into Zimbabawe to fight for freedom and the ownership of the land. They knew the place could not be searched properly, although they searched it diligently.

Mount Nyangani is also the home of the Ancestors; the ancestral spirits who welcomed and protected their own boys, the *vanhu ve'ivu*, the Freedom Fighters, but who did not love the irreverent strangers who now climbed the mountain for amusement, who worshipped white gods and had neither respect nor knowledge. Only half laughing, Joyful Masvingise had warned them not to mock, insult or abuse the mountain; for its fierce spirits would take a large revenge, would steal away the people who treated them without respect and exact a punishment that was neither life nor an easy return to the home of the ancestors, the place of spirits.

As the eastern mountains had sheltered the freedom fighters, so they could also shelter other less noble warriors, the *banditos armados*, the part pirate, part political, part crazy gangs who might perhaps indulge in a little kidnapping for reasons of their own.

All three explanations for the disappearance on Mount Nyangani are offered with equal force. Nature, gods and politics compete here in the lands above the escarpment, beyond the frontier, compete for power, for the right to define destinies.

In David's case there was a fourth possible explanation. The young soldiers who found her at the foot of a pile of shattered rocks and carried her to the road reported that, although barely conscious, Clare had muttered repeatedly that she had killed David.

They asked her what had happened; over and over again they asked her what had happened.

And she said, 'I don't know.' Or, 'I can't remember.'

Of course this was not all, was not enough. They pressed her for better answers. She pressed herself for better answers.

Apart from the things that she could not remember, there were also the things that she could not say.

She had heard Chirikudzi, the mermaid spirit of the Pongwe, singing.

The mist had been filled with the dark voices of the ancestors whose language she could not speak.

She had wanted David to be dead.

She was asked so many times what had happened that it became a story; even in her own mind it was a story with a beginning and an end, even if neither she – the narrator – nor they – the hearers – knew what the end was. It had the structures of a narrative, the urge towards tension and resolution. There was a secret and surprisingly powerful need to leave out everything that did not fit into the story.

'Tell us,' the police said.

'What happened?' asked her brother Joseph, and Peggy and Joyful and David's insurance company and her own dreams.

'I don't know,' she said. 'I don't remember.'

'Begin first thing that morning,' they all said.

'Tell me,' Anni was to say, when six months later they were sitting together high up on the hills above Skillen. They would lean against the rock; it would be very quiet, but not silent, the wind moving the grass. Anni rarely acted like an older sister, but she would then.

'Tell me slowly, from the beginning.' She would not look at Clare, but at the eagles over Cranach Head.

'I don't know the beginning,' Clare would say. 'I don't know where to begin.'

'Clare,' Anni would say patiently, gently but inexorably, raising the binoculars to her eyes and still watching the distant circling of the birds around the shoulder of the dark mountain. 'Begin with that morning. Begin where you can remember.'

All the questioners had different agendas.

The insurance people wanted David to have killed himself, or she to have killed him. The flat was valuable, the endowment mortgage assigned to her. Next best they wanted him to have

4

been not killed but kidnapped, possibly alive somewhere in the Mozambican interior, to turn up again for propaganda or ransom.

The Zimbabweans, mostly, wanted to be able to demonstrate that Zimbabwe was safe; a safe place, a happy place for tourists to come and spend their western currency, not a place where people disappeared mysteriously off mountains and were never seen again. But not all: some wanted, or almost wanted, to demonstrate the continuing presence of the spirits, to prove that the western currency-spenders were as nothing compared to the ancient power of the ancestors; that a young man and a young woman riddled with western decadence could not with impunity climb the steep sides of Nyangani and mock the older laws. Some wanted more attention paid to the constant incursions of the MNR from over the border, wanted to prove yet again that South Africa was actively engaged in destabilisation, undermining the brave attempts of the young country to be a model for Africa, the home of the brave.

The soldiers and the villagers who scoured the wild terrain for three weeks, searching for some sign simply wanted to find one, wanted their persistence and determination to pay off – they wanted at the very least some mangled remains to be found in some crevasse, some gnawed bone, some bloody garment, some evidence that although the mountain was difficult and dangerous, they were wiser and stronger.

Most of Clare's family wanted proof that Clare had not shoved David off the edge of the fissured rock, because they did not want the person they loved to turn out to be that sort of person.

They all wanted to know. So they asked questions, and over the months Clare knew that she did not give them good enough answers.

They would ask demandingly and then when she said she could not remember they would reassure her that post-traumatic amnesia was not unusual, was normal, that everything would be all right.

They cut off her right hand and it was left behind when she left Africa.

She had wanted him dead and he was dead.

10th August

A T THE BEGINNING of the second week in August, Clare found
herself, without ever having quite planned it, on King's Cross
station waiting for Anni.

After she had been brought back from Zimbabwe, Clare was
in the hospital for over three months. It had been warm and safe
there. Her family came to see her.

'Goodness,' said one of the nurses, amused and kindly, 'what a
huge family.'

'You haven't seen half of them yet,' said Clare and felt again
the mixture of pride and embarrassment that the number of her
siblings had given her in childhood.

'How many of you are there, then?'

'Seven. Seven children; and Mummy and Daddy of course; but
Louise, who came today, is my brother's wife.'

'Oh, I thought perhaps she was a friend of yours.'

Clare realised that it was her family not her friends who visited
her.

Her mother came regularly, catching an early train, spending
the morning with Clare and then going off to see her own friends,
or to visit Felicity or Anni or Louise. Once Clare was out of danger
and moved to the orthopaedic ward, Hester set about the business
of getting everyone organised. She brought chocolates for the old
woman in the next bed; she spent time cheering up a young man
the other end of the ward who had lost both legs in a car crash;
she helped the nurses with recalcitrant patients.

'Your Mum's amazing,' the nurses said.

'Yes,' said Clare wearily.

'Oh God!' said Anni loudly, overhearing this on one of her
regular flying visits. She brought books which Clare could not find
the energy to read and she brought a calm and patient attention, a

willingness to listen that frightened Clare. But now they laughed together at their mother's energy. 'Oh God, it's lucky really that she's so moral, otherwise she'd be the last of the great *grandes horizontales*.'

Almost before Clare had realised that she had lost her hand, Hester had completed her researches into amputations and artificial limbs and arranged the best possible treatment for Clare. Clare was now the lucky possessor of a state-of-the-art myeloelectric prosthesis. She knew Hester had put a great deal of work into acquiring this high-tech gadget for her. She felt guilty about criticising Hester, and she was not able to tell anyone that she loathed it. So now she smiled weakly with Anni at the thought of her mother as a courtesan.

But although Clare had always been closest to Anni, it was Felicity who came to visit most often, usually complaining how hard it was for her to find the time.

'It's OK,' Clare said, when Felicity informed her yet again of the difficulties and labours of fitting Clare into a day already full of Alice and her commitments to the Deaf Association for whom she worked. 'I'm wonderfully petted, you don't have to come.'

'Don't you want me to?' Felicity fidgeted her soft hair back into the velvet band she wore and fretfully rubbed her thin face and sounded almost sulky, unlike herself. Clare tried to feel concern, but the cotton-wool protection of the hospital cut her off from everyone else.

Joseph came late in the evenings and also frantically busy; hastening elsewhere, a couple of times in a dinner jacket, but with magazines, more books and helpful advice about lawyers and insurance companies. Even Tom came once, looking awkward and revoltingly healthy; and Caro, his wife, sent flowers, not bouquets from shops, but bunches and swathes from her own garden delivered, dripping wet and sweet-smelling, by a string of friends who just happened to be passing through London that morning. Caro and Tom had another baby, still tiny and unsuited to hospital visiting, but they sent funny cards, faintly vulgar jokes toned down a little in recognition of her invalid status.

Ceci also sent cards, though not funny ones; nor Clare noticed, touched by the delicacy, religious ones: floral pictures and some rather lovely photographs of the convent's cloisters and gardens. Clare saw without curiosity both the austerity of the Carmel and the fact that one of the sisters at least had an extremely good camera. The rest of her family always looked at the pictures with interest; it was strange to see the pale fine wooden floors of Ceci's home in pictures when in the fifteen years she had lived there none of them had ever seen the reality, had ever passed through the plain doors into Ceci's enclosure.

Even her mother would pick up Ceci's cards and inspect them, almost greedily. The black-and-white photographs of the plain brick cloister, the sparse cells, and the path down the middle of the garden, gave a physicality to Ceci's life which they could never learn sitting in the cosy visitors' room and talking to Ceci through the wide hatch in the wall.

'Where's Ben?' she asked her mother once the days had settled down into a pattern and she became aware that she had not seen him.

'Oh. Oh, darling, parish life – you know how hard it is for priests to get away,' but even in the swaddled safety of the hospital she could sense an evasion.

'Where's Ben?' she asked Felicity, and Felicity blushed.

'Have you seen Ben?' she asked Joseph.

'Not recently.'

'What's going on?' she asked Anni. 'Where on earth is Ben?'

'Monastic servitude.'

'What?'

'We're not meant to tell you, it's supposed to upset you; but he got himself in trouble and his Bishop resigned him, and packed him off to the monks to repent of his wicked ways.'

'What sort of trouble?'

'Guess. Gay clergy trouble. Unamusing pictures in our favourite Sunday rag.'

'Hasn't Mummy fixed it?'

'Oddly enough, now you mention it, no. But she's been pretty hectic; a couple of days later you fell off your mountain and gave the Sunday tabloids something else to bother with. Mummy's been fixing that. And your hand, of course.'

'Sunday tabloids?'

'What did you expect?' Anni sounded brusque. She had been caught out. She rallied and said teasingly, 'You can hardly be a well-known society photographer and get spectacularly lost, and lose your glamorous financier lover, *White Mischief* style, and announce to your rescuers that you killed him and expect the noble British Press to pay no attention at all.'

She looked down and saw that Clare had been startled out of her passivity.

'Do you really not remember any of this?'

It wasn't that she did not remember, it was that she had not thought. She did not want to think. She closed her eyes and listened for the dark music that lurked waiting beneath the pain.

'Post-traumatic amnesia . . .' she muttered. She had heard it said enough times in the darkness. It was a safer thing to say than 'Chirikudzi took him.' Or, 'I'm glad he's gone.'

Anni was baffled.

'If it's any comfort to you, the general view of the family and, it looks increasingly, of the police, is that it's rubbish. The sort of thing anyone might say after being lost up an African mountain for six days.' The heavy irony that had punctuated Anni's adolescent conversations still emerged sometimes in moments of embarrassment.

But Clare was not listening. She drifted in the comfortable peace that the hospital provided, where there were priorities greater than the whole outside world; priorities like what was for lunch and how physiotherapy was.

Physiotherapy. Physiotherapy was the worst part of being in the hospital. It was physically and mentally demanding, at a time when she wanted nothing to be asked of her. It was also the stuff of nightmares, that met and clashed with Clare's own dark dreams and restless sleep. Physiotherapy, learning to use her new hand, forced her to recognise what had happened to her and at the same time made it more difficult to distinguish what was real and what was imagination. The real owner of her electronic prosthesis, her new hand, was a bright young computer wizard. She tried not to think of him as Dr Frankenstein, and of The Hand itself as Frankenstein's monster, yearning, angry and malevolent.

Dr Frankenstein adored his creation and wanted Clare to prove herself worthy of it. He made her work. As she got physically better he made her work harder. The new hand functioned by picking up the electronic impulses from the severed nerves of her lower arm and converting them, via solenoids, into movements that were supposed to replicate the movements of her original hand. But it was not so simple. Actions which had become entirely involuntary, which were patterned into the right hemisphere of her brain, sets of spacial responses, had to be consciously transferred. The Hand's creator and lover thought this challenge ought to be exciting for her, he thought Clare should worship at the shrine he had built for his modern godling. Clare hated him and she hated The Hand.

'How fascinating,' Joseph said one evening, picking The Hand up from the bedside cabinet where she had inadvertently left it. She gave him a lethal stare, and he put it down again almost guiltily.

The one thing she did learn speedily was how to stop anyone ever mentioning her handlessness and its consequence in her presence.

It was only when she had left the hospital and emerged into the world that she had realised how safe she had been in there. Outside, her own daily life felt nightmarish. She was an amputee, a cripple, stared at discreetly and pitied; or completely ignored, invisible in the embarrassment of strangers. At the same time she was also a possible murderess, stared at surreptitiously by those who knew her and were curious about what had happened to David.

She slowed down; exhausted, weakened, she was no longer able to resist the loving force of gravity exerted by her family. Until, at the beginning of the second week in August, she found herself almost to her own surprise, on King's Cross station waiting for Anni. The tickets for both of them were in her bag, together with the seat reservations.

Clare and Anni did not look like sisters when they met on the station, slightly too early in the morning for either of them. They hardly even looked as though they belonged together. They were both tall, fair women, but they appeared to come from different worlds. Clare saw Anni as she came up the steps from the tube, and felt immediately both aggressive and secretive about the fact that she had come in a taxi. Until she saw her older sister, Clare had not given a moment's thought to how she was dressed, but instantly she felt artificial: made-up, overdone, self-conscious. She knew that Anni had genuinely given the matter no thought at all. Anni was wearing her usual jeans and T-shirt; she had a slightly battered backpack and a plastic carrier bag. Clare noticed for the first time that Anni's hair was going grey; not elegantly silver, but faded, dusty looking, as though someone had emptied an ashtray over her head. Practically the first thing that Clare had done on leaving the hospital was to go to her hairdresser, an old and trusted friend, and have her highlights put back in; they had shaved her head after the accident and the new hair was still fluffy and babyish, but it was fair still, and deftly and discreetly blonded and immaculately cut. Despite the grey hair and the scrubbed, slightly lined face Anni looked younger than Clare, with a sort of cheerful innocence, somehow childlike, not at all appropriate to a schoolteacher; to the head of the science department of a large girls' comprehensive. Clare felt a pang, and did not know whether it was envy or pity. Anni never seemed to bother with the things that haunted Clare.

It turned out, however, that she was no more oblivious than Clare was.

'Dear God,' she exclaimed as Clare and she located each other and celebrated the moment with a customary hug, 'that is the most outrageously beautiful jacket I have ever seen. Whatever is it made of?'

Clare felt an immediate cringing guilt, compounded by knowing that Anni's admiration had almost certainly been sincere and innocent.

'It's not new, you know,' she said almost apologetically and then, brazening it out, 'Distressed silk.'

'Distressed? If I was that silk, distress would be the last of my emotions. Distressed Louise, I should think.'

There was a joyful cosiness in the bitchery. Joseph's wife would indeed be envious; her envy would join Anni and Clare together regardless of the fact that Clare felt guilty paying more than a month's worth of Anni's salary for a jacket, and Anni, had she known how much the jacket had cost, would have been appalled.

They looked at each other, grinning almost shyly. Since Clare had left the hospital she had not seen so much of Anni; there was a gap, one they were both happy to accept. The hospital had shifted the balance between them too much.

Once they had been so close, so tightly bound together that it had annoyed other people; now they had to forge bonds of intimacy by disparaging their sister-in-law, and laughing at their relatives.

'I have the tickets and Mummy, I need hardly tell you,' Clare said, 'has reserved our seats.'

'I'm surprised she didn't ask the guard to keep an eye on us.'

'We don't know that she hasn't yet.'

They both grinned again. Hester had, as always, organised everything impeccably. She had rung Clare ten days before to reassure her that the tickets were in the post and would arrive in good time.

'Mummy, I'm still perfectly capable of buying my own ticket.' On the phone she had allowed some of her exasperation and tiredness to spill out.

'I know you are, darling, but is Anni?'

'Yes.'

'I'm sorry. Am I interfering?'

She wanted to say 'Yes' again, but did not.

'It was meant to be a present, that's all. I know you're only coming up because I want it, so why should you pay for it?'

Why indeed? 'Thank you,' she said, and could hear her own infantile sulkiness. 'What shall I bring?'

'Fresh veg would be nice. As usual. No, better if Tom does that. Fresh veg from central London is a bit silly isn't it?'

'Fruit?'

She bought a box of avocado pears, fresh basil and oregano, and two pineapples. More for herself than for anyone else she also bought several packets of coffee: Lavazzo in shiny hard packets, red and silver. They were easy to pack, necessary to her comfort – her mother had never seemed able to understand about

coffee, happy with powdered instant or a bitter, over-boiled perco-
lated brew.

Anni tossed her rucksack on to the trolley which already held
Clare's suitcase; she turned the trolley deftly and together they
walked down the platform looking at the carriage letters. So they
had walked along railway platforms in their teens again and again,
neat then in school uniforms, or almost as neat in their family
uniform of jeans and Barbours, and more alike than they now
were. Sometimes, especially when Felicity and Cecilia were there
too, the four of them, all fair, all so nearly the same age, all
carrying themselves with that innocent arrogance that they had
inherited from their mother, had attracted considerable attention:

'Are you all sisters?' people would ask, smiling to cover their
curiosity.

'Yes,' they would say, giggling.

There were only four months between Anni and Clare; barely
two years between the four of them. Sometimes curiosity would
win over discretion.

'Which of you are twins?'

'None.'

Gleefully they would watch their interrogator try to work it
out. On some lucky occasions the questioner would become
embarrassed. It was a rigid point of honour between them never
to explain. Felicity and Cecilia might have allowed good manners
or even real kindliness to overrule this code, but Anni and Clare
were adamant.

Now they would not even have been taken for sisters: Clare so
glamorous, Felicity so neat, Anni so dowdy, and Ceci, her blonde
curls shaved off and half her face invisible behind the wimple;
and yet, after a quarter of a century, Clare and Anni could walk
easily along the platform at King's Cross, still buoyed up by the
memory of their unusual relationship, able to ignore the differences and difficulties that had come between them. They found
their seats and Anni said, 'Bags I face the engine.'

Clare replied, 'It's not fair, you always face the way you want.'

'That's because I'm the oldest. You could have bagged it first.'

'I don't care; the train turns round at Edinburgh and I won't
swap.'

Anni grinned, 'You're meant to say "yah boo sucks".'

'Do they still say that? Kids I mean.'

'Lord no. They say "Piss off" . . . if you're lucky.'

Despite the goodwill it was a ten-hour journey from London to Inverness, and ten hours is a long time to sit in a public place with someone who used to share your bedroom, your dreams and your secrets, and with whom you have not had a sustained conversation since you lost your hand and your lover halfway up a mountain in Africa.

It was more than the events themselves: the accident had forced changes on them, on their established feelings and their well-tested ways of dealing with each other. Now compassion and pity for Clare's losses tempered Anni's fierce teasing; now defeat and fear modified Clare's compassion and pity. Now Hester's instructions to sensitivity and carefulness, which both of them, knowing their mother, knew would have been issued, made Anni the older sister again, a rôle she had never relished and had deliberately abandoned. Clare felt that although her jacket was indeed beautiful and Anni had admired it with simple sincerity, it was only an outer layer, and inside she was ugly. She had no right hand and no lover, and could not say for certain how she came to lose either.

Somewhere, six thousand miles away, under the shadows cast by a different sun, a midday sun that stood directly overhead and reduced shadows to tiny pools of blackness that coiled like black cats around the feet of their owners instead of fleeing away northwards. Somewhere what little remained of David's once beautiful body, broken by the weather, eaten by scavengers, was lying unfound, unburied, unloved. Had she pushed him? Had her right hand reached out and pushed him over the side of some dark pit? Had he clung to her right hand while slowly the sharp, fractured rocks cut into it? Had she screamed in pain, had he screamed in fear?

She had wanted him dead and he was dead. Did that mean that she had killed him? They had climbed a mountain together; a mountain haunted with tragedy, haunted by sudden mists and thunderstorms, haunted by terrorists whose habit was destabilisation, haunted by the spirits of ancestors who resented her angry presence, who resented David's arrogant presence.

The questions would not go away. She tried to hear, tried over and over again to hear the gentle voices of the nun-nurses in the hospital in Mutare telling all the questioners to leave her alone, telling them that post-traumatic amnesia was not uncommon, especially when the victim was concussed as well. It was normal not to remember. She did not remember. David had disappeared and perhaps she had killed him.

She knew too the reality of Anni's curiosity. Anni wanted Clare to tell her what had happened to David, and their relationship could never be close again until she had. Clare's heart sank; she must be mad to be going on this holiday. For the time being the train protected her as the hospital had, but to the north of them were the wide open hills and the intimacies of childhood.

Anni was offhandedly solicitous and subtly protective. It was she who trekked down the carriages to collect cups of coffee, and later sandwiches, beer for herself and gin-and-tonic for Clare. Clare knew she was being looked after and resented it, but equally she knew that she did not want to have to trust The Hand to behave itself; to carry flimsy boxes of balanced liquids past all those lounging people. The sleeves of her shirt were long, but she could see The Hand poking out of one, groping round to see what mischief and distress it could cause.

Clare suspected that Anni was going to ask her if she had killed David. So she asked, 'Did you have a good term? How do all these educational reforms actually work out?'

In fact, it had not occurred to Anni to ask whether Clare had killed David. There was nothing Anni wanted to know about David; she had disliked him for nearly a decade and was delighted by the permanence of his absence.

She heard Clare's question with innocent pleasure, and, as she often did when subjects interested her, began an excessively detailed reply, about Special Needs funding and the GCSE science results in the inner-city girls' comprehensive where she taught. Behind the pedagogical tone was a purity of commitment that made Clare envious.

As though she felt some flicker of her sister's withdrawal, Anni

15

said, 'I do go on, don't I? It's so old-fashioned to go on believing in comprehensive education; I can't bear the thought that we'll lose it. How many of your friends in the last ten years have asked you to forgive them for taking their children out of state education? Of course they know it's wrong, they say, but their child is special. And if I try to explain, I can see them thinking, "It's all right for you, you don't have any children, you poor thing." '

After a pause she added with a fierceness that was startling: 'Do you ever wonder, Clare, if we were right about feminism? I mean, did we just give ourselves a language of self-fulfilment so that we had the power to earn enough money to ruin an education system? On cold winter mornings I wake up and wonder if those ferocious old Trotskyites weren't actually right and all this personal development and "the personal is the political" stuff wasn't actually a brilliant evasion of the real questions about class. Treachery.'

It was the 'we' Clare heard and heard with joy. David had said much the same thing to her, but he had said 'you'. 'You' and later 'they'. 'It's time for a post-feminist perspective; *they* don't have much to ask for that doesn't belong in some welfarist programme, do *they*?'

'Rape,' she had wanted to say to him. 'Rape and porn.' And, as Anni was explaining to her now, she could also have said, 'Confidence, access to the full science curriculum, and equal wages and child-care provisions,' but she seldom had; David's '*they*' had distanced her effectively from her own feelings. She had almost forgotten how to express them, how to feel the fierce straightforward anger that his patronage deserved. But Anni said '*we*' and it felt like a homecoming.

They had gone to their first Women's Liberation movement meeting together more than fifteen years ago. When Anni had been studying biology at Imperial College and Clare history at LSE they had shared a flat, clothes, friends, a whole life.

'I don't need it, Clare,' Anni had said when Clare had first suggested they might go and find out about this 'women's lib thing'. 'I don't wear a bra.'

Then one afternoon Ceci, still at school wrestling with A-levels, had visited them. She had looked very young, her chubby knees under her school uniform skirt creating a barrier between her and her blue-jeaned sisters.

'I do like your flat,' she had said. 'Much more fun than Felicity's college.' Felicity had been in Durham training to be a social worker.

'You can come and live with us next year.'

'No thanks. I won't be in London.'

The two of them had looked affectionately interrogative.

'Actually I'm joining a religious order. I'm going to be a nun,' and she had laughed, half-proud, half-embarrassed.

'Ceci! No, darling!'

'Yes. It can't be that much of a surprise.'

But it had been. She looked like a child; she was a child.

Anni had taken a deep breath, 'So you're going to nurse lepers in the slums of Calcutta.'

'There are no lepers in India,' Ceci had said, 'and no, I'm going to be a contemplative. A Carmelite. Well, as a matter of fact, I'm going round the world first. I promised Mummy.'

'But Ceci, the food! They'll have horrible lentils all the time.' Anni had not been a vegetarian in those days. 'No cream buns; no ice-cream, you'll hate it.'

All three of them had laughed cosily: Ceci's sweet tooth an ancient nursery joke. After the laughter, after absorbing the fact that Ceci neither protested nor complained, they had asked,

'Ceci, why?'

'Well, Mummy thinks I'm a bit young and she's right of course; and anyway I think it will be fun; I want to go to Japan, I always have, and to the Himalayas, to Tibet; and to the Holy Land of course. Better see it all now.'

She had been calm, but she had also been like steel, armoured against their love, against seventeen years of being the youngest, of doing what they told her.

'Not "why round the world?" silly. Why a nun?'

'I want to,' Ceci had said. 'It's what I want to do.'

'God's call, eh?'

'I hope so; but really it's just what I *want*.'

She had looked at them almost pathetically, her curls bobbing round her plump face. They had both known that there was nothing pathetic about Ceci, that she was cheating them. They had not known what to do, what to say.

'Is that why you became a Catholic last year?' Clare had asked shrewdly.

'Yes.'

'You didn't tell us.'

'No, there wasn't any point then. I didn't want a drama. And I don't want one now. Anyway I do believe in universality, and the Apostolic See.'

After Ceci had left they had still not known what to do. Clare had made some coffee and Anni had stayed very still, sitting on the floor looking intently at the carpet. Suddenly she had said, 'Damn Mummy.'

'Or Daddy.'

'No. Mummy for this one and you know it. What's that you've been saying about women's lib meetings in the pub?'

'Anni . . . ?'

'No, I mean it. And it's Wednesday today. Perhaps this is a sign from God.'

'Don't . . .'

'You're the one who's been on about it. We could have a look; it's just round the corner.'

They had gone to see, slightly self-mocking.

'I became a feminist,' both of them would say later, 'because my little sister became a nun.' Anni would add, 'That's the power of sisterhood.'

The meeting had been in a pub. They had bought beer at the bar and gone upstairs, and both of them had been reminded too forcibly of their school.

'Are you twins?' they had been asked. Over the next couple of years, until Clare had gone to Italy, they had been asked more often if they were lovers; sometimes it had amused them, they would exchange covert glances, and unselfconscious giggles, but that first time . . .

'We're not even sisters,' Clare had said, and Anni had been offended. They liked to be sisters; although they had grown out of the schoolgirl rules about it, they did not often explain the relationship between them. When Clare denied that relationship, Anni had known that there was something going on that was important to Clare.

When they arrived the meeting had been discussing the failure of the anti-discrimination legislation, which had, they learned, been talked out in the House of Commons the previous Friday. All the women seemed vastly well-informed, highly articulate and they laughed continually at references that neither of them could quite follow.

'Is this your first meeting?' someone asked them afterwards.

'Yes.'

'What do you think?'

'I think,' Clare had said, 'that you need, I mean I need, a beginner's group.'

'O hell! Was it that bad?'

'Oh, no,' said Clare, with great clarity. 'That good.'

It had taken Anni longer to understand. 'It's OK for historians, Clare, of course I can see there are gaps, there's been a bias against women. But it's changing – equal pay, education. All the anger is just silly. Anyway it's all so subjective. I'm a scientist; this women's lib stuff doesn't have anything to do with me.'

They had been brought up in the Fabian tradition; a progressive and charitable socialism, a pious pacifism, an anti-imperialism based on a mixture of class guilt and Christian morality. They did not have the sins of the fathers to drive their anger. Anni had felt superior to those reckless, furious young women then. She had not understood why it had so excited Clare. She had failed to understand for over a year, until the Child Benefit campaign had shown her the connection between the politics of poverty and the politics of gender. But once she had forged the link it had been unbreakable. She seemed untouched by the Thatcherism of the eighties, unmoved by the pluralisms and high theories of post-modernist feminisms, somehow dowdy in her constancy. Often the simplicity of her commitment made her sound self-righteous, which she sometimes was, or stupid, which she certainly was not.

'Bugger representation,' she would say. 'Could we please talk about violence against women?' It made people guilty and alarmed because she was so uncompromising, dislike her or feel sorry for her because she was single and did not wear make-up and refused the casual glamour of middle-class libertarianism.

Now she sat in the carriage realising that although she had followed then where Clare had led, now her understanding of women's politics had nothing whatsoever in common with Clare's, except a vocabulary learned together. Time had changed them both; Anni mourned the change in Clare, denied it in herself, and tried not to feel either superior or inferior in the face of Clare's lovely jacket.

She wanted to ask how Clare applied mascara left-handed, and why she bothered. She had a strong feeling that this was not just a petty curiosity, but it was one that Clare would hear either as a criticism or as an intrusion. Once they had been more than sisters: best friends, special best friends, and now they were going home on a train as they had done then, but with nothing to say to each other.

'I miss you,' Anni wanted to say. 'If you really want to know, I'm glad he's dead because he stole you from me. Apart from how you feel about it, I'm glad.' But she could not. She was afraid that Clare would look at her blankly, would not know what she meant.

'Are you working yet?' she asked instead.

'At what?' Clare said, and there was an edge of anger in her voice. 'I have had quite a lot to work on, you know.'

'I'm sorry.' Anni said it mildly. 'I meant professionally, of course. You know me, I'm the old puritan who thinks work is the antidote to all poisons.' It was true and a good-natured gift.

Clare accepted it. 'I don't know,' she said with unusual openness. 'I don't know what to do.' Involuntarily her right hand, which was not hers but belonged to the hospital or worse still to itself, clenched and flexed. She looked at it with annoyance.

'Won't it take photographs then?' Anni was delighted at a chance to talk about Clare's hand.

'They say it will when I learn to use it properly. But I rather doubt it will delight the yuppy puppies' doting mothers who pay me; it might upset their little darlings, don't you think?'

She would not get much sympathy from Anni, she knew, because Anni did not approve of the charming family portraits that had made Clare's professional name, but it was not sympathy she wanted. After a pause, she went on boldly, 'I don't think it will ever take the pictures I want to take. And I don't think I ever want to take another picture of someone's cute blond baby.'

'I thought that's what you were famous for. Stubbs for horses in oils, Kerslake for children in high-gloss finish. The tasteful fashion accessory for the 1990s.'

'Shut up, Anni!' but she could not help laughing. 'It wasn't like that.'

'Damn it, after the accident they said in the papers: "Society photographer". And you never told me you took the baby royals. It all sounded dead posh to me.'

'It was. It was also unutterably boring.'

'Why did you do it then?'

'I . . . it paid the bills.' She could not tell Anni that she had done it because David expected her to. Because it gave him access to people who impressed him.

'Distressed silk, and Malibu Beach, eh?'

'We never went to Malibu.'

'I was joking.'

'Anyway, I took other pictures.' Clare knew she sounded defensive: she felt defensive.

'I lost my camera in Africa,' she said, and realised immediately that she had said it only to remind Anni of what a hard time she had been having. She was ashamed of her own self-pity and her shame made her angry: it was not her fault that Anni was so damn pure.

Anni was irritated too. It was obvious that Clare was not telling her the whole truth. She tried to tell herself that it was none of her business if Clare wanted to have secrets. She had always had them, but when they were young she would always tell Anni in the end. Why must Clare insist on making her do all the emotional work?

Crossly she shut herself off from the conversation and took out her book, almost blushing in the knowledge that she had chosen it mainly to impress Clare. She wanted Clare to be reading something that would endorse her own intellectual superiority, some sex-and-shopping paperback with a preposterous high-gloss cover; it was a petty wish. She wondered what Clare did read these days. Clare, she saw out of the corner of her eye, was not reading anything: she was looking out of the window, probably seven thousand miles away, reliving an incident that Anni could not begin to imagine.

Anni was wrong. Although Clare looked out of the window at the passing of the Midlands, she saw little, and that through a veil of guilt. David had always called Anni, the Schoolmarm; 'How's the Schoolmarm?' he would ask.

At first she would say 'Who?' and he would reply, 'Oh come on it was only a joke.'

Later she would snap, 'Don't call her that,' and he would complain, 'Sometimes you can be neurotically sensitive, you know.'

Finally she had begun to call Anni that herself, though never without noticing, never without a stab of self-contempt which converted itself slowly into hatred of him.

So now, with a determined act of will, Clare turned away from the countryside outside the window, and back to her sister.

'What's it about then?' she asked, flapping at the book.

Anni looked up quizzically. 'The philosophical implications of Cantor's proof that there are different sizes of infinity.'

Clare knew that Anni was giving her permission to mock; which meant that she had been mocked too many times. Clare sympathised. She would at least try to do better; she said seriously.

'I'm not too good at infinities, they leave me cold.'

There was a pause; Anni did not look disappointed but she held Clare's eyes, still uncertain of herself. Clare was saddened by this surprising timidity; she tried again:

'What does it mean?'

'Do you really want to know?'

'I've talked about practically nothing except my lousy health and my complicated life for three months, Anni; I'd like to know anything interesting.'

'Well, a mathematician called Cantor proved that infinities can come in different sizes. I could try to show you if you wanted me to; I try and show my kids, but frankly they're not very interested.'

Clare could see the yearning, and although part of her was laughing at Anni and her preposterous seriousness, she said, 'Well, you could try to show me.'

And Anni's face lit up. She took a pen and a pad out of her plastic bag.

'Do you know what a set is?'

'Er . . .'

'It can be a group of anything really, but for now it's going to be numbers. So,' and Anni wrote a large X on her paper. 'X is a set. P(X) is the set which contains all the subsets of X. This is called the Power Set – which is rather neat, isn't it?'

Clare smiled, as much at Anni's pleasure as at the abstract notion.

'I mean, for example, if X is the set with elements {1,2,3} then P(X) equals {ø} (that's the set with 0 numbers of the elements in it) and {1}, {2}, {3}, {1,2}, {1,3}, {2,3}, {1,2,3}. So if X is the set with the infinite number of numbers, then P(X) is still larger than X. Yes?'

'Faint but pursuing,' said Clare. 'Am I allowed to ask what "larger" means here?'

Anni was delighted, 'That's very clever actually; but think of same-sizedness in infinite numbers just as though they were natural numbers – that is, you can match them to each other. So you can see that infinities made up of say, natural numbers, even numbers and prime numbers are the same size.'

'The trouble is,' said Clare, almost reluctant to break the flow, 'the trouble is that as soon as you say "infinity" I can only think of theology. Of God and Mummy and such distracting notions.'

'Fair enough, discourse shifts and all that; it's a real problem.'

Clare was not sure what Anni was talking about, but she did not interrupt.

'As a matter of fact that's the answer to your initial question; what this book does is ask what mathematics means if Gödel is right and you can't prove what you know to be true within any given logical system; and Cantor is right and you can only get to his absolute infinity by faith.'

'What?' If infinity was difficult, hearing Anni say 'faith' was nearly impossible.

'Well,' said Anni, 'there are an infinite number of infinities. Until you get to Cantor's Absolute, the infinity-est infinity you can have, and you can't get there reasonably because it will always include itself, which means there's a bigger one. It would need a different way of thinking, like religious faith. So when Mummy and her ilk speak of an infinite God, we have to face the fact that she's not merely speaking of an infinite God but of the God of infinities.'

'I thought people like Hawking were trying to eliminate God, not expand him.'

'Her.'

'It. Not that either of us believe in Them.'

They both laughed.

'Anyway,' said Anni, 'Hawking has ideas above his station; all cosmologists do. They only want to get rid of God so they can be God. Not very useful. Did you read it?'

'Yes.'

'Good Lord, if you'll excuse the expression, I didn't think anyone did. Except pseudo-scientists like me.'

'David loved it, and I read it mostly because he didn't think I was up to it. And because it made him think he was God.'

They giggled conspiratorially, and then both remembered that David was dead.

'More coffee?' Anni asked, and stood up abruptly before Clare could respond.

After Anni brought the coffee back, placing the cups carefully on the table, pushing Clare's black one towards her and fishing her own sugar and little milk pots out of her pocket, they both watched the beautiful profile of Durham Cathedral swim past the window of the train and did not dare to share their pleasure with each other.

Anni said only, 'I love long train journeys.'

'You went to Japan by train didn't you? Across Russia?'

'Yes, it was wonderful.'

'It's a long time since I went anywhere by train. David didn't like trains. He always wanted to drive.'

'Yes. I did love his car, you know; if I'd had one of those I wouldn't have gone by train either.'

David had driven a classic Jaguar; a beautiful sleek thing with a deep smell of leather, that had purred under his hands.

'I hated driving it,' Clare said. She had never felt that he had quite trusted her with it; 'but it was blissful to be driven in.'

'What's happened to it?'

'I hadn't thought,' Clare said, startled. 'It must still be sitting in the garage. I suppose I'd better sell it.'

'Don't.'

'I'll have to. I'll never drive it.'

She ought to be able to drive it, but she knew she never would.

'He loved it.' She wasn't sure whether that was an explanation or a new topic.

She hastened on, 'So it's years since I went on a long train journey.' She cast her mind back for a nice little story to offer Anni. Then she wished she hadn't. The last train journey she could remember was when she came back from Italy. Her sudden departure had meant that she had failed to book properly. The only service that could provide her with a *wagon lit* had been via Berne. She had woken uncomfortably in the morning to see mountains and villages so neat and clean that it was impossible not to believe that the Swiss had risen at dawn and combed the grass, that Heidi was not about to skip round a corner, her pinny starched and frothy, to wave to the train. In contrast she had felt dirty and muddled.

She had fled from Italy in a moment of panic; leaving the dazzling sunlight too abruptly and waking up in the chilly cleanliness of Switzerland. That running away had been a disaster, a terrible mistake. All her life she had had a tendency to panic, to be shaken too suddenly from self-control into terror. David's clarity and order had protected her from that, until . . . until they had been caught in a mist on the side of Mount Nyangani. She knew now that she should have stayed in Italy whatever had come of it; that long train journey had changed her life. The four years she had lived in Italy had been the happiest of her life, and she had abandoned them on an impulse of fear.

She had gone to Italy first for a holiday – laughing southwards after her finals, with nothing in particular to return to. Anni had an extra year of university still to do, because of changing courses at the end of her first year, when 'biology' had come to seem a feminised soft option. They had joked together about how unfair it would be if Clare started working, started earning, while Anni was still studying. That had merely been an excuse: nothing had prepared her for the suddenness with which education would cease. It had provided her with the framework for her life since she was five years old; she could do it well, everyone was pleased with her, and now suddenly there was an enormous emptiness So she had gone to Italy for a holiday, and for an escape.

In Rome the contrast between the sun on the butter-coloured walls and the pools of black shadow, the light refracting off fountains and bouncing shadows of light into corners of shaded white marble; the baroque churches, the fabulous trompe l'oeil effects, the lifting up, up up of her lines of sight had made her suddenly excited, a visual excitement precisely balancing the intellectual excitement which had structured her childhood and the excitement of the senses which alarmed her. Before she had left home Hester had lent her the family camera, used for years to fill drawers with snaps that would on a day that never quite arrived be stuck into a family album.

'Take some photos for me, darling; I do so love the Holy City.'

Without thought Clare started to play with the camera, play with the light. It was just a holiday hobby, but she wanted to see what results she was getting so she had the first rolls developed, and then she was smitten.

'You'd better go to Venice,' someone said, 'because the water makes a third sort of light.'

'You'd better go south because in Sicily . . . in Calabria . . . in Greece, the houses are whiter and the sky is bluer.'

The one place not to go, they had all thought that long summer, was home, home to getting dreary jobs and becoming grown-ups.

When it became clear that Clare was going to stay a while, Hester had used her influence, and, without effort, almost passively, Clare had found herself installed in a high-ceilinged room in Trastevere with a job assisting a middle-aged art historian with his research.

He was an outrageous Anglo-Catholic homosexual, whose family, as grand as Hester's, was only too delighted that he should stay in Rome, where he could be referred to affectionately as 'artistic' and cause no one any embarrassment. He was always on the verge of converting to Roman Catholicism and never quite able to give up the eccentricities and privileges of Anglicanism. He was vaguely in bondage to Hester, a mixture of devotion and fear, and although he did not particularly need a research assistant, he was more than content to have this beautiful blonde daughter of his dear friend around.

'Let's show off, darling,' he'd say, and take her by the arm across golden evening piazzas to restaurants where people were impressed by their style.

He bought her beautiful clothes and taught her how to wear them. The regulation scruffiness of studenthood slipped off her with unexpected ease, and she flourished. He laughed at her seriousness, and because she was in a foreign country, because it was not her business she was free to laugh too, and to abandon politics in favour of conversation. More importantly, he laughed at her parents, though gently, in a way that was useful to her. One week during her first winter, her father had led a pilgrimage to Rome and she and Stephen had arranged to meet him for dinner.

'Whoops,' he had said, 'not that frock, darling; it has a slight whiff of immoral earnings about it.'

'Daddy won't notice.'

'Nor will he; what a shame for him.' They had giggled like children together, and she had begun to shake off the guilt at her own sensuality that her parents had so unconsciously imbued.

Underneath everything he was immensely kind. When he realised that she did not really want to research the religious symbolism of flowers in early Renaissance paintings – 'though why *not*, darling, I can't imagine' – he had introduced her to an American photographer, and Clare had begun her apprenticeship.

Four wonderful years; and in a moment of panic – just because a beautiful woman promised her, 'When we make love the stars will explode, will flash and crash and die for us. When we kiss there will be fireworks,' – she had thrown it all away, and come home on a long, miserable, uncomfortable train journey. She had tried to drown the memories of the sunlight and the fountains and the crazy passion in the minute demanding details of being a good and successful young woman. The train journey had led inevitably to David, who had wanted all that success and virtue; who had affirmed it and structured it for her.

Now she did not even want to think about long train journeys, let alone the more difficult things.

'You look tired,' Anni said.

Clare was tired. She was on the train in order to escape the tiredness.

It had been warm that spring in London; warm but pale, as though the city had been too long in the wash and the colours had bled out of it. The washing had not cleaned it however; the dirt and decay struck her as it never had before. The warmth filled her with a vague dread; summer was approaching too fast and she would then have to think about whether she had enough courage to wear T-shirts, to wear sleeveless dresses. She watched strangers, on buses, in shops, on the streets themselves, to see if they noticed. Mostly they did not seem to, although once she heard a mother whisper piercingly to her toddler, 'don't stare', so ferociously that she knew the mother had herself been staring. But although she heard she did not mind. She did not mind anything much.

With acquaintances she more quickly grew accustomed to the surreptitious glance down to her right hand, and back, blandly meeting her gaze. They knew what they were looking for. Or so she thought at first. Soon she learned that their glances of covert inquiry ran swiftly from her hand to her face because there was another question to be asked and they were searching for an answer.

She was invited to dinner by some old friends of David's, people she had come to think of as her friends, although they were mainly older than she was and had known David for a long time, even knew his first wife and asked him or told him about her when they thought Clare was not listening. She had been pleased, happy to return to a world she understood, touched almost that they should have remembered. It felt easy; a lovely early summer evening, a pleasant dinner with civilised people, work and social worlds meshing comfortably, just as the delightful sitting room and charming garden meshed together as they drank delicious wine. There was even a black-and-white portrait she had taken a couple of years ago of their three children sitting on a rug in the garden; a rather nice composition, an acceptable presentation of family values and youthful charm, now well-framed and hung. Clare felt reassured, normal again. They drank, talked, laughed; seven successful, delightful professional people, and the food thoughtfully prepared so that she could eat one-handed and not have to ask someone else to cut up for her.

It was not until they had finished eating and had moved from the gleaming Italian hi-tech kitchen to the calm chic of the sitting room, and she had been settled solicitously on to a low sofa and given some brandy to go with her coffee, that her hostess said with warm kindness:

'Can you tell us what did happen to David, then?'

She did not want to talk about it, but acknowledged to herself that they were old friends of his, they must care, she owed them an explanation.

'I don't know,' she said and looked up. She saw at once that this was why she had been asked. Not because they cared about David, but because they wanted some intriguing gossip. It had been planned.

'I don't know,' she said again.

Someone tittered in a way that might just have been meant to sound sympathetic, 'We're all terribly discreet you know, you'll be safe with us.'

That was going too far: she sensed rather than saw her two hosts make surreptitious eye-contact. She inhaled, pushing down her fear. She was not going to gratify them.

'I really don't know.' She would not let herself sound defensive. 'It's extremely embarrassing for me, as you can imagine. We got up in the morning and went out to climb a mountain. I remember parking the car and setting out . . . and then I don't remember anything at all. It's called post-traumatic amnesia, and believe me, it's weird.' She tried to smile. 'They – the medicos – say I may wake up one fine morning remembering or I may not.'

She was not doing too badly, she thought. She got some help from one of the other guests: a dark pretty woman whom she had not met before said quietly:

'Other people have disappeared from that mountain, haven't they?'

'Oh yes,' she said, trying to find a tone of abstract interest, 'but usually adolescents. The Zimbabwean press offers three explanations. The terrain is very rough, the mists very sudden, perhaps they just fell down crevasses.'

They were still waiting, this smart dinner party, still hoping for something more revealing than a little rough terrain and mist. Clare drew a deep breath.

'But also Nyangani is right on the eastern border, the Mozambique border; some people think the MNR may kidnap tourists.'

'MNR?' said someone.

'RENAMO. They were a South African funded terrorist group. Well Rhodesian funded originally. Now it's a bit more chaotic. South Africa says it no longer funds them and they certainly make efforts to demonstrate their independence. But it's as though no one is in charge. I don't really understand about Mozambique, it's all too complicated. They're anti-FRELIMO and supposedly a Mozambican nationalist opposition. But they, the dispossessed bandits, freelance terrorists, guerrillas, there isn't a proper language . . . Anyway they specialise in South African style destabilisation along Zimbabwe's eastern border. Blow people up; a little shooting, a little torture, the odd farm destruction job. Not nice.'

'And you think they killed David – and are responsible for all these other disappearances?'

'The trouble with that explanation is that they never ask for ransom, or say they've got these people. Two of the adolescents were daughters of a Government Minister.' Clare said it patiently, as much for herself as for her audience. Did she remember gunfire? Did she remember voices and people in the mist, did she remember David looking frightened? looking angry? looking appalled? Did she remember being marched cross-country for over twelve miles till she fell and they left her? Was her hand coldly and deliberately hacked up? Did she fall and become a liability? Did she try to escape? Did David help her to try and escape? Had she and he already separated, already got lost when they captured him? Had she betrayed him to them by some accident? Deliberately?

The pause lengthened.

'There's a third explanation, you know. It might amuse you. Nyangani is a cultic mountain, haunted. It's said to be the home of a powerful spirit, an ancestral-type spirit who doesn't like foreigners climbing the mountain. They get stolen by the ancestors.'

'Really?'

'They really say so.'

'That wouldn't seem to cover the Minister's daughters.'

'Their mother was white American. Perhaps they had lost their cultural values. Worse than being a foreigner in some ways.'

'Hard to imagine David cavorting with spooks, somehow.'

'Yes,' she said. 'Very hard.'

It was hard to imagine him dead, if he was dead. 'But up on the mountain, it was a great deal easier to believe, I can tell you.'

She could remember the sweet beauty of Chirikudzi singing for David; she heard the dark throaty singing every night in her dreams. There were other spirits, too.

In the silence that followed she noted with interest that they had not asked her which of these explanations she preferred. They had not asked her for the obvious details: why were you both there? what were you doing in Zimbabwe? did you take any good pictures? what are you going to do now? She knew why. She summoned up another smile, carefully constructed.

'I wasn't paying attention at the time, but did our papers suggest another explanation?'

The sophisticated polish to the company stayed in place, but it was stretched, fragile. No one wanted to answer.

'Did they suggest I killed him?'

She had to know, and her family would not tell her. Tomorrow, she told herself in the silence, I must go and research the clippings. I shall have to. These people had asked her here so she could tell them whether she had killed David or not; to give them the greatest social *frisson* of their lives. That was what they wanted: there was nothing she need be embarrassed about asking them.

31

The pretty dark woman broke the silence. 'There was a certain curiosity.'

'Which you share?'

The room was very still. Clare reached out her hand for her wine glass. Her host laughed, nervously.

'Oh, come on now, Clare. Would we?'

But the woman who had claimed to be discreet tittered again.

She distracted Clare's attention for a moment and, ignored, Clare's new prosthesis continued to close round the glass. Its plastic skin received no tactile information and so sent none to her brain. Therefore her brain did not instruct it to stop its inexorable closing until the sound of crushed glass shattered the tension of the room.

The hostess leapt up from the sofa, whipping out a handkerchief, and then stopped abruptly. Clare shook the glass splinters to the floor, and ruefully turned her new palm upwards. She looked at it, blankly.

'It doesn't bleed,' she told them, and then started to apologise for the damage.

'How does it work?' the dark pretty woman asked deftly.

'Solenoids,' Clare said, relieved. 'It's super hi-tech stuff. A myeloelectric prosthesis. It picks up the left-over electronic buzzings, charges, from the nerves still running down my arm; then the solenoids raise the power output and it does what I want it to.'

'More or less,' grinned the woman, dusting away a few more shards of glass. Then she tentatively reached out her own hand. With the sensitivity that she had developed in place of a new skin, Clare knew that the woman had neither compassion nor disgust, only curiosity. She could cope with that, though not with the flinching from other of the guests. She held herself as still as she could, and watched the woman touch it delicately with her fingers.

'I'm not too good at it yet,' said Clare, 'that's why I break things. They make me practise on eggs: you should see us all at the training sessions, worse than a public meeting at a general election – splattered yolks everywhere.'

The two of them smiled at each other against the tide of revulsion and pity in the rest of the room. It was surprisingly intimate, the first time she had let anyone touch this strange new part of her body, feel it and fiddle with it. Like adolescence: the first time you let someone touch your nipple, except The Hand did not respond with tremulous excitement and fear. It was a good thing, the delicate curiosity of the woman. Clare felt happier.

But on her way home in a taxi she found she was crying.

Immediately after the accident Clare did not remember what had happened. Nor did she particularly want to. Post-traumatic amnesia is not an uncommon result of concussion and shock. Faces, black faces and white faces, leaned over her sometimes, looming somehow different from the faces of her dreams, and voices, dark voices and bright voices, sounding somehow different from the voices of her pain, and they all asked: 'What happened to David?'

'I don't know. I can't remember,' she would whisper, and she would try to concentrate, try to find out if this was a satisfactory answer, if they would be pleased with her and leave her alone, but she drifted away again into the dark land.

Gradually she came to remember some things; and she learned some others, and dreamed still more. She remembered that she was Clare Kerslake, a photographer. She remembered that David was her lover, and had been for eight years. She remembered that she and David had been on holiday in Zimbabwe. She remembered that they had set out from their lodge at Udu Dam to climb Mount Nyangani. She remembered that she had wanted him dead.

She learned that David had disappeared, she learned that she was glad about that, she learned that they had cut off her hair and her right hand. She learned that some things must be kept secret. She learned that on a sunny day in February, on the highest mountain in Zimbabwe, she had lost her lover, her hand and her memory.

She did not want to think about it. So, by and large she did not think about it. She had enough else to think about. By day she worked hard at learning to pick up eggs, to write left-handed, and to cope.

There was a lot to cope with. The legal procedures for any missing person were complicated: they were doubly complicated when the missing person had been rich, had gone missing in southern Africa and his sole beneficiary was still the subject of a police enquiry about how he came by his death, if he was dead. Her brain clogged with the complexities; several times she was even reduced to consulting with Joseph. He found the problem fascinating, delightful, exciting. She found it deadening. It sucked at her time, her limited resources of energy and health. She tried to make lists with a hand that didn't know how to write, lists of priorities: settling the legal issues, doing her exercises, mourning her lost lover, sorting out her lost memory, thinking about how she was going to earn a living, accepting her amputation. Too much. Too much for anyone to cope with.

At the same time she found she was bored. She had not realised just how much of her life she had spent running about: hustling for work, travelling to work, ingratiating herself, socialising, managing David's life, a constant busyness which had suddenly gone away and left a huge hole with nothing to fill it up.

There had been no escape from those nightmares in sleep. Down in the deep drifts of sleep the dark voices were waiting and she could not silence them.

She dreamed of the mountain itself, the three ridges shouldering up out of each other to the crest above the moorland that was so like the hills of Sutherland, the mountains of home. She dreamed the wide, the infinite view, breaking through the clouds; of hills behind hills, eastward to Mozambique and the dawn, westward toward the Pongwe River, the escarpment and the plain. She dreamed of the lightning, the pure descending power of heaven and hell, with the growl of hungry thunder behind it, the lightning crashing down on her like a knife, slicing through her wrist, exploding in a cloud of burning stars.

She dreamed of the *banditos armados* breaking cover from behind the smashed boulders, their smiles violently white and greedy. She dreamed of Selous, with a face like David's but more golden, killing his way northwards towards the mountain, and of José Rosario Andrade, with a face like David's but darker, fucking his way southwards towards the mountain. She dreamed of the revenge of the African warriors on these newcomers.

She dreamed the huge fierce power of the spirit of the mountain, the first ancestor, the place of beginnings, the violated Spirit angry and unforgiving, and the warnings of the N'anga. And within them the shining voice of Chirikudzi. She dreamed of Chirikudzi, the mermaid spirit, who lives in the source waters of the Pongwe River, making love to David. Chirikudzi was shadowed and wraith-like; her arms reached out for David, her crab-like pincers held him, tore delicately at his flesh, stripped him to the bone and he responded with joy; the ancestors took his flesh, claimed him back and he enjoyed it while she watched.

She dreamed of David. She dreamed that she lured him, as shadowed and lovely as Chirikudzi, she lured him up, up a sharp pinnacle of rock, and from the very top in a whirling moment she saw the distant hills of Mozambique folded together; she saw the wild beasts below, waiting, waiting while she twisted carefully to one side and he fell slowly, slowly towards their iron claws and blood-red teeth.

She dreamed other dreams too, and would struggle to wake up from them, pulling herself as though by desperate effort up from the pit of sleep. She added insomnia to her problems and lost weight.

So when her mother had said, 'Come to Skillen with us, darling. Just come and have a holiday,' she was too tired to resist.

And later, riding on the train with her sister, returning to the home of her own ancestors, she could smile a brave smile and respond to the remark 'You look tired' with a gentle,

'I am.'

Suddenly that was not enough. This was Anni, not some goggle-eyed dinner-party guest.

'Anni,' she said, 'you don't know how tired I am.'

She wanted to say, 'Tired in all directions. I don't know anything any more. I've lost my lover and I don't know how; I've lost my hand and my job, and unless they decide pretty damn quick what they want to do about the insurance money I'm broke. I hear voices in the night and I don't even know if I want to hear them. I am empty.' But she did not know how to begin.

'You ought to be tired, Clare,' said Anni with great tenderness. 'You ought to be tired. Be nicer to yourself, you don't have to be superwoman.' Now Anni did want to ask, 'Did you kill him?' Or, more accurately, 'Whatever makes you think that you might have killed him?' but her personal opinion that anyone who bumped

35

David off was performing a valuable service for the universe made it too difficult.

Instead she said, 'I'm glad you decided to come. Even if it was only because you were too tired to resist Mummy's pressure. It'll be good to have some time.'

They understood each other better than this exchange might have suggested. They wanted to talk to each other and could not do it on the train. That was enough for the time being. They smiled a little tentatively.

Clare said, 'There's a point of tiredness that doesn't make any sense any more. Everyone keeps saying, "you're supposed to be tired," and "try to remember" and they seem to me to be opposite instructions. Like learning to swim: relax and kick harder, you know.'

Anni said carefully, keeping a wary eye on Clare as she spoke, 'When I was talking about maths earlier there was something else I wanted to say; there's this newish sort of computer maths where basically you get the computer to repeat, loop-feed, computations and then make the results visual on a screen; the point is you get these extraordinary patterns, different kinds according to the equation you used in the first place, they're called things like Julia sets and Mandelbrot sets and . . .'

'I know what they are,' interrupted Clare relieved; 'like wildly beautiful paisley patterns; I did some photographs of them. Someone wanted me to illustrate a book on natural fractals. I read quite a lot of stuff about them.'

'You did?' Anni marvelled.

Clare felt sad. It sounded as though Anni no longer even hoped that they might have anything in common.

'The idea was that I would do all these close-ups, waves and tree branches, and sand patterns. I was fascinated by him, the man who wanted to do it – do the text, I mean. There was something about the scaling, the way they kept repeating themselves at different scales.'

'It's called self-replicating; they are self-replicating across scale.'

'That's right. I thought . . . I don't know . . . once he had shown me what to look for, I couldn't stop seeing them everywhere: fractals, fractal relationships. Actually it made me think about

36

how the personal is supposed to relate to the political and doesn't, and he, this guy, wanted me to take some pictures for him. So I did some research.'

He had been called Mark. David had rung her from work: 'Darling, I'm bringing someone back for supper.'

'Not tonight, David, I'm . . .'

'Clare, this is work. He's a total nerd, you needn't do anything special, but he's a computer freak and I want to pump his brains about JNC, you know, the firm I told you about that we're doing the share issue for . . . he works for them, has worked for them, and I want to get a feel.'

'I'm supposed to be taking those pictures for the dancers . . .'

'Those bloody hippies. Darling, there could be a lot in this for us.'

'I promised.'

'OK then, sweetheart, pop round and click at them a few times and I'll take him out for a drink first . . . we'll see you about eight, OK? Must run.' He made it sound as though he was doing her a favour.

Mark had looked like a nerd; young and rather clumsy in a puppy-like sort of way; he had yet to use his thick spectacles to give him authority instead of making him look like a very gauche sixth-former. She had been bored and cross. Except that after a fairly dreary supper, during which she could easily sense that David was not getting whatever it was he had wanted, Mark had come back from the loo holding some of her photographs; a set of pictures of a garden path. They had been part of a commission, illustrations for an article about town gardens, but she had become fascinated by her own technique and by the intricacies of the crazy paving, and the tiny plants growing between the gaps. For her own sake she had shot them closer and closer up, tightening the focus. They had been a waste of valuable time, and they were now rubbish. But not to Mark. Almost stuttering, he had started to explain fractals to her, about Mandelbrot and his fractal geometry of nature, and why people were cheapening it with bad reproductions and how . . . how beautiful . . . how he wanted to combine computer-generated imagery with natural forms and was she interested.

She had been interested. He had given her reading lists; she had taken pictures for him in the park – trees against the winter sky, and a wonderful unfinished series of little ripples on a pond superimposed repeatedly on each other. And because she was not absolutely sure what she was doing, she had experimented with developing the negatives herself, and since she normally only printed she had had to borrow darkroom space from a colleague she had not seen for ages. She had become excited by the pictures, by the chemistry of developing, by the contact with old workmates and, oddly, by Mark himself. He had an open-eyed enthusiasm, a sense of wonder, and a completely infantile sense of humour. They had swapped riddles; she had forgotten all about riddles: 'Knock, knock . . .' jokes and elephants-in-the-fridge jokes, and a whole group new to her: 'Doctor, Doctor' jokes, which they had somehow missed out on in her childhood. It had been enormous fun. Mark had reminded her of her youngest brother, Tom, in the idiotic exuberance of his humour, and they had spent hours together repeating this infantile babble and talking about chaos theory and fractals. She could not be entirely surprised that it had annoyed David.

'Of course,' David had said, 'I can see that it is rather amusing to be admired and looked up to, to be mummy to a cute kid, but a bit narcissistic, eh? Bit fag-haggy. You'll turn out like your esteemed Mamma if you're not careful.'

She had been stunned.

'Or do you fancy him?'

'Fancy Mark? Are you mad?'

'Well then, it's not very fair on him, is it? Pretending you're professionally interested. He fancies you.'

'David!' She tried to sound indignant, but she knew he had an uncanny sense for other people's sexuality. He was probably right. He rather approved when other men fancied her, it turned him on. 'Anyway,' she had said hastily, 'I am professionally interested.'

'Oh come on Clare: if you want to take jolly pictures of trees in the park, you can find someone who'll pay you decently for it. You don't have to play mummies and babies with some pimply adolescent.'

'It's not the pictures, it's the technique.'

'But yours is great anyway,' he ran his hand down the back of her neck and she was cross with herself because she could not help responding to his fingers like a teenager.

She blushed, remembering, and then heard Anni saying,

'I thought you only did people.'

'I did lots of things. The children were only the most public. I did people's houses and gardens, for magazines and things; and I was thinking about doing some other sorts of things altogether. The fractals were one of them.'

'Science things?'

'Nature things. But hard, not soft. Perhaps I'm menopausal.'

'No; return to infancy more like.'

'What do you mean?'

'I've still got a picture you did, years ago, when you were in Italy; you gave it to me for my birthday; a sort of double picture of sunflowers in a field and a piece of stone carving, very elaborate, rococo I'd guess, but taken so that the two look like each other, and at the same time look like nothing on earth.'

'I don't remember.'

'It's lovely, actually. I've always liked it because it's so weird; you'd probably say "hippy rubbish" but that wouldn't be fair to yourself. I'll show you. I'd be dead chuffed if you wanted to go back to that sort of thing: highly technical, but not cold.'

Clare wondered how it was that Anni so precisely wanted for her what she wanted for herself.

'I want to live in the country,' she had said to David.

'You don't really.'

'I want to have a baby . . . Live in the country . . . Take different pictures.'

'You don't really,' David would say, and with immaculate logic demonstrate why she didn't.

'I know you better than you know yourself,' he would say, smiling at her, and she would feel her fear and her desire for him melt together.

Anni, of course, did not hear that voice, she was still pursuing the extraordinary patterns, the self-replicated bifurcations of waves on beaches, trees in winter, wind on sand.

'Do it. We can collaborate. I'm pissed off you never got me in as a consultant.' Anni sounded quite hurt. Clare could not tell her that she had not done the book because David had made her feel so self-conscious around Mark that the delicate beginnings of a friendship had collapsed. Clare could not tell Anni that she had not done the book because David had laughed at her, scoffed at her arty pretensions. She did not even know if David had done those things deliberately. If he had wanted to wreck her friendship and her developing work, or if he had just not noticed.

Now, hearing Anni's eagerness, her enthusiasm for them to work together, hearing the trace of sadness in Anni's voice, knowing their loss of each other, neither could Clare tell her that she would take no more pictures. She only said,

'It didn't work out. He couldn't get a decent commission. Anyway, that was a diversion, you were saying something about chaos theory . . .'

'If I'd known you knew all this stuff I'd have got it said hours ago. I was going to point out that it is only on the boundary between chaos and order that the beautiful patterns of the Mandelbrot sets appear; perhaps if you want something good to emerge you just have to live on that margin.'

Clare was silent again, Anni shrugged. 'I don't know what you do to me. I'm waxing all philosophical again.'

It was all too delicate. Anni used the new tender shoot of intimacy restored to say, half laughing,

'Stuff philosophy, try scandal. What do we feel about poor old Ben?'

'Stupid idiot,' said Clare. 'Not you. Ben. Have you seen him?'

'No. He's lurking.'

'Is he coming up?'

'Mummy hopes so.'

'Is she being enormously forgiving?'

'Yes. And worse than that, she seems to have persuaded Daddy to be so too.'

'Then it's brave of Ben to come.'

'Yes. Her public position is that it's only the Sunday tabloids and everyone knows what they're like. But, like you said that day in hospital, Mummy didn't ring any bishops to get things sorted.'

'That serious. She knows it's true then?'

'She must. VICAR IN GAY DRAG ORGY. I think it's the stupidity she minds, him getting caught, though of course she can't say that.'

'You can pity her.'

'Clare, the real problem is that he never told her.'

'Told her?'

'Told her he was gay.'

'He must have.'

'Well I thought so, and anyway I just assumed that she must know – Mummy, I mean. She's not a baby. But he didn't and so she's hurt and guilty on top of everything else and how has she failed her children and so on and all that.'

They both smiled, Anni from deep affection for her mother and Clare at the image Anni summoned up so deftly. They noticed simultaneously that they had lowered their voices.

'I still don't think he should have let the Bish resign him,' Anni almost shouted.

'We're not very nice to her are we?' Clare said almost at the same moment, but slightly less loudly. Anni was quickest to reply.

'Neither you nor Ben seem exactly to have planned on shock horror headlines.'

'Lucky no one made the connection. EARL'S GRANDCHILDREN IN MYSTERY MURDER AND VICE RING. Christ.'

'It wasn't a vice ring, it was a party. But you've got a point. No . . . I think Mummy could cope with a tender and loving romantic relationship, it's the idea that it was "just for fun".'

'Well, quite honestly . . . I think it upsets me.'

Clare thought of Ben, her favourite brother, and could not connect the child he once was with the man he had become. She needed to see him, to graft the picture of him in leather and the nipple-ring on to the older image: the gentle, humorous vicar in his shabby clergy house. She had hardly seen him out of his dog collar in ten years. The last time they'd been together he had asked her to come and take pictures of his parish's celebrations for the opening of the social centre in the crypt. It had been a massive and courageous undertaking for an impoverished run-down inner-city church. He was a good liturgist, she realised, infusing the quite old-fashioned Solemn High Mass with an intimacy and affection commonly missing. He had been warm with his flock, hugging children and teasing old ladies; rumpled and relaxed. He had been polite to his Bishop and to the assorted wealthy sponsors drummed up partly of course by Hester, but also by his skilful manipulation of Joseph's and David's and her acquaintances and connections. He had made a witty and appropriate speech of thanks, but his energy, his love, had been so obviously directed towards his parishioners. His devotion was like their father's, but had an immediacy, a sort of personal involvement that James had never shown. Then, presumably, he had returned home, dropped his cassock in his untidy bedroom, exposed his nipple-ring and gone out into the night. She found it hard to imagine.

Anni was saying, 'What, the promiscuity? I think some people just like sex a lot, don't you?'

'Ben?'

'Oh yes, I think so,' Anni said. She was completely matter-of-fact; Clare knew she was right and was sorry she had not thought it out for herself. She did not want Anni to know that she had never told David that Ben was gay; she had lied when he had asked. She did not know why.

'That's not quite what I was getting at. I meant the whole . . .' she didn't know how to say it. She did lower her voice, '. . . the nipple-ring.'

'How did you know that?' said Anni, genuinely surprised.

'Felicity told me. She was in tears and nearly sick. She said "And it's illegal now," sort of squeakily. But I find it hard to think about it.'

'No different from having your ears done,' Anni said.

'Yes it is!' Clare's false hand, they both noticed, had covered her own breasts protectively; they exchanged a knowing grin. 'It makes me feel funny though . . . I can't imagine. I suppose I want to say I can't imagine it being sexy, but I can and I don't want to. Sado-masochism and . . .' She was feeling her way; she did not want to say that thinking about Ben's activities had opened her eyes to her curiosity about them all: the questions you do not ask yourself about your own family – what did Felicity and Bob, Joseph and Louise, Tom and Caro get up to in their bedrooms? Did nuns masturbate? Did her parents still . . . ? Who did Anni do what with? And the shadow of David, David and herself. She was relieved when Anni, changing the subject abruptly, said

'If you've been talking to Felicity, do you happen to know what's eating her?'

'No. She was a bit, I don't know, put upon earlier in the year. But I've hardly seen her since I came out of hospital; she's always so frantic. Except for Alice's birthday, and she was fine then, wasn't she?'

'Mummy asked me what I thought the matter was and I hadn't noticed anything.'

'Maybe she's pregnant?'

'God. I hope not. It's genetic. Did you know that?'

'What, Alice's deafness?'

'Yeh, some recessive gene thing. There's a really high chance of it happening again.'

'Well Felicity would say that was no problem.'

'Come on, Clare. Don't be such a bitch.' Despite the reprimand she sounded affectionate. 'Ah ha, have you been getting "disablement is no disability" lectures from our poor sister?'

'No . . . but I thought maybe she was thinking it was unfair that I was getting so much attention. She can say what she likes, it can't be fun . . . I mean, it must be bloody hard work. I'm not surprised she gets downhearted sometimes. Exhausted.'

'I hope you're right. Perhaps we can spare Mummy yet another mid-life crisis then.'

Clare leaned her head back against the seat cushion. She tried to resolve not to let herself compete with Felicity for the senior suffering award. Felicity would win. Then she smiled at Anni, wanting her to go on talking, but suddenly feeling a new wave of exhaustion.

They were beyond Edinburgh now; the last of the wide urban views had slipped away southwards and the train ran through the wilder valleys of the Highlands. It was evening and Clare was more than tired; the dull ache of exhaustion was back in her arm, making it impossible for her to forget its injuries. The ache was inevitably at the join, the join between the real and the artificial, but it always seemed to spread in both directions, pain reporting in from the metalled fingers and latex palm as nothing else did.

She ought to have put The Hand to bed; like a small child it became fractious and difficult once past its bedtime.

She was tempted to take it off, but the emptying train had become more intimate, more domestic, since Edinburgh. Even though she and Anni had not exchanged more than a couple of sentences with anyone else all day, the smiles and shrugs had accumulated into a little companionship. To take The Hand off now would be exhibitionism, would attract shock or compassion from too many people. Would be shameful. Surreptitiously she massaged her elbow through the soft cotton of her shirt. Surreptitiously Anni watched her, alert, curious.

At last Anni said 'Last lap,' and stood up, gathering, tidying, sorting. Folding her *Guardian* and Clare's *Independent* loosely, pushing them to the end of the table and chucking away the rest of the detritus.

'Who's meeting us?' Anni asked. The question marked the end of that phase of the journey.

The answer emerged, large and warm, in the fading light of the platform: Bob was there, with Alice. They had come in Tom's car. Alice hurled herself on Anni with delight, and more circumspectly on Clare; her enchanting five-year-old face turned upwards for the expected kiss. Clare felt a wave of love for her.

The grown-ups exchanged more formulaic kisses. Clare and Alice rode in the back of the car. In front of them Anni and Bob chatted peacefully, catching up on a couple of months of common interests. Clare let herself be lulled in the soft dark, half waking, half sleeping, on the long remembered road which she had not travelled for ten years. Bob drove fast, well. Alice relaxed and dozed against her; she could feel the little warm body and in contrast the hard angular box of the hearing aid, jutting out of her chest. There was nothing to do but consent to her tiredness, accept the gentle forward retreat into the terrains of childhood, while the soft light faded to the right of the car and the darkness hovering in the east prepared to take over.

By the time they had driven through Carnith it was too dark to see more than the silhouettes of the hills, a flicker of the loch waters picked up by the headlights. They went over the bridge at the loch head and doubled back, suddenly going south again along the single-track road. She knew that they were nearly there.

Anni hopped out to open the wrought iron gate; Bob slid through and waited till Anni shot the white painted bolt. She came back to the car, but on Bob's side, not her own.

'Go on,' she said, 'I'll walk.'

'Sure?'

'My legs want to . . . and my head too; five minutes to prepare for regression.'

Bob grinned, let the clutch out and the car drifted away with Anni raising a hand in mocking salute.

'Are you awake, Clare?'

'More or less.'

'Is Alice?'

'No, sleeping.'

'She really wanted to come. We said it was past her bedtime, but she insisted, and she slept more or less the whole way there and back. You'd better wake her.'

'Alice,' said Clare. 'Alice.'

'You have to shake her.'

'Shit. Sorry.'

Alice made peculiar noises as she woke up; the completely unmonitored verbalisations of the profoundly deaf; then she leaned forward to tap her father's shoulder and give him a thumb's up sign.

Clare was frightened suddenly; in two minutes she would be with her family again. Bob honked the horn as he pulled the car round and manoeuvered it in between two others on the gravel. Then the front door opened, flooding the sweep with golden light. She groped out of the car, her arm still round Alice. Hester came out and stood under the porch, silhouetted against the open door. There were a lot of voices; a lot of light; she was sleepy. She was hugged and kissed, welcomed. Alice left her for her father, running round the car swiftly.

Then they were all in the long panelled sitting room; there was a crowd of people, all intimately known to her, all here. Nothing changed, nothing ever changed, except that she had changed; and her father was smiling and Felicity was putting down her sewing and standing up and Joseph and Louise and Tom and Caro had been playing bridge but had stopped at the sound of the car, and absolutely nothing changed and Joseph was walking towards the drinks table under the not surprisingly peevish eye of grandpapa's first royal stag, neatly labelled 1881, and was about to say . . .

And Joseph said, ' "For malt does more than Milton can, to justify God's ways to man." Want one, Clare?'

'Gin, please,' she said. 'Keep the whisky for Anni, she's walking down.'

And nothing ever changed. The first time she had come to them out of the darkness they had been assembled in massed ranks like this too. It had not been here, but in the vicarage playroom in Manchester. That made no difference. The sense of being inspected as she had been then laid its ancient weight upon her, accentuating her tiredness, her distance from them. It had been the morning of the funeral and all of them had been dressed for it already; seven cousins all wearing kilts; the boys with green wool jackets, the girls with Fair Isle jerseys. And she, still different from them wearing the red cotton dungarees she had travelled in; a consequence of a fight between her aunts, settled too late, with Hester's complete victory. They had stood in a line and inspected her – her cousins, all of them known to her and now, forced into new intimacy, total strangers.

Of course she probably didn't really remember: she had been only five. There were odd details to the memory. They would never have stood still in a line, from oldest to youngest, ranged tidily for her inspection – Joseph, Ben, Anni, Felicity, Ceci, Tom. Could Tom even have been born then? and Ceci must have been a toddler too small for even the smallest kilt. But Clare remembered remembering. The wall of them, impressed by the dignity of her status, awed by what they could understand of disaster.

Even before Hester could move to make her welcome she had been accepted by them. She had known it by some shifting in the ranks, some implicit welcome . . . but that was silly, no five-year-old knows such things; she had remade her past to meet this moment, because the moment was a hard one. She had come to them once, battered and defeated, and now she came so again; wishful thinking projected the old welcome, not memory. Anyway it was not the same: Joseph, Felicity and Tom had acquired spouses, and even though their children were in bed they filled the room with difference. They were all the grown-ups now, and could not inspect a newcomer with wide-eyed curiosity. She had been received with so much love, so little resentment, that she could not blame that single moment of silence, even if it had ever happened, for the gulf between them now. The separations came later, not then, not from that old arrival.

Her mother and father were of course also in the room, as they must have been then. She had not seen her father since she had come out of hospital; his dry kiss was more a homecoming than anything else could have been.

She was back in the present moment. A room full of cheerful holiday people, her brothers and sisters, her family. And there were real and normal things to do and say: gin-and-tonic and Caro getting two plates of cold roast beef and salad, then apologising and slipping all the roast beef on to her plate and returning to the kitchen for cheese for Anni. The room was warm, gracious, comfortable. She grinned suddenly, catching Tom's eye.

'Who's missing?' she asked.

'Ben. He's supposed to turn up tomorrow. And Ceci's in bed. I think she's finding us a bit raucous.'

'I'm not surprised,' Clare said, 'You dear brother, after all those sweet and silent sisters would be a shock for anyone.'

She noticed that she was already playing their games, the endless bruising banter which was the only way her family had of expressing its affection. She was too tired. She felt a wave of real communion with Ceci. The two of them might have found different ways to escape, but the intention had been the same. Ceci's was more effective; she had made herself free to go to bed early in a way that Clare knew she could not manage.

She looked at her plate and almost laughed. Caro had cut up her beef into neat squares, but had then plonked the slices she had carved for Anni whole on to the plate. One level of consideration obscuring an earlier one. Caro was infinitely good humoured and kind. Anni was smiling gratefully because she had not needed to remind anyone that she did not eat meat. Clare was grateful too because she had not needed to remind anyone that, like Caro's children, she could not cut up her food. She folded the slices neatly, left-handed and ate them with her fingers. Then she ate the salad, and the pre-cut rectangles, left-handed too, with a fork. Then she realised that nobody was looking anyway.

'Where am I sleeping?' she asked Hester.

'In the girls' passage. Ceci took the first room, and we've put Amanda up there this year – she wanted the end room, because of the windows – but the two next to Ceci's are ready for you and Anni. Hot-water-bottled and everything. You do look tired, darling.'

'I am.'

'Do you want to go to bed?'

Clare stood up; after a tiny pause the proper ritual came back to her and she went round the room to kiss everyone. Tom's cheek was scratchy; Hester's soft; Louise's slightly reluctant. At the door she said, 'Good-night then everyone.'

'Sleep well.' 'Sweet dreams.' 'God bless.' 'Don't be late for breakfast.' The last was accompanied by an old and shared laugh. Hester said,

'Eight-thirty; but you could sleep in if you wanted.'

'I wouldn't dream of it.'

'Fine. Mass'll be at eight.'

'Tea or Eucharist?' Joseph said. Like the malt and Milton quote it was an old family joke: house guests at Lord Halifax's home before the First World War were said to have been so questioned by the butler. Her children thought that it caught the flavour of Hester's morning energies perfectly. It was a joke Clare had not thought of for years, and it briefly deflected her tiredness.

'You can bring me tea if you like, Joseph; sugar and a dash of milk.'

'I don't do that even for Louise. You're taking pretty casually a rare chance for a lie-in; don't push your luck.'

Clare knew that if she responded as part of her irresistably desired to do, she would stay downstairs and play with them; and then it would get late and they would sit round the fire and someone – she cast a shifty glance around the room wondering who – someone would ask her something she did not want to answer. They were waiting, biding their time. There was probably already an organised conspiracy of love, which would have been carefully plotted, entirely for her own good.

So she smiled weakly and Hester said,

'Tom, carry Clare's bag up, will you?'

'I can manage.'

But Tom was already on his feet.

Hester said, 'God bless and keep you, darling.'

Clare said nothing. She followed Tom up the stairs, both of them self-consciously hushing their footsteps to pass Ceci's door, and into the neat little room. Nothing changed. There was an old rug on the floor, candlewick bedspread on the single bed, and faded chintz curtains already drawn across the window. Clean, spartan almost, like a convent cell; and she sensed Ceci's peaceful sleep through the wall.

She waited until Tom had departed before she took off her hand, shut it up in the top right-hand drawer and plugged in the battery recharger. For a moment her arm felt a sense of relief, but the ache remained. She looked at the stump, imagining her hand and fingers, beautiful in memory as she had never been conscious of them in their lifetime. She could hear the night silence, soft with the noises from the burn, the mutterings of the secret world outside. When they had been small they had all believed that plants and trees grew in the night when no one was watching them. It was not true of course; they grew in the sunshine, photo-synthesising, but she did not hear the darkness here at Skillen as threatening, but as busy, vibrant though secret. She walked down the passage, aware of the others, still awake, talking, laughing, downstairs. She wondered if they would talk about her; but she was too tired to care. The water in the old taps was brown and soft; she noticed that and so, for once, was not conscious of how strange washing one-handed was. The bare floor of the girls' passage sounded noisy and she walked carefully so as not to wake Ceci. Without even being aware of it she took a longer stride to avoid the squeaky board between the first and second of the little rooms.

Back in her own room, she did not unpack further, but stripped naked, climbed into bed and fell asleep, like falling off a wall. That night she did not dream. She did not need to. She had come home to the dream world, to the place of her childhood, the land of memories.

The house was a cradle of dreams; rocked itself by the soft lap-lapping of the loch, it rocked them all, even Tom and Caro's littlest baby who smiled and snoogled herself in her pile of satin-edged honeycomb-weave blankets; the dreams before words that no one can ever know the content of, which remain forever unreachable.

The house was long and low; built for pleasure, built for innocence despite the fact it was also and deliberately built for killing. Less than twenty yards from the front door, across the lawn, laid out once for long skirts and croquet, and now for children's swings and see-saws, was another low run of buildings: the boathouse running out over the water, poised to reach for the little trout; the game-larder with its huge ceiling hooks, waiting to receive the corpses of the red deer, whose entrails had been left on the high mountainsides to feed the golden eagles and carrion crows, but whose heads lolled down still dark-eyed, bleeding on to the concrete floor.

It was a house designed for the joys of death. The bedrooms were small and insignificant, but the baths were long and deep to welcome back bodies that have been soaked and worn by long days of killing. The kitchen was roomy enough to feed the hungry hunters home from the hill, but not as huge as the gun room with pegs for rods, racks for guns, ingenious devices for drying lines, storing flies, keeping cartridges, hanging binoculars, balancing telescopes: all the instruments and equipment for orderly and sporting murder. There was a solid wood table in the middle of the room, scrubbed white, for the careful recording of victories.

11th Sept 1884. South Hill. 12 pt. stag. Lord Mereham. Stalker: Alan McLeod.

12th Sept 1884. High Loch Cheildh. 36 brown trout. 13lb 5oz. 3 rods.

The log books of over a century of dead deer, hare, trout, salmon, snipe, ptarmigan; and only the rabbits, polymorphous vermin until myxomatosis taught them a lesson, were given a plural form to multiply their destruction.

And how to balance this killing, this killing which was the sign and substance of privilege, against the sweet delights of a century of huge meals truly enjoyed, and pale dawns seen from the high scree, where the pattern of valley and lochs far below, replicates the boulders and pools of the upper burns, both born out of the morning mist, shining like jewels in a necklace of purity; and in the very distance the sea, and the first sunlight catching the waves as they break against the rocks, palest pink, white gold. The deep, ancient satisfaction of stalking a living prey, where intelligence must be set against senses, rationality against instincts, the thinking mind against ears and eyes and nostrils more sensitive, against limbs more swift and strong; the long days of hard walking, careful breathing, silenced whispers, real skill, real intimacy, and the wide spaces, the clean wind of the high moor; and beyond every shoulder of mountain another shoulder of mountain, muscly, hard, bare at a distance, beflowered, bemossed, butterflied, beetled, alive, under your very nose as you crawl across it.

All this, together with the sense of freedom that summer holidays bring to town-raised children, installed deep in the memory long before the conscience had been informed of new laws of liberal sensitivity and political repugnance.

Skillen was, inevitably, a house of dreams.

Clare did not need to dream that night, on her return to the place of childhood, because the house itself was dreaming them all; dreaming the children they had been, the child their mother had been, the men their mother's brothers might have been if they had lived and not been stalked and shot, mown down on the killing fields of northern France.

The girls' passage, with the whole house, was heavy with sleep. Anni and Clare and Ceci, all breathing as deeply now as they did twenty years ago. Only Felicity had deserted them for the double rooms on the other side of the house; and instead they had Amanda, their niece, thrilled to have joined the aunts, the big girls, at last. So there were four little girls, still, and all sound asleep, in the darkest hollow of the night.

11th August

CLARE WOKE IN the brightening morning. She did not drift up from sleep but sprang from it in a sudden fear that she might have slept through the gong, missed breakfast, that she might be late and disgraced. She smiled at herself because that was too strong, she was a grown-up, there would be no disgrace, but she didn't want to be late. She groped for her watch and was glad to see that it was not yet seven, over an hour to – what was it Anni had said as they had arrived together last night? – over an hour to prepare herself for regression.

She climbed out of bed and went to the window, pulling the curtains apart and flinging up the sash with an urgent desire to smell, as much as see, the Small Loch and the hill above it. The rough mown lawn ran down to the edge of the loch; it was very bright green against the soft brown water and the muted heathery hill beyond. She considered briefly how she might best catch the vivid contrast and then stopped herself abruptly: she was thinking photographer's thoughts and she must not. Then, as she breathed in the soft peaty air, she was suddenly free in the sunshine and the innocence of morning.

Her skin felt soft in the coolness; she turned away from the window to look for her cigarettes. Without thought she reached towards the bedside table with her right arm, and was brought up short; the stump looked particularly ugly at the end of her naked body. She tried not to pay any attention to it. Instead she noted with pleasure how adept she was becoming at extracting a cigarette and lighting it one-handed; she inhaled, pleased, and looked around the simple room; the iron-framed single bed, the chest of drawers, scratched and old but beautifully clean, and the shabby curtains; the chastity of childhood given back to her. A place of safety. She was glad she had come.

She turned back to the window, to lean again on the sill and to enjoy the view, and the childish pleasure of believing herself the only person in this crowded house who was awake.

It was a delusion; she was not the only person awake. Even while Clare had been lighting her cigarette, Felicity had come out of the house, and when Clare went back to the window, she saw her younger sister sitting near the water edge, already dressed, her back to the house. Clare considered calling to her and then decided to leave her to what was clearly a chosen moment of solitude. They were rare enough here. She turned away from the window and faced the chest of drawers. She drew a deep and determined breath and began the practical, fiddly business of getting The Hand to co-operate with its morning duties.

Felicity used to enjoy the half-hour she gave herself as a daily gift before Alice woke up. At home in Ealing she would give herself that brief respite in her kitchen with a cup of coffee and the radio; here she took that same small break outside, beside the loch, although she no longer enjoyed it. Each morning for the last six months when she sought the old peace, she could not find it. She knew why, and she knew it was all her own fault.

Bob wanted another baby.

I want her to talk to me.

One night last winter, in the harbour of their bed with his arms round her, his voice muzzy, lost in the softness of her breast, even while she reached with a practised hand for her cap, Bob had said,

'Felicity, don't bother.'

'Don't bother what?' her hand was still reaching.

'Don't bother with that damn bit of rubber. Let's have another baby.'

'Oh Bob,' he had caught her by surprise, and she heard the desire naked in her voice.

'Well then?' Along with the desire, he must have heard the undertow of sadness, because he lifted his head and laid it on the pillow beside her, his hand still on her stomach.

'We can't,' she said. 'You know we can't.'

'Why not?'

'You know why not . . . the geneticist said . . . the risk . . .'

'So?'

'Bob!'

'So maybe we'll have another deaf baby. We'll almost certainly have a fair-haired baby, and one that will grow to be taller than average. OK. So what?'

'No.'

And five years of work and argument and learning and demanding crumbled in her hand. Bob really did not mind that Alice was deaf.

He said, 'Wouldn't that be rather neat for Alice?'

And after a long pause he added, 'We've learned so much stuff now, it won't be such hard work, and we'll get the diagnosis even sooner.'

He reminded her, 'Darling you've always argued . . .'

Felicity had argued with the world: 'There's nothing wrong with being deaf, only the way we treat the deaf. Alice is different, not better nor worse; she is special, and so she is especially loved. We would not want her other than how she is.'

I want her to talk to me.

She tried to tell herself that it was different for Bob, because he got to go out to work every day, he got to spend time with other people, with hearing people, with people who spoke to him in his own language. It was different for Bob, but not for that reason. It was different for Bob because he truly believed Felicity's rhetoric; he really did not see Alice as a handicapped person. He saw her as Alice. Felicity had thought she did too, but she, who badly wanted a baby, did not want a deaf baby.

He said, 'Would you want another baby if I could promise you it wouldn't be deaf?'

He had not sounded accusing, but she had felt accused. She accused herself. She had felt Bob, that night, silently smiling beside her. She had known he was smiling at the thought of another little baby. Bob loved neo-natal babies; she had often thought, with a great tenderness, that they made him feel good about being so tall. That night she had ruthlessly obliterated the tenderness, she had stamped on his silent smile.

'I won't risk another deaf child,' she had said to him, turning away from his arms. He had wanted to comfort her, but she could not let him. She had learned the truth now. She had been living a lie; her life was a lie and had been for five years.

I want her to talk to me.

Since then there had been no peace in her mornings. Bob had never brought the question up again. Perhaps it was only her hyper-sensitivity that made her feel he spent more time with Alice, engaged with her more lovingly, tried to compensate his daughter for the betrayal of her mother.

Felicity watched him, and knew that he was different with Alice from how she was. She could not understand why she had never noticed this before. Her signing was much better than his, more fluent, more grammatical and with a wider vocabulary, but none the less he communicated with Alice better than she did. Because . . . because he didn't mind. He saw the barriers only as a challenge, a game between Alice and him, a game that together he and Alice would inevitably win, because in his generous love there was no loss. She saw Alice's communication as a project; he saw it as a joy.

In five years Felicity had become a deaf expert. She had worked hard to learn Sign; to speak both ESL and sign-supported English. She and Bob were honoured members of their local deaf club. At one point she had even been grateful to Alice because Alice had given her a confidence in her own ability to learn things: to learn a language, in which Clare had so excelled as a little girl; to learn sciences – biology and linguistics and statistics and psychology – in which Anni had so excelled as a little girl. She went out and gave lectures, initially at women's clubs, but more recently to health visitors and social workers and academics, on a child's right to its own language and on deaf-world culture. She had taken on the Local Education Authority, not just on Alice's behalf, but on behalf of other deaf children. Deaf parents wrote to her and asked for her support, for her ability to deal with the speaking, hearing, prejudiced world when they needed it.

Felicity had become passionately committed to Sign, and therefore had spoken openly against oralism. She argued that in terms of normal development even the smallest children need access to language, a broad range of language, a density of concepts and ideas. Verbal language could not give them that: even at best it was a slow and ridiculous way to try and give profoundly, prelingually deaf children a language. The seduction of oralism, of forcing children to lip-read and speak, was nothing more than a denial of their deafness; a denial of their difference, of their unique culture. She had publicly criticised oralist parents for their 'possessive selfishness', and for a cultural arrogance that truly handicapped deaf children. Parents, teachers, social workers, officialdom, by insisting on rigorous oralism handicapped children. Deafness, she argued, was not a handicap; being deliberately deprived of language, of access to good Sign, was a handicap – a wilfully inflicted handicap. She had been asked to write a book: a book that would combine her and Alice's experience with a political agenda for the parents of profoundly deaf children and a history of the deaf community. This pleased her; it increased her confidence and her sense of her own standing, once too easily subdued by her big sisters. She had thought she believed what she preached. Deafness had become her profession.

But she made Alice wear her hated hearing aid. She refused to have another deaf baby. She refused to raise any more lovely babies for another community. Brood-mare and wet-nurse for the deaf community. It wasn't fair.

I want her to talk to me.

So she did not have the right to be Alice's mother.

Bob would not love her any more and she could not blame him. She was hideously angry with Bob. He should be on her side, not Alice's.

Worse still, God was entirely on Alice's side. God always sides with the little ones, children over adults, the sick over the healthy, the minorities over the powerful. Felicity did not see this in terms of politics, in terms of the Liberation Theology that Ben preached, but in terms of relationships. God loved her and God loved Alice, but in any struggle He would side with Alice, because Alice was deaf. It was this knowledge, this certainty that made it possible for her to fight so hard for Alice, but the same certainty made it impossible for her to fight for herself.

I want her to talk to me.

Over the last months she had had to dodge God. She had even

tried persuading herself that God did not exist; but she could not convince herself. God existed all right and wanted more from Felicity than she had to give.

'It's not fair,' she wanted to scream. And the well-informed voice of her conscience would argue that no one said it was fair; that the crucifixion wasn't fair. She could and should demand justice for others, but not for her privileged mean little self.

Even the Psalms, which she had always looked to as a very present help in trouble did not seem to meet her need:

> Out of the depths I call to thee, oh Lord,
> Lord hear my prayer.
> Oh let thine ears consider well
> the voice of my complaint.

She had nothing to complain of. She was not afflicted with a handicapped child. She was blessed with Alice. The complaint was against her; that she was too lazy and too selfish and too greedy —

I only want her to talk to me

too lazy, too greedy, too selfish, to have a child that was not of her choosing.

'You can't tell a gift when to come,' she preached to herself. 'Is it so wicked to want her to talk to me?' she asked.

Her God answered 'Yes' and she did not want to hear that, so she thought of more and more virtuous deeds to perform, and hid from herself the fact that Bob looked anxious, that Alice was more inclined to tantrums than she had ever been and that her mother made extra visits to London to be with her. When Hester wrote 'it would be especially lovely for me if you could all come to Skillen this year, please darling,' Felicity had thought instantly how totally exhausting it would be to take Alice somewhere different while at the same time giving her aged parents pleasure, so she accepted at once.

Now she sat in the peace of the morning and knew no peace. She heard the window open behind her and hoped that whoever was looking out would call to her, would distract her, but with the sulkiness of a child she would not turn. Whoever it was ought to want to talk to her. She stared stubbornly ahead, and then felt bitterly disappointed because there was only silence.

The silence was preparatory to Mass, and eventually Felicity got wearily to her feet and went to join her mother and father in the library where they always celebrated at Skillen.

Since his Ordination, forty-three years ago, James had only failed to say his daily Mass three times; twice when he was in hospital and once when Hester had gone into labour with Cecilia. They all teased Ceci about it still, 'You had to become a nun, reparation for causing grave sin.' James would looked pained, 'It was not a sin, it was a necessary consequence.'

Hester had received Communion every day since June 1942 when the church that was being used as a local shelter had been hit by a fire-bomb and a young woman sitting next to her had said that if she got out alive she would take up religion. The next morning Hester had committed herself to daily reception: it had been a thanks offering not for her own survival, but for the woman's repentance and its acceptance by God, because she had not survived though Hester had. Now, nearly half a century later, she would no longer have considered herself bound by such a promise, but she had discovered that she needed the Mass, needed Communion for herself. She let the promise stand, because she thought it drew less attention to her own piety than suggesting that it was her own spirituality that craved the daily reminder of the incarnation and resurrection.

James and Hester made no drama about this pre-breakfast activity. There was no pressure on the children or guests to attend. 'God has no grandchildren, only children,' Hester would say when asked. Until their Confirmation all of them had been rigorously schooled in religious devotion of a highly romantic Anglo-Catholic variety. The day they took those promises for themselves it became their own business. Hester never asked. Not that she did not know, or care; only that she did not ask.

'It is one of the things I find most endearing about Mummy,' Anni had once confided to Clare. 'It is an extraordinary generosity.'

'That makes it worse,' Clare had said, 'You can't even complain. You have to be grateful while obviously hurting her.'

As she went back into the house, Felicity wondered who would attend. Ceci was already on her knees. Felicity sat on the floor beside her sister, folded her legs, straightened her spine and glanced around; she could see only the white edge to Ceci's wimple and the tip of Ceci's nose. Perhaps she could talk to Ceci? Perhaps that disciplined faith, that honed singleness, could help her. Perhaps Ceci's deep prayer would work where her own more Martha-like activities had failed. But she did not want to acknowledge that Ceci had 'chosen the better part'. Felicity often caught herself thinking that nuns had it easy, despite all the sacrifices: no insecurity, no distractions, no demands. Ceci, who had been her closest sister in childhood, now rather scared Felicity. She thought crossly that she did not like her family. She wished she had not come at all; today she remembered there would have been the outing to the seaside organised by the Deaf Church's Sunday School. She acknowledged, irritated, that it was odd to miss the church while trying to avoid God, but the Deaf community there was more than just a congregation: it was the mainstay of her support network, the one place where she and Alice were equally valued, where she did not have to fight for Alice's rights, and where she did not feel judged, as she did at Alice's school, for being unable to sign well enough.

Hester arrived and smiled at both her daughters; Felicity shut her eyes as though in prayer. She could hear Hester moving round the room, checking that everything was in readiness, and then James arriving and helping her. She knew instinctively when they were ready to start. At the last moment the door opened again and, curious, Felicity opened her eyes. It was Joseph; he sat down quickly on the broad window seat and looked out.

The 11th of August was the Feast of St Clare; Hester, James, Ceci and Felicity all wished that Clare had come. Joseph did not think about it.

With the detached, careful precision of his generation James raised and spread his hands and said,

'In the name of the Father and the Son and of the Holy Spirit.'

Four right hands crossed themselves with a tidy flourish. 'Amen,' they all said; Hester cheerfully, Ceci very softly, Felicity formally and Joseph a tiny bit louder than everyone else.

'The Lord be with you.'

'And also with you.'

Only Felicity had her eyes open; she had become so used to seeing the liturgy as well as hearing it that she was temporarily distracted by the stillness of the room.

After Mass they all had breakfast.

Breakfast was Hester's favourite part of the day. Breakfast with her family about her was as near to heaven as Hester looked for in this life. She sat at one end of the table casting a benign smile on her household; marshalling her troops, organising the day.

Clare, determined to get it right, entered the dining room punctually. She saw her mother glow when she arrived, and was pleased. Since she had come out of hospital, people had been kind to her. She knew they had been kind and she could not explain why the kindness itself was so exhausting: realising that she gave her mother pleasure simply by consenting to be here, she recognised with a tiny rekindling of hope that she could still act, could still choose, and whatever her own motives in coming here she had acted kindly.

She saw also, and with relief, that she was neither the first nor the last to arrive. She poured herself coffee from the side-table, went to the long table, pulled out a chair and sat down. Nothing changed. Her mother was sitting at one end of the table with the grandchildren around her: Amanda, Joseph's oldest, neat, sweet and well behaved; Tom's three, at various stages of highchairs, cushions and their mother's breasts, already dirty, already noisy; and Alice eating with the concentration that she always gave to the task, uninterrupted by the cacophony around her.

Her father sat at the other end. And in between them the chairs for the generation between.

Joseph was standing by the window eating his porridge. He smiled at Clare, but she knew he was embarrassed. Too much intimacy had been imposed on them and Joseph wanted to recreate a proper distance.

As soon as she heard about Clare's accident Hester had reached for the telephone and spoken to her oldest son. She thought he had better go to Harare and bring Clare home.

'I know how busy you are, darling, but someone's got to and

really it had better be you. I mean, Anni or Ben . . . Can you imagine?' Long long ago Hester had decided that Joseph was the sensible one.

Although Joseph put up a token resistance – he was busy, he had an important case coming up, Louise would have to be consulted – he had known as soon as his mother outlined the problem that he would agree to go. He liked being the sensible one; it gave him a small edge, a tiny area of complacency, in the face of his feckless, crazy but more beloved, more attractive younger brothers and sisters. In any case very few people who knew her offered more than token resistance to Hester's plans for them, it was simply too tiring.

At the same time, Hester also rang a friend of her brother's who worked in the Zimbabwe High Commission to solicit his assistance for Lord Mereham's niece, and the Bishop of Harare's office, just in case that should later prove useful. Then she went to Mass; and with her usual brutal honesty inspected her conscience to see how she would feel if Clare had indeed killed David. It made no difference she decided, it was egotistical to assume that it did: both of them were in need of her prayers and she prayed for them. Hester lived with an unusual combination of intelligence and piety. This made her life so constantly difficult that all her daughters had chosen one or other – Clare and Anni the intelligence, Felicity and Cecilia the piety. It made Hester sad sometimes that none of her daughters seemed to see that the two were not mutually exclusive; that God was fun and that all a woman's resources could find space there. The boys had managed better she thought, all three of them carrying their faith more casually, more comfortably. In fairness she tried to remember how much more difficult it was being female nowadays than it had been for her when she was learning how to go about it. At that moment she remembered that Ben was carrying his religion a great deal too lightly and felt furious because he had distracted her from her prayers.

After Mass she had made James his breakfast, enquired with genuine curiosity as to whether he would say Requiem for David, and then sat down to ring all the other children so that they would not learn the news from the papers. They had all had quite enough bad tidings from the press for one month. She disciplined her anger against Ben, which in these early days still surfaced violently, erupting, throwing out clouds of sulphurous gas. She went into her own sitting room and spent a further quiet half-hour in prayer, for Clare whom she loved, and for David whom she did not. Then, confident that there was nothing more that she could do, she turned her attention to her weekly lecture on the history of western spirituality which she would give at the local theological college.

Joseph was more than sensible, he was highly competent. Three days later he was in the hospital in Mutare, calling Clare.

It is hard to resist the voice of your oldest brother, who was, even when small, given the authority to summon you; who has bossed and commanded and protected you for more than thirty years. Clare did not want to surface from her darkness even though the dreams there were not kind. She did not want to face the pain and the brightness, but Joseph called to her and reluctantly she turned her feet from the dark journey and came back into the world.

It was a world of pain, but still more of confusion: she did not know where she was or why Joseph was there. The sky was bright and hot outside the window, a different quality of light, but Joseph was solidly there.

'Hello, old thing,' he said.

He met a question in her eyes and added, 'Mummy sent me.'

'Hello, old thing. Mummy sent me.' It would be impossible to count how many of her meetings with Joseph had begun like that. It did not answer Clare's question exactly, but it made her feel safe. She drifted off into a gentler sleep.

Later Joseph's voice was mingled with the many others who asked her, 'What happened? What happened to David?'

Joseph was the first person to whom she tried to give an answer.

'I don't know,' she whispered. She tried to peer into the blackness. But the effort hurt.

'What's happened?' she asked Joseph. 'What has happened to David?'

Joseph was a good person to ask questions of, because he always gave sensible answers.

'You went to climb a mountain, you and David, a mountain called Nyangani, here in Rhodesia . . . I mean here in Zimbabwe. You didn't come down again. When they went to look for you they couldn't find you, either of you. Not for five days; then they found you miles away from where you should have been, much further north, with your head bashed in, and your arm. They still can't find David; they are afraid he may be dead.'

She nodded slowly.

'And you are still very ill and Mummy sent me to bring you home.'

She smiled at him, because that was less effort than anything else.

'Would you like that?'

The dark voices called her, that was what she wanted, to stay and listen to them. Joyful would know. She did not want to go back to the mess she had left behind her in London. But she kept smiling because she felt so terribly ill and muddled and because that was what Joseph wanted.

'Good,' Joseph beamed back, pleased with her, with the progress they were making.

Later, he had added, 'The thing is, they won't let you go home until you tell us what happened.' His confidence wavered suddenly and she started to drift away into her own dream world, but he was firm.

'Clare, the soldiers who found you, who carried you down from the mountain, they say that you told them you had killed him. Now, we know that's nonsense, but you must try and concentrate, remember, tell us. There is a problem because David has disappeared; tell them about it and then I can take you home.'

Clare smiled again, and knew that Joseph thought she was smiling at the thought of going home. She was lying to him. She was smiling because David had disappeared, because David was gone. She knew that was a secret that she had to keep or she would never get home again.

Joseph did not spend all his time leaning over Clare's bed. He spent a great deal of it negotiating, arguing, consulting. He wanted to take Clare home. Until he was given permission to take Clare home he was going to make a highly skilled nuisance of himself.

His uncle's friend in the High Commission became exasperated and weary. Clare was very ill and not getting any better. In the end, inevitably, Joseph won.

The journey home was horrendous. It was worse for Joseph, who had to organise it all, than for Clare, who simply slipped away into the dark place which had only one centre, a centre fixed in the pain in her right hand, and in the low voices of the mountain.

At Harare airport she surfaced briefly, on a stretcher on the tarmac, in the sun. She was restless, anxious.

'Joseph.' It was not Joseph's face that appeared, but the face of a nurse whom he had hired to accompany them.

'Are you all right, dear?'

'Joseph.' Her agitation increased, she struggled to sit up.

'He's coming, dear.'

He came, irritated now by the delay that was keeping them waiting here.

'Calm down,' he said, and then, 'What's the matter?'

'Joseph, where's my hand? What did they do with my hand?'

He was startled. They had decided not to tell her about the amputation. 'Did you know all the time?' he asked.

'Oh yes,' she said, although until that moment she had not had the energy to think about it.

'I can't leave without it,' she told him with real clarity, but then lapsed into fretful mutterings, 'it might be lonely . . . I don't want to leave without my hand . . . I want it.'

'Nurse,' Joseph called. 'Nurse, can you come over here a moment? I must talk to someone, find out about this delay. Can you take over, please?'

The nurse was kind. She smothered Clare's anxiety with her kindness.

'There, there, dear,' she said. 'You'll be on the plane in a few minutes and then we'll have you home in no time.'

I'm thirty-six years old, Clare tried to tell herself, I'm not a baby. But it was good to be a baby. She drifted off again and when she woke, somewhere high over the Sahara desert, she felt only a vague sense of loss, of worry. She imagined it was for her camera. Another thing she had lost in Africa: a camera, a job, a lover and a hand. A pretty impressive list of losses even for her.

But throughout the spring, when they visited her in hospital, none of her brothers and sisters teased her about it: it was one of the ways she knew the situation was serious.

Joseph and Clare had never chosen closeness, never exposed weakness to each other. Looking at him now, sleek and grown-up, standing in the sunny window, she knew that he did not want to have to remember her weakness, and his failure to extract from her any coherent narrative, or set of facts that he could go to work on. Since they had returned to London he had been immensely efficient and helpful; the complicated dealings with the mortgage and the insurance companies were grist to his well-organised mill, but he did not want to have to deal with her neediness. He wanted to laugh it off.

'Well,' he said, 'here's a surprise. Clare's on time for breakfast.'

She grinned a little sheepishly, her breakfast-time-banter skills rusted from disuse, but managed a riposte:

'Did you rise at dawn for the delight of being earlier than me?'

'I,' he said, waving his porridge spoon at her, and smiling to show he meant nothing by it, 'have been adding my little ha'p'orth to the sum total of world virtue: I have been at Mass.'

'Peace be with you,' she said, relieved that he could still tease her.

'And also with you.'

'If you would shut up that might be possible,' she said.

She sipped her coffee, but she was not left in peace. Joseph's son, William, was normally a child with extraordinarily good manners, a small, contained boy who seldom asserted himself. He was his father's pride and joy; which meant that Joseph was remarkably strict with him. Joseph looked at his brother Ben with bafflement and disapproval, and had persuaded himself, long before the scandal had proved him right, that Ben's lifestyle, his lack of realism and responsibility, was a direct consequence of being encouraged to show off when he was a child. Joseph knew, though never articulated, that his mother preferred Ben to him: he was the sensible one, the son and heir, the oldest, the best, but not the most beloved. He would not have called this jealousy, he would have called it impartial objectivity; but one result of it was that he was severe with William, knowing that he loved him, enjoyed him, took pride in him in a way that he did not with Amanda, his daughter. The boy grew up proper and tidy:

'You should have called him Charles,' Anni had once said to Louise, in a moment of unusual exasperation.

'Why?'

> ' "The nicest child I ever knew
> Was Charles Augustus Fortescue;
> He never lost his cap or tore
> His stockings nor his pinafore;
> In eating bread he made no crumbs,
> He was extremely fond of sums"

and so on and so forth.'

Louise, as so often when she had to encounter Anni, had not known whether or not she was being laughed at.

That morning, however, William was in an unusually elated mood. Joseph and Louise had begun the day with a minor fight about Amanda being allowed to sleep in the girls' passage.

'It's not that I mind where Amanda sleeps,' Louise had declaimed plaintively, 'it's just that your mother's so high-handed; she ought to have asked me first.'

Wrestling with the business of shaving, and not very interested, Joseph said, 'Well, she's the hostess; it's her job to decide where her guests sleep.'

'But this isn't guests, it's family.'

'Mummy wouldn't accept the difference; you know how polite she always is to children, it's something she believes in. She loves Amanda and wants her to have a good time. Why shouldn't she sleep in the girls' passage, anyway?'

'That's not the point. She should have asked me first. She's always trying to undermine me. Just because Caro spoils her children rotten and Alice . . . well, poor little Alice, but it doesn't mean . . .'

'Discuss it with her, Lou, she'll be very understanding.'

'It's too late now.'

'Then let it go.'

66

'You always expect me to manage the children and then complain when I don't.'

Joseph was left thoroughly annoyed by the whole thing:

'I'm going to Mass,' he had said with a slightly dishonest assumption of virtue, then pulling on his clothes he had left the bedroom. On the landing he encountered William on his way to show his mother he was properly dressed and ready to go downstairs. Crossness was replaced by pride, and his pride had been stung by Louise's suggestion that he didn't do his part in bringing up the children.

Without thinking he said, 'Will, I've been thinking. If Amanda is old enough to sleep on the girls' passage, do you think you're old enough to come on the Boys' Stalk?'

He saw the child's eyes light up deep inside with a simple joy that so pleased Joseph he was briefly carried away, and went on:

'We've got rifle practice this evening. You've been shooting pretty well with the .22 – if you want to try, you can have a go with the big rifle. If you shoot decently . . .'

He had gone too far. Louise would be furious and probably rightly, but he could not go back now. He said,

'No favours, mind. Duncan will have to decide. And it will be a long day; you'll have to walk with us, properly.'

There was a pause while the full significance of the promise registered with William. Joseph lost his nerve,

'Will, don't tell your mother just yet. She's in a bit of a bait this morning. This is just men's stuff.'

'Yes, Dad,' he said, but there, on the landing, he had crossed his Rubicon and he knew it. His father went downstairs to Mass and he reported to his mother for matutinal inspection. She was still annoyed and expressed it by fussing: his hair was a mess and his socks twisted, but he distanced himself proudly, feeling a complacent compassion for her because she believed she still had the right to straighten his shirt. He arrived in the dining room for breakfast in a mood of greater self-confidence than he had ever been aware of before.

So when Louise told him, aloud so they could all hear, that he was to carry his cereal *carefully* from the sideboard to the table he did something he had been longing to do. He sat down in the empty seat on his Aunt Clare's right and asked, rather louder than he had intended,

'Aunt Clare, I know it's a bit of a cheek, but, please, can I see your hand?'

'William,' snapped Louise from across the table, 'don't be rude.'

Putting Louise in her place was a better way of reclaiming her dignity after her sudden and all too visible flush than repressing a small boy. With an act of will Clare stopped the instinctive withdrawal of her right arm into hiding under the table and said, 'Leave him alone Louise, it's a perfectly natural curiosity.'

She said to him, 'Look, it's pretty clever.' In front of them all and with an almost aggressive nonchalance, she pulled her sleeve back so he could see the join and the strap. 'Here's where all the machinery is. If you want to, you can unscrew it here and see the insides.' And with her left hand she started to untwist the whole hand at the wrist.

'Yeugh, gross!' said Caro impulsively, but everyone else was sitting in stunned silence.

'I won't do that now,' said Clare, responding. 'Then you put the batteries in here, and turn it on. You can do that.' His small fingers fiddled with the tricky business of finding the subcutaneous switch, but without her own repulsion, only with fascination. 'Then there's all this circuitry stuff. Did you know that your nerves work by electricity, little electric messages that hop from your brain down your arm? Well, this just keeps them going. Clench your fist.'

He clenched it, looking at it with interest.

'How did you do it?'

He looked mystified.

'Your brain told your hand to. Now I will, but it's a bit slower because I have to think it more carefully.'

She put her elbow on the table as though she was about to engage in an arm wrestling contest, and quite slowly but inexorably the plastic hand closed beside his. She sent a little message of gratitude to the pretty dark woman from the dinner party who had taught her that this was possible. 'It's clever computer trickery, and something called solenoids, little magnets which can turn tiny electric currents into strong ones; just like when you start a car. I'm sure Anni or your father can explain it to you, better than I can.'

'Wow! Bionic!' said her ten-year-old nephew, wide-eyed, enormously impressed. Oblivious to her lurking embarrassment, he put the questions that none of the grown-ups had dared to ask: 'How does it stay on? Do you take it off at night? How long do the batteries last?'

She answered, and as she did so Alice came round the table to her left side and stared with intensity at The Hand.

'Electronic toys,' Clare said to William, and tapped Alice's hearing-aid box very lightly, 'really powerful stuff. Magic, Alice and I carry scientific magic around with us. We're modern witches. Electronic witches.'

Alice, knowing she was being talked about, snuggled closer into Clare's side, but looked away to her parents for a translation.

'Felicity,' said Clare, 'can you tell her The Hand can't talk Sign?' She stopped, alarmed, and then realised that no one at the table could see the capital letters.

'You mean you can't.'

They had all been supposed to learn because Felicity had asked them to and Clare knew with shame that she had done less about it than anyone else at that table.

'I mean I didn't, that's true; but The Hand can't.'

'Irish Sign is done one-handed,' Felicity said.

'Felicity, I'm sorry.'

But Alice reached across her and took her right hand and placed it very gently against her own ear and smiled.

'What else can't it do?' William asked, anxious to return to his position at the centre of attention.

'Swim, tie complicated knots, find things in the dark,' said Clare. Make love, but she didn't say that, take *my* photographs, make me feel good about it. 'When I first got it and they were teaching me how to make it work I had to make a list of all the things I most wanted to be able to do, and they could tell me if that was possible and how. So if they weren't on my list I might not know. There's probably lots of things that I can't do anyway, that it couldn't do even if I could. The beautiful sewing Aunt Felicity does, for instance.' It was offered as an apology, but she could not tell from Felicity's face if it had been accepted or even understood. 'And I don't know yet if it can manage to de-bone a trout, so you can help me find out, if anyone caught a spare one yesterday.'

She was pleased with herself; only twenty-four hours ago she would not have dared consider the eating of a small fish at her family's breakfast table.

Felicity got up and left the room; Clare could not tell if it was coincidental, or if her feelings were really hurt.

'Daddy caught two, but I think he promised Mummy one; and Uncle Tom caught one but it was very little, Aunt Caro said that it would have to be for Bitsy.'

Emily, Caro and Tom's three-year-old, hearing her pet name, squeaked, 'Me too,' at the top of her voice, and looked around for attention.

'Quite right, Ma'am,' said Joseph, deciding that he would intervene before Louise did, 'Where are our trout?'

He put his bowl on the sideboard and lifted the silver lid off the dish on the food-heater. 'Scrambled eggs and sausages. Very nice but . . .' He stuck his head through the serving hatch and called, 'Lucy!'

A pleasant Australian voice replied, 'Coming.'

'No, I just want to know where my trout is.'

A froth of dark curls appeared in the serving hatch.

'What?'

'My trout. What have you done with it?'

'The fish you caught last night? I made them into some mousse for Anni, for tonight. The rest of us are having ham.'

'Oh Lord,' said Tom. Did nobody tell the poor girl? Lucy, my poor antipodean chum, you have just committed the worst crime in the country.'

Hester interrupted, 'Don't tease her Tom. It's my fault. Oh, Joseph, I am sorry.'

Lucy continued to stand at the serving hatch, looking puzzled.

Louise said, 'Hester, honestly, it really doesn't matter.'

'It certainly does,' grinned Tom. 'Joseph will serve a writ upon you, Mummy; you know how he values customary usage.'

Caro said, 'Shut up, Tom. Ignore them all, Lucy. People who

catch them get their own trout for breakfast: they'll be in the fridge all cleaned and gutted, and you are expected to roll them in oatmeal and fry them in butter and arrange them on a flat plate in order of size. That's how they can have a good fight about who caught the biggest one every single morning; it's a family tradition.'

Anni said, without any note of conciliation, 'Goodie, goodie, I am extremely partial to trout mousse.'

'I don't think it's fair that picky eaters should get special privileges.'

'Tom,' said Hester, 'stop stirring.'

'Vegetarianism,' said Anni, her eyes lighting up gleefully, 'does not count as picky eating; it counts as high principle and nobility of soul. Treasury of merit stuff which certainly earns me something – and I'd rather have trout mousse than eternal salvation.'

'Anni,' said James, suddenly re-connecting to his household, with a smile of great sweetness, 'stop stirring.'

'Which reminds me,' said Anni, returning his smile with one nearly as sweet, 'I have brought you all a rare gem. It is a book which you will all find soothing to your wicked consciences. It's by Pastor Ammon and he – bless his name and alleluia – is the executive director of Sportsmen for Christ. His helpful little volume is called *The Christian Hunter's Survival Guide*; and he will tell you that God positively wants you to kill animals – only you call it harvesting them instead of hunting, shooting, fishing, stalking, trapping or whatever – anyway God loves it if you off them so long as you take helpful biblical texts, called memory verses, out with you and chant them as you wait in hiding for the harvest-on-the-hoof.'

'I don't believe a word of it.'

'No, honestly, Joseph, you'll love it. I'll go and get it right now.'

She jumped up and left the room; Hester started making arrangements for lunch and supper, and for shooting practice that evening. Anni returned with the book and she and Joseph and Tom fell on it with glee.

'Listen!

Before you enter the field digest this: if anyone out there is

71

expected to live by the rules it is the Christian Hunter! With God in you, you can think more clearly, give more and be more patient than the unsaved hunter . . . as you sit eating your breakfast put your Bible and the state game law in front of you and vow to obey them both this day.

Praise the Lord Jesus.'
'Amen, Sister.'
'Alleluia.'
'You're making this up,' said Ceci.
'No, wait, give me the book back; there's a deeply moving witness somewhere. Hang on. Here we go, he's just shot a beautiful little white fan-tailed pigeon, this was of course "Before I was saved" when he was, and I quote, "the King of slobs". He says, "My life changed that day because of that pigeon; God used his death to bring me to Him and deliver me from being a slob hunter." '

Their differing views on blood sports were entirely forgotten in their shared delight.

'Who is easing whose conscience?' Ceci asked, but she came round the table to share the book with them.

Clare tried to listen and knew she had lost, perhaps for ever, any taste for this particular game. After a while she went to find Felicity.

Nowadays Felicity very seldom did the beautiful embroidery to which Clare had referred. Sometimes, when Alice was out of the house, she felt the tight band of concentration that bound her to her daughter slacken and she was free; but normally she did not give herself over to anything that could not be laid down easily. Although Alice was playing quite happily now with her cousins, Felicity did not relax: the habit of attention was ingrained.

Alice had been a perfect baby; the first of many perfect babies Felicity had thought. She had imagined, as an adolescent, that she would marry a priest, because in her mind that went with having lots of children. Of course she had not, she had married a school teacher and she was happy with that choice.

She and Bob had been unusually perceptive. She had known by the time Alice was six weeks old that something was wrong: she had mentioned it to her GP at the post-natal check up. And the GP, oh blessed chance, oh cause for praise and gratitude, did not tell her to calm down and stop being silly, but said, 'Show me.'

Felicity had known because she loved Alice. She had known because Hester had taught knowing, had taught observing and following one's instinct when it came to babies.

The doctor said, 'Show me.' Then he said, 'Honestly, Felicity, I'm not trying to fob you off. I don't know how. . . . She might be . . .'

Felicity's imagination had run through an appalling list: brain damaged, spastic, neurologically impaired, terminally ill, dying.

'I wonder if she might be hearing impaired.'

'Deaf?' gasped Felicity, but it was a gasp of relief. It sounded infinitely preferable to anything on her own list.

'We'll keep an eye on her, shall we? I don't know . . . quite frankly, I've never had to work with a baby this small. I'll find out.'

She had told Bob; and, telling, what she had felt was shame.

'Do you feel ashamed?' she asked Clare quite abruptly when her older sister found her in the sunny sitting room, five years later.

Clare stood poised in the doorway like a deer, not yet frightened, but wary.

'Ashamed? Of what? Of not learning Sign? Yes a bit.'

She wanted to say, 'So you think I killed him do you? You think I killed him and I'm lying.'

Felicity said, 'About your hand.'

'Embarrassed, do you mean? When people stare, or flinch. Of course. I broke a glass the other day at a party, everyone was looking. I felt embarrassed then.' She could talk to Felicity about this as to no one else, because of Alice.

'No, not that. When Alice was first diagnosed I felt this extraordinary sense of shame.'

'They told me in the hospital that everyone does. I don't know why.' There was a pause. 'I thought about you and Alice a lot, you know. When I was in the hospital.'

Alice had been formally diagnosed at ten months.

'Profound hearing loss.' The consultant who had performed the electronic tests, under general anaesthetic, had looked compassionate. 'Give yourself time to mourn.'

By then they had not needed to mourn. They had already known; they had run their own domestic tests on Alice. Long before the doctor gave them his kind permission to mourn, they had moved on. They had already started to look for ways of dealing with the future.

'Do you know there's something that calls itself a 'deaf church' in Southern Street? I hadn't noticed before,' Bob had said one Saturday evening. 'They have a service at eleven on Sundays. Let's go and have a look.'

'What's a deaf church?' Felicity had said.

'I don't know. Ring your mother and ask.'

'The minute I ask her, we make it public.'

'Mmm, yes. Is there anyone else we could ask?'

They rang Ben. He said, 'Sure, why do you want to know? There's a whole network of churches for the deaf. The C. of E. have a field officer or whatever they're called nowadays. I don't know a lot about it really, but they . . . actually the one in Milton Keynes asked me to come and do a service one day in Holy Week last year. Bloody typical – the only people who want me to preach for them are deaf. It was rather moving: we did Stations of the Cross and they were all taken off the wall, the images I mean, and handed round and touched by everyone. Actually, Felicity, it nearly made me cry. It wasn't just the deaf, there were a lot of people who were deaf *and* blind. I had an interpreter. I'm told they do a lot of social stuff too. Are you planning some good works? And they all talk this weirdly beautiful language, if that's the right word, called Sign.'

So Bob and Felicity went, the next morning, and found a home, a heaven, a place of glory. The Eucharist was transformed for ever: the dancing sacrifice. The liturgy not of the Word, but of the Body. The Word was made flesh and danced among them, and they beheld its glory.

As a small girl, Felicity had been the only one among her sisters who had wanted to go to dancing class. Anni and Clare's derision at such 'sissy' desires had prevented her ever speaking of them to her parents; dance remained somewhere deep inside her as a romantic and delightful idea. And now, this connection between meaning and movement was given to her as a gift precisely when she needed it. She had been awestruck at the grace and authority of the priest, at the silence and devotion of the congregation.

The verbal dexterity of her family, which had so often made her feel slow and clumsy, had not prepared her for the beauty and directness of Sign. Because she knew the words of the service so intimately, she did not need to listen to them; the dimension that this strange language added to the old and well-worn faith was instant – she saw and she believed. After communion she found herself wiping tears from her eyes and smiling at Bob over the soft, elegantly formed head of her precious baby.

Alice had been six months old; Bob had carried her, still crumply, in a blue canvas pack on his chest. After the service the priest had greeted them, hands fluttering in the language they neither of them spoke. Then he said,

'You're new?'

'Yes, Father.' He smiled a jovial pleasure at the form of address.

'Just visiting?' A welcoming voice, but a hint of suspicion also.

'I don't think so,' Bob said. Then after a little pause, 'We think she . . .' and he ran the two smallest fingers of his left hand over the top of Alice's silkient skull, 'we think she may be hearing impaired.'

'We say deaf,' said Father Harris. He had not been ashamed. 'You might like to meet Elspeth,' he said. 'Nicky, her youngest, must be much the same age as yours, but the other way round. She's deaf, he's hearing.'

Elspeth, who taught in the Sunday school, could change nappies while talking to her baby with her hands; Felicity was impressed.

Father Harris, interpreting for the two mothers, said 'She says, you talk to Nicky while she talks to . . . ?'

'Alice,' said Bob. Elspeth took Alice from him, and propped her up in a baby seat. Alice watched her face with a concentration that surprised both her parents.

'Hello, Nicky,' said Bob, with half an eye still protectively on his daughter. The baby did not look at his face but at his hands. Suddenly he laughed, a splendid baby chuckle.

'Elspeth,' said Father Harris, 'says, "are you learning Sign?"'

and to tell you I am only an interpreter. Talk to her not me and I'll simply translate.'

'How do we learn?' Felicity asked, still looking at the priest. He did not answer, but fluttered his fingers at Elspeth. She grinned and answered.

'Here,' said Father Harris, still looking at Elspeth. 'Beginners' Sign classes on Tuesdays at seven. Play group for children between 2 and 3.30 on Wednesdays, babies very welcome. How to manipulate social workers, special class for mothers, sorry for parents, Monday evenings at 6 p.m. Bridge, played in Sign only, Thursday nights. You won't need the old age pensioners' lunch club details just yet.' He and Elspeth were laughing. 'And I'm not to interpret the last bit!'

'I have to go,' he said. 'You'll find it difficult at first. Don't worry, but if you want to ask anything, I'm usually around to interpret. If Elspeth isn't bossing me about you can even talk to me if you want to.' He handed them a card, touched Alice's nose welcomingly and went off smiling.

By the time Alice was eighteen months old it was their home, but right from that first day it was not just social provision, it was the silent beauty of the liturgy: the signed Mass, the priest dancing at the altar, the God who came to them through this power and shapeliness, the unashamed welcome. There Felicity had found a strength that had carried her triumphantly through the next five years.

She had thought she had made it. She thought she had got it right, and in one little moment the whole thing had evaporated, vanished, disappeared. She had discovered in herself a hard wall, a solid barrier of egoism, that she had not dreamed of. She was not a nice and good person, she was a mean, selfish one. She did not know this person who must be herself and she hated her.

She had never mourned, and so now she had to learn new emotions. She had to try and learn everything again. Now Felicity wanted to know from Clare how it was to be disabled, to be handicapped.

'I thought about Alice in hospital,' Clare said.

'You're the only one who didn't even try to learn Sign.'

'I know,' said Clare. 'I'm sorry.'

'It's no good being sorry.'

It wasn't much good, thought Clare, but what exactly was Felicity punishing her for? With an odd clarity she knew that Felicity was jealous.

Felicity felt that Clare got everything. Clare even got more sympathy than she, Felicity, did. Than Alice did. Clare always stole from her. She did not know why she felt that way. She would not let herself remember.

'We must be kind to Clare,' Hester had said when Clare had come to live with them. 'She hasn't got a mummy and daddy now and she hasn't got any brothers or sisters.' The four-year-old Felicity had not wanted to be kind.

'I think we might let her sleep in Anni's room, don't you?' Hester had said, 'so she doesn't feel lonely.' Felicity, who had been longing for her promotion from the nursery to Anni's room, who had been longing to be a 'big girl', just as Joseph and Ben were 'big boys' had seen Clare and Anni become 'the big girls' while she and Ceci had to be the 'little girls'.

She did not remember any of this now, but she heard her own voice, slightly shrill and childish, saying, 'It's not as bad as all that you know, losing a hand.'

'It's pretty bad, Felicity.'

Felicity, although she was appalled at her own meanness, had found someone to punish and could not let it go.

'You've got a replacement. Electronic magic you called it, I heard you.'

Felicity did not care whether her sulk was about the moment of closeness she had seen between Clare and Alice at the breakfast table: that Clare, who had not bothered to learn Sign, had a bond with Alice that she could not share; or whether it was about Clare attracting the attention and concern that were due to her and Alice.

'So does Alice.'

'But it doesn't work. We bombard her with sound, enough sound to damage a well person's ears, and it doesn't work.'

'Nor does my hand.'

'And Alice hates it.'

'Bloody hell, Felicity, so do I.'

77

They are five and six years old again and there is nothing they can do about it. They are standing on the top landing of the Vicarage. They are fighting. They fight a lot. It worries Hester, who loves them both. Clare's right hand reaches out and pushes Felicity. She loses her balance and slowly, slowly, slowly tumbles backwards down the stairs. Time slows down relatively in a strong gravitational field: Clare's hand reaching out, pushing, and Felicity's slow descent, bump bump bump, and the long horrid moment of silence before they both start to scream. Neither of them remembered this now.

'So why do you wear it then?'

'Why does she?'

There was no way out of this. For either of them to point out to the other that they were behaving like children would be to consign the other to the nursery.

The nursery saved them. The door opened and Alice came in. She smiled sweetly and went to her mother; immediately Felicity refocused. Clare was touched by the complete attention that Felicity gave her daughter. In that stilled moment she was able to detach herself too, to recognise the weight and weariness of that perfect gaze – the gaze her mother had at prayer. The two of them spoke in a foreign language, the one that Clare had failed to learn. She had not earned the right of being privy to their conversation, but it ended with smiles.

Alice skipped over to a green baize card-table that stood in the window and from it brought something to Clare, which she held out with solemnity. Clare hesitated.

'It's your jigsaw bit,' said Felicity with a smile. 'Alice is really taken by the idea. We got ours yesterday.'

Every holiday since either of them could remember Hester had provided a huge 5,000 piece jigsaw puzzle. At one point they had all competed to find the most complicated, difficult or original puzzle for Hester's birthday present. Round puzzles, abstract paintings, monochrome monstrosities without edges. Finally, 5,000 blank white pieces, identical on both sides, had defeated them: frustrated and annoyed they satisfied themselves now with major art works, crowd scenes, or views of trees with complicated green and brown sections.

One Easter, when he was about fourteen, Ben had got up in the night and, working until the chilly dawn, had completed that holiday's puzzle all on his own. The rest of them had been outraged and Hester had introduced a new twist to the tradition: when the puzzle was taken out of the box everyone was given a piece of their own, to keep. The puzzle could only be completed when everyone was present.

Remembering, Clare smiled and held out her hand for the little chunk of cardboard. Alice did not hand it to her. There was a pause. Alice looked meaningfully at The Hand and Clare was surprised by her own deep reluctance. She had to draw a breath, let it out slowly, and then, overcoming her reluctance because of the pleasure in Alice's face, because only half an hour before she had told Alice that they were Electronic Witches together, something to be proud of, she held out The Hand and received her jigsaw piece.

It was black and white, tightly drawn parallel lines.

'Thank you,' she said to Alice, mouthing carefully and smiling. 'Have you given Anni hers?'

Alice turned from her abruptly to demand a translation from Felicity. Then snatching another piece from the table she danced out of the room.

The two sisters looked at each other.

'What's the picture, then?' Clare asked Felicity, to fill the momentary silence.

'Escher; people going up stairs in all dimensions that melt into each other, you know.'

'All black and white?' Clare knew the picture too well; the hospital psychologist had had a copy of it on the wall of her office.

'Yes. Alice likes Escher,' Felicity said. 'Anni gave her some socks for her birthday with Escher fish on them, all interlinked, and I have difficulty in getting them off her and into the wash, but I think they're spooky.'

'How odd, that's just what I was thinking,' Clare said.

The two sisters looked at each other.

'I'm sorry.' It did not matter which of them had said it first.

There were of course other times, easier to remember. Times when Anni's infuriating oldest daughter status obliged them to

79

combine their talents in a full assault on her privileges. Times when Ceci was the baby and it was their obvious, mutual, moral duty to put her in her place. And times when all four of them, so close in age, so tightly bonded by class and domestic life, united in an unbreakable team against the other children in the parish, the other girls in their school, or against the grown-ups. These times could be remembered more comfortably, and they relaxed and smiled at each other.

None the less it was with the distinct feeling of sneaking off that Clare made some excuse and left the room. Felicity sniffled a bit, privately, but knew she was not really going to cry.

Clare could not escape her own fears. These increased as she crossed the hall, for there on the table, on top of the pile of post was a letter from Peggy, her mother's best friend, the last person who had seen her and David together, unmistakable in its blue air-mail envelope and brightly coloured Zimbabwean stamp. Her fear mounted almost to panic. Whatever Peggy had written, Hester would want to talk to Clare about it.

The infantile mood created by her squabble with Felicity remained with her: she debated stealing the letter, to read it first and then to burn it. She paused. The Hand reached out for it spontaneously. Tom came across the hall.

'Clare,' he said, on a sudden impulse, 'I thought I'd take a boat out on the Big Loch. Do you want to come?'

'Yes!' she said, with such enthusiasm that Tom was surprised.

'I'm escaping my paternal duties,' he said, 'and a planned trip to the seaside; what's your line?'

'I think Mummy may want to pray over me.'

'Little talk time, eh? She's in a Lady Marchmain mood, is she?'

'I don't know, but there's a letter here from Peggy.'

'Ho hum. I get it. You were staying with her when you disposed of David weren't you?'

'Tom!'

'Only joking.'

'How this family managed to produce someone with so little sense of good taste is a constant surprise to me.'

'Watch it or I won't row. Look, let's make this snappy. I'll get a couple of rods, you get us some lunch.'

'Tom . . . bring me the little one. I've never tried left-handed.'

'Big Sis, I may have no sense of decorum, being but a country yokel, but I am not entirely stupid. You're on, so long as you're ready in the next three and a half minutes.'

They were running away, and the childish delight of it got them out of the house and out of sight behind the copse of fir trees that stood between the Small Loch and the Big Loch. They ran out the heavy rowing boat, with its flat wooden platform over the bow to sit on: Joseph and Ben had built it together one teenage summer, and it made casting a great deal easier.

The wind was firm and gentle, chasing alternate bands of sun and shadow across the dark green water, and the mountains circled around them, purple-grey, green-gold, violet-black responding like the water to the wind's patterning of light and shade. The clouds were high and silent.

Tom managed the boat, sitting not on the rowing bench but in the smaller seat towards the bow and keeping it all the time square to the wind down the long gentle drifts, now and then dabbing one way or the other with an oar and casting expertly across the water the rest of the time. At the end of each drift he turned square on his bench and pulled the boat strongly and steadily up to the top of the loch again while Clare sat in the stern and ran out her line. He exercised a beautiful and unexpected tact, turning the boat's bow always to the northern shore so that she could more easily cast over her left shoulder, tying her flies, untangling her cast not once but twice without comment and managing to make all the extra chores he had to take on because of her handlessness into acts of male pride, not compassion for the handicapped.

She hadn't fished for years and, lulled by the peaceful rhythm and the silent beauty around them, felt pleased with herself, especially when she found the confidence to use The Hand to steady the bottom of the rod. It did not give back the soft warmth of the cork handle the way it should, but she did not mind.

Tom watched her neutrally, but after about forty-five minutes he said, 'That's very pretty, Sis,' as cast after cast went out straight, delicate, almost splashless, on to the water.

'Thanks, that's a compliment.'

'Can I ask you something?'

'What?'

'Why don't you just do it with your new hand?'

Clare considered the question. 'Two reasons, I suppose; one is that there isn't a great deal of wrist flexibility, and what there is I'm not very skilled at. Fly-fishing wasn't on the list of the pressing needs that I had to give my physio. But more, well, it's a bit odd, but you don't get any information back through it. It's good for controlling things, but not for receiving them. So, I suppose, I, I didn't really think about it, but I suppose you wouldn't feel the fish strike, you'd have to be looking all the time.'

'You should be anyway.'

'Like you are now.' They grinned at each other.

A little later when she felt the definite down twitch of the line and struck with a prompt clean response, she trapped the bottom of the rod between her thigh and the boat edge to leave her left hand free to play the fish, although in no very impressive style, Tom once again stopped looking at his own fly. He produced the landing net at exactly the right moment, and was delighted for her. She had forgotten and was freshly reminded of the tiny but absolute thrill of landing even a rather small trout.

'Lucky it wasn't bigger,' she said.

He grinned because it was true, but generously.

'Never mind, it's breakfast. And as a special treat I'll gut for you.' He made a nice little practical suggestion about fitting a clamp on to the edge of the boat for her and they discussed one-handed fishing techniques. They didn't catch much and they didn't talk much, until after a couple of hours, at the bottom end of the loch, they let the boat float gently into the shallows and ate their sandwiches.

'What did you get?'

'Beef or cheese. Beer or nothing. You didn't give me much time.'

'Which do you want?'

'No one was looking, I got plenty of both.'

'Beef to start with then. And beer. Do you want me to open your can?'

'No thanks. Beer cans — along with wine corks — were definitely on my physiotherapist's list of imperatives,' and she hooked her metal index finger into the aluminium ring on her beer can, and pulled away from it with her left hand.

'That's neat,' he said. 'God, it's a relief to have one member of this family who is relatively normal.'

She looked up at him so obviously startled that he was provoked into further comment.

'I am, of course, assuming that you did not, in fact, bump him off. That's why I'm the only one who can joke about it. Mummy thinks it has to do with religion; Anni thinks it has to do with politics; Joseph thinks it has to do with sex . . .'

'Sex!'

'Joseph thinks everything has to do with sex, haven't you noticed? It's because he's become such a prude; he thinks everything has to do with sex and as he can't use any dirty words it's very difficult for him. But I, as I was saying, think it was just bad luck . . . sort of thing that might happen to anyone.' He glanced at her quickly to make sure she knew he was joking. 'Think of that poor guy up that mountain who cut his friend's rope to save his own life and then the bloke lived. Double bad luck. If you climb mountains, accidents happen. That makes you normal, not abnormal.'

She looked away from him across the loch and saw, miniaturised in the distance, the children spread out across the field above the house.

'Mushroom risotto for supper,' she said, to cover her confusion.

Tom looked round, too, and the memory of those treasure hunts for mushrooms encouraged him.

'Well, you know what I mean: there's Joseph and Anni both in their different ways sinking into middle-aged old maidery and covering it up by pontificating as though they were both the Pope; and Felicity wrapped in pious good works. I don't understand what the hell Ceci's up to. So there's just you and me left to have a reasonably agreeable time.'

He smiled at her, but her next words broke the spell:

'And Ben.'

There was a pause as though the sun had gone in.

'I can't,' said Tom. 'I can't even think about him.'

He leaned over the side of the boat, washing the breadcrumbs off his hands, and then reached down and scooped a small round pebble off the bottom. He held it between his fingers, not looking at her.

'Confession time,' he said. 'Mummy rang us all the morning it was in the paper . . . you were already away but she rang us all, bless her. So I knew, and it shouldn't have been a shock. We, Caro and I, were going out to lunch, pleasant people, lots of kids, family meal, and someone had the bloody rag, just reading it after we'd eaten. And he laughed and turned the picture to me and said something like "look at this, Tom old man, here's a naughty, nancy clergy-boy with the same name as you." Something like that. And I, damn it Clare, I laughed. I laughed as though it simply wasn't possible. Caro was braver . . . She said, "actually that's my brother-in-law, so shut up will you." And the bloke was really upset and apologised and said of course you couldn't believe a single damn thing a paper like that printed and went on to some other juicy rubbish. But if Caro hadn't, I wouldn't. I'd have laughed and pretended.'

He sat in silence fiddling with his stone and then suddenly threw it with great violence into the water. 'Frankly, I think what he did was revolting. Quite apart from the scandal, and poor Daddy. It's just, it's just revolting in itself. I don't know how I'll be able to talk to him.'

The ripples from his stone bounced against the ripples the breeze was already making on the loch surface and fragmented into little scatters of light, each intricately linked with the other. They were exactly the patterns that Clare had tried to photograph for Mark, for herself. She almost told Tom about it, but at the moment when the ripples from the wind overcame and blotted out the ripples from his stone, he said with obvious pain.

'I wish to God he wasn't coming.'

'Oh, Tom.'

He turned in his seat, gathered up the pieces of cling-film, the empty beer cans and the paper bags and neatly stored them in his fishing basket.

'Very eco-freako, we've become, you see.'

'You were never cut out to be a litter-lout anyway.'

'True, but now we can feel morally superior about it instead of mere snobbish superiority; much more satisfactory. Lend us your feet.'

He scrambled on to the central bench; reached backwards for the rowlocks and oars, settled them into place, then looked at Clare expectantly. The boat had never had a decent footboard. She sat forward and braced herself against the seat, and with an old practised gesture squared her knees so he could use her shins instead. He was wearing canvas tennis shoes; not the fashionable clunky trainers of the London streets, but worn light school plimsolls with brightly coloured children's laces in them. Clare found that rather sweet.

'Once you've seen him,' she said, 'it won't bother you so much; it'll just be Ben.'

He was rowing so hard that his body swung towards her and away, making his voice rise and fall, and he was beginning to pant a little.

'It's the nipple-ring,' he said, his head nearest to her breasts on the word. 'That's too much. I'll know he's wearing it you see.'

She resisted the impulse to cover her own nipples with her hand, trusting Anni's tolerance more than she trusted Tom's.

'Perhaps he can take it off.'

'Have you ever seen one?'

'No, not my thing.' Yet she couldn't help wondering what exactly her various siblings did do in bed. And how Tom would feel if she told him what she and David had done. What was Tom's thing? What was hers for that matter?

'Well, thank God for that. I think if Caro had it done I . . .' he paused.

'Doesn't fit with breast feeding, eh?'

'She's not just an earth mother, you know! And anyway, it tastes delicious!'

He was boasting. The blatancy of Ben's sexuality, dragged out into the public arena, had triggered something in Tom. Although he was teasing her, some real nerve of sexual curiosity had been stirred. It was true of her too. They were testing each other delicately, both wanting to talk about sex, but at the same time leaving plenty of space to retreat into juvenile coarse humour. She noticed for the first time in years how remarkably good-looking her youngest brother was, in a way that none of the rest of them were. It was more than good health and fresh air. She could see him all too clearly suckling Caro's breasts, both playful and passionate. The image gave her a sudden lurch of desire, as he swung towards her with the rhythm of the oars. She remembered vividly that David had commented at Tom's wedding,

'I bet an extraordinary amount of bonking will go on in that household.'

'David, don't!'

'Don't be prissy, Clare. They'll do it outside and in gymnastic positions, and I bet he's bought her naughty undies for the honeymoon.'

She had not liked it then, but now she wanted to ask Tom if it was true. She opened her mouth to pursue it and then realised that the moment she asked him she would give him the right to ask her about her sex life; and she did not want to have to think about that. She joked,

'I'm told it's especially tasty on cornflakes.' Then, looking up over his shoulder added, 'We're getting to the top of the loch now, don't row us into the trees.'

The suppressed tension of the moment evaporated, and she could not be sure whether Tom was relieved or disappointed. She realised with mild surprise that she had never talked about sex with any of her family.

They made two more long gentle drifts and were soothed. Tom caught three trout and she lost a second through inattention. The rhythm of the water on the boat against the rhythm of their casting was soothing. Fishing, thought Clare, was not like other blood sports; it did not raise adrenaline levels but smoothed them off. She knew Anni would call that casuistry, but Anni had resources that she did not. Tom, she noticed, did not look middle-aged; he did not look like a father of three, he looked very young and boyish, untouched by grief; more innocent and attuned to the quiet air around them than Anni could ever be.

Apart from a few remarks about the fishing and the occasional joke, they did not talk any more. She knew he was relieved to have admitted his cowardice about Ben, and she was somehow touched to have been chosen as his confessor.

'That was nice,' she told him when they brought the boat in during mid-afternoon. 'Thank you.'

'Mutual,' he said. 'We'll do it again. Caro squeals the whole time.' There was too much affection for any disloyalty, but she knew he had enjoyed the peace as she had and was pleased.

'You've burned your snout,' he commented as he gathered their gear together, leaving one basket all packed away for her to carry.

'Damn,' she said, feeling her nose with The Hand, but so habitual was the gesture that she failed to notice the lack of information now conveyed, 'I always do.'

'It's because it's so big.'

She swung her basket low in front of him, the strap catching him just above the ankle so that he tripped laughing. They strolled along the river towards the Small Loch and the house.

Ben suddenly appeared on the path walking towards them. She dropped her basket and ran into his arms.

'Clare.'

'Ben.'

'For Christ sake,' he said.

They were locked in each other's hug. Ben was the best hugger in the world, a huge, generous embrace which had something, but not a lot, to do with his size. She had once told David how wonderfully well Ben hugged, and David had looked cross. She enjoyed that memory.

They separated and, still close, inspected each other; they had not met since disaster had overtaken both of them. God, she thought, he looked tired; but tired was not the right word, he seemed weary, and defeated.

He returned her gaze and said, 'Well, we've both been in the wars, haven't we?'

'I love you, Ben.'

They had both been humiliated, shamed, in public. There was a new bond between them, however strange and unwelcome.

'Thank God for that. Me, you, too and also,' he said, and his arm tightened round her. It was a quick aside, for Tom, patiently carrying both baskets, came up to them.

'Hello, Ben.'

'Hello, Tom.'

There was a brief pause, both of them uncertain. Then, as though according to a prearranged plan, they each threw one arm over the other's shoulder, a strange greeting that, Clare realised suddenly, all three of the boys used for each other; an ancient easy habit, like the way they would punch each other, often quite hard, on the chest. She did not think she had ever seen David touch more than the hand of another man. She knew that Tom had been honest in the boat, and knew also that she had been right; the habit of affection was stronger than the new disgust. They had sorted something out in that oddly male moment, even though she could never know what. She was glad that nothing needed sorting between her and Ben, and felt sorry for both of them.

Ben said, 'I have come partly to give you the joy of the prodigal's return, partly to warn you that you are both in deep disgrace, but it's worse for Tom than Clare, since she is supposed to need the refreshment of a little fish murder, whereas he has failed in his paternal duties. Prepare your defence.'

'Oh shit,' said Tom. 'Hang on, I was supporting Clare. Could it have been your idea, Clare? Perhaps you begged me to take you out for the whole day.'

'Oh, I should think so. He was dead nice, Ben, and he's going to gut my trout for me, so I think it would be fair to make it my idea and Tom just helping me towards a healthier lifestyle.'

'Perhaps he could say he thought you needed a peaceful loch to confess all, for the good of your soul and the family's nerves.'

That was too near the bone. They all knew that Hester would have had a little talk with each of them about Clare's problems, but he should not have been so candid about it. Ben had missed the careful balance that they all preserved between teasing and intruding. He had been more damaged than Clare had realised.

Tom was embarrassed. He glanced at his watch. 'If we want tea before rifle practice we'd better get a move on, gang.'

'Fruit cake,' said Ben.

'Caro's plum jam.'

'Scones?' Clare asked hopefully.

'Bread I think; Lucy is a great baker.'

'Yummy, yummy.'

Ben took one of the fishing baskets and Clare's rod. They turned towards the house, Clare walking between her brothers. Though David had not been small, she was too tall. She had forgotten the sensation of walking with men who towered over her, their voices flittering across her hair.

By the time they had put away the gear and Tom had cleaned the fish, tea was already well under way in the sitting room. The loaf was three-quarters eaten, and used plates sticky with jam were stacked on the trolley.

'Tom, you wretch,' Caro shrieked at him, but Bitsy rushed over and hugged his knees so they knew no one was seriously angry.

'I'm sorry, Caro,' Clare said. 'It was my fault. I really wanted to fish, and I didn't think I could manage the boat on my own.'

'Well . . . lucky for you, Tom; but you might have told me you were going.'

Tom shot Clare an affectionate wink and cut her a slab of fruit cake.

'What's this?' Ben asked, helping them through their useful little lie. On the table beside the trolley was a large pile of printed papers, all identical. James was sitting in his usual chair with one in his hand, and Amanda, William and Alice all had copies on the floor along with a jumbo pack of coloured felt-tips.

'Joseph's game.'

Clare felt a stab of guilt; she had entirely forgotten her familial obligation to provide a game for the others.

'Don't worry,' muttered Ceci, catching her expression. 'No one does it now but Joseph.'

Clare picked up one of the sheets of paper and looked at the diagram on it:

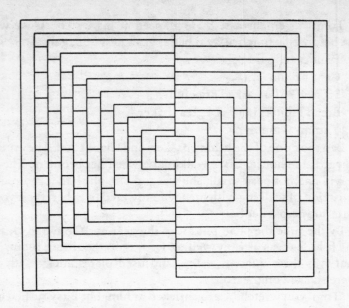

'What is it?' she asked.

'The four-colour problem.'

'What?'

Joseph said, 'You know, there's a theory that four colours will always be enough to colour in any map so that no two countries, or areas with shared borders, have to be the same colour. Experience will suggest that it's true, but there's no way of proving it. It's one of the great mathematical mysteries. This diagram is the ultimate test. Can you fill it in using only four colours? I'm betting that you can't.'

'Of course you can,' Anni interrupted, 'it's been proved.'

'No, it hasn't,' said Joseph, 'not mathematically.'

'Scientifically,' said Anni. 'Experimentally.'

'That doesn't count.'

They both sounded quite irritated. No one else knew what they were talking about.

'Look,' said Joseph, 'a mathematical proof is a logical, followable process. It's a sound piece of reasoning, which if you can understand the language – and I'm not saying I can – can convince you of the truth of some assertion and show why it's true. It's not a computer programme that reduces the mathematician to the level of a lab technician, someone who just sits and watches the mixture bubbling away, and then notes what he observes.

'Don't be such a snob. You can't elevate mathematics above other sciences like that. Theorise, experiment, adjust theory to match experimental data. What's wrong with being a lab technician? with being a chemist or a field biologist?'

Clare felt confused. On the train yesterday Anni had said, with patent sincerity, 'I increasingly incline to the idea that mathematics and theology are the same thing.'

And now Anni said explosively, 'Bloody men!'

'Please, Anni, what has that got to do with it?' James looked up from his tea offended by the violence rather than what she said.

'Do you really want to know, or do you just want me to talk more civilly?' It was unusual for Anni to get het up; even the children looked up from the floor. 'OK I'll try. In the mid-seventies these two mathematicians called Appel and Hagen produced a proof of the four-colour conjecture. It may seem like a game to you, but apart from Fermat's last theorem it was about the most famous puzzle in mathematics. Their proof was a new kind of proof; they had taught a computer to do maths that they couldn't do themselves, that no one could do. You can check the programme, but it's impossible to do the calculations, or to see how they're done. So Joseph's right really, it does change what a proof is. It changes it in a good direction and whenever anyone does that, the people with power – in this case male formalist mathematicians – say the methods don't count. Do things our way or don't do them at all. Join our club or stay out in the cold.'

'Ah,' said James, 'I see. That is why, of course, theology was called Queen of the Sciences; it approves both methods.' They were not sure whether he was joking or not.

Suddenly Anni smiled. 'Poor Joseph. On this one you're out-of-date; but such a stupid struggle. People really don't want machines that do things better than they do; it offends their androcentric universe. Same as Galileo's telescope. Same as sexism.'

Her ill will evaporated. 'It's a pretty game though. And possible. I'll bet you, Joseph, one of us can do it over the next week.'

'Stakes?' asked Tom.

'Steaks,' said Anni.

'Huh?'

'I'll eat a steak, a real beef one, rare if you like, if no one has done the damn thing by the end of the week.'

'Against what, Joseph?'

'There's no deal; what can I put up? A bowl of muesli and a lentil stew, although disgusting, are hardly on the same level.'

'A fiver for the successful colourer-in?'

'The children,' said Louise, 'are calling it "the aunts game" already.'

They all laughed; the four sisters caught each other's eyes, delighted at the idea.

Amanda said, 'You'd better each choose a colour then. Aunt Ceci can be blue, and Felicity red.'

'Ceci should be white really.'

'And Anni should be red.'

'OK,' said Felicity, 'I'll be yellow and Clare can be green.'

'Clare's not green,' said Anni. 'I'm greener than Clare.'

'You're redder as well though, so it's not fair. I won't be pastel.'

'You could be black,' said William.

'Is that better?'

'Well, you said you were a witch, and you went to Africa, didn't you?'

'Don't be cheeky,' Louise said.

'I think it's time for rifle practice,' said Felicity. 'We can't keep Duncan waiting. Who's coming?'

Duncan, the stalker, was scrupulous and James and Hester had always stood by his punctiliousness. Anyone who wanted to stalk had to do rifle practice: it was not just practice, it was a test. To grown-up guests it was sometimes described as 'a chance to get used to the rifle', but Duncan would not stalk with anyone who could not shoot well enough.

Felicity said she'd rather take a walk with Alice. Anni volunteered for baby-sitting duties and looked invitingly at Clare, but she wanted to spend some more time with Ben and replied, 'I'm even more useless at baby-bathing now than I was before. No, I'll go watch the murderers prepare themselves.'

James offered to help Anni, and everyone else began to divide themselves into car loads. Clare had thought she would walk down to the practice field with Ben, but Tom got delayed, paying for his day off by being firmly delegated to pyjama finding and supper supervising by Caro, so in the end Ben and Clare rode down, later than the others, with Tom. Even as they parked outside Duncan's cottage they heard a shot.

When they walked out into the field, Louise was getting up, handing the rifle back to Duncan and looking modestly pleased with herself. She was easily the best shot of them all with a rifle, though despite Caro and Tom's urgings she did not use a shotgun.

'I don't like seeing women shooting,' Louise would say.

'Thanks,' Caro usually snapped.

'Unless they're very good of course.'

'Oh, don't be so stuffy,' Tom would say, but there was always a tinge of envy because she could pick off bulls'-eyes, and indeed deer, with a stunning accuracy.

As the three of them drew near, Joseph had just lain down. Duncan handed him the rifle.

'Evening, Duncan,' the three of them chorused.

'I was sorry to hear about your accident.'

It was not clear which of them he was talking to, but it was easier to assume it was her rather than Ben.

'Thank you,' she said. He did not even glance at her hand.

After Joseph and Tom and Caro had all taken their trial, there was a pause.

'Lady Hester?' said Duncan.

'Do you think you can get me up the hill?'

'We've got this new all-terrain vehicle his Lordship bought me. It can carry you up anything, better than the ponies even. You'll see. Nothing to it. You won't even have to walk.'

Hester lay down and addressed herself to the target with adequate efficiency.

Since Ben had been ordained Duncan had never known what to call him, so he just looked at him enquiringly.

'Not this year, Duncan.'

William said, 'My turn.'

Louise said, 'Don't be silly, Will.'

93

Simultaneously Joseph and William interrupted,
'Daddy said . . .'
'I told him . . .'
Everyone was sensitive to the silence, and Clare said, 'I'll have a go.'

There was a sigh of relief; followed immediately by a sense of surprise. Clare lay down on the sacking and looked at the target. She looked at The Hand. There was no reason, no reason why it shouldn't shoot; in fact, there was good reason why it should, steady and unfaltering. Duncan reloaded and handed her the rifle. In a way it was just ancient habit; a regression to childhood, when they had all shot ten rounds at a paper target with a .22 before breakfast and Hester had given half a crown to anyone whose holes, with their cartoonish burned edges, would all fit under the coin. Clare snuggled the butt into her shoulder, tucked her left elbow well under the barrel and squinted down the little mounted telescope. The gun felt good, solid. She did not fully understand her own impulse. Once comfortable, she considered the next problem: how to get the index finger of The Hand into place accurately enough so as not to set off the trigger until she was ready. The fishing had helped.

'Tom,' she said, 'I need a hand.' They all laughed as though she had made a joke and it took a moment before she realised they thought she had said it deliberately.

'I'll be watching,' said Duncan, as though this was a procedure he had to learn, not an experiment.

Tom squatted down beside her and helped guide the steel and plastic finger though the loop. Then he stood up and stepped back. Clare had not fired a rifle since her teens. She besought The Hand not to make a fool of her. Her left arm tightened against the kick and she silently instructed The Hand to pull the trigger.

The Hand did not pull in the old sense. Its mechanism gave her a strong pincer in place of a thumb and index finger. Years ago, in this very field, she had been taught, 'Don't pull, squeeze,' which had always seemed impossible. Now at last she could obey the instruction. With her will, rather than her sense of touch, she squeezed the trigger. The Hand was better at this than her own hand had ever been. Now she could shoot smoothly.

94

The Hand gave back no information. She could not discern from it the gradual moving of the trigger, so the moment of the explosion startled her. She had not known exactly when it was going to happen, which was why it was smooth, efficient, without the jerk, the tiny nervous reflex that they had tried to train out of her with a .22 rifle before she was ten. She had forgotten the unexpected loudness and the cleanness of the bang, the living leap in the gun.

'Very nice,' said Duncan. 'A little left, but we've all been having that problem this afternoon. Would you like another turn?' and he knelt down and reloaded for her, slamming the bullet in deftly, and then, with the same gentleness as he had watched in Tom, helped her rearrange her fingers.

'Just a shade, a breath to the right,' he murmured.

She was quicker this time and less nervous. It was a perfect shot, clean and accurate. Duncan was pleased with her and she lapped up his pleasure, and found she was sweating. When she had felt the gun jump, shaking her whole upper body, she knew why she had wanted to shoot and she was sweating in the realisation of what might have happened. She had wanted to shoot to see if she could remember any shooting on the mountain, whether, along with the thunder, there had been gunshots on Mount Nyangani. But the explosion had triggered no memories. Now she was trembling with relief that no memories had stirred her. More darkly, under the relief, there was a new terror. The Hand loved the rifle, wanted to shoot, wanted to blast, kill, destroy.

'You wait,' the physiotherapist had said, 'you'll find there are some things it can do even better than your old hand could.'

Well, she had found one; it could shoot better than she could. She would not stalk this week. She got up and tried to smile at the pride her family were taking in her.

Louise was looking haughty, but William was looking excited, Clare knew who had won that little fight. The rifle looked huge in William's hands and he was biting his lower lip in tension and anxiety. Duncan was gentle, explaining how much more of a kickback he should expect from this than from the small rifle he was used to. 'We'll not score with the first one,' he said. 'That's for you to get the feel of it.'

The recoil jerked the child's whole body, his feet in their neatly tied trainers drummed on the grass. Joseph looked anxious.

'Wow!' said William. 'I see what you mean.'

Louise shrugged her shoulders.

'All right, Duncan. I'll try properly now, please.'

Duncan, for the first time, lay down on the ground beside the boy, talking to him almost inaudibly. William fired. Again his body jerked, but the shot was well within the allowed zone.

'One more,' said Duncan.

'It might have been a fluke, mightn't it?' said William bravely.

'Everyone does two,' said Duncan. 'At least two. You've been working with the .22 though, haven't you?'

It wasn't a fluke. The second shot was not as good as the first, but good enough. There was a silence in which too many of them were thinking that the whole thing ought to put Louise in her place. Duncan patted the boy's head and said, 'You take after your mother don't you, not this sloppy lot. There's none of them who could shoot like that first time out.'

Louise relaxed, smiled.

'Thank you,' said Hester to Duncan as they walked back towards his house.

'It was nothing, Lady Hester; they're all like that. No doubt you were when yours started. He's a good little lad though. Will he come out with the gentlemen or shall we set up an easy day for him?'

'They'll draw on Thursday, they always do. Shall we see how that goes?'

'Do you want to see his Lordship's new toy? This all-terrain vehicle, an aga-cat they call it. The army have had them for a while.'

Hester walked with him round the corrugated-iron garage. On a flat trailer sat a small khaki-coloured object, like a sailing dinghy but with caterpillar wheels.

'You're joking, Duncan,' Hester smiled, 'that won't carry me.'

'Me, you, and your stag coming down. It's made of fibreglass, and, apart from the motor, it weighs nothing; the motor can pull it up anything and because it's flexible it doesn't tip over. They're very good. Lots of people have them now. To replace the ponies. Do you remember the ponies?'

When she had been a little girl they had kept ten or more ponies to carry them up to the steeper heights, and to carry the dead stags down again. They had kept ten or more ghillies, too. Now it was just Duncan.

'It's good for the business, this toy, I told his Lordship; the Americans like them.'

'I'll walk,' said Hester, proudly.

'No, we'll take it and go up the north side; you haven't been there in ten years. I'm looking forward to it.'

'Very well.' They were old friends and smiled warmly at each other.

The grass smelled of sunshine; Duncan's spaniel, let out now the shooting was finished, ran in loose circles through the meadow. William was walking beside his mother, the two of them sharing his pride. Hester glowed. All her family home for dinner. They would climb to the high deer runs, and the sunshine and the love and the wind would remind them all how good God was and they would be happy and well. She wanted her bath now, and her whisky. She could still shoot as straight as her children and Clare had managed the whole business without any fuss. There were sturdy grounds for hope.

Ben and Clare walked along the riverside together.

'I fucked up,' he told her, quite casually.

'So did I,' she answered, and then, turning towards his particular silence, 'Christ, Ben.'

'Do you think I wanted to?' He could ask her and no one else that question.

'I don't know,' she said. 'Do you think I killed him?'

'I don't know. You tell me.'

'I don't know either.'

There was a pause. Finally she said, 'Are you all right?'

'Physically?'

'That first, anyway.' She waited on his answer without breathing.

'I don't know.'

'Join the gang. We don't know much, do we?'

'What?'

'Never mind.'

'I'm tired,' he said, 'and I've lost my job.'

'Join the gang on that, too.'

There was another pause and then he said, 'It was so bloody stupid. It wasn't even that much fun, you know. It was stupid, I got drunk and I talked too much. Showing off. If I was going to get into trouble I'd rather have got it for doing something I really enjoyed, cared about. Not that night. Tacky.'

They stood, baffled, beside the stream which in its movement was unmoved by all of this.

'Are you going to talk to Mummy?' Clare asked.

'That's why I came.'

'You're brave.'

'I didn't want her to know. I wanted there to be something about me that she couldn't be more understanding about than anyone else in the world. There's a sick AIDS joke I keep thinking of: "The most difficult thing about telling your parents you've got AIDS is persuading them you're Haitian".' And after a pause in which she did not laugh he said, 'It's not very funny.'

'Mummy must have known.'

'That makes it worse; if she knows, she's also known for years that I didn't tell her.'

'No wonder you look so tired. Poor Ben.'

'Undeserved sympathy probably. Compared to what you've been through.'

'I'm alive,' she said, and for the first time knew that it was true and she was glad of it.

'So am I,' he said. 'Every cloud has a silver lining.'

They laughed together.

'I might have killed him, Ben. I really might have.' She could not quite say 'I wanted him dead,' but very nearly. Ben heard her anyway.

'Was it dire? You and him?'

'Pretty shitty.'

'And you couldn't leave.'

He did not even ask it as a question. She did not know how he understood, but he did.

'Why didn't you leave him?' was the question she most dreaded. For at least two years she had been asking herself that question and had found no answers. Why was it so impossible to say 'stop' to a relationship which was increasingly devoid of pleasure? She was thirty-six years old, she was financially independent, she was child-free, she was not unattractive; she was not even married to him: there was no reason, but . . .

She had moved into the place of spells: love potions concocted not so that he would love her, but so that she would love him. Simple spells practised before he returned to their flat of an evening: a long bath, an excessively generous gin and tonic, a cute joke, a promise to herself not to nag or complain. And then the magic words, 'I love you, darling' because if she could say the words they would become true. They were true, anyway, because if she did not love him she would leave him. He knew she loved him and he had to be right. He would not listen if she tried to say otherwise. He simply ignored her: it was almost impossible to say difficult things to someone who would not listen, who denied that you meant what you said.

She created rituals, rules for grace. More complicated and elaborate than the religious rules of her childhood: novenas of sex, first Fridays of smiles and charm, confessions of devotion, candles of intercession.

She bought him expensive presents, because if she was generous then she must be loving. She indulged his every whim and demand, especially if she did not want to, because if she was unselfish then she must be loving.

Above all, she never told her friends how she felt, because once said it might become true. Instead, she displayed her aesthetic attributes, how long-legged and blonde and successful she was. And when friends who knew her too well would see her changing and challenge her, she avoided them, looked for new friends, found the sorts of friends who needed for reasons of their own to see and believe that lots of money and physical beauty do certainly and surely make for happiness.

When she had first met him, soon after her return from Italy, his golden certainty, his clear framework, his sturdy belief in his own power had created her afresh, created her as a woman who could love and be successful and get on with her life. His managerial skills had enabled her to order her chaotic ideas. She had wanted to take photographs, he had shown her how to become a photographer – how to market herself and her work.

She had come back from Italy panicked by her own dreams and desires, by the suddenness and violence of her lust. His complete conviction that he knew what she would enjoy, that he would introduce her to pleasure that was guaranteed and definite, measurable had made her feel safe. He would protect her from her fears, he would help her to control herself, he would make her safe, if she would let him. The passivity he demanded from her had been a relief. She was grateful to him.

The price of his protection was her obedience. If she was good, he would love her. The small print in the contract was hard to read; if he did not love her, she was bad.

She became a child; she let him become her God. Like God he had created her, made her from dust. Like God he knew all the answers, and only his love could sustain her, could keep her safe, could make her lovable.

Because he was like God, she was forced to use chants, incantations, liturgies, rituals in all her dealings with him.

Gradually she taught herself blacker and more dangerous spells too.

There was sex: engaging in ever more exotic sex; running risks; exposing more and more of the lust for humiliation she found within herself to match his wish to humiliate her. Because a woman who can do that is a woman who loves her man.

There was lying: telling herself that she did not feel what she felt, so that the dull weight of misery in her gut was constantly ignored, dismissed, renamed. She was tired and ill and did not acknowledge it, and then she worked like a maniac to explain the tiredness, and to reward herself with money and fame which might give her value in the eyes of the lover she denied not loving.

There was the morning mantra: enchanting herself, by repetition, into believing that her expectations for a relationship were too high; if she lowered them enough then the relationship would be fine. He was fine and the only thing that was wrong was her. She was too demanding, childish, stupid, romantic, deluded. She was too idealistic for the times, which was the fault of her child-hood, of her family, her own self. So she avoided her family, for they undermined her discipline by holding up to her other happier images and higher ideals. Her family and their religion were preposterous. He, he alone, was sensible and sane and if she abandoned him out of some adolescent fantasy she would be abandoning truth and progress; she would be regressing to the place of wildness, to the place of hopes that cannot be met, and will not be met, to the place of betrayal and danger.

He and he alone could keep her safe.

Safe.

She knew the damage she was doing to herself; and in the end it was easier to hate him than to face up to that truth.

'And you couldn't leave,' Ben repeated.

'Oh Christ, Ben.' She turned into his arms. As they hugged again it was not the warm welcome of the sunny afternoon, but a more desperate clinging. Even in their separate needs they could feel each other's fragility. The desire for comfort, and the desire to comfort were balanced, in a strong and careful tenderness.

'Oh shit!' said Ben, and then added: 'Have you ever noticed that the members of this family who claim not to believe in God always swear by his name, and those of us that do use sex and lavatories?'

'Anni always uses "God" as an affectionate prefix,' Clare said with gratitude. ' "Dear God," she says perfectly casually. But I've never heard Ceci say "fuck".'

'True,' said Ben considering it, 'But I do. As well as "shit". That's how I know I still believe. And that you don't, you lucky cow. When I was staying with the monks, I think it was my obscene language more than my obscene behaviour that upset them.'

'Why did you go?'

'The Bishop asked me to. They always do — "get thee to a nunnery" stuff. It was nice there anyway: I got a lot of reading done, and mowed the lawn for them. It was something I missed at All Saints you know, a garden. When I decide what to do, I'll make sure I have a garden; a real one.'

'What will you do?'

'Shit, I don't know. The usual thing is to teach at some minor public school, isn't it: bit of RE, bit of Latin, and supervising cross-country runs – and, in this post-Esther Rantzen era, I have sort of ruled that out for myself. Probably quite right too, but it's a pity because I might have liked it. So long as it had a garden: I have a hankering for irises, as well as striped lawns. I expect I'll have to become an AIDS expert: it's the new trendy thing for disgraced clergy. I'm not very well-equipped for secular life – like the sacked steward, you know.'

'Who?'

'You really have escaped haven't you? The parable bloke, remember? "Dig, I cannot; to beg I am ashamed."'

They laughed together, in relief and companionship, and the laughter brewed up out of shared disaster and the soft sunshine of the highland evening carried them through a dangerous place, and back into the security of their childhood.

It was hard, though, to imagine what Ben would do. He had been a cheerful outgoing child, not particularly marked by religiosity, but at the same time there had been an inevitability in his ordination. Clare could not remember when he had first announced his intention, any more than she could remember when she had first known he was gay. He had proceeded reasonably happily with the process of education, gone to King's London and read theology, got a first, sung in his college choir, and then spent two years working for a major Housing Association. After that he had presented himself to the Church as a suitable candidate and slightly to his parents' surprise, since they would have expected him to have trained somewhere more aggressively catholic, had gone to Westcott House as an ordinand. 'But Mummy, I'm quite bright you know; I want to do proper theology.' It was a normal, healthy way to become a clergyman, but it did not leave room for much else. Clare pushed away the questions, which she did not want to deal with now, and said,

'One moment you say you want a garden, and the next you say you're too refined to dig.'

'Umm, well . . . perhaps I can get in a "youf" to do the heavy digging.'

They laughed.

The laughter, the love within it, and the good feelings of the day gave her a new confidence. At dinner she cut up her own ham, and felt comfortable even to the point that she could enjoy the Cumberland sauce and listen without impatience to a tedious discussion about recipes for its preparation. When, over coffee, Hester asked them what they wanted to play that evening, Clare was bold.

'Do you remember,' she said, 'at breakfast I was explaining to William about the list I made for my physiotherapist of skills that were necessary to my well-being? I put Racing Demon on the list.'

It was true, too, although originally she had only done it to tease the physiotherapist, but her family did not need to know that. The energetic young woman she had been working with at that point had gone away and learned the rules and together they devised a set of strategies, of techniques. It had been one of their happier sessions.

Now she said, 'But no one in the hospital could play well enough to give me a challenge.'

They all laughed.

'Count me out,' said Bob good-humouredly, 'I'm never playing cards, or not that hellish game anyway, with you lot again. Once was enough, the worst humiliation of my life; as my score went into the three-figured minuses and my pile had about two cards on it, everyone just said "be grateful Clare isn't here, she always wins".'

Clare was amused and happy that, for over ten years, since she had last played the card game with her family, her speed and concentration had remained in their memories, a bench-mark of excellence.

'Have we got enough packs of cards?' Louise asked, and she and Tom got up to sort out the table.

'How do you do it?' James asked Clare.

'I hold the pack in my right hand and switch off the works. Then it's quite stable and I do everything else with my left one. The only snag is turning the cards over again. I've grown much neater.'

'I didn't mean that. I meant, how do you make your mother so happy with one sentence?'

Clare looked up, surprised, and saw that Hester was indeed quietly glowing.

James smiled at her, 'It's her favourite game, and she'd never have suggested it because of your hand.'

Even the resounding defeat that followed; even the compassion of her siblings for that defeat, the first realisation they had had of what she had really lost, she who used to be the only one of them who could challenge Hester in this tiny arena of excellence, could not deflate her hopefulness. She went to bed childlike and sleepy, her nose still pink from the sun and her back still warm from Ben's hug.

She did not dream about David. She dreamed she was still a child, she was a child in primary school studying caterpillars. She and Anni, in the dream, were busy with caterpillars. They fed the poor things until they were bloated; then they watched them build themselves cocoons, and drew cute pictures of the cheerful larvae in there, busily at work growing wings and lengthening their little stubs into antennae, ready to pop out.

In Zimbabwe, Clare had learned that this was a damned lie.

In Zimbabwe, she and David had met a peculiar English woman, a Mrs Mildenhall. She had been staying in the same hotel in Harare. She was a naturalist.

'I thought she said naturist,' said David, laughing with Clare afterwards in their bedroom.

At dinner one night she told them a lot about butterflies. It had been alarming. Clare had found the elderly lady not sweet and eccentric, but gleeful and somehow malevolent. Now, even in her sweet dream, she could not escape the shadow of Mrs Mildenhall. She had always thought that caterpillars were basically butterflies without wings. Mrs Mildenhall had taught her better.

'If you'll excuse my language, my dear, that is a damn lie. It makes me very angry. Children should not be so deceived. Truly horrific events occur inside a cocoon. First there is a total disintegration. Everything that was the caterpillar breaks down into primal ooze, a sort of amorphous smear.' She had smiled sweetly, pecked at her dessert and continued. 'And only when the caterpillar has consented to that total annihilation can the butterfly be constructed. The caterpillar has to risk all for the emergence of the butterfly's beauty. That is why, for the mediaevals, the butterfly was used as a symbol of the resurrection: you have to die, you have to be destroyed first, even if you're God. Now a cocoon is supposed to be a place of safety and comfort. So is God of course, which is very odd.'

'Do you think she's kinky?' David had asked in the privacy of their huge bed, the mosquito netting drifting down like butterfly wings.

'It's not kinky to talk about theology,' Clare had retorted.

'Don't be obtuse, Clare. I was referring to the enthusiasm she had for the sexual practices of insects; all that gleeful stuff about not being able to separate after mating.'

'You're obsessed by sex,' she had said to him.

'Jolly good,' he had replied, 'it's very important to pander to the obsessions of obsessives. Come here.'

'David . . .'

'Come here.' The laughter evaporated, he was commanding, stern. She had obeyed.

And now in her dream she watched the caterpillars disintegrate inside the cocoon, break down not merely into ugliness, but into nothingness. There was a wailing of loss, a disordered silence, that could not carry meaning into the void; a silence like the sounds that Alice made when she was unhappy, involuntary senseless agonies.

In her dream Clare picked up a chrysalis in her own right hand and watched the struggle of the butterfly to emerge from that vacuity. It was a terrible labour, worse than the films she had seen of babies' births, and when the chrysalis finally broke open and the butterfly crept out it was deformed. It was wingless, and with her pink right hand, with its delicate fingernails and exquisite daintiness, she fitted the maimed butterfly with myeloelectric wings, which did not work. Flapping painfully, it crashed off her hand and was broken on the stone slab at her feet.

Clare fought her way up from the darkness, as she had fought her way up from the darkness in the hospital in Mutare. And through the dark of the night she lay sweating, too frightened to sleep again.

Only when the dawn had paled through greys and pinks to fresh gold; only when she could sense that the dreams were dying down and waking consciousness was stirring across the loch and through the house, could she bear to go back to sleep.

12th August

HESTER WOKE HAPPY. She was surrounded by all her children. Skillen was the place of her childhood. She and her sisters had, long before her daughters, slept along the girls' passage, each autumn. She never woke here without a start of surprise that she was not in her own little room with her nanny at the end of the corridor where Amanda now slept, but instead in the room that was really her own mother's.

The war had disrupted the gentle security of Hester's growing up. She had been too young to take part in it, but too old to be protected from its horrors. By the end of the War she had been working in East London, at what had started as well meaning welfare work among the 'very poor'. Shocked by the bombing and the destitution; moved beyond anger by the sufferings and dogged irony of East Enders in contrast to the grumbling continuance of civilised life among her parents' friends; ravaged by the death of her brother, she had been changed. The God who had ordered her childhood from a polite distance and would scarcely have had the impertinence to interfere in the life of her father the Earl, came to make a new sort of sense there in that devastated world. In the impassioned and romantic socialism of East End Anglo-Catholicism she found a new home.

After the war her family had wanted to pretend that nothing had changed. She had tried to be obedient and optimistic. Pinning her long tartan sash with the traditional Celtic silver pin and wearing her mother's priceless pearls, she had become a debutante. But she had been too weary to be amused by the balls after the Clan Gatherings; full-length white gloves got shockingly dirty and champagne was extravagant. She made her curtsey to the King too late to be impressed, too exhausted to be excited, conscious only that her dress would have provided meals for a whole Sunday school of children for months on end.

She told her father that she had voted Labour in the post-war election, and the Adam fireplaces had been shaken with his wrath, but she had not. A year later she had told him with the same fine calm that she was going to marry a sweet and clever curate, whose family was unmentioned in what she was already calling 'Mamma's Stud Book', and no, neither of them wanted Daddy to speak to his friends and find James a good incumbency. She never used her title. She had returned her mother's letters unopened, with 'not known here' scribbled on them for over two years until she had rammed her message home. She devoted all her enormous energy to her husband's parishes and to her children; but still, as she would say to her confessor, it was impossible to escape from privilege. She had spent her dowry on charity, and sent the children to the local grammar schools; but Joseph had served his articles in first-rate chambers, and Clare's magic hand, and Alice's extra needs were met by intimidating first her father and then later her brother.

'Class,' she would say sometimes, self-mocking, 'has us all in a half-nelson.' All, of course, except her own children, whom she believed she had set free from that bondage.

The family holiday was a part of it: she had worried about it when she was younger, but now she accepted those things about herself, not with complacency but at least with clarity. Every year since Joseph had been born she had brought her whole brood for a fortnight's holiday at Skillen. Normally, since the children had grown up, the organisation of the holiday was straightforward.

Sometime in the spring she wrote to her brother to arrange the dates. It never occurred to her that every year this assumption of her right to a fortnight of his lodge infuriated Lord Mereham, who would otherwise have rented Skillen out to his own friends, or to rich Americans.

'She doesn't live in this century,' he would mutter when her letter arrived; but he never quite felt like exerting himself against Hester's will and anyway the poor girl had quite enough to put up with.

Once the dates were fixed Hester used to let the children know what they were and then wait and see what happened. This year, however, it was all different. There was a tide sucking out the still waters of her family life. James was going to be seventy that autumn: the obligatory retirement of the clergy was something she had always approved of, but now it was a threat. In a way that was untypical of her she had made very few plans. She supposed that they would move to the country and James could help out in some parish. She was not convinced that it would work for him and she was almost certain that it would not work for her.

She was, moreover, worried about her children. She who had tackled with serenity the wild gyrations of their adolescence found the soft sinking of their middle age heartbreaking. She had wanted, that spring, to recreate their childhood, to reclaim them, bring them back around her and oblige them to be children again. She knew, of course, that this was folly. But she did not care.

So, having succeeded in persuading them all, she ought to be thanking God and enjoying herself, but it was not so simple. She woke that morning happy, but as she struggled up through the opaque layers of warmth, her worry met her, ready and eager. Immediately she began the effort of collecting her household together in her heart and praying for them. Recognising her anxiety, she knew it would be hard to pray properly and so lay instead invoking the children's patron saints.

She had not chosen her children's names; she had thought that would be presumptuous. They were each named after the saint on whose feast day they were born.

'Thank God I wasn't born on St Eggfroth's day,' Anni used to say as a teenager. 'Annunciata is more than enough of a burden to carry around.'

'We're all lucky, come to that, and Mummy did stop short of Perpetua. Felicity is a good deal easier to live with.'

'Wilfred, Lioba and Walpurga; luckily we got born before Mummy's Anglo-Saxon phase.'

Hester had learned to ignore their teasing: she was prepared to accept that it had been a pretty silly idea in the first place and could remember, by the time Tom was born, a certain sense of relief that she had been able to abide by the tradition without making any of them too ludicrous. Sitting up in bed and watching the dawn break on the loch she could smile at herself and begin her morning litany:

'St Joseph, guardian and foster father of the Holy Child, pray for him.'

'You named me,' Joseph had once said irritably, 'not only after the only married male virgin in the Church's calendar, but after the only bloke in history who would take his pregnant girlfriend on a trip without booking in advance.' Joseph would never fail to book; that constant care and grave middle-aged attentiveness that the Church had foisted on to St Joseph, she had also foisted on to her oldest son.

In fact there was a different, wittier connection between the two and Hester smiled as she always did when she remembered it: Joseph, wonderful efficient Joseph who would never fail to book in advance, had in fact failed to get his wife to hospital when his son was born. William had been born in the back room of a pub because Joseph had run out of petrol. Hester grinned to herself in the morning light, and heard again his voice on the telephone, half confessional, half angry, and her laughter and his plaintive reiterated requests that she should not tell any of his siblings, 'Only because Louise would be so embarrassed.' She hoped, and even sometimes prayed, that Joseph would find some way to share this rather delightful error of judgement with his son. A little lapse was reassuring. It was easy to be grateful for the intrinsic sparkle of her other children, but it was hard always to bear in mind Joseph's continual thoughtful goodness.

'Holy Joseph, pray for him.'

St Joseph, younger than usually depicted and distinctly better looking, glanced up from his work bench and grinned at Hester.

'St Benedict, father and doctor, pray for us.'

Her heart leapt with joy just naming her second son. He had always been her favourite. He ought to be her favourite now, her pride and joy, her baby priest.

Then her heart sank, lurched downwards in grief and anger. She heard the 'us' of her prayer; her relationship with Ben needed praying for as much as he himself did. And, taken unawares, she discovered again just how angry she was. How dare he?

His voice had been cringing on the phone.

'Mummy, I think I had better warn you. I'm in trouble.'

'What sort of trouble, darling?'

'News of the Screws trouble.' There was a pause. 'I'm sorry,' he had added.

She drew a sharp breath, and to cover up the physical shock had become efficient. 'True or libellous?'

'True enough.' But she knew at once that this was not the reaction that he wanted.

'It's not your problem,' he had said, and the telephone crackled. 'I just thought you should be warned. And I'm going to take the phone off for the rest of the day, so you won't be able to reach me.'

'All right,' she said; but it wasn't all right. Three days later Clare had disappeared off a mountain and there had been no chance to make it all right.

How dare he what? she made herself ask herself.

How dare he keep so important a part of himself secret from his loving mother? She who had spoken out so boldly against prejudice and bigotry in the Church; she who, as he very well knew, directed the souls of at least two young gay clergymen, and supported the vocations of others. Hester berated herself for her vanity, but the wound was deep and she was angry with him for inflicting it.

How dare he drive a wedge between her and James?

'You can do what you want to change the rules, Hester,' James had said; 'I know you think they should be changed, but the Church does teach that the genital expression of homoeroticism is wrong. There is an onus on a priest; there simply is. It's not a question of being willing to forgive, it's a question of accepting that there is something to forgive.'

Later James had said, 'Hester, you won't like this, but I have to tell you that if you exert the old, and I admit effective, influence of your family and your wide acquaintance with the bench of bishops to get special privileges for your son, I will not only take it as an affront to the Gospel, I shall also have to regard a large part of your life – such as the denial of class privilege and the Labour voting and the solidarity with the poor — as a lie.'

James had apologised afterwards. He had nearly wept. He had even tried and she knew it was hard for him, to address his feelings of shock and disgust; but it was still said, and could not be unsaid, and it was Ben's fault that it had been said.

How dare he do it? The two pictures of him that had adorned the breakfast tables of the nation had been well chosen: the wedding picture, taken at his Church door, the tall priest smiling down on a particularly sweet looking young couple, contrasted nicely with the leather trousers, dark glasses and nothing else. No, not nothing else, he had a small metal ring in his right nipple. And how many times had she hugged him without knowing that? How dare he do that?

She tried to ban the thought, 'How dare he get caught?'

How dare he do something that made her feel so guilty? He had raised doubts about her identity as mother, from which she had always drawn a serene self-confidence. How dare he?

'St Benedict, father and doctor, pray for him and pray for me because I cannot pray for him.'

But St Benedict in his mystical eyrie, high up in the hills south of Rome, did not turn from his meditation.

'Holy Gabriel, Archangel of the Living God, pray for her.'

And there is a flutter of feathers, sweep of light, and Gabriel laughs. Gabriel's joy was to visit determined young women and offer them wild and improbable consolations. The passing of pinions tickled Hester's nose and even in her careful prayer she smiled.

It was with happiness that she turned in her mind to Anni. When she had first rung Anni about the holiday she had asked her if she would make a special effort to turn up this summer. Anni had teased her. She told Hester that she was letting the side down inviting rabid socialists who wouldn't change for dinner at Skillen. Uncle William would have an apoplectic fit, and she, Hester, would have to shell out for something suitable to wear at the funeral, because Anni had already committed her entire year's salary to the Commies Against Blood Sports League.

'Please,' Hester had said, knowing that Anni was the one child she could beg from. And Anni had come: partly from goodwill and affection, partly because she was moved still by the beauty of Sutherland in the late summer and partly, Hester suspected, because despite her high principles, Anni really liked good food and really liked to torment her siblings.

Hester's friends tended to compassion not entirely free from glee when they spoke about Anni, with her cropped hair, her extreme opinions and mysterious single life. But Hester recognised in Anni her own self. Of all her four daughters, Anni was the one she had long felt most easy about. Clare so patently successful, Felicity so patently good, and even Cecilia, so patently holy, filled her with a nervous tenderness from which her relationship with Anni was entirely free. With that freedom went a deep gratitude, for Anni had taught her what 'Blessed are the pure in heart' could really mean. Recognising what it meant in Anni, she had understood it in herself, so that now it no longer bothered her when people called her 'sensible', a harsh euphemism for the harsher 'bossy'. She did of course pray for Anni's conversion, but knew it was more dutiful than passionate.

By what lucky chance did some children get born in joy? When Hester had felt her first contractions late on the evening of the 25th of March, James had teased her. The 26th was the feast day of St Ludger: very nearly as bad as the fictional Eggfroth. But Hester was in labour for less than two hours. Anni was born ten minutes before midnight: Annunciata Margaret, her first daughter, propitiously born and lovingly celebrated. And now angels' wings wrapped Anni in Hester's imagination, although she no longer told Anni this. Once at Anni's flat Hester had picked up a gold volume of poetry and found heavily scored in green ink the lines:

> You say you will shelter me,
> Your wings giving me comfort:
> I've got news for you
> I'm allergic to feathers.

Hester had written beside it, in pencil so that Anni could rub it out if she wanted to,

The angels keep their ancient places,
Turn but a stone and start a wing.
'Tis ye, 'tis your estrangéd faces,
That miss the many splendoured thing.

She never knew if Anni had read that, but she never again made public reference to Anni surrounded by feathered guardians.

'Holy Gabriel, Archangel of the Living God, pray for her.'

And Gabriel, as androgynous and sturdy as Anni herself, smiled on Hester and murmured, "Continuously."

'St Clare, Virgin and Foundress, pray for her.'

Yesterday had been St Clare's feast day, but it was not Clare's birthday. Clare had been named according to a different code, and Hester did not have to labour the connection. She was happy with the name though, St Clare had been a beloved friend even before the child Clare had come to join the family. Usually when she thought of St Clare, Hester saw in her mind the pile of soft gold curls, kept in their tiny treasure chest in Assisi, since Francis had cut them off for her in 1211; their undimmed prettiness, a mark of how much the brave young woman was prepared to give up, always struck her as singularly moving. But this morning, St Clare manifested herself quite differently; ravaged by disease and penance she stood at the wall of Assisi and held out in her right hand the monstrance to drive back the pagan soldiers of the Emperor Frederick. Clare had no right hand. Clare had taken no vow of radical poverty. Hester wanted her tucked securely under the protection of the monstrance, of the Sacred Host, and did not know how to offer her that place of safety.

Did she believe that Clare had gone out to Africa and deliberately killed the man she had been living with? She was prepared to entertain the idea. 'Entertain' was not the right word – there was nothing entertaining about it at all. How could that contained, self-disciplined child have grown into a woman whose mother might consider the possibility of her being a murderer? What, in God's name, was one meant to do if one of your children was a murderer? Hate the Sin but love the Sinner she had been taught; but it was a silly dualistic distinction; or else it was one so subtle that only God could make it.

114

Guilt ate at her. In what way had she failed to meet Clare's needs that first she would entangle herself with a man whom Hester could not bring herself to like, a man of immense worldly charm and, so far as she could tell, no depth at all; and then kill him? If she had killed him. It was ridiculous; of course Clare had not killed him, it had been an appalling accident. Hester's guilt grew; why was she even half-way convinced that her daughter had killed him? She should not be. Disaster had shaped Clare's life from its beginnings. She had done all she could to protect her from the legacy of death and craziness that Clare's natural mother had left her only child. That woman.

Hester stopped herself sternly. That too had been an accident; and it was too late to hate her sister-in-law. She had to love Clare more, not less. Clare was greedy for love in a way that her other children were not. She had tried to supply that; tried to give it. Clare had turned her back on the source of love, on God; not with an intellectual clarity like Anni's which Hester could understand, sympathise with, even admire, but with petulance, somehow sulkily, as though she was afraid. Of course Clare needed more love, more reassurance than the others did, that was inevitable, but why then did she need always to reject it, always to run away from the offer, and seek out people who could not really give her what she wanted.

As her sense of guilt rose so did her irritation. Surely Clare must, at some level, know whether or not she had killed him? If she didn't, she ought to be trying to find out. Why wouldn't Clare at least talk about it? Tell her. If Clare would explain, repent . . . But, she told herself, Clare had been ill, Clare had been very ill indeed. Through the long thirty hours when they thought Clare might die six thousand miles away, she had not worried about whether or not she had killed David. But . . . of course there were no limits to love, unconditional love, as God offered us in Christ, while we were yet sinners. And Clare was still frail, had lost a part of herself more essential than any hand.

Hester knew she had to keep trying to understand. She thought about Peggy's letter.

. . . we still have no firm news here about Clare's accident.

The papers have more or less forgotten it, you'll be glad to hear, and the local police when I enquired last week seem to have decided that ascribing it to the MNR is the easiest solution. Of course, it is not my business really, but we felt there was a lot of tension between the two of them and that Clare was in some way ripe for folly, to use an old-fashioned expression. I feel guilty towards you, that I did not make more contact with her during the couple of days they were with us, although I know that's silly. She seemed quite het up. A friend of mine, Joyful Masvingise, who was staying with me at the same time, saw more of her, and feels the same way. I don't know how one goes about provoking memory, and Joyful is, somewhat mysteriously, insistent that it would be wrong to try, but I hope for her sake, and even more for yours, that Clare will somehow remember and make it all right. I would find such questions about myself an intolerable burden to live with.

On a happier note, you must have the whole tribe with you at Skillen now; I shall think of you each morning striding the hills as we did together half a century ago . . .

Tension, Hester thought, what sort of tension? She would write to Peggy later that very day; Peggy was a lifeline. Blessed Providence had placed her best friend at the scene of her daughter's accident – 'Thank you God for Peggy; St Margaret, pray for her' – and she must go on trying to be gentle, safe enough, loving enough, so Clare could relax and remember.

'St Clare, pray for her.'

St Clare would do so, her stern, pale face assured Hester, but perhaps she was too fierce and dangerous a saint for that battered and guilty daughter.

'St Felicity, Virgin and Martyr, pray for her.'

When Felicity was born on the feast day of Perpetua and Felicity, Hester had been tempted. James had been amused.

'I won't let you,' he had said. 'I have to draw the line somewhere and I draw it at having a daughter called Perpetua.'

'It's pretty,' she had said, cradling the unnamed daughter in her arms.

'And so is she,' said James smiling. 'Call her Felicity. Call her after the slave girl, not the aristocrat. You ought to like that.'

Perpetua was a favourite saint of Hester's.

'What would we call her? What will they call her at school?' James had insisted.

'Pet? Petal?'

'Dearest Hester, don't you think that is just a little camp?' She remembered it vividly. How could that laughing young man, who had been ironically amused at high churchery, have turned into the man who would speak to her so about Ben? There were things better not thought about. She had given in and called Felicity after the slave girl, not the aristocratic martyr.

Felicity meant 'joy', and as a child Felicity had seemed born for her name. Now there was a shadow over that joy, but Hester felt that Clare needed attention most. Felicity was probably just exhausted from the effort of taking such good care of Alice; the rhetoric of deafness was one thing, the daily grind was quite another. Hester understood that. Felicity must have agonising decisions to make about having more children too; but Felicity had both God and Bob on her side. Hester smiled with pleasure at the thought of her son-in-law. How nice he was, and the Deaf Church had secured Felicity within the structures of Christianity more certainly than Hester could have done. Felicity would be all right.

'St Felicity, Virgin and Martyr, pray for her.'

St Felicity although too busy gritting herself to the harsh unspoken language of the arena to turn and smile, none the less assured Hester of her prayers and protection.

'St Cecilia, pray for her.'

Hester did not have to spend too much time thinking about Ceci. Her youngest daughter, more than any of the others, had escaped from the family. By doing exactly what her mother would most like she had slipped through her net, but it did not matter. With a detached eye and a great deal of experience Hester sensed that Cecilia's vocation was solid; neither neurotic escapism nor immature sentimentality. Sometimes when Hester thought about Cecilia she was struck with awe, with the knowledge that something quite mysterious was happening to Ceci and it was better that her mother did not interfere.

Hester believed there was a sort of holiness that was a perfect concentration. Ceci's ego was not destroyed or transformed by her relationship with God but compressed, squeezed, compacted, to the very point of collapsing under its own mass. The gravitational force of her passion had become so strong in her that light could not escape outwards, and she gave little joy or comfort to those around her. She had become a black hole: there was a perfect dark night of her soul. Time slowed down in that gravitational force; as if in slow motion once the irrevocable process had begun she was stretched, twisted, warped by the plunge; and everything that was Ceci was sucked towards the singularity; and thence into an alternative universe beyond the laws of physics and psyche, into the new universe, into God.

This was death; but could also be life, depending on the position of the observer. The saints on the other side of the singularity watched with excitement the slow transformation, understood the breaking down of the rules – where self-love and self-hate, masochism, aloneness, egotism, and self-giving lose their differences.

Hester, awed and even frightened, knew she could leave Ceci safely to the prayers of the saints.

'St Cecilia, Virgin and Martyr, patroness of music, pray for her.'

And although she had no mental image of St Cecilia beyond the standard stained-glass windows from Bourges, she was content that her prayer would be answered.

'St Thomas, pray for him.'

Not the flamboyant Archbishop of Canterbury who had stage-managed his martyrdom with political astuteness; not the Apostle with doubts, both of whom might have suited her Tom rather well, but the Dominican intellectual. It was hard to find much common ground.

'Mummy,' Tom had said as a teenager, 'There's absolutely no point in my being clever, or wild, or good or bad; the big kids have done all those things. I'll just have to be nice, it's the only unfilled vacancy in this family.'

He was nice. He would have burned no Albigensians. He gave her no anxiety. He never had. A cheerful, adored baby, he had grown into a cheerful young man. Life always seemed an easy thing for Tom; and if he drank a little too much and spent a little more money than he quite had, it didn't seem to matter. Even parenthood did not seem to shake him. Getting him and his family to Skillen was never a hassle; when the appointed day arrived, and about three hours later than they planned, he and Caro, his jolly wife, would pack their three tumbling babies into the back of their Renault Savannah, congratulate themselves because they weren't typecast by a Volvo, and drive up through the night. The children were never car sick and always slept. Hester was never able to understand how people so lightweight could be so happy, so golden. She checked her own impulse to Presbyterian dourness: they seemed to breed joy, and it was a gift not to be despised.

'St Thomas, Father and Doctor, pray for him.'

St Thomas looked up from his industrious scribbling and gave her a jovial wink. At the moment he was busy with a tricky proposition and had little time to waste on one who so clearly lived in the sunshine. Be glad of it.

She completed her litany with a small sense of accomplishment.

Next to her James was still asleep. He lay, as always, on his back, tidy. His white hair ruffled up in the night and he looked sweet: a sweet old man, with large veined hands outside the blankets. He was not sweet at all: in reality he was a fierce madman and she knew it with joy. He was not a modern sort of human being; nor was his God. For forty-five years she had woken up beside him, and there had been, long ago, many mornings when she had sworn to herself that this would be the last time. His combination of detachment and dependency was intolerable, his rigour exhausting; but now she knew who he was and rejoiced in it. Not 'all passion spent', she thought; no, not at all, a quite different place of acceptance: not acceptance of him but of herself. He was her man, by the grace of providence. She prayed for him with a simplicity that she could never find with her children: 'May the Lord bless you and keep you, may the Lord lift up the light of his countenance upon you and give you his peace.'

And finally she prayed for herself, as she did every morning,

Accept, O Lord, my entire liberty, my memory, my understanding and my will; for all that I am and have thou hast given me and I give all back to thee to be disposed of according to thy good pleasure. Give me only the comfort of thy presence and the joy of thy love; with these I shall be more than rich and shall desire nothing more. Amen.

She was old enough to know it would not work, old enough to go on trying to make it work even knowing that it would not.

She put on her dressing gown, picked up Nadine Gordimer's new novel and started to read. This was her holiday and she did not have to think about breakfast, because Lucy was paid to do that. Ten years ago it would not have occurred to Hester to employ anyone to perform her duties for her. She was not sure that she liked it; but this morning, with James's folded hands rising and falling on his chest and the Small Loch turning to fire below her window, she was thankful.

After a while she heard the front door slam and a car engine start up; that would be Tom and Caro leaving for their shooting party. Hester, as she had promised, kept an ear open for the waking of Tom and Caro's two elder children, for they had taken the baby with them.

'Glorious Twelfth,' Tom had said after supper the night before. He and Caro were getting up at some preposterously early hour to go and kill grouse with some friends.

'It won't be a posh shoot,' said Caro, 'but it will be fun; we haven't seen Mike and Janey for months. If you're sure you don't mind looking after the children?' They would drive for two and a half hours at both ends of the day just in order to walk for miles on the hillsides and shoot a few small birds.

So Tom and Caro were absent from breakfast, but the children were good; a brief murmur of 'I want my Mummy' from Bitsy had been silenced by Anni's cheerful reprimand:

'Your Mummy's gone off to have a good time; you should be pleased about it.'

The child smiled over so novel a notion and Anni turned to the rest of the household.

'Glorious Twelfth,' she said loudly, 'how wonderfully exciting.'

'Don't start,' said Louise, 'just don't start being sarky before I've finished my second cup of coffee.'

Clare lifted the lid of the breakfast dish. There were eight trout neatly fried and arranged in order of size. Hers was probably the smallest one.

'Before Anni gets warmed up to elevating prayer quotations from Pastor Ammon, can someone tell me if anyone took out an almost criminally undersized trout yesterday, or if this one is truly mine.'

'Mine was a bit of a midget too,' said Amanda, and came to join her, 'but not *that* small, I don't think.'

The courage of yesterday evening seemed to have dissolved, 'There's a wee little trout here for anyone who fancies one,' she said. 'I can't face it.'

She lifted up the other lid and looked at sausages and a heap of dark grey mushrooms. 'The mushroom hunters did better than the fishers yesterday.'

'That's Alice,' said Amanda, 'she's *really* good at it.'

Felicity smiled at her, and nudged Alice to pass on the compliment. Alice was shovelling down her cornflakes and staring intently at a copy of Joseph's puzzle. Felicity took it away from her gently. Alice looked cross.

'No, seriously: listen,' said Anni. 'The Glorious Twelfth isn't glorious just for mass feathered murder among the landowning classes. It's also the Perseid shower, and it will be particularly fine this year.'

'What are you talking about?' Felicity asked.

Joseph looked up, smiling.

'I'd forgotten,' he said.

'I checked,' Anni said. 'It should be dark enough and no moon. And a lovely high radiant.'

'Poor old Tom,' said Joseph complacently. They all knew at once that he was jealous not to have been invited grouse shooting.

'Come on, what are you two talking about?' Clare asked.

'Joseph and I have a show for you,' said Anni, 'tonight about ten, perhaps a little later. A spectacular.'

'Give us a clue.'

'Nope.'

Felicity said, 'Who's it for?' She sounded peeved, frustrated by not knowing.

'Everyone.' Joseph glanced at Amanda, then Alice. 'Grown-ups, and bigger children too.'

'Inside or out?'

'Out.'

'But not far. Feet not cars.'

'Where?'

Anni looked out of the window. 'We'll tell you later. Who's doing what in the meantime?'

Bob said, 'Felicity, remember the garden we read about: Mickle something or other? How far is it?'

'Why don't you two go and we'll look after Alice?' Hester offered too quickly.

'Yes, please,' said Bob even quicker.

'Do you think you can cope?' Felicity asked, looking slightly put out. 'You've got Bitsy and Malcolm already.'

'Clare'll help, won't you Clare?' said her mother.

'I was quite keen to go to the craft shop actually,' said Clare. 'Ceci, you would too, wouldn't you? We could take a car and I could experiment with driving.'

'Poor Ceci.'

'I'm sure Clare is more than competent,' Ceci said smiling.

'Come with us,' said Felicity. 'We'll go to the garden first and then drive up the coast. It'll be pretty.'

'Do we,' asked Anni, 'sense a certain avoidance of intimacy among the middle Kerslake girls?'

'Shut up, Anni.' Felicity and Clare spoke simultaneously, and reached out to shake smallest left fingers with each other, laughing.

Hester looked disappointed, though whether at her failure to get Clare on her own, or at Felicity's apparent unwillingness to be alone with her husband, or at Anni's lack of tact was not clear.

'I'll stay and help you with the bratlings, Mummy. I'm not too good at gardens or pottery-and-macramé.' Anni smiled at her mother, 'And my Sign's better than anyone else's.'

'Boast, boast.'

'But true.'

'No, go if you want to. I can manage.'

'Dear Mummy, could you face up to the possibility that I'd like to spend the day with you?'

'Anyone else? Louise?'

'Not me. We thought we might take our two up to Loch Saidhe with the dapping rod.' Louise pronounced the Gaelic names with a confidence that the others could scarcely fail to admire.

'Why don't we take Lucy?' Ceci said. 'She hasn't been out of the house yet.'

'Good idea; can we take your car, Louise? It's the biggest.'

The isolation of Skillen meant it took a very long time to get anywhere else. It was a long day's drive, across the vast deserted hillsides; with views opening and closing of tiny lochs and folded mountains.

'Once,' Ceci told Lucy, as they drove up a long shoulder leaving an enchanting wild river below them, 'all these hills were densely forested. And full of wild Picts, the painted men that the Romans were afraid of. That's why they built Hadrian's Wall; they couldn't conquer them so they thought they'd just keep them out.'

'Hadrian's Wall,' Felicity said, 'was a second shot at it; there was another wall right up where Glasgow is now but they couldn't hold it.'

'Really?' Clare said. 'I never knew that.'

At Ledmore they turned southwards and then right off the real roads and headed towards the sea. The land flattened out, into a strange world of bogs and tiny pools.

'I don't like this bit,' Bob said. 'It doesn't look like the highlands on the calendars. Bleak.'

'No,' said Ceci. 'I like it; it's a breathing space before the ocean. The Summer Isles only work because of it.'

They reached the shore eventually. The sun came out and the islands danced on the sea.

'You can't count them,' they told Lucy. 'The tides and the sunlight and the mists come and go. They're magical. At midsummer it never gets dark.'

'Is this what you call the land of the midnight sun?' Lucy asked.

'No. You have to go much further north for that. It's not that the sun shines, it just isn't dark; there's a sort of green dusk that goes on and on until it's a green dawn.'

'Mermaids live on those islands,' said Bob smiling. 'They have beautiful green hair which they comb.'

'Not mermaids; seal women,' Felicity said.

'Are they different?'

They had stopped the car and climbed out; they were on a small headland with a perfect miniature beach on either side of them, with rocks and crumbled sea-weed along the tide line and the islands floating beyond.

'Of course they are. Mermaids belong on coral atolls; seal women belong in the northern waters.'

'Do you know,' Clare said, 'that in Zimbabwe they have stories about figures that have been translated as mermaids? There's a character called Chirikudzi "the mermaid spirit of the Pongwe". But there's no sea there at all, it's completely landlocked. She behaves just like a European mermaid, except she doesn't have a tail or a mirror.'

Joyful had told her about Chirikudzi, the naiad of the source waters, who hid behind trees and rocks and sang to seduce passers-by. She stole you away and kept you prisoner, but if she loved you she would teach you her secrets, and you would return eventually to the world as a great N'anga, knowing the stories and thoughts of the ancestors.

She thought if she could introduce Chirikudzi into a family seaside trip she could diffuse her power. It did not work. The low voice of Chirikudzi sang still, calling David, through the mist on Mount Nyangani.

'Do you think it was a mistranslation then?' Bob asked with genuine curiosity. 'That "Mermaid" was the best English could offer?'

'She sounds more like a seal woman anyway. Seal women look like ordinary women, they don't have tails and green hair, but they aren't . . . you fall in love with one and then she turns back into a seal and swims away.'

Bob put his arm round Felicity's shoulders, as though to hold her against vanishing. He noticed his own gesture and was ashamed.

'It's so beautiful here,' said Ceci, almost dreamily, noticing none of the tensions around her.

'It's a sad country though, isn't it?' Lucy said.

'What do you mean?'

'All the deserted fallen-in cottages we've seen, where people must have lived such lonely lives and now they don't live at all.'

The rest of them were reminded again of the region's long and desolate history; a history of violence and defeat that stood against the beauty of the sea.

'There's an island, way out there,' said Ceci waving her hand westward, 'called St Kilda's; and just after the war the few remaining inhabitants decided to ask the government to rehouse them. They were dying by inches; inbred and struck by diseases they had no resistance to. There's a weird film about it. They were taken off the island. And they had had a ritual, a sort of rite of passage, where the young men proved they were grown ups by climbing up their cliffs and gathering gulls eggs in the spring. And the spring before they all left the men took the children, even the little babies, and carried them up the cliff strapped to their backs, so that they could grow up. It always makes me cry . . . that last gesture, so that the children could be grown-ups.' There is a strain in Ceci's voice as though even here in the dappling sunshine she has to fight with her tears of longing for the island to which there will be no return.

'It didn't work,' Clare said with a brutal casualness. 'They couldn't settle anywhere else; they trusted the authorities and they were betrayed. They didn't even try to keep them together, to find them a new place. The health visitor who went to work with them sort of bullied them into it, and then they got nothing; they were split up, and housed here and there on these brand new Glasgow housing estates, all mod cons, and it wasn't any good and they all died. They were conned.'

'That's what I meant,' said Lucy cheerfully. 'It's a sad country.'

'Let's go find Felicity and Bob's garden,' said Ceci. 'Gardens here aren't sad at all, they're triumphant.'

'Doesn't it get too cold in winter?' Lucy asked.

'Not really, there's the Gulf Stream.'

'What's that?'

'Central heating. A vast warm-water current delivered direct from the Caribbean. Perhaps the mermaids are carried up here by it.'

They drove up the coast, with the island-speckled sea lying tranquil off the indented coast beyond tiny bays. The road was a single track, but all morning they encountered nothing on it except a few sheep; it twisted between sapphire blue lochs and purple bogs, turning to face the sea so that sudden shafts of refracted light would bounce against the car as they turned sharp bends to find themselves again beside the sea.

Quite suddenly round a sharp curve in a narrow road that ran beside a desolate loch, they saw a small craggy tower with green gardens running down to the seaweed. In this improbable isolation some nineteenth-century eccentric had restored an ancient castle, set back from the sea in a sheltering fold of hill; and between the shaggy grandeur of the keep and the treacherous brightness of the sea had made herself a garden.

'You've tricked us,' Clare exclaimed with delight. 'It's not a Scottish garden at all. Scottish gardens,' she told Lucy, 'are full of woodland walks, leafy glades, and masses of rhododendrons. Highly romantic. This is an Italian garden.'

It was, against all the odds an Italian Renaissance garden with tidy box hedges marking out parterres, filled with solid hedges of lavender and each corner marked by statuary. There was a fountain close under the castle itself and it was channelled down towards the sea through patterned stoneworked canals.

Clare looked at it, laughing with recognition. 'It's a copy – sort of – a miniaturised copy of the Mosca garden in Pesaro, but with the wrong house.'

She ran down from the castle towards the sea. 'Come here and look,' she called to the others; and when they followed her down she showed them how the hidden fountains were designed to catch the innocent visitor, squirting water into the face of the unwary or the over dignified. 'It's a pretty childish joke. I wish they worked now. They have them at the Villa Lante too, in Tuscany, but the garden at Mosca is littler and better kept.' She turned towards the sea; ' The wrong house, the wrong view, and of course the wrong smell. Mosca smells of lemons, but this really is it.'

'Do you know Italy well?' Lucy asked her. 'It's one of the places I'm hoping to get to.'

'Clare lived there for about four years,' Ceci told her.

'In Rome really; but one of the first real jobs I had, properly commissioned stuff, was doing the pictures for a book on Italian classical gardens. I was just the photographer, I don't know that much about it.' She remembered though; she remembered her eagerness, not just professional but greedy for the experience, delighted to be there to walk in the gardens and catch the light. Stephen had arranged the job for her, and had travelled north with her. Stephen had continued to keep her under his wing, and still showed her off as his protegée, but with increasing pride, increasing equality. The wind blew across the garden from the sea at Pesaro too; and the terraces had been laid out so that you looked down from one to the other.

'Did you like it there?' Lucy persisted.

'Italy? Very much.' And then, carried away by the sweetness of these memories, she added, 'It was the happiest time of my life; I should have stayed.'

'Why didn't you?'

'I was in love with somebody and it went wrong.'

She stopped abruptly aware that this was news to her sisters. And they both looked away, faintly embarrassed; it was not permissible to have love affairs around your siblings, she thought.

I was in love with somebody, she had said. She had heard herself say it. She had never admitted it before, but it was true. She had been in love with Julia, and Julia had been in love with her and it had scared her and she had run away.

'Is there a guide book or something?' she asked Bob, as this was not the moment to pursue such self-revelation.

They found one in the ticket booth on leaving, and all was revealed; the Victorian gardener had been deserted by her husband, who had run off to the continent with a chorus girl.

'Princess Caroline lived at Mosca with her lover after George III threw her out,' Clare explained to them. 'It can't have amused Lady Whatsits' Highland neighbours much.'

She was full of gaiety. She remembered Julia's smile. Her own siren, mermaid, seal woman, Chirikudzi.

The rest of the winding road to Lochinver filled her with joy; the hills and bays and inlets were still haunted by the ghosts of clansmen long dead, by the blood of the Forty-Five and by the sadness of the Clearances, but they were lit with sunlight and promise. High up on a pass above the little town they stopped and counted islands in the seven bays below them. The air was light with salt and sunshine. After lunch, Bob drove with Lucy sitting beside him, and Clare felt a childlike glee at being squashed in with her sisters. They had travelled like that a thousand times, the four of them.

'We wouldn't fit all four of us across the back any more, would we?'

'One nice thing about a habit,' said Ceci unexpectedly, 'is that you never feel fat in it.'

'Don't you stop caring about being fat?'

'Not a chance. You all teased me too much when I was little.' It was true, they had. Her three tall, skinny sisters had kept her as their baby, their puppy, and her smaller plumper build had made that easier. They had not always been kind to her. No longer the real baby once Tom was born, but still the youngest of the sisters. Clare remembered the teasing with pain; she had hated it throughout her own childhood and now felt a tender and apologetic empathy with Ceci. But Ceci was smiling faintly, as though the memory was a pleasant one. She had been feeling guilty of the sin of vanity for four days. She had been wearing her habit because she preferred to be seen as too pious by her siblings, than to be seen by any of them, especially Louise, as dowdy in the ugly slacks that she had had for years. Admitting even in jest, that she cared about getting fat was an expiation given her by the same memory as moved Clare: they had been children together in cars like this and the other three had always accused her of chubbiness. Infected by Clare's ebullience she too relaxed. Bob, catching a glimpse of her face in the driving mirror was struck by how extraordinarily becoming a wimple was, emphasising Ceci's eyes and giving dignity to her round smooth face.

At the pottery in Lochinver, Clare bought Lucy a plate. A soft blue-and-green glaze with grey-white sheep processing across it.

'You shouldn't.'

'Why not?'

'Well . . .'

'Plates , bowls, pottery, are good things to buy in foreign places. You can get them everywhere and they're all different.'

Julia had bought her a bowl in a little shop in front of the cathedral in Orvieto; not pseudo Umbrian folk art but contemporary, though using traditional colours.

'It's the first piece; when we live together I will buy you a whole set so that you can throw them at me when we fight. Much more fun to break something really expensive,' Julia had said.

'Will we fight?' She had been flirting.

'I hope so; fighting is about passion.'

'Not for me.'

'You are always trying to avoid the strength of your feelings.'

'I don't like fighting.'

'I will break down all that nice English repression.'

She had not wanted that, then.

She had bought a spotted bowl, as John Chitaukire had recommended, from a roadside stall outside Great Zimbabwe. Black with brilliant turquoise spots on it.

'It's a bit gaudy,' David had said, 'but quite ethnic looking.'

'It's pretty.'

'Not really; not my cup of tea. But at that price you can hardly lose.'

He had wanted to buy her ivory bangles. 'It's bound to be a good investment.'

'We're not allowed to import them.'

'Smuggle them in.'

He would not have been amused if she had broken a gift from him in a moment of abandoned passion.

Felicity liked Lucy's plate, but she would not buy one; nor would she let Bob give her a long elegant fish plate, scaled with the same soft sea colours, even though her fingers reached out to touch it.

'It's lovely,' said Ceci, with real delight. 'Do get it.'

'It's extravagant, I don't need a fish plate.'

'Oh, come on Felicity,' Clare said, 'it's not outrageously expensive.'

'We're not all as stinking rich as you are, you know,' Felicity said with a kind of dogged perversity. Bob looked suddenly sad.

Clare to her surprise was not stirred to defensiveness, but to compassion.

'OK,' she said tentatively, 'I'll buy it for you.'

'No thank you.'

'Why not?' But Felicity was not going to give her an opening; she slipped across the room and made Lucy help her choose a china sheep for Alice.

'What was that about?' Clare asked.

Bob said, 'She just hates being given presents at the moment. Or I'd get it for her myself.'

'Oh dear,' said Ceci, 'what's she feeling guilty about?'

'Guilty?'

'People who won't accept presents are always feeling guilty: hadn't you noticed?'

Bob stood absolutely still for an instant. 'I'm so stupid,' he said, 'I never thought. Thank you.' He continued to look thoughtful, but also relieved. He crossed the shop after his wife.

'Clever clogs,' said Clare to Ceci. 'Shall I buy you a plate?'

'If you want to, but I wouldn't have much use for it. And you should never forget that Felicity has been jealous of you for a very long time.'

Clare received the rebuke, and its information, in silence.

The sheep was duly chosen and paid for and they wandered out into the sunshine.

'I'm sorry,' Lucy said, 'but I must be getting back or we won't have any supper.'

'We have to stop at Carnith for the potato scones,' Felicity reminded them.

'Aren't we going to walk to the waterfall?' Ceci asked.

'No.' They both spoke a little too firmly.

Ceci said, 'That's the second time today Felicity and Clare have spoken simultaneously.'

They were both grateful to her; the uneasiness between them evaporated as, once more, they shook the ritual little finger.

Felicity hastened to offer a reason for her emphatic refusal.

'I do think we ought to get back to Alice. It was sweet of Mummy, but she's had quite a long chunk now.'

'She'll be fine.'

'I know she will, Bob, but I'd like to get back and if Lucy's in a hurry . . .'

Clare was relieved that no one asked her why she did not want to linger. She did not ever want to see another waterfall again.

They found the family having tea when they got home; great sections of the jigsaw puzzle had been filled in.

'It's been perfectly peaceful,' Anni said. 'Alice has been wrestling with Joseph's puzzle most of the day and I have heroically not been helping her. Did you remember to get potato scones at Carnith?'

'Yep.'

'Great, because I didn't make a cake.'

Ben came in from an eight-hour walk, weary but relaxed. When Hester smiled at him he bent over and kissed the top of her head, an old affectionate gesture he had not bestowed on her since his disgrace.

Clare excused herself from kitchen duties on the grounds of left-handed incompetence, but laughed about it and volunteered instead to pyjama the babies.

'But no baths.'

'I'll wash, you dry,' said Louise, cheerfully, and did not seem to notice the others' surprise.

Later, after supper, bundled against the summer night – 'put on something warm; there may be a bit of hanging around' – they walked away from the house, round the shoulder of the hill and started up the forestry track.

The minute they turned off the road, they were out of sight of the house and its faint golden glow. The darkness pounced. And then sight came slowly creeping back. The moving dark of the loch lay separated from the still dark of the hills. Above them there was a delicate darker seam, where the hood of the sky lidded neatly over the hills.

'Where's the moon?' asked Amanda.

'It has set,' Joseph told her; and teasingly, 'It's a baby moon so it has to go to bed early.'

'We're better off without it,' Anni told her, 'a bright moon dims the stars.'

They all looked up and saw the stars undimmed, infinitely distant. It ought to have been scary, Clare thought, and remembered the last time she had been out at night. That had been frightening.

She and David had gone to the Victoria Falls, as all tourists to Zimbabwe should. The Victoria Falls had undone her; all the doubts and miseries about her life had become focused there.

She had tried, all the three days that they were there, to deny her fear. She read the guide books with unusual care and endeavoured to reduce the power of the Falls to a set of statistics.

The Victoria Falls are between 61 and 105 metres high and 1,688 metres wide. About 545,000,000 litres of water pour over them every minute in flood season, sending spray some 500 metres into the air.

One hundred and fifty million years ago, the whole of Southern Africa was wracked, skewed, destabilised by volcanic activity; a 300 metre thick lava blanket was cast down casually by a crazed God experimenting with his toy. It hardened into igneous basalt. Then the land cooled and the blanket shrunk, just like mud in a drought. It cracked along both its warp and its woof, fractal patterning on a vast scale. Slowly, so slowly, the cracks were eroded open, stretched, etched, widened, into crevasses.

Then it rained; and it rained and it rained; a flood with no ark to bob upon it, until the whole land became a lake, a sea without salt. And molecule by molecule, lime and clay filled the crevasses, and turned into rock themselves. Not the hard rock of the burning times, but the soft rock of the wet time; and there was nothing to give consciousness to the growing rock, as it had grown in Clare's soul.

Then when the Zambezi River started its long push to the Indian Ocean, it forced its way down through the limestone network, taking it easy as it could afford to do, ignoring the harsh basalt, passionately consuming the limestone which was its own child, water-made. Pushing its way along the fissures laid down for it; emptying them and then crashing into them. Breaking its way from crevasse to crevasse, carving back as rock face after rock face collapsed before its tireless progress; great falls of rock and the river calmly reorganising its own fall another fifty yards further up its course. And now it crashes over the basalt lip into the pit it has carved for itself. These are the Victoria Falls, renamed after a fat little half-German queen who painted watercolours of her children and sent her heroes out to possess the earth.

Before Livingstone came there was an enormous booming and a profound silence. 'On sights as beautiful as this Angels in their flight must have gazed,' the good doctor wrote. After the fall of rock, not in eternity but in time, the Falls were created. Angels never flew here: after the Fall there were no more angels; they were cast down in spray, into the bottomless pit where hope never comes that comes to all, and then there were no more angels.

Clare knew perfectly well, here on this Scottish hillside, that the guide book had not said any of this; that she was making it up, that her terror was irrational – there was nothing to fear.

The children were excited. Amanda and William had come, and Alice; 'especially Alice,' Anni had said. They were bubbling with late-night glee. Ben sang with them, waving the big torch he had brought like a baton. It was not scary; it was childlike, the thrill of being out after bedtime.

But the terror remained. At the Falls the solid facts had not protected her. Everything that she had been frightened of since she went to Africa, everything she had been frightened of for years without knowing it, had all been there. The contrast between those enormous waters and the drinking of sundowners on the terrace of the hotel with flame-necked Rhodies and the rich international tourists, was unbearable.

David did not understand.

He had wanted to have fun. Within a couple of hours he had uncovered the treats of the resort, and dragged her out to the craft village to buy charming model animals, in wood and stone and clay. Then they took a hotel bus out to a little strip airport and boarded a six-seater plane. It was too small, too insecure for Clare, but David was grinning and happy and she was too scared to tell him she was scared. They flew over the small town and out across the gorge. The Zambezi River had lain below them, the snake laid out twisting and turning, hissing and tossing off venom, the cloud of spray from the lip of the cliff, and from the boiling cauldron underneath where waters crashed into pools too small to contain them.

'It's called the Flight of Angels,' David told her, leaning close to her ear to be heard above the engine. 'We're like Livingstone's angels.'

Clare had felt more like one of Mrs Mildenhall's butterflies, unable to uncouple, drifting perilously on the wind. She had felt afraid. It was not just the flight that scared her, although she was always nervous of flying, and especially in so small an aeroplane. The Falls themselves frightened her; the two of them had gone out, clad in hideous black plastic cloaks against the spray, to inspect the waterfall from the other side of the gorge; only fifty yards away the wall of water plunged downwards, half seen through the spray, enormous, roaring like an animal, and what Clare felt was not delight but awe.

There had been too much beauty and power; it had been to escape this sense of powerlessness before a greater power that she had given up Christianity. It was not that she could not believe, when the priest, when her father, raised the circle of cardboard-flavoured bread, that the Divine Word, the power that exploded the whole cosmos into being, had not been fully present. It was the fear of what that truth might mean: her insignificance, impotence, fragility in the face of infinity.

David did not understand.

Finally he insisted that they go to see the Falls by night, under the influence of the moon.

'You go,' she said, when he shook her awake, in the chilly depth of the night. 'I'm too sleepy.'

'Come on,' he said, 'it'll be spectacular. The moon's full tonight.'

'I don't want to, David. It'll be scary.'

'Rubbish, darling, grow up. Don't spoil it for me. It won't be any fun on my own.'

She had given in and they had gone out. The moon had been so bright and near, creating moon-bows of spray; the moon and the upthrown spray conspiring playfully to make the coloured lights that are more properly the business of the sun and the downfalling rain. The dark night was alive with light, flames of water, a new alliance, an alliance against her.

The Livingstone Memorial Statue, commemorating the Victorian hero who had served both God and mammon so well, stood, stern and powerful at the top of the Devil's Cataract. Here was safety and control, for the statue had been placed in the one position where people could watch the falls without getting wet. David had learned that here was where they should come to take pictures of the dawn.

It was pitch dark, and she had stumbled on the narrow pathway, aware of the trees and undergrowth crowding in around her.

'I can't see where we're going, David; this is dangerous.'

But David had sensibly borrowed a torch, and its wide beam picked out a path for them.

'I don't want to . . .' she tried to say, although nothing came out.

There were eyes watching them, two low, close-set jewels.

'Hare,' said David.

'Baboon . . . bushback,' as the eyes reappeared at a higher level.

'Owl,' he said as the darkness was filled suddenly with great white power that came and was gone before she could inhale the freshness of the air against her face.

'David . . .' she whispered.

'It's only an owl, silly.' How did he know? Mrs Mildenhall had told them that owls were birds of evil omen to the Shona.

When they arrived at their vantage point the roaring of the water was too loud; there was an immense din in the darkness and she could see nothing. But David had timed the expedition perfectly; they only had to wait a few minutes before the light changed to grey and the air was filled with spray, and with the rushing, pouncing water only yards from them.

Without warning, in the pre-dawn light the spray rising from the Falls turned to blood, owl's blood perhaps, or David's or hers, an explosion of blood; and so beautiful that she could not breathe. She could not breathe. And she did not know why the sparkling, the red blood dancing, were so lovely and terrifying.

The red faded, slowly, to delicate shell-pink. She had been brought up to see the beauty of nature in silence and here there was no silence, never silence: the noise was enormous and constant; she hated it but was grateful to it because it meant that she did not have to talk to David.

Quite suddenly the sun, bright orange and yellow, leapt up out of Zambia and everything was normal again.

'Wow!' said David, and grinned at her, a grin that was both boyish and openly inviting.

'I forgot to take any photographs,' she said.

'Idiot,' he said affectionately. 'We'll come back tomorrow morning.'

She pretended not to hear him, turning away from the magnificence and starting back along the narrow track. She could see her own footsteps and his, clearly imprinted in the muddy sand, and a third set, bare with long straight toes. And then on a turn in the narrow path, with the trees close around them, she saw, laid across her own footprint, the enormous pugmark of a leopard.

She froze, and David following behind nearly bumped into her. He put his arms round her, a warm hug that she did not want. He saw what she had seen.

'Jesus Christ!' he said, and then after a pause, 'We should have brought a gun.'

Then he released her, and walked on, placing his footprint over the leopard's.

She hated him. She wished he was dead. She was terrified of her own hatred which had some connection with the paw print at her feet. She wished that she was dead, for all her certainties had been eroded by the weight of water.

'You know,' he said casually, when they were far enough away from the face of the Falls for normal conversation to be possible again, 'you can sort of understand why the sentimentally inclined might want to call that a spiritual experience.'

Looking up she saw a section of the hideous metal bridge

that spanned the gorge just below the Falls themselves, linking Zimbabwe to Zambia.

'You're like Cecil Rhodes,' she said. 'You would have built that bridge; so that white people on fast-moving trains could enjoy the spray from the waterfall.' Then she smiled at him, pretending it was a joke.

He smiled complacently. 'Cape to Cairo,' he said, 'and a good thing too.' Then he added, 'Mr Rhodes wants his breakfast.' He led the way up the narrow track towards the hotel.

And here she was once again climbing up a narrow track, though now it was at the beginning not the end of the night. They climbed steeply for about ten minutes, spreading out on the track according to fitness and determination. Then the path levelled off for a bit and ran across an open stretch of land, heather and rough grass.

'Lie down,' said Anni. 'Lie down and look at the sky.'

She threw herself on her back.

'What are we looking *for*?' Bob asked, trying to relay the instructions to Alice, and having difficulties in the dark.

'Just look.'

They all lay down.

Ben said, 'If Joseph and Anni can arrange this with so little squabbling then whatever we're going to see is bound to be impressive.'

They all laughed, and fidgeted themselves comfortable. Clare looked up, content to wait. It was quiet, with very little wind, but the night itself was stirring softly. As her eyes adjusted and waited, she was stunned by the intensity of the stars. Joseph was instructing his two children on the constellations: the Big Dipper, the Pole Star and Cassiopeia, and brilliantly bright almost overhead Vega the key star of the Lyra, the little summer constellation. The Milky Way was extraordinary; each star precise, a pinprick on the velvety blackness but so many and so many and so many; Clare felt herself reeling.

'In Zimbabwe,' she said aloud, 'I saw the Southern Cross. It was so strange, to have read about it and read about it and then someone just said "there it is, that's the Southern Cross" and it was .'

John Chitaukire, a lawyer from Mutare, had shown her the Southern Cross after he had taken David and her out for supper.

She remembered the evening perfectly. John, whom they had met quite casually in the hotel, had taken them out to a craft market in one of the townships.

'We don't say township any more, we say high-density area,' John had informed them.

The square houses with corrugated iron roofs, each in its own minute colourful garden, had looked picturesque, but the loafers, mostly young men in shabby jeans or colourful shorts, had seemed menacing to Clare.

'All visitors buy crafts; here you can find the real McCoy.' John had obviously been delighted by his own slang. Clare had bought lengths of cloth and carved wooden spoons and earth-turned bowls.

'They'll break,' John had warned her, 'and anyway, if you want bowls you should buy the black, charcoal burnished ones, and the spotty pots from down in the south east. Here you should buy baskets. And perhaps a hat.'

There had been a stall with high piles of loose-woven straw hats. She had tried on several, the men laughing at her, and she laughing back.

'You ought to see the N'anga's stall,' John had said to Clare.

'What? What's a N'anga?'

'Hmm. That depends where you stand. A N'anga is a healer, a traditional healer. But Zimbabwean medicine doesn't work like western; it's more -- would you say religious? A N'anga first has to decide what made you ill, so some N'angas are like mediums, they consult with the ancestors. They don't just deal with illnesses, but with other things that go wrong, or with the future; fortune telling. Also, if something goes wrong it may be that someone else in your family has done something wrong, not you. You see,' he had smiled, 'we are natural socialists in Zimbabwe. But anyway, after diagnosis, you may have to take some medicine or get some-one else to, and then you go to the N'anga stall to get it. Over there.'

At the side of the market, under some trees, there was a hut with open sides and a thatched roof. They had strolled into the

N'anga's shop, past an old man and a small boy squatting motion-less on the wooden step, identical in their dark abstraction. It was dusty and dim inside; she had to take off her dark glasses.

One moment she had been a tourist, relaxed in the sunshine, the next instant she entered a dark new world. The place was full of messages she could not read. There were piles and boxes; shells, twigs, dried powders, tin crucifixes. There were sealed pots too; and on higher shelves glowing glass jars. And there were bars of Nivea soap, their blue paper wrappings an entirely different tone of colour from the faded neutrals of the earth's dross.

'What are these?' she had put down her hand at random.

John had looked over her shoulder, 'Monkey's paws I should think.'

She had lifted her hand abruptly and looked. Skeletons of tiny hands; not soft and wide like babies' hands, but rather the dwarfed hands of old women.

'How about pickled snake?' David asked, reaching for a golden jar. ' "Eye of newt and toe of dog".'

She realised that he was finding all this funny. 'Clare, ask the old bloke if you can take some pictures; they'd be great. Colour supplement stuff.'

'I'm not allowed to work here. You know that.'

'They wouldn't know, and this isn't exactly a military instal-lation, is it? Just jolly tourist interest.'

But Clare knew power when it touched her. The place was full of power. She had not known if it was good power or bad power. She wanted to keep the power and her fear of it away from David.

'And this?' she had asked John, fingering some powder in a small open bowl. 'What's it for?'

'I do not know. I'm a Western-trained lawyer, not a N'anga, and even if I was, it's quite local.'

'How do you get to be one?'

'That depends. There are different kinds, you know. The really big time is to be a medium, the representative, the person the ancestor will talk through. There are different grades of ancestors, different amounts of power. You are born that, it just has to be discerned . . . recognised, is that a better word? . . . and trained of course. I don't really know much about it. Healers are less,

less . . . I really don't know. Why should you care? This stuff here. A lot of it will be charms for one sort of trouble or another; some of them will be bribes for the dead, and I expect that here in urban areas lots will be love or fertility things. For big troubles you'd have to go back to your communal lands anyway. The ancestors tend to stay at home. It's one of the problems. Leave it alone, just enjoy it. Here's crocodile teeth, see.'

She turned to search further and the old man from the step outside was near her, too near. Right in front of her. He reached out and touched her right hand with one finger, almost surreptitiously. She noticed the bloom of white dust on his skin.

She tried to smile graciously, and turned away. The old man spoke to her. She looked for John.

'What is he saying?'

John and the old man talked a little. 'He wants to sell you a fertility spell; for twin boys. He says you would make a good mother and should not wait too long.'

'Rubbish,' David said abruptly.

'Did you make that up?' Clare asked.

'No,' John said, but he caught the tension between her and David and was amused by it.

'And now,' he had said, returning immediately to his jovial manner, 'shall I take you out to supper? Not hotel dinner, real Zimbabwean food. Sadza.'

They went to a small eating house, immensely crowded, immensely noisy, immensely hot. There was a lot of beer, and no other women. No other white people either. But no one paid them any attention.

'All white women are mad you see,' John said, 'so we just don't judge them.'

John ordered, and three pots of food arrived. 'Sadza – which is mealy porridge, our staple food. Meat – don't ask what kind – but stewed. And peanut butter.'

There were no plates or cutlery, and once again Clare was aware that John was teasing them. With a gesture that seemed both ancient and elegant, entirely appropriate and entirely out of keeping with his smart suit, John scooped out a glob of sadza with his two fingers and thumb, swirled it in the stew pot and tucked it into his mouth. Clare and David had looked at each other.

'It's easy.'

It had not been. It had been messy.

'You can have forks if you want. Like spoons for people who can't manage chop sticks in Chinese restaurants.'

The peanut goo had been delicious.

'We wanted to be exotic,' David laughed, plunging in. And John had been grinning, tolerant, pleased with them and himself. Later in the meal, Clare, her beer in her right hand, had reached casually towards the pot with her left.

'Don't do that!'

'What?'

'Never, never eat with your left hand. Or greet people, or give them anything, or receive a gift. It's . . . what shall I say . . . a breach of etiquette. No, worse. It's very rude. Even I, appallingly westernised though I am, can't suppress instant shock-horror.'

Clare blushed.

'No, no. I'm just telling you. Don't be upset.'

But she had known. She could remember Peggy, on one of her visits to Birmingham telling them as little children that in Africa it was rude to use your left hand. She was ashamed. Her whiteness meant that she burned, and meant that she carried a burden of shame, and that she had been rude, rude to this big kind man who had given them a day they had not deserved, as a gift. David was finding it funny. The silent eyes of the N'anga had been fixed upon her; upon her immodest white knees and her blunted soul. She wanted to go home. She had known that she would never be able to explain her shame to David, who would call her a bleeding-heart liberal and would be right; who would accuse her of being both a neurotic and a spoilsport; who would laugh at her.

They had walked back to the hotel after supper, companionable in the darkness.

Apparently inspired by no external event John said, as he walked beside her, 'I should warn you. Don't get too romantic about N'angas. Among other things it is said that they have a recommended cure for AIDS which is to rape a white woman.'

141

She did not know how to respond, and they walked on in silence.

And then, as they paused at the hotel gate before going in, 'Look,' John said. He touched her shoulder very gently, and then pointed. 'The Southern Cross.'

The four stars glowed bright above them, the stars you could not see in England, only read about. The scent of flowers from the hotel garden had been rich and giddy as though she had never smelled flowers before.

'Thank you, thank you,' she had said to John, 'you've given us a wonderful afternoon. A gift.'

'No. At least a very small one. I had fun. I really like English people you know. I miss it sometimes. Anyway, have a good holiday. I'm off home at dawn.'

He had shaken hands with David, turned towards the door and disappeared through it into the light.

David had said, 'What a show-off.' Then he had put both his hands on her shoulders and kissed her, not a gentle kiss for a lovely and unexpected holiday evening, but a demanding, claiming kiss. She recalled, with a tiny spurt of irritation, that it always turned him on when other men fancied her.

Now the flowering garden of the hotel was so far away and David was dead and John would not fancy her again because she had no right hand, and the stars above her head, like the stars still above the garden in Harare, evinced not the slightest bit of interest.

Joseph said, almost crossly, 'Don't toss the Southern Cross in now, you'll muddle them up.'

Felicity said, equally crossly, 'How long is this going to take?'

Alice, who had been lying flat out obediently looking heavenwards, squawked one of her strange sounds, sitting up and banging Bob on the chest. All the grown-ups looked away from the sky and at the child.

Amanda said, 'What's that?' and then almost immediately, 'There, again.'

They all looked up and after a waiting moment saw a single sharp flash across the sky, and then another apparently moving just as fast in the opposite direction.

'Shooting stars,' said Ben, and they could hear and share his wonder.

'Watch!' said Joseph.

They watched.

They saw a display of outrageous flamboyance, each star a streak of fire fanning out from a centre and plunging away. Every one was greeted by a cry of delight from the children. With a dark sky and no moon, they were seeing shooting stars, nearly two a second. Alice squawked afresh for each one; Anni and Joseph smiled at each other as proud as if they had created this display themselves. Ceci gave a tiny sigh with each star. Felicity and Bob reached for each other's hand, a moment of tender awe. Ben lay quite still, relaxing because now he had found something outside himself that he could give himself over to.

Anni, her voice deepening in some sort of internal passion, explained the performance.

'A meteor is a chip of something, usually smaller than a marble, up there in space. There are bigger ones, there can be ones so big that they survive the heat and friction of entering earth's atmosphere. Some people think that it may have been a really huge one crashing into the earth that killed off the dinosaurs. There are millions of them, they are everywhere, there are lots of different kinds, all too small for us to observe them in space; mostly they're made from broken up chips of material, left over from the epoch when the planets were being formed.

'These ones, though, aren't lost little planetoids; these are the dust of a passing comet. As comets, which are weird astral bodies made up of ice and crumbly particles, whizz through space, they shed dust. Just as you would if you ran through the house in shoes that were caked with dry mud. And when the earth – which is moving really fast too, over one thousand eight hundred kilometres a minute – crosses a comet's orbit, this dust is sucked into our atmosphere, and the meteors, the dust particles, vaporise and disintegrate in a flash of light.'

Anni paused, took a deep breath and added, more quietly. 'In a flash of glory.'

They knew she had embarrassed herself.

Ceci said comfortingly, 'I know. God is such a show off.'

Anni went on with her lecture in a much more pedantic voice.

'The process is the same as with the sporadic meteors, but because we know the orbits of both the earth and the comets we can tell when we're to see this sort. These ones are called the Perseids, because they seem to be pouring out of the constellation named after Perseus. I know they look as though they were fanning out from a fixed point, but they aren't: it's an effect of perspective, really they are all parallel with each other.'

'Anni,' said Ben, but affectionately, a laugh in his voice, 'enough, enough.'

Joseph said, 'Tell my gang later, when we can draw a diagram for them.'

They all lay together watching the sky; watching star after star – impossible, whatever Anni said, to hold in their minds that these were just marble-sized chunks of waste matter, crumbly dust left under the bed of some comet that will not return for thousands of years – watching star after star hurl itself headlong into the atmosphere – impossible, whatever Anni said, to hold in their minds that the meteors were not moving towards them, but that they were charging on the meteors.

Bob said, 'Do you think the story about Perseus being conceived by Zeus disguised as a shower of gold came from observing these showers?'

Anni said, 'I must admit that's more interesting than what I was saying.' The grin was back in her voice and they all relaxed.

'Not to me,' said Joseph, though whether he was comforting Anni, rebuking Bob, or simply asserting a preference for science over mythology was not clear.

'I've always hated Perseus,' Felicity said. 'Complacent creep. There was Andromeda, waiting for her monster: no one ever asked her if she wanted Perseus to save her. Perhaps she half saw on the wave's crest the cruel beauty of her sea dragon and discovered that that was what she really wanted. And then, b-boom, b-boom, along comes Perseus all sweaty, muscle-bound and glowing with gentlemanly virtue and rescues her, and she was obliged to be grateful for ever and ever.' Her voice sounded slightly sad.

There was a moment of stunned surprise.

'Felicity has had a feminist insight,' said Anni, mockingly.

'I thought the same thing at the Victoria Falls,' said Clare. 'I thought: "No one ever asked Livingstone if he minded when that vulgar Stanley burst into his life without apology and became a hero." Perhaps he wanted to be lost forever, to lose his way and find his own life.'

Joseph said, 'I still find Anni's lecture more interesting than all this mystical speculation.'

'Both/and,' said Ben, 'Mythology and science; not either/or. And do shut up all of you. There's enough to see, without this pedagogical commentary.'

Clare reached out her arm, remembered that it was the wrong one, rolled over and tweaked his nose with her left hand.

'It's pedagogical to use words like pedagogical when trying to stop people being it.'

They all laughed and lapsed into silence; a true desire to return to the shared delight.

Clare felt the quietness settle around her. She forgot everything, now, perhaps for the first time since she had come back from Africa. Each shooting star was suddenly and completely surprising and yet the whole show a preposterous dance of power. They were too many, too many, and each was alone in a space too huge for comprehension, so that comprehension was no longer needed. Anchored in Anni's knowledge and Bob's humanism, perhaps there could be some safety and yet . . .

And yet . . . star by star they vaporise and die in a burst of glory, the fireworks of God, the fall of the angels. They explode in the heavens and die in a burst of glory.

Ben said, 'It feels like there's a pause in the darkness, an audible silence, almost unendurable, between each one. Like when you're a kid and a grown-up lights a firework and you know it's going to go off and the waiting is unbearably exciting. Like . . .' and he stopped abruptly. Clare knew he had been going to say, 'like the moment before you come'.

Anni, who probably heard the same ending to Ben's arrested sentence, said with a chuckle, 'That's built in deliberately. It's simply to give the person with the taper a chance to run away; so much beauty is very dangerous, it can burn you up.'

Clare jerked physically as though she had been hit. She had been hit by memory. Not the mountain and the voices of the darkness; not the roll of thunder and the mist. But before that, long before that, when she was a very little girl:

Her parents, her real parents, before James and Hester, before this was her family, her real parents had been powerful magicians. In older times her father would have been an alchemist, turning base metals to gold. In those same times her mother would have been a witch and burned. As it was they had been pyrotechnicians: they made fireworks. Occasionally they would demonstrate some new model they were working on.

'Stay inside,' they would say. 'It's very dangerous. You can watch through the window.'

'Yes, Mummy; yes, Daddy. I know it's dangerous.'

Then she would press her nose against the windowpane and watch their scuttling shadowy figures on the lawn, watch one of them advance with the taper, light the touchpaper and retreat to safety; she would endure the unendurable pause between the moment when the fire embraced the touchpaper and the moment when the firework came alive. Then she would see the garden turned to light, the heart of the magic, the dancing fire, the stars brought down from heaven, the rain turned silver, gold, incandescent, glorious. And she knew it was dangerous.

Her parents' best display was their last, on a crisp November evening. She had knelt on the broad window seat quivering with anticipation. Her mother had advanced into the middle of the lawn and lit the fuse. Then she had joined her husband against the laboratory wall. When the pause ended all heaven broke loose: there were stars and flames and explosions; the window shattered, cold glass diamonds joining the hot fire ones. In a flash of sulphur lightning she saw them embrace, and explode.

Clare watched her parents explode in a cloud of stars.

For the second time that year she was on a mountainside and the heavens were exploding around her and her parents died so and David died so. She knew she must not scream because the children would be frightened and her brothers would laugh at her.

She must not scream. Had she screamed on the mountain when

David had died? She knew she must not scream on this mountain, because this is the mountain of childhood, the mountain of her own ancestors, her own roots, and she was balanced on the edge of chaos and above her the stars continued to fall, needle rips of dying light as her parents had died, explosions, guns, meteors, the fall of the angels, the loss of innocence. 'On sights such as these angels must have gazed.' She had known at the Falls that there was too much blood, spraying up into the morning.

There were too many stars. And it was in the beauty that the fear lay.

'Clare,' came Anni's voice. 'Clare are you OK?'

What had she done that made Anni, in the dark, think that she might not be OK?'

'I've just remembered something,' she said, and lurched to her feet. She started to walk down the hill; while she was still in sight or sound of the children she must not run. Soon she ran. She ran through the dark night while the world smashed into the meteor cloud, and all she can see is the garden lit up with wild light and her parents in each other's arms, laughing, laughing. They had laughed and embraced and exploded.

She fled into the sitting room at Skillen and there were her mother and father. They were sitting in the golden glow of the peaceful room, and her father was reading aloud to her mother, who was knitting. It was a place of safety; when they were small her father had read like this to all of them. Hester was sitting by the fire, her back to the door, so it was her father's face that greeted her first.

Whatever her expression was, his reflected it back in mild alarm, in half rising, and she wanted those thin cold arms, that disciplined distance, but Hester read from James' face something of what was on Clare's. She turned quickly.

'Clare, darling!' she cried, and stood up. She came at once to her daughter's side. And Clare, still panicked, still the little girl who watched her parents die in a meteor burst of their own creating, reaches out almost desperately for her mother's hug, for the kisses and sticking plasters of infancy.

But, so that there should be no moment of rescue and comfort, The Hand was ready; when Clare lifted her arms to embrace her mother they were the arms of childhood which had no knowledge of The Hand. The weight was wrong and The Hand hit Hester sharply on the side of the face so that her glasses were knocked off. There was a moment of recoil; not even Hester could cope unmoved with a hard slap on the face from a beloved and distressed daughter. Especially a slap from Clare who has always been controlled, economical with her contacts and gestures.

Clare had not felt the blow, because although The Hand responded to her thoughts and desires, it did not give any information back. The Hand looked innocent now, craftily disguised as a normal hand that had been instructed by a normal brain to hit a comforting and loving mother on the face and knock her glasses off.

The blow and the shock were both strong enough to bring tears to Hester's eyes. She stood there with the tears springing unbidden and unforbidden; as impulsive and accidental as the blow. She raised her own hand to her face and Clare realised what had happened.

Coming out of the wild and dangerous darkness, coming overwrought and stretched, confronted brutally by her own handicap that prevented her even seeking love with assurance, Clare said the first thing in her mind and it was not a kind thing.

'You never told me they were laughing.'

Had David been laughing too?

Hester had no way of understanding. 'Clare, what is it? Have the boys been teasing you?'

'I'm sorry,' Clare drew a deep breath. 'Mummy, I'm sorry. It was an accident; I can't make this damn thing behave.'

The Hand flexed its metal and plastic fingers and wriggled evilly. It was laughing at her, as her brother had laughed when she was little, as David had laughed. She hated it.

She bent apologetically to pick up her mother's glasses.

Hester was immediately comforted; a malfunctioning hand called in practical straightforward ways for sympathy and love. She smiled tenderly and bent down to pick up her glasses.

Their heads rapped smartly together.

They both said, simultaneously, 'I'm sorry.' They looked into each other's eyes and laughed.

James said, 'Have you two quite finished beating each other up?'

Clare reached for the glasses with her left hand and gently restored them to her mother's nose. They both stood up.

'What is this about?' James asked gently.

But the moment had passed. Clare said, 'It's this stupid prosthesis. Or stupid me, I suppose; it's a bad workman who blames his tools. I forget that it's fake.'

Hester smiled, 'They did say when we talked to them about it that it could take a while to get used to.'

'There's too much to get used to,' Clare said. 'They're very good at the clinic, but they want you to do two contradictory things at once: to accept that you're an amputee — that there's loss, you have lost part of yourself, there's . . . they want . . . there's a mourning process they want you to go through, but at the same time they sort of imply that it doesn't make any difference; the myeloelectric prosthesis, this thing, is so wonderful that it doesn't make any difference. They're terribly proud of it. They want you to be too, they want you to love it and learn everything and perform well. They want you to pretend it's just like your own hand. But . . . but I've spent so long trying to learn that my body is who I am; getting away from the idea of the self as a soul stuck into a bit of machinery. They want you to learn too many things at once and be grateful.'

'Hard for you,' James said, 'because you have the other mourning to do, too. For David.'

Hester held her breath.

Clare said, 'Yes.'

For both her parents that was better than nothing. Clare added, 'If he is dead, of course.'

They said nothing, looking at her with too much compassion; loving, serious, concerned.

'Honestly honestly, I do not know what happened. I can't remember. I can't remember.'

'You must go on trying though,' Hester said. 'You'll feel more at peace if you can remember, whatever it was.'

Clare smiled, 'That's exactly what Peggy said.'

'Really?' Hester smiled gratefully.

Peggy had come to visit her often in the hospital in Mutare. After Joseph had arranged for her to come home, Peggy had come with Joyful to say goodbye.

'What happened?' everyone had asked her. And she had always said, 'I don't know.'

But that last time Peggy and Joyful had come to see her they had woken her up from a deep sleep. 'What happened?' they had asked, and with the quiet sweetness of sleep still on her she said, almost mischievously, 'Chirikudzi got him.'

Peggy looked startled, almost excited, and said, 'Darling, did you . . . ?'

Joyful interrupted, almost rudely. 'Rubbish,' she said, 'Chirikudzi does not live on Nyangani. She lives in the source waters of the Pongwe River.'

At the very end of the visit Peggy said, 'Try to remember. You'll feel much better, whatever it was.'

'I'm not so sure,' Joyful said grimly.

'Write to me anyway,' said Peggy, 'whatever happens.' Then she kissed Clare and Clare had begun to cry.

'Yes, really,' said Clare, and she could almost smile at her mother's smile, 'But, Mummy, it's not a conscious act of will you know; it can be simply physical – "post-traumatic amnesia" isn't the same as neurotic repression. It can be something that just comes with concussion, with a severe blow to the poor old brain.' And then more boldly because she was anxious for her mother to understand, 'A sort of subliminal amputation. With no prosthesis.'

'Have you thought about hypnosis?' James asked, deliberately making his voice sound neutral.

'I don't believe in hypnosis,' Hester said. 'What the mind doesn't want to remember shouldn't be tricked out of it.'

'Then you're really saying that you don't accept Clare's explanation; that you think the mind does choose, neurotically if that's the technical word for it, does choose to reject the material.'

Hester looked put out.

Clare said, 'Daddy, the thing is I don't know. Perhaps it is repression. The soldiers, the ones who rescued me, you know what they said.' She did not know why they should lie.

'The hospital say "wait". They say that whatever happened it was shocking, in every sense. They say very likely the memory will come back.'

The doctor who had tried to explain it to her had been very sweet. 'You can't force it,' he had said, 'but you can dodge it. You can refuse but you can't insist, like a child learning to speak: the child can refuse, consciously or unconsciously, but it can't make it happen, it has to build up the blocks one by one.'

'Of course, there are things you can try,' he had said. 'You can try telling the whole story to someone; start where you can remember and just go on till you can't. If you can tell it often enough you may get a little further each time. You can try returning to the scene of the accident, re-enact it.'

'I'm a neurologist,' he had said. 'I think it's fascinating what has happened to you. I hope you'll come and tell me when or if you do remember; but in your case there are too many traumas – the concussion, the amputation, the death or loss or disappearance of your partner' – even then she had noticed with some amusement how well he handled the neutral term – 'so I don't want to jump-start your memory just for my curiosity; electric shock or hypnosis or repeat experience. I can't know if that would be in your best interest.'

'Have you been asked to?' she enquired.

He had looked embarrassed. Then taken a deep breath, 'Yes, we have. But not by the police. By your partner's insurance company. That's their problem, not yours or mine. You are my patient; don't worry. Not their needs, nor my curiosity: you are the person whose life it is. I might try if you asked me, but not yet. Why don't you wait and see? Give it some time. Often the memory just comes back, very gently, like a growing process. Also, you've probably seen it in films; sometimes it happens very suddenly. Very suddenly. Something triggers it, some trivial daily event, some repetition or *aide memoire*. That can be frightening. I ought to warn you.'

It had been frightening; that sudden surge of returning memory. It had sent her crashing down the mountainside.

She said, 'That's not what upset me. We've got distracted. Do you know what Anni and Joseph wanted us to go and look at?

Something called a Perseid Shower, a whole lot of shooting stars that perform regularly.' She felt no response from them. 'A sort of astral firework display,' she said, and Hester flinched.

When she was little they would never take her to firework parties.

'It did something to me . . . I remembered my parents. Perhaps I should have tried hypnosis years ago. I had forgotten how they died. Why did you never tell me they were both laughing?'

She saw the empathetic pain in Hester's face. Hester put her arms out and Clare, keeping her arms by her side, leaned into her mother's shoulder. She almost started to cry, the choked tears made her sound angry, insistent, resentful.

'Why didn't you tell me?'

'Clare, darling,' said Hester. 'We thought . . . ah, dear Clare, don't be like that, it doesn't matter . . . we wanted . . .'

Suddenly, although they hadn't heard the outside door, the room was full of returning stargazers.

William was saying, 'Grandpa, gosh it was good, have you ever seen it?'

Alice, in an urgency of excitement, desperate that she should be able to tell her grandmother before anyone else did, was tugging demandingly at Hester's skirt.

Anni was listing for Ben and Ceci the other occasions in the year that eye-visible meteor showers could be observed and the difference between fast white and slow yellow ones.

Louise appeared from somewhere else and was telling her children that it was long past their bedtime.

Clare withdrew her head from its resting place and tried not to feel resentful. Hester with her extraordinary powers of concentration had already said to Amanda, 'You can tell your mother, Mandy; Alice is going to tell me.' She led Alice to the sofa so that they could be close. Hester could not sign well, but she noticed Alice's need and payed attention. She earned a grateful smile from Felicity, and an understanding one from Clare.

As the room filled with noise and people, James came to Clare, and spoke quietly but clearly:

'We didn't tell you, because we didn't know. We weren't there. Nobody was there but you. We could only tell you what you gave

152

us to tell you. You cannot blame either of your mothers for that.'
He spoke with the voice of authority.

Then the familial confusion was multiplied by the arrival of
Tom and Caro, back from a long hard day of killing.

It took the house a long while to settle down that night. The
sky was too enormous over the loch, and although the brightness
of the Perseid Shower had vanished still the earth turned crashing
through the meteor cloud and last sputters of glory spun out of
the constellation of Perseus, restlessly.

When Clare tried to take The Hand off it hurt. It did sometimes.
Her own hand had been amputated just above the wrist; in the
London hospital they had tidied the stump so that it could fit
tightly into the bowl at the upper end of the prosthesis.

'Talcum powder,' the technician who had fitted it had said
laconically, when she had asked him how to deal with the problem. Clare felt he saw her stump as useless and therefore as
insensate. Certainly he had never had to put the thing on or take
it off, against not only the repulsion of the imagination, but
against the healing skin of the wound itself. Talcum powder
helped, but it did not stop the process being painful and embarrassing: a striptease performed reluctantly.

If it hurt, then the nerves of her arm would instruct The Hand
to clench or twitch. Trying to remove an inanimate object which
flexes and shifts was bizarre and humiliating. The easiest thing to
do was to turn it off first. Tonight Clare was convinced that The
Hand had set its own will against hers. She hated it. She decided
that she would never wear it again, and then she remembered the
shame. When she finally got it off she yanked out the batteries and
plugged them into the recharger; she would need them tomorrow.

She was afraid that if she slept she would see again the deep
explosion; the world turned to fire, the moment of her apocalypse
and her first parents wrapped in each other's arms, laughing
wildly. They had known that it was dangerous but they had
still gone ahead, they had not thought of her. They had blown
themselves up and laughed at her in their moment of glory and
destruction.

David had laughed at her. They had climbed the mountain and

she had heard the distant roll of thunder and he had laughed at her fears.

Sleep seemed very dangerous.

Anxious, overstretched, for the first time since the accident she missed not David, but sex. She wanted the mechanical certainty of orgasm. He had been able to do that for her, over and over again. It had, she had discovered, nothing whatever to do with love; orgasm worked to silence fear, just as bread and water worked to silence hunger. David had been a mechanically brilliant lover.

She turned on to her front, wriggling her hips; longing, both for comfort and escape, mounting, she conjured up his presence and reached down with her own hand and . . . and then she hit a wall. It had always been her right hand. Always. Alone or with others it was her right hand, her dominant hand, the hand that had led the way and taught her body as a child and which knew the soft corners and the hard pressures. And her right hand was now rotting somewhere under different stars.

Loss caught her by the throat; and with it yet more memories she would rather be without. It was true that David had been a highly skilled lover; he had also been an imaginative and adventurous lover. He liked to play games that she did not like to play; games that included her humiliation. He loved to watch her masturbate. His ghost would be watching now and laughing; he had never thought of trying to make her do it left-handed. If he had he would have made her. No, he never made her; there was no force other than the force of his personality, but she would have consented. He like to sit, fully dressed, on the chair beside their bed and tell her pornographic narratives in a slow inexorable voice; and watch her masturbate. It always worked: she would reach a point of uncontrol when the need to come and the desire to withhold that from him would topple into fear and the distant rumbles of thunder and crashes of explosion. And in the end she would submit, submit to his voice because she could not bear to hear the edge of anger that would creep into his voice if she resisted him. She did not want to have to remember the shame and the relief and the slow, irresistable physical pleasure.

He was sitting beside her now, his tie neatly knotted. He had no face because the wild dogs of the eastern highlands had devoured it; she had pushed him down a crevasse and the scavengers had eaten his face away.

He was sitting beside her now, his hair neatly brushed. He had no face, because the *banditos armados* had cut it away. In Lalaua, Mozambique, RENAMO once massacred over a thousand people, stripped the supermarket shelves of produce and stacked the severed heads there. The stench of death became so strong in the village that the terrorists had themselves abandoned the town and set up camp outside it. RENAMO always left survivors, to flee and tell. You cannot govern by fear unless there are victims to spread that fear; David had known that and she was alive.

He was sitting beside her now, his shoelaces neatly tied. He had no face because Chirikudzi, the mermaid spirit, had kissed away his skin and nibbled his bones. Chirikudzi sang to him, low and sweet. Chirikudzi had a face; Clare was not sure if it was Joyful's face, or her first mother's face, or Julia's face. She wanted Chirikudzi to sing for her, but she sang for David, who had no face. The ancestors did not need faces, they were voices who spoke through the lips of the N'angas. David did not need a face any more.

She needed to escape: she knew no other escape than masturbation. She had not tried, she had not thought of trying since she had lost her hand. She could not work it out. Her left hand, friendly and willing, was as embarrassed as a pubescent girl discussing things in the night. It could not lose its consciousness, its guilt and its sense of being too young and too good for such things. In Africa, as Clare had learned, the left hand was the hand for such activities, but in the north that was not so. Those patterns laid down in childhood, with exploding fireworks and the wild manic laughter of departing parents, and . . . why is humiliation the place of safety? The one way to calm the panic, to comfort the soul and stomach.

She was briefly tempted to get out of bed, open the drawer, extract The Hand and see if it was possible, if its hard alien fingers could do for her what David had done, but she would not humiliate herself by failure or let The Hand into such an intimacy.

Clare and The Hand were not friends, not lovers.

'Don't worry about it,' her physiotherapist had said when she had tried to explain the hatred and the fear. 'You'll fall asleep one night and wake up in the morning and find it has become second nature.'

Clare had thought then that this was very likely true but was no comfort at all. She wanted first nature, not second.

She did not dare to go to sleep. She did not know if she were awake or dreaming these dark dreams.

In her dream, she heard the words of Chirikudzi's song:

> You watched your parents explode in a cloud of stars.
> You saw their fiery embrace, their wild smiles.
> They found the fireworks worth the risk.
> Risk must be desired like El Dorado,
> hunted like the unicorn, feared like the Amazons,
> embraced like the caterpillar in its cocoon.
> Beauty and danger walk hand in hand and cannot be
>   separated.
> There is no beauty without risk.
> The only safety is death.

She dreamed that The Hand, her miracle of modern technology, shivered with dread in its drawer.

13th August

BY FAMILY TRADITION — though God knows why, Anni grumbled, since there must have been a time when none of the boys shot at all — the first day's stalking in the holiday was always the Boys' Shoot.

The three brothers came to breakfast slightly over-excited, and trying to disguise the fact with a display of ironic teasing.

'Well, Joe,' Thomas said, 'can you bear to be seen out with us scruff bags?'

There was a point to this: Joseph was dressed in plus fours and a tweed jacket. The rest of them were more shambolic: Thomas wearing an extremely ancient pair of jeans, tucked into non-matching socks, and an ex-army jersey.

Joseph smiled and looked patient and grown-up.

'I consider myself properly and traditionally attired, as a matter of fact, and moreover plus fours have all sorts of genuine advantages, the which I do not need to spell out to you. In addition, I appear to be the only person round here with half-way decent manners: we could not but note that you didn't go to Killraven yesterday wearing what I can only describe as a costume suitable to The Yokel in an amateur theatrical production. But we do understand how difficult it must be for one who hunts with the Pytchley to take seriously a mere family outing.'

Tom laughed with some admiration.

'And,' Joseph continued, 'as we can't expect a poor stipendiary clergyman' . . . the atmosphere quivered, Joseph paused in his peroration, and then boldly plunged on . . . 'to afford or even worry about matters so material as decent attire; and as William didn't know he was going to stalk and therefore didn't have time to get himself measured for a proper kit, and Bob is too pleasant-natured to want to show you up by stunts of sartorial elegance, we are forced, Tom, to conclude that you are the only scruff bag on offer, but in view of your extreme youth I will, in fact, agree to let you come out with me.'

'Posh, isn't he?' said Tom.

'City gent type, that's all,' Ben replied.

'Does he know you have to walk, do you think? Joseph, did anyone warn you that you can't do it in a golf buggy?'

With a deftness that excited admiration from everyone watching, Joseph, who had appeared to be placidly buttering his toast, suddenly flicked a glob of marmalade off his knife neatly on to Thomas's cheek. William was awe-struck. Tom looked for some form of retaliation; observed all eyes upon him and laughed. Their pleasure in each other was touchingly obvious. Clare could not help thinking how appalled David would have been at such infantile ragging; how little he could have understood the loving regression which could not be spoken between the oldest and the youngest of her brothers, which had no acceptable form except this constant barracking.

'I never want to see you do that,' Joseph said to William, but smilingly, and went on eating his toast, his eyes alert for any revenge.

Eventually he wiped his mouth with his napkin and said, 'OK, Mummy, do the spoons.'

Hester smiled. 'Who's in?' She looked round the table, 'Bob? Ben?' She got up and opened a drawer in the long sideboard. Each of the children had been given spoons, identical but with their initials engraved, as baptism presents. Each year they drew this way for who would actually shoot. Bob, who never shot and privately disapproved of it, always allowed himself to be in the draw, as though it might be rude to refuse. He had been allocated Felicity's spoon the first summer after they were married. On the occasions when he won he would auction his place in aid of whichever deaf charity he and Felicity were at that moment supporting. It had become as much a part of the ritual as the draw itself.

'Not me,' Ben said. 'William can have my spoon.'

'He'd better not, you might change your mind sometime and muddle us all up.'

'He'd better have mine,' said Ceci.

' "C",' muttered Hester, sorting through the spoons. Clare's 'C', added later to the collection, was different from Cecilia's; but they both knew that Hester would not get it wrong. The relevant ones were put into a carrier bag. The little children each gave it a shake, William carrying it round the table for them, slightly solemnly; the first time he had not shaken the bag, but been in the draw itself.

Hester drew Thomas's spoon first.

'Give it to Will,' Caro said. 'You get to shoot more than anyone else.'

'No,' said William with a dubbed vitriol. 'No. I don't want it.'

Hester smiled at him. 'It's against the rules, I'm afraid. It doesn't matter whether you want it or not.'

He wanted to be one of the big boys far more than he wanted to shoot a stag.

'And . . . ?' Tom asked. Sometimes they would get a second stalk in the afternoon. They drew for that too.

'And . . . and William.'

'Let me see,' he said suspiciously, and they all laughed. It was Ceci's spoon with the curly 'C' on it and the child smiled happily.

What did they think they were doing, Anni wondered, while keeping her nose in her coffee cup and watching her family over the edge of it. What were they doing, to turn killing into such a treat? But she said nothing, watching her mother with bemused affection.

Then there was a good deal of disturbance; of back-slapping and joking and looking at watches and complaining about other people's lateness and finding boots and hats, and quite abruptly, with their departure, a gentleness returned to the house. A house of women and children and an old man. A quiet house.

Hester said, 'Shall we go to the sea this afternoon?'

'All of us?'

'We've got enough drivers. And Duncan said we could borrow the new Land-rover.

'I didn't drive yesterday,' Clare said, half apologetic.

'Why worry?' asked Anni, genuinely curious. 'Couldn't you just latch it on the steering wheel and get on with it?'

But Clare could not trust The Hand. She could see it lurching on the steering wheel, pulling the heavy land-rover over a cliff, smashing all those soft little bodies, adding to her game bag, the tally of those she had killed.

'Yes,' she said waspishly. 'Yes, I probably could, but I haven't yet, and I don't want to experiment on a Land-rover with my small nephews and nieces in the back.'

'OK, calm down,' said Anni. 'I only asked.'

Even thinking about it Clare tensed her arm and The Hand started to close evilly round the imaginary steering wheel. Suddenly there was a strange violent noise from under the table. Felicity was on her knees in a second.

'Alice, what are you doing?'

Alice was sitting on the floor holding The Hand. She had been holding it, and Clare did not know for how long. And now it had closed round Alice's hand; gripping it. It was hard for Felicity to get into a position where she could sign to Alice and see her replies. She scrabbled further on to the floor. Even though The Hand was clearly squeezing Alice's right hand hard, she was still stroking it gently with her left one. Alice had taken her hearing aid off, laid it tidily on the floor, and shut her eyes. She was cut off from Felicity, from the whole world.

'Clare, let her go!'

'What?'

'You're hurting her, let her go.'

'I didn't know she was there,' Clare was shocked by what felt like an intrusion; to have your hand held, tenderly stroked, and not know it. She suddenly, absolutely, could not make The Hand relax.

Felicity put her mouth right against Alice's ear and shouted, 'Open your eyes,' and at the same time she put her hand firmly on Alice's eyelids; but there was nothing she could do. Alice did not choose to obey her.

'Let her go.'

'Felicity, I can't.'

'You're hurting her.'

Clare slipped off her chair and joined Felicity and Alice on the floor. She was both embarrassed and frightened, but she was also worried. The Hand could, if it chose, grip extremely tight; she really could hurt Alice. She had to be calm. There was no point being angry with Felicity. As gently as she could she wriggled in beside Alice, her amputated arm now lying across the child's lap. She put her left arm gently round the child.

'Felicity, I'm sorry, but you're in the way. Can you move? Look, she's not hurt.'

Beyond Felicity were the ranks of her sisters, her mother, waiting, puzzled. She shut her own eyes; rocking Alice gently backwards and forwards, comforting her although she did not need to be comforted. Slowly she relaxed, trying to loosen The Hand's grip. Sometimes this happened if the batteries were running down, but they should be fine at breakfast. It was the shock. It was difficult to concentrate on relaxing. She opened her eyes again and found that The Hand had released Alice but Alice was still holding The Hand.

She lifted her arm, shaking it slightly, and Alice opened her eyes. With her left hand she reached for the hearing aid and offered it to her niece. Alice shook her head, pushed the aid away from her, and tightened her grip on The Hand.

Felicity's face reappeared under the table. Alice let go and started to sign to her mother.

'What's she saying?' Clare asked.

Felicity laughed a little shakily, 'She wants to swap; she says your hand speaks Sign really well. Why did you squeeze like that?'

'I didn't know she was there. Don't you understand? I can't feel anything. Not if you're as gentle as she was.' They all crawled out from under the table. Clare stood up.

Anni smiled at her lovingly and said, 'You win. I think you'd better not drive.'

So when they went to the seaside, Clare sat in the back of Felicity's car and Alice held The Hand the whole way.

They went, this time, not to the lovely island-splattered west coast, but up to the north shore of Britain, where the long waves rolled down from the ice cap, tinged with green. They broke here, on the gritty sand of wide bays; bringing with them memories of three thousand years of seafaring, of mermaids and drowned sailors and the war ships of the Jutes, eager for killing and spoil.

The wind, cutting cleanly, sang harsh songs of the whales' journeys, of challenge and danger. The foam was brittle-cold; despite the brightness of the high noon, the full summer sunshine, the long days of light, the water was always too cold for swimming, and no one lay still to catch a tan from the bright yellow sun.

Clare and Hester walked along the beach together.

The other women played nearer the water with the children, who shrieked with nervous excitement when they tried to paddle in the bitter water and settled down with businesslike calm to the construction of massive sand fortifications which would provide no defence against the incoming tide. The little ones were gleeful, forgetting that jerseys and wellingtons were not the usual seaside gear; and Amanda, sulking at the unfairness of her younger brother's elevation, wandered off to explore the rocky pools at the end of the bay.

All the women knew that Clare was being subjected to one of Hester's interrogations. By mutual consent, though with differences of sentiment, Anni, Felicity and Ceci kept their distance. Caro and Louise, briefly united as outsiders, smiled in amazement, but they too knew there was little point in trying to stop Hester once she had determined on a course of action. And equally little point trying to rescue Clare, who would not accept that from any of them. Instead all five chattered idly and joined the babies' endeavours, glancing up only occasionally and surreptitiously as the two tall women walked along the coarse sea grass above the bay.

'Tell me,' Hester said to Clare, tenderly, but firmly. 'Tell me about Peggy.'

'She could not have been kinder to us; she was wonderful. We had a lovely time with her before . . . before the accident; and afterwards, she . . . she . . . I expect Joseph told you.'

'What's her home like? How does she live?'

'Mummy. You've got pictures; you probably know as well as I do.'

'Darling, I know you find it hard to talk about, but she's my best friend. I do want to hear. I won't ask about anything else, if you don't want me to, but just tell me some things about Peggy. Please.'

It was fair. Clare knew it was fair, but it was hard to talk about, hard to know what to say that was safe and where she would run up against the dark voices, the strange magic in Joyful, the places where she did not want, did not dare to go.

'The earth round her house is very red. A really strange dark red colour. The dust is red, red dust on white woodwork.'

Red, the earth was around Peggy's home, dark red.

'They say that Zimbabwe has a really good infrastructure, compared to say Zambia; but the road to Peggy's house was dire. We were nearly in despair by the time we got there. It was a long drive from Great Zimbabwe, where we'd stayed the night before.'

She recalled it now with great vividness. Off the metalled road the red track cut between the fields like a gash. Their car bumped alarmingly on the ruts.

'Where the hell are we going?' David asked angrily.

Clare was too tired to answer him. The day had been too long. The whole holiday was exhausting her. Since the Victoria Falls she had lost any sense of balance.

They had driven to Great Zimbabwe from Bulawayo. Bulawayo fitted into the stories of childhood, a colonial township still with wide roads, lined with bushes of bougainvillaea. There the museum had tried to link the African past to the imperial past and both to the new national present. It was not a happy story, or even a creditable one, but the connections had been there, explaining to Clare and David their presence in this country. At Matopos they had climbed up the World's View and seen Rhodes' grave, where he could lie and survey the wide lands he had claimed and won. Below in the rocky woods there had been caves and cave paintings; ancient kraals, and the hiding places of resistance movements for more than a century. It was spectacular: the enormous views, the secret caves, the vast, balanced boulders which threatened every moment to collapse and crush the tentative hold that the roads and tourist huts had made on the place, yet it was sensible, it had history and meaning.

But at Great Zimbabwe, the ancient ruin which is the heart and mother of the brave new country, she had been overwhelmed by a lack of meaning, a lack of history or narrative. The beauty of the lower site was undeniable; lying in a broad green valley, tucked safely under the steep cliff. And hovering over the palace, or market, or city, was the grandeur and strangeness of the citadel, or sanctuary, or whatever it was, carved into the cliff itself so that it was impossible to tell what had been made by geology and what by history.

The huge walls were thick and solid, the entrance ways narrow and welcoming; despite their size they were made of millions and millions of tiny slivers of rock, dry stone, and bonded by their weight and the skill of their masons. The walls curved round, vast and embracing.

The great elemental booming of the Victoria Falls was silenced at last by a thousand million tiny stones laid with exquisite care, one upon the other without mortar, and she had no knowledge of why or who by. A place that was both fortress and temple; but which protected no one she knew and honoured Gods who were not hers.

Clare read the guide book feverishly. Who had made this place and why? Who were the builders who had made the walls with such elaborate care but had consented to, had worked with, the rocks and the heights, not challenging nature but co-operating with it.

The guide book could not help her, though that was not its fault. At the turn of the century, with a perverse arrogance, a white archaeologist – convinced by prejudice alone that so sophis-ticated a structure could not have been devised by Africans – had thrown away as 'rubble waste' two metres' depth of Shona artefacts looking for evidence that the Phoenicians, or Arabs, or someone, anyone who was not these dark and dangerous people, had built it. Underneath his rubble there was nothing: he had stolen the story and now Clare had to look and look with no clues as to what she might be seeing, for the histories, stories, memories were gone, thrown away, lost.

David had got her up too early. He had insisted that they climb to the holy place, the heart of this heartless structure, and watch the sunrise. The sanctuary path was narrow, steep and twisted; natural splits in the rock, seamlessly united to artefactual walls, hemmed them in, claustrophobic, alarming. The place was impregnable. What eyes above them now permitted their ascent?

Trapped, they tunnelled upwards, both of them panting a little and, despite the early softness of the morning, sweating; the mosquito bites Clare had got the evening before started itching. And then they emerged; suddenly a long view away up and down the valley reeled before them. A view radically different from the view at Rhodes' grave. There the infinite distance was a claim of supremacy; here the view was useful, designed to watch and see from, but who had watched what along the river bank beneath?

'I need to go down,' she said to David, while he was still consulting an empty diagram.

'Breakfast?'

It was easier to agree than explain her terror, her sense that she had no right to be here watching the sun rise, admiring the beauty, surveying the kraal below and not knowing, not being able to imagine, what it was all for. How would the aspiring cathedrals of northern Europe, the baroque churches of the Mediterranean, look when the stories that built and sustained them were lost? When the roofs had fallen in and the barbarians were through the gates and some strange black historian had thrown away all the signposts, all the statues and candles and books, in a reckless search for proof that the pallid, decadent natives of this distant chilly land could not possibly have built with such confidence and certainty?

But when they had come down she did not want to return to the pretentious hotel. With David muttering behind her she admired some dawn-playful monkeys and walked along the ridge-way to the Great Enclosure. It had been impressive the afternoon before but now in the cool light of the early morning it was magical. She stopped outside the first narrow opening and then turned away and started to walk round the outside. It was import-ant to walk all round before she went inside.

'What are you doing?' David said.

'Oh, do go away. I want to be alone.'

He put his arm round her shoulder affectionately and started to walk with her, but she shook him off. She was scared for a second but he shrugged and dropped his hand – too smug, she thought, to be offended.

'If you're having a silly fit, I'll wait in the car,' he said.

There was no one else there; it was bright, silent, dense. Once the curve of the wall had hidden David there was no one, no one else, just those high, incomprehensible walls. When she emerged from the shadowed side the sun had increased its brightness, winning over the softness of morning, and David had vanished. She stepped through the narrow opening into the enclosed space. At the north exit, where the inner passages and the wide central passage met, she knew absolutely that there was a purpose; that all this had been built for a purpose, and yet it was nonsensical to her. There was the huge solid tower that no one could ever have climbed; there were the curves of the walls which carved out shapes that were not rooms; there was the implicate detail, the intricacies; there were two small red-and-green butterflies skittering on some tiny bright blue flowers – and she did not know what any of it was for.

She was defeated. She walked slowly back towards the car and found David, leaning against the side of it looking resolutely patient. It was so still, so heavy with lost meaning, that she could feel the air trembling. She felt a stirring of anticipation, and then nothing happened.

'Are you OK?' David asked. 'You need breakfast.'

After breakfast David swam in the pool while she packed and he came back full of energy, bouncing, raring to go. She felt lethargic, dopey, too vaguely ill-at-ease to resent his driving power. She gave in to it; let him make things how he wanted them to be, let him make her and the holiday and their life. Her wishes no longer mattered because she did not know who she was or what they were. She blotted out the silent voice of the ancient ruins.

As they pulled out past the terrace of the hotel David lifted his hand from the steering wheel and waved at a large golden man and his wife still sitting at breakfast.

'He was swimming with me. Nice guy. He said that once we went over Birchenough Bridge we should be careful. Not stop in isolated places or get out of the car.'

'Leopards?'

'No,' he grinned, pleased with himself for knowing so exotic a detail, 'Guerrillas. Bandits.'

'I thought that was in the west.'

'Different lot. These are Mozambicans; RENAMO types. South African funded forces of destabilisation.'

She could tell he was excited, that some part of him wanted to encounter fierce, alien soldiers, that he liked the adventure of it. She felt her own belly quiver with fear; she knew that he would like her to be frightened. She was driving into unknown territory with a man who enjoyed her fear.

Looking out of the car window she let a memory catch her unawares. She was frightened of thunderstorms. She always had been. But years before, when she was little, whenever there were thunderstorms Anni would come and climb into bed with her and hold her, seldom saying anything, just holding her; she had not been ashamed. David made her fear into something to be ashamed of, a thing to be hidden: David had laughed at her fears.

One night, while the demons outside had hurled themselves down from heaven, blazing, crashing, assaulting her, she had lain beside him literally gripping her pillow in terror, desperate not to wake him, resolved not to expose her childishness to him.

'Get up,' he had said suddenly, while she had still imagined him sleeping. He had been awake and amused the whole time.

'No.'

'Get up.'

'David, please.'

'Come on. This is silly. It's time you grew up.' He had been amused, but coldly determined. And she, fearing his coldness even more than the thunder, had got out of bed. He had taken her pillow away from her and led her to the window, both of them naked.

'Look at it; there's nothing to be frightened of. Look at it.'

She had tried to resist him, but his will was stronger than she was. She had stood shivering at the window of their bedroom and the storm had beaten over her head. The rain had pounded on the London street, and then overhead a double crack of lightning accompanied by a pure noise; pure volume, naked decibels, not rolling thunder, nor crashing thunder, but pure, infinite thunder and she had screamed. From a level deeper than her fear of displeasing him, deeper than her desire to be a sensible grown-up, a sane human being, she had screamed a wild insane scream and fled. She had slipped from his grasp and fled into the bathroom, slamming the door, pushing the bolt. She had lain on the floor, curled up like a child, keeping her eyes closed uselessly against the lightning, shivering with fear and cold, and she had not come out until the morning.

'I'm sorry,' he had said, over their coffee. He had not sounded sorry, he had sounded pleased. 'I'm sorry,' he said, 'but it's so stupid. It's only thunder: only electrical currents in the air; it makes more sense to be neurotic about the electric kettle.'

She had been ashamed.

Now in the car, frightened again, she was, for the first time, angry that he had made her ashamed. She had thought he would keep her safe, he was so solid in the world and calm and efficient, but all he taught her was how to behave properly.

He had taught her well; she could not name her fear, but denied it in the face of the beauty of the long drive. She was a silly neurotic child and David was right and strong and there was nothing to be frightened of.

The rich commercial farms, the beef lands, green and heavily treed, gave way to the dryer communal lands, with the little homesteads of rondevaal and concrete sheds close to the road. From the beaten smooth earth of the enclosures children waved to them. In the distance were ranks of small pointed mountains, and above were wide skies with clouds processing grandly in deep fronts with hot bright sunshine in between. She wanted to stop and take photographs, but her fear prevented her. In their smart car they sailed past the land which might appear stunningly lovely, but which she knew was impoverished and barren. The road itself was wonderful; later when she took over the driving she realised how wonderful, straight and smooth and empty – and it was impossible not to rejoice for the pure pleasure of driving.

Once David said, 'You were right, you know, up the Falls; I am like Rhodes. If I were Rhodes, I'd have done it too. I'd have claimed this country, just to ride across it and be buried at Matopos.'

'It didn't belong to him.'

'I'd have invented some politics, some ideal that let me do it.'

He would have done, she thought, and for a while could not see the beauty for her own guilt; guilt because she knew it was true and because she did not dare to complain.

In the mid-afternoon the eastern mountains raised themselves up to greet them, solid and commanding. They crossed the Sabi River at Birchenough Bridge, and began to climb the escarpment. A steep climb with red table mountains either side of them and weird baobab trees and beautiful flowering acacia. The road narrowed and twisted, and as they climbed huge downward views opened up for them — westward to the plain below stretching into mistiness a world's distance away; northward towards the higher mountains, or East, over ever more hills towards Mozambique.

The road was lonely and the afternoon gentling down towards evening; the valleys filled with shadows although the sky was still bright.

'Stop a minute,' David said.

'I thought we weren't meant to.'

'Just so you can look properly.'

She turned the car on to the verge. Far below them, through the trees beside the road they could see a curve of the Sabi, grey for the water and mud flats, green around it and the golden plain reaching away towards the sunset. It was worth stopping for: there were two neon yellow butterflies dancing on a branch, not two metres from the car, larger than British ones and brighter, dancing one above the other.

Clare looked down and, without thinking, switched the engine off.

There was no wind. There were the butterflies dancing, a cliff of broken rocks above them and below the valley still golden in bright sunlight, and the curve of the river. She heard the silence, and within the silence a noise which might have been the sound of her own awe.

David opened the door with a rattle.

'Don't!' she said.

'I'm just going to pee,' David said, straightening up. From outside the car he bent down to look at her.

'Don't panic so,' he said, 'you're being silly.'

She wanted to say, 'You don't know that.'

She wanted to shout, 'Why repeat frightening stories told to you by some overweight colonial in a swimming pool, if you don't mean to take them seriously?'

She wanted to yell, 'There are guerrillas and bandits out there. You told me so. It's you that's being silly; what the fuck are you playing at?'

She watched him in silence.

He left the car door open, and walked away; she could not reach to shut it without undoing her seat belt. She didn't want to make that move.

The peace talks between FRELIMO – the governing party in Mozambique – and RENAMO had broken down again, far away in Rome, although Clare and David did not yet know this. Not that it made any difference to them, high on the side of the escarpment. RENAMO could not control its own out-lying forces. And far beyond even the outer fringes of guerrillas and nationalists there were gangs of armed bandits who might or might not be part of RENAMO, who might or might not be armed and equipped by secret elements within the South African military establishment, who might or might not recognise the border when they came to it; who might or might not want to punish Zimbabwe for holding the Beira oil pipe, who might or might not just feel like a little killing today, on a border which had been destabilised by drawing it in the first place, over a hundred years ago.

Clare resolutely tried not to watch David's back as he stood five metres away. She watched the citrus swallowtails dancing instead. There was no wind and it was completely silent on the road. David wanted her to be frightened. If she called to him he would suggest they took a walk. She needed his firm anchorage in a sensible and orderly world. She forced a grin on to her face as he turned, buttoning his jeans.

'Shall I drive?' he asked, coming up on her side of the car and putting one hand on the frame of the open window.

She wanted him to drive. She was exhausted and she wanted to see the view. She wanted him to take responsibility too, so that if something . . . if something happened it would never, ever, be her fault. But if she let him drive he might stop again. He would stop again and open the door of the car and get out and walk in among the trees and she would not be able to stop him. If she let him drive she would have, herself, to undo her seat belt, climb out of the car, walk round, exposed to the cliff above them. She would have to get out of the car. She was being stupid. She knew she was being stupid. Perhaps, even, David had made up the instruction that they should not stop, that they should not get out of the car. He liked her pain, he enjoyed her humiliation.

Up the cliff there were eyes, there were broad waiting grins in dark faces. They prowled as the leopard at the Falls had prowled. They were holding flame-throwers in their left hands. She did not want to get out of the car.

'No,' she said, 'I'm fine. You'd better do the navigating.'

His face did not register disappointment. She had made the whole thing up; no one would be so sadistic. She was crazy. It was a perfectly beautiful evening, near the end of a perfectly beautiful car journey, and she was just being silly, crazy, childish. David dawdled his way round the front of the car; stopped by the door so that she could only see him from the groin to the ribcage, and then climbed in, smiled at her, tapped her knee.

'Nothing to worry about,' he said. 'Let's go.'

She did not feel fine; she felt weary and lethargic. Within half an hour she cursed herself silently for not letting him drive; for her stupidity and paranoia. Her insect bites swelled and were sweaty. The spectacular beauty, the green trees and occasional glimpses of enormous vistas, made her feel dirty and sad.

They turned off the main Mutare road and on to a strip road. They turned off the strip and on to the red road; red dust at first and soon red baked clay, cut into deep ruts. Remembering the highlands of Scotland she tried to drive on the ridges between the ruts, but the car bumped and slithered. She was exhausted.

'Where the hell are we going?' David asked.

She was too tired to answer.

Then there was a white painted gate standing open, a clump of high eucalyptus trees, with dark pools of shade underneath them; there was a raspberry pink bungalow with a flowering vine winding up it. There was a terrace with cane chairs and a wide table. There was Peggy.

'Darling,' called Peggy, walking toward the car with a black cocker spaniel at her feet.

'Darling,' called Peggy, as Clare opened the door and straightened up stiffly.

'Darling,' Peggy said, and Clare was wrapped in a warm hug which had the same smell as her mother's hug.

'Foul drive isn't it? Hello David. I, as you may have guessed, am Peggy. Come on, leave your stuff. You must both need a long drink. Down Chim . . . she's called Chimurenga. She's terribly sweet actually.'

They sat on the terrace; and although her mother would never have worn shorts, and a Mancunian vicarage had little in common with a raspberry-coloured bungalow with a corrugated iron roof, they were the same place: her mother's world.

Clare sipped her drink, smiled warmly at Peggy and felt the tension in her stomach relax with a gentle hiccup of homecoming. Of course they talked about home: long lists of names, while David tried to keep his expression benevolent and interested, and she knew that he was bored. Peggy wanted news of her whole family, one by one: Hester, and James, and Joseph, and Ben, and Anni, whom Peggy still called Annunciata, and Cecilia, and Felicity and Thomas. Then Hester's grandchildren, by name too: Amanda and William and Alice and Emily and Malcolm and George. Clare was comforted by the litany of names.

Every now and then Peggy said to David. 'You must find this all incredibly boring. Just let me get them all out of the way and then I promise I shall return to being a normal and proper sort of hostess. I expect Clare has told you that Hester is my oldest friend. I'm greedy for news of her. Clare, darling, I cannot tell you what a delight this is. It has been too long.'

'When we found the house,' Clare told Hester now, speaking into the brisk wind of the coastland. 'When we found the house, it was such a relief. It's a very pretty house, and Peggy is so absolutely . . . well, she's like you actually. Except she wears shorts; quite long rather neat brown linen ones. But she doesn't change.'

Hester smiled.

'She had a floppy black cocker spaniel called Chimurenga.'

'Called what?'

'Chimurenga. It was the name for the uprising, both Nbele and Shona, at the end of the nineteenth century. And for the independence war: the Second Chimurenga.' Clare paused, her curiosity bubbling up out of the corners where she had buried it in her determination not to let her mother know too much. 'Mummy, do you know what Peggy was doing during the liberation war?'

'What do you mean?'

'I don't know . . . there's something. They have this expression, "a Rhodie", for people who are still, well, Smith types, and that is what Peggy ought to be really. Really, I mean by class and everything, but she isn't. She calls herself a "white Zimbabwean" and . . . never mind. She had a friend staying with her anyway; a lovely woman called Joyful.'

'Yes, I spoke to her on the phone once, after, after you were . . . hurt. She seemed very nice.'

'She was a guerrilla.'

'Clare!'

'Really, Mummy. Armed and trained in Yugoslavia. She left her village at fourteen, crossed the mountains into Mozambique, crossed them not far from where David and I had . . . had our accident. Later they sent her to the States as a sort of ambassador, PR person. But not till she had been in the army, gun in hand; it is hard to come to terms with somehow, sitting at supper with Peggy looking just like you and a woman who has infiltrated rural villages, up in the Zambezi valley and, presumably, killed people. She was amazing, but also Peggy was amazing with her.'

Joyful. Joyful Masvingise.

They had sat with Peggy for a bit, as she chatted about her house, their trip, the things they had seen, all very civilised and affectionate. Finally Peggy had glanced at her watch and said,

'Goodness me, I have been running on. Look at the time. Do you two want to go and unpack and change? We're pretty good on hot water. One thing these highlands don't have in common with the Scottish version. Dinner will be in about forty-five minutes. And turning towards the house she called, 'Luckmore!'

A young man appeared round the end of the house. He was

wearing jeans and a white T-shirt. 'This is Luckmore,' Peggy said, in the identical tone that Hester used when she introduced her cleaning-lady. Clare was touched that after over twenty-five years in Africa Peggy should still have that gentle guilt.

'Luckmore's my house manager. Luckmore, this is Clare and David. Could you help them with the luggage and show them their room?'

Luckmore smiled at them both, but he started speaking to Peggy in Tishona. David walked over to the car and opened the boot.

'We really don't need any help,' Clare said.

Luckmore showed no particular signs of offering it. After David had lifted out their two bags and accompanying rubbish, he came over and picked up one of them casually. Clare knew that David was surprised. It was easy to get used to the level of service that they had received since landing in Africa. She did not know who Luckmore was. She felt again that she had no social skills here, that she did not know how to respond, what to expect. She looked at the backs of the men, both carrying identical suitcases. Luckmore and David were much the same height, and were dressed almost identically, except that David was wearing shoes and socks. She fished around inside the car for her camera and handbag, and followed them in.

The spare room was comfortable but plain. It had French windows that opened on to the garden; standing beside them Clare could see Peggy sitting in her cane chair with her feet up. The curtains were local cloth, dyed and patterned brightly. The pictures were Zimbabwean. The floor was bare, with a speckled rug. The bathroom was a marked contrast; a huge bath on raised feet in the middle of the room, and a deep pile carpet – an unexpected level of luxury.

'OK,' said David grinning. He bounced on the bed, suddenly carefree and unselfconscious. She wanted to ask him if he had been teasing her or bullying her when he got out of the car on the drive up.

'I'm going to bathe,' she said. She lay in the hot water with the door open watching David move about the bedroom. He was better than she was about unpacking; putting all his things away in the drawers and cupboards. He brought his wash things into the bathroom and arranged them neatly on the little table beside the sink.

He stripped off his shirt and said, 'Can I use your water? Is it still hot?' She wanted him to look at her long brown body stretched out in the water. She wanted him to desire her, even though she felt no desire.

'Come on, get out. I want to enjoy the grand colonial.'

'She's not grand colonial.'

'And how large a staff beyond the idle Luckmore do you think keeps this place looking so good? Do you think she'll have invited some beefy coffee farmer plus little woman to dinner. I do hope so.'

'So you can laugh at her?'

'So we can.'

He stripped off his jeans, and she got out of the bath. The towels were wonderfully thick and fluffy. There was a pile of them on a stool in the corner of the bathroom. She wrapped herself in one and wandered through to the bedroom, still annoyed with him.

'Are you going to wear a tie?' she called.

'Why?'

'Just wondering what to put on.' She went to the window to see if Peggy was still sitting there in shorts. As she looked out, a small battered jeep turned into the driveway, and bumped across her view.

'Looks as though you were right. Your coffee planter or equivalent has just arrived.'

'Don't forget to ask him his golf handicap.'

'Get out of there and get dressed,' Clare said. 'I'm not facing him on my own. He'll have a pink neck.'

'With a bit of luck he'll be Peggy's lover.'

'Then you won't get the little woman, who might be amusing.'

There were splashing noises from the bathroom; she knew David was getting out of the bath. 'Don't you believe it. We've seen *White Mischief*; we know what these upper-class backwoods colonials get up to.'

'Peggy!' she laughed. 'I think she's more of a missionary.'

'Pious virgin? Clare, don't be silly; you've seen her. I bet you there is absolutely nothing virginal about your mother's chum.'

'How can you tell?'

But he always could, she knew that.

It was not a backwoods upper-class colonial with or without wife. It was an elegant middle-aged African woman.

'Clare, dear, this is Joyful Masvingise; Joyful; Clare Kerslake, David Holland.' The smooth formal introductions which Clare thought that no one except her mother ever made any more.

So ordinary and proper a meeting. Was it always so, that one met at the turning point, on the road, and did not recognise what you had been given?

'Are you enjoying Zimbabwe?' Joyful was clearly at home here, settling back into a chair with a habit beyond the guestly.

'Yes,' said David, 'enormously.'

'Enjoying?' said Clare. 'I'm not sure if that's the word.' And then, worried that she might seem ungrateful, added, 'It's so beautiful. Somehow no one ever tells you that.'

Joyful ignored the second half of the statement. 'What is the word?'

She seemed so relaxed, so at home, that Clare relaxed with her.

'Different . . . different is the word. I think of myself as cosmopolitan, I travel a lot, I thought I could be at home – no, not at home, but a competent guest – anywhere, but here is too strange.'

Joyful smiled.

'David said today in the car coming up that he could understand Rhodes wanting it for his own back garden, but I think I wouldn't have had the nerve.'

'Very wise. Though there are milder but equally devastating options. Selous, for instance.'

'The Victorian Nimrod? I'm ashamed to say,' said Clare, 'that he was a friend of my grandfather's. I was brought up on the exploits of the Great White Hunter.'

'There you are. He came up from the Cape, and didn't bother to claim the land, he just killed the animals. Or there's Andrade and his like.'

'Who?'

'José Rosario Andrade: he was a Portuguese trader up in the Zambezi valley. The Portuguese had a rather different relationship to imperialism; they didn't claim the land, they simply impregnated the women instead. The people of the Dande carry his bloodlines still. Don't be afraid of Rhodes, there are plenty of other ways to own a place.'

Her laughter filled Clare with courage, 'We were at Great Zimbabwe yesterday, this morning. I couldn't . . . to be quite honest I couldn't cope. I couldn't fix it – I didn't know how to look at it.'

'Ah, but you see that's very good, I wish more people felt that; if you had asked me I would have said don't go to Great Zimbabwe until you've been to Serima.'

'Serima?'

'It's a mission, north a bit, but it takes you across the worlds. Christian stories done in Shona art; a tiptoe in. That can make the next step easier. But you are right to be afraid of Great Zimbabwe; it's the womb of a nation still in labour for itself. It's hard enough to know your own mother let alone deal with other people's.'

Clare was startled. She looked up from her drink, caught the ironic smile on Joyful's face, and changed the subject.

'What do you do?'

'I work for ZINATHA. Do you know what that is?' She glanced at Clare, but did not stop for an answer. 'The Zimbabwe National Traditional Healer's Association, to put it in full.'

There was a pause. Clare tried for an expression of intelligent interest, rather than blankness. She was half aware of David charming Peggy on the long low leather sofa across the wide room.

'You're meant to say *witch doctors!* in appalled accents so that I can give you my little lecture,' said Joyful with a smile.

'Give it anyway. When we were in Harare we went to see a N'anga's shop. I found it fascinating.'

'Yes?' There was no judgement, but not a great deal of interest either. 'The short version of the lecture goes a bit like this: since Independence, ZANU has been actually encouraging, not just tolerating, traditional medicine. There's a pragmatic reason for that which is real but quite boring: the missionaries and colonialists tried to stamp it out and replace it with European-type clinics, but there were never enough and there still aren't enough, and people don't limit their getting ill to fit what's available.

'But more interestingly there's simply a difference of approach: Western medicine treats disturbances of bits of the individual, traditional medicine treats disturbances of bits of the community. So you can't exactly compare them: it depends on what model you have of wellness. In the urban areas people may have a choice and they'll choose treatment according to what sort of illness they think they've got; but at some point about three-quarters of all Zimbabweans will consult a traditional healer.'

'We met someone in Harare who was explaining that to us. A lawyer, from up here I think, John, John . . . David, what was John's surname – the guy from the hotel who took us to the market?'

'Chitaukire,' said David.

'You met John,' Joyful said, 'Peggy, they met John Chitaukire in Harare.'

'He's a good friend of ours,' Peggy said, smiling.

'He's a bad lot,' said Joyful and the two of them laughed together; and Clare sensed that Joyful liked her better, trusted her more, because, by chance, she had met John Chitaukire in Harare.

Now Hester interrupted Clare's memories and asked, 'Do you think she, this Joyful, was . . . was she Peggy's girlfriend?'

Of course she was, although Clare had not until this moment thought about it; she must indeed have been returned to infancy, there in the house of her mother's friend. She remembered almost wryly David's certainty.

'Pious virgin? Clare, don't be silly; you've seen her.' It would have pleased him to be proved right.

How did one discuss such things with one's mother?

'Really, Mummy, I didn't ask.'

Hester said, 'I've always thought that . . . well, of course we didn't think it when we were growing up. It wasn't a thing I even knew how to think. And then after the war Peggy got engaged to this Rhodesian, he'd volunteered for the British army, he was very suitable and . . . she got engaged, but she wouldn't marry him here. She went out with him, after the war, and then she broke off the engagement. There she was in a country where she had no roots really, and no useful training, and yet she didn't come home. It took me years to think why. It's not the sort of thing you think about your close friends. Then last time she was here I wondered and I wanted to ask her, and I think she wanted to tell me but . . . but those things aren't easy, especially when you're our age, and when you've been such close friends. When I rang her, while you were lost, and this woman, Joyful, answered the phone and did not seem to explain herself, I was so pleased for Peggy and wanted to tell her and knew that I wasn't allowed to. I envy you lot sometimes, just to be able to say it.'

They both knew that Hester was telling her that she was sad that Ben had not said it to her, sad and angry, when she was so obviously happy for Peggy and would have been willing to be happy for Ben if he had let her.

'Mummy, I didn't think about it then, but if it's true then you should be glad for her. They are very lovely together. Joyful is a good bit younger than Peggy, but they do sort of fit nicely. But I don't know if . . . Zimbabweans are, well reticent . . . I was never sure, there's a sort of purity which is quite repressive; I think they would think of it as Western decadence, so I don't know. Emotionally perhaps.' It was too difficult, she went back to the descriptive narrative:

'Joyful doesn't live there, I mean in Peggy's house. She was, like us, just staying there for a few days, a holiday. It was such a relief getting there. I hadn't been enjoying it at all, the holiday I mean. I was frightened.'

'Frightened?' asked Hester, puzzled.

'It was too strange, as though I didn't know how to do anything right. As though I might offend at any moment. As though everything I was certain of was suddenly misted, foggy; a culture gap too big. None of the stories fitted there. It was my mood; David loved it.'

When she had been in the hospital, after Joseph had called her back from the dark places, she had been endlessly cross-examined, and though weakened and confused she had known that she must not answer the questions honestly.

'Why were you in Zimbabwe?'

'We were on holiday.'

David and Clare had gone to Zimbabwe for a holiday. It had

been from the start a stupid and ill-conceived plan, a greedy, infantile clamouring for the contentment which evaded her.

'Why did you choose Zimbabwe?'

'We thought it would be interesting. We had neither of us been to southern Africa. And my mother has friends there.'

'Miss Wetherby?'

'Yes, Peggy.'

'And Dr Masvingise?'

'My mother never met her.'

'So you came to stay with Miss Wetherby?'

'Not really; we came to see Zimbabwe, but of course we stayed with her. She was like an extra aunt. We came because we wanted a holiday.'

'I want to get away,' she had said to David one evening, pouring him a drink, all steady and determined to explain to him as nicely as possible that she needed some extra space, that she needed some time for thought and for decision. She had not wanted him to be angry and she did not want to have to argue, so she said it with a carefully constructed combination of casualness and tenderness.

'Great idea,' he had said, grinning. 'We've been working too hard. Where shall we go? Somewhere exotic. Let's do it after Christmas, I can probably grab a couple of weeks in the new year, there's always a lull then.'

As so often, she could not afterwards remember exactly what happened to the conversation next, exactly how it was that they ended up going to Zimbabwe for a holiday which was, in effect, entirely planned by him; although it remained in conversation her idea, her indulgence, her adventure.

'Where did you stay?' the voices had asked.

'We stayed four nights in Harare, at the Green House Hotel.' And without meaning to she smiled.

'Who did you meet?'

'A Mrs Mildenhall . . . an English lady.' She had not mentioned John; she had not wanted him to get into trouble, because he was a friend of Joyful. He would be a witness for me, she had thought without even knowing what he was meant to be a witness to, because he was a friend of Joyful and Peggy.

'What else did you do?' they had asked her. 'Where did you go? Who did you meet? What did you do? Did you like Zimbabwe? Have you ever been to South Africa? to Mozambique? to Portugal? Why did you come? Where is your camera?'

And, 'Do you love your husband?'

'He's not my husband.' It was for some reason crucially important to her to say this, every time, over and over again.

'Did you love Mr Holland?' The question meant, 'did you like him?' and 'did you feel like pushing him over a cliff? and 'do you mind that he has disappeared?'

Did you kill him?

Her eyes would fill with tears and Joseph, or Peggy, or the nurses would rush in soothingly and remind everyone that post-traumatic amnesia and distress were entirely normal. Surely these questions could wait until Clare, until Miss Kerslake, was feeling better.

'I was frightened,' she said to her mother, now. She wanted to add, 'The country made a nonsense of my life,' but she did not. Instead she felt a deep wave of sympathy for Ben: there were things you did not tell Hester precisely because she would understand them so sensitively.

'I was frightened,' she repeated. 'I was frightened until we got to Peggy's, and then Peggy was so like you that I forgot to be frightened and we had a lovely three days.'

Peggy was like Hester in lots of ways, and in some ways she was not like her at all.

'I told her she must come over here soon and we would all return her hospitality.'

'You should come home more often, Mummy would like it so much,' Clare had said the first evening.

'This is home, Clare.'

'Yes. Sorry.' She had felt rebuked.

But once it had not been home; once Peggy's home had been in Scotland like Hester's, her friend and Clare's mother; once the two women had been children together. She had wondered then in the long shadows of that southern African evening if it was possible to change one's home and not be amputated. And now, remembering that, she felt the join between her arm and The

181

Hand ache in the cold wind that flowed unceasing from the sea and across the sand.

Clare wanted to give Hester something, a little gift to take away the sting of Peggy's rebuke and of the ache in her arm.

'Peggy is better at the servant problem than you are,' she said, turning her head a little to smile at Hester to show that she was teasing.

'Practice, I should think,' said Hester wryly.

They had gone through to the dining room for supper; a dark panelled room that could have been an upper-class dining room anywhere in the world. After supper they wandered gently back into the sitting room.

'Play?' Joyful asked Peggy, looking at the piano.

'I want to talk,' Peggy said, and put a record on the gramophone. She opened the French windows on to the veranda, and smiled at Clare.

'Does your mother still play?'

'A little. More when she's on her own, I suspect. She accompanies us sometimes. Ceci and Ben sing.'

Peggy smiled, very sweetly.

'It's the most beautiful evening: let's sit outside.'

There were lights on the side of the house, half-hidden among climbing plants, and a light about fifty yards away, hung high on a tree; but they were golden not bright, they deepened rather than disturbed the night. The stars were immense; and their constellations entirely other from the ones that Clare knew. She knew none of their names. Then in a comforting moment she felt again John's hand on her shoulder as in Harare he had pointed out the Southern Cross and she reoriented herself looking for that unmistakable pattern, but even that small city had dimmed the stars – here in the mountains they were brighter, more plentiful; she felt giddy with the nearness of them, the strangeness of them.

'Where's the Southern Cross?' she asked.

'You can't see it from here at this time of year; the mountain is in the way,' Peggy said, and Clare felt a wave of loss.

'It's better,' Peggy said, 'to fix from Aldebaran, that very bright one, there. Huge, isn't it? People often mistake it for a planet.'

'No,' said Clare, 'it twinkles.'

'I miss the seven sisters, Cassiopeia,' Peggy said. 'I think they were the first constellation I ever identified. That was at Skillen; your grandfather's stalker pointed them out to me one night when we were staying with your family,' she said, perhaps to Joyful or David as an explanation, but really, Clare thought, to remind herself.

Clare said, abruptly, as though she were depriving Peggy of something she had a right to, 'I haven't been to Skillen for ten years.'

She knew that Peggy was about to ask her why not, and was relieved when Joyful said quite unexpectedly, as though to reclaim Peggy back from the land of her childhood, 'You know what you were saying about not having any stories: Peggy has stories for everything. She has a Great Zimbabwe story; she claims it was the home of the third wise man, the black one of your Christian tradition.'

'Well, it would be nice, bringing everything together, don't you think? And you like it when I play Bach,' Peggy sounded almost plaintive.

Joyful laughed. Clare watched Joyful's profile in the soft light. Perhaps she really was a witch, or a medium; perhaps she really could explain the song inside the rushing waters of the Falls, the low humming among the tiny stones of Great Zimbabwe.

'It's a dishonest notion,' Joyful said, but smiling. 'It's an imperialist plot through and through; take our city, the largest city in sub-Saharan Africa in its time, take our place of pilgrimage, the mother place of our nation, and drag it into your decadent Western commitment to the everlasting Christian story. Peggy,' she said, grinning at Clare, 'remains, despite everything, a Rhodie missionary at heart.'

'Rubbish!' Peggy said. 'You'll confuse them. I'm no missionary, I'm a white Zimbabwean, and Mugabe says I am a creative force for unity. We can build a Zimbabwean culture that embraces the best of all our roots. Joyful's Shona, you see; they are very arrogant, they want all Zimbabwe to be theirs.'

'It is ours, we are *vanhu ve'ivu*.' She was quite suddenly not talking to Clare and David, but to Peggy, and talking with a depth of teasing affection, of intimacy. Clare knew this was an old conversation, probably an old argument, which was also, mysteriously, the warp thread of a friendship of great strength: a whole cloth now woven out of the intricate threads of love.

Peggy, though, wanted them to understand. 'That means, *the people of the land*. It is important. The closeness of the people and the land is how it is to be indigenous, what it is to be of Zimbabwe. Historically, that is the perspective of people's lives — even if they're living in the towns now. The whole history, the national identity, is wrapped up in that. In owning the land, and it owning you. You can't talk without understanding that. The people, the land, the land of the ancestors, the ancestors of the land. It doesn't just find expression in what we call "culture" — songs, dance, stories, customs — but deeper: like traditional medicine, because a person isn't an autonomous body to be treated in little chunks, but a part of the story of the land, the family. That is why we won the war, why ZANU were bound to win it once they had decided to fight. That's why really it's so ironic that the single factor that shaped Zimbabwe as a country was the racial division of land, telling people where they could and couldn't live, and things like that after the British came.'

Joyful said, 'Peggy is romantic about it . . . what you might call convert's zeal. We take it easier, breathe it. It doesn't matter the way Peggy makes it, it just is, and it can go horribly wrong. Just don't forget they are cutting the sacred trees for firewood, and that I have very little doubt that Mr McNeil's foreman is sacrificing babies.'

'And Mungoi protects his village.'

'In Mozambique!'

Almost impatiently the two women tried to explain to David and Clare what they were talking about. The road to Chidenguele in Mandjacaza district, is a road of death and fear. It is the heart of the civil war, the slow, apparently inexorable, tearing apart of the free country of Mozambique. The road threads its way through fields that have not been planted and villages that are desolate and deserted. Along the roadside are the corpses of blackened lorries, and there is little traffic.

But the pink and blue houses of Mungoi are bright and brave: the village is peaceful and prosperous. The guerrillas do not attack Mungoi because the spirit of Augusto Sidawahane Mungoi, who died thirty years ago, has returned in power to protect his people; he comes to them through the body of a woman, a traditional healer . . . Or else, Joyful had told them ironically, the woman who is the medium for his spirit is collaborating with the MNR and growing rich on duplicity and bribes . . . When his children are kidnapped he enters the bellies of the MNR commanders and will not let them sleep or eat or drink until they have freed the captives and made reparation.

In Mungoi's compound, where his white grave is surrounded by palm and mango trees, the women dance out of their hut, led by the medium. They sing softly; clapping, dancing, praising their ancestral father, inviting him, welcoming him. The medium wears a man's suit and a blue hat with a feather. She prays and clacks her fingers. About ten metres from the grave there is an ancient tree; it is hung with the skulls of small animals. The spirit speaks to the curious.

'This is not a simple war,' he says, through the lips of his medium. 'I told my enemies I want my family, and because you have kidnapped them we are at war. I paralysed them. They had to apologise and free the people.'

Now the raiders no longer dare to come into Mungoi's territory and his people are at peace.

Clare felt at peace also. She liked to look at the faces of the two older women who told such different stories and had such different histories and who were such good friends. She wanted to stay there all night and watch the movement of Joyful's face, which expressed things she did not know how to understand; and the huge strange stars overhead glowed in the darkness.

She felt at peace and then there was a stirring in the branches and unbidden she heard the breeze say, 'Woe to the false prophets who cry "peace, peace" when there is no peace.' The peace negotiations between the government and RENAMO had collapsed that morning in Rome, and, despite the protestations of the government that since the Nkomati Agreement in 1984 South Africa was no longer supplying the MNR, unmarked helicopters continued to deliver arms and ammunition across the border by night.

David was looking sullen; she knew certainly, at least for that moment, that he had indeed been trying to frighten her when he had climbed out of the car, trying to reduce her to begging and whimpering, and if it had not been for the citrus swallowtails dancing on a thorn bush he would probably have succeeded.

'Round Peggy's house,' she told her mother now, trying to catch for herself the sweet soft darkness of the Zimbabwean night, 'there are eucalyptus trees. They are planted all over the place in Zimbabwe. Apparently early settlers introduced them from Australia. It turns out that they're a total disaster ecologically speaking; they rob the soil, and undermine natural balances and all sorts of problems, but they are very beautiful; tall and graceful and they have pearly grey barks that seemed to sort of glow in the dark. We sat outside after dinner all the evenings we were there, and you could see them in the darkness.'

Alien trees; more beautiful but as deadly as the Scandinavian firs with which the Highlands of Scotland had been reforested.

'Somehow,' Clare said to her mother as she had said to Joyful, 'I hadn't been prepared for how beautiful it was. I don't just mean Peggy's house, although that was very lovely, but the whole country; it took me by surprise.'

Hester's glance range along the beach, sweeping over the children playing, and taking in the beauty of the soft firm sweep of the hills running down to the cream-coloured sands which hemmed in the blue-green water. The turning caps of the waves were brilliantly white in the sunshine, out beyond the shelter of the bay.

Clare said, quite gently, 'It's her home now. She was very clear about that.'

'Yes, of course,' said Hester in an admonitory tone, as much to herself as to Clare. 'So . . . what else did you do there?'

'Lazed. Peggy arranged for us to go to the club, to play tennis with some friends of hers.' The club had been very strange, like something out of a 1930s novel; on the gate out to the golf course there had been a notice informing members of the maximum permitted caddy tip. Clare had felt as alien there as she had at Great Zimbabwe.

'David got on really well with a couple we met there and went off in the afternoon to see their farm. I think he was a bit fed up with perpetual family reminiscences. You couldn't blame him really.' She did blame him though, and she knew she did, and she knew that her mother knew she did. She could feel Hester poised to use this opening to enquire further about David, so she rushed on: 'and I went for walks with Peggy and Joyful – and Chimurenga, of course.'

Even the thought of the delightful black spaniel with her long silky ears could not reduce the walk to a Sunday afternoon in the shires. She found she did not want to tell her mother about the walk, but she had left herself no escape. She tried to flatten out the memories, retell them blandly.

'Joyful is collecting local stories. Not old ones, new ones. She gets the kids in the schools, the high schools, to write their version of traditional tales. There's a theory, you see, she gave me a book about it . . .'

And where was the book? *Peasant Consciousness and Guerrilla War*, by some professor at some English university. She had thought that her camera was the only thing she had lost, apart from her hand and her lover of course, but now she could not remember having seen it since the accident. She pushed the thought aside, and stubbornly returned to her narrative.

'. . . a theory that one of the reasons why the freedom fighters were able to succeed was that they incorporated themselves into the mythology, the lore of the people; that they fitted into the expectations and patterns of the stories. They worked with the mediums, with the ancestors. Like Cortez, and the Aztecs expecting white bearded strangers to appear and conquer them – only in reverse; ZANU appeared and claimed, helped the peasants claim, the ownership of the land. Joyful thinks that stories change, grow, reflect changes of consciousness, shape consciousness even. She was telling me about it on the walk.'

Afterwards, over tea, Joyful showed Clare some stories, written on soft ugly paper, not white paper, you could not use ink on it because it bled into confusion and collapse. Pencil-written stories from the mission schools, which Joyful had collected as part of her work.

Joyful said, 'There is a tendency to think that culture is something static, fixed; traditional values mean fixing the peasants for ever somewhere before colonisation; traditional means old-fashioned, rather than born on the roots. Look, look at these stories: that is a living culture, not imposed nor grafted on, like Peggy's Christian one last night. Have a look.'

Luckson Mazango

I heard that long ago babies were able to talk as soon as they were born, but nowdays they are not able because of what happened long ago. I heard that the mother of a baby new born left her sleeping in the kitchen when she was going to fetch water outside. Then the father stole a piece of meat from a boiling pot and he struggled to swallow it before his wife turned up; but he failed to swallow it because it was too hot and big to pass through his oesophagus, or gullet; so he hid it in his back pocket and the soup commenced to flow from the pocket down. As soon as the wife entered into the house she was told by the baby what happened in her absence. The scene spread like veld fire and the wife was very shameful with her husband, so she put a piece of yam in the baby's mouth to stop her from denouncing old people. From that day until today no baby was born speaking and no baby is born speaking.

Lions and Soldiers: as told by Shepherd Chanengeta

There was a young man called Muchuchuzombi. He was a tall and fatty man. His eyes were very large and were always red as if he smoked *Mbanje* – the green tobacco.

One day in the late 1970s he went to Mozambique, where he wanted to be trained as a soldier. He headed for Moza alone with his bag fulled of tinned food. He arrived at Chimoi camp during the night and he was welcomed by other soldiers. He told them that he wanted to be trained to become a soldier and come back to Zimbabwe to fight for our liberation.

For six months he was trained and he departed for Zimbabwe with ten other trained soldiers. Before they had travelled very far they met a group of lions, then they ran away but they were too late. Only Muchuchuzombi managed to escape by climbing up a tree. The other nine were all perished.

After some hours he climbed down and tried to call the other nine. There was no answer. He walked for some distance and found the leftovers of some of his partners. He went to the nearby mountain and prayed to the spirit mediums telling them that they had done something bad to let some of his friends to be eaten by the lions. A voice came from the stones near him saying, 'Son of the Soil listen to me,' and the voice stopped. Muchuchuzombi then said, 'I am listening, my Lord.' The voice then said, 'Take all what you have except the clothes that you are wearing and burn them here; that's all. No question, no answer.' Muchuchuzombi did all what he was told. When the fire was about to put out he found his nine partners standing behind him.

I was once told this story by my mother and then by my uncle.

by Taurai Daka.

There was a girl who was an orphan. Her mother and father had died during a war. She then lived with relatives of her parents. The relatives treated her very bad and in a cruel manner. Most of the time she troubled herself thinking about her life.

When she was fast asleep one day it happened that her mother who had died spoke to her through a dream. She had a short conversation with her mother.

In the dream her mother was very ashamed by the way she was treated by the relatives with whom she was living. She felt compassion to her daughter.

Then she told her to go into the bush, and there she would find an egg. When she had seen the egg she was supposed to sing beautiful songs and she had to have some dancing and ululations around the egg. She was to take everything she found in the egg and go away with it to a far away country.

It happened that from the egg there came a hundred cattle, fifty goats, many hens, a lot of money and nearly all the things that are used for domestic purposes. The girl was very happy and excited. She managed to take all the things she had and drove the animals away to a far country so that those relatives of hers would not see where she had gone.

This girl became very rich, she had a nice family and her living conditions changed greatly.

My name is Taurai Daka. This is my own story. I am the God of the above story.

'You see,' said Joyful. 'ZANU, the boys, come and the stories change to greet them, to acknowledge them. The women join the struggle and so they need to enter the stories.'

Clare had tucked the papers into the book: she remembered doing so with a sudden vivid clarity, she had not wanted David to see them, to laugh at them, to have them to use against her.

Joyful told her about Chirikudzi, the mermaid spirit of the Pongwe headwaters, who hid behind trees and sang to seduce passers-by. She stole you away and kept you prisoner, but if she loved you she would teach you her secrets, and you would return eventually to the world as a great N'anga, knowing the stories and thoughts of the ancestors.

Joyful told her about Nehanda, one of the most ancient, the most venerable of the ancestors, whose medium had been executed after the first Chimurenga in 1898, but who had and always would return to fight for her own land, and for the people whose land her land was. She was a grandmother of the nationalist struggle: they had been her children, they had needed her guidance, and she had supported the war.

War zones had been named for her and her songs were sung, even, necessarily, at the height of victorious national socialism. On the night of Independence, Joyful told her, by the light of a thousand fires her songs were sung, were broadcast to the new nation.

Startlingly, Joyful, walking along the red path on the hill behind Peggy's house had sung. Strange music on that sunny bright hillside where the red path cut through the high dry grass and Chimurenga hunted nose down and tail straight out behind her, feathering in the slight breeze. Joyful translated, still singing. 'We sang in many languages,' she said with a smile:

> Grandmother Nehanda
> You prophesied,
> Nehanda's bones resurrected,
> ZANU's spear caught their fire
> Which was transformed into ZANU's gun,
> The gun which liberated our land.

Joyful told her how the ancestors liked to be remembered and how beer should be poured on their graves to keep them happy, and how their neglect could make you ill.

Clare heard the shadows of the religion of her childhood, a religion where everything was bound in a seamless cloth that could not be ripped or shredded. She asked more questions, probing towards a clarity, a desire that she herself could not name: that what had gone wrong with her could be cured perhaps by contact with this simple and deep magic where the mediums could consult with the past and offer cures.

'Holism,' she said, 'is something we've lost in the West. How does one become a medium?'

Suddenly it was the wrong question; she had crossed a line that she did not know existed.

'Oh, come on,' said Joyful, 'they are not your ancestors. Don't go trying to put your reading on our stories; it is the one thing we kept from the white people for a very long time: I cannot tell such secrets. Go home and find your own, if that is what you want.'

There was a silence.

'I'm sorry,' said Clare, and Joyful said it simultaneously; and laughed, suddenly girlish. Clare thought, with a surprising wave of loss, of Anni with whom she had giggled ten thousand miles and thirty years away. So she showed Joyful how, when she was a child and you said something at the same instant as someone else you had to shake little fingers with them and mutter an incantation.

And then Joyful gave her a thousand presents to compensate for the one she would not give and for which Clare should never have asked: telling her stories about the birth and childhood of a country which should never have existed in the first place. Stories of her own childhood, and how her mother had seen the uniform she had to wear at the convent as a proper punishment on her for being too clever; but how her father's brother, the head of her family, had been determined to get her educated; and how their bitter quarrel had gone on over the head of her own father who had tried constantly to please both parties. 'Enough to make a revolutionary of anyone,' said Joyful with a smile.

Everything was fine between them, but Clare knew that she had been warned off, a foreigner always in that place even though Chimurenga, who hunted beside them, had been bred through English bloodlines and was registered with the British Kennel Club.

They had come home from their walk and Joyful had picked through the soft pink skin of Chimurenga's underbelly to remove ticks and had then, with the same kind but dispassionate fingers, done the same for Clare's legs. The fat black ticks were squeezed gently out and the two women, like monkeys with their grooming done, sat in the drawing room and drank tea from Peggy's Crown Derby cups.

Later David had come in.

'Well what did you get up to?' he asked her when they both went to change for supper.

'Not a lot,' she said casually. 'More fond reminiscences of schoolgirl days in the 1930s.'

They returned to the veranda and sipped their gin in the shade of the house where the flowering vine absorbed the last of the heat and converted it into warm gentleness. It reminded Clare of Italy: they need not have come all this way to sit on cane chairs, comfortable against blue-and-white striped canvas cushions, and drink gin and tonic with viciously neon-coloured lime slices in it. They could have gone to Umbria and left her world intact – to central Italy, where the cathedrals, Romanesque or baroque, cradled the stories that she knew; the little baby Godling, the Christ Child, the crucified, whose schemes she had seen through in her teens, and felt slightly superior to ever since. Those were her ancestors and Joyful was right. They had not needed to come to the blood red waters of the Falls, or the shapeless vastness of the walls of Great Zimbabwe.

The phone had rung and Peggy had gone to answer it. She had come back glowing with pleasure. She had smiled at Clare but spoken to Joyful.

'That was Marnie; she and Tove have a cottage at Udu Dam for the weekend and something has come up and they can't use it and she wondered if we wanted it, and I said that these two might.'

'Oh yes,' said Joyful, 'wonderful.'

David and she were going to Nyanga National Park the next day; they were planning to find a hotel, hoping to pick Peggy's brains about it; but suddenly their plans were being taken over. The simple lodges beside the lake at Udu Dam would be much better they were told, and cheaper and more agreeable and more convenient. Clare looked towards David, anxious lest this interference with his plans should irritate him, but he had heard of the park cottages that afternoon from the couple he had visited. He thought it would be fun.

She could hear him already, saying, 'That's where the locals stay, you know; of course you can't book them as a tourist, you have to know the right people.'

She drifted out of the conversation. David had taken over; he and Peggy, who had seemed to have nothing in common, generating a shared enthusiasm almost as though their previous distance made it necessary.

David and Peggy arranged to swap cars for three days so that David could have a four-wheeled drive one – 'It's not absolutely vital,' Peggy was saying, 'but you'll have more fun. It's self-catering of course,' so Luckmore was summoned and sent off to discuss with the cook what provisions were available.

A map was produced: 'Here is Udu Dam and here is Nyagombe, and you can swim in the pools above it, and here are the Pongwe Falls.'

'Where your mermaid lives?' Clare asked.

Joyful nodded, 'Well, almost. She is supposed to live in the headwaters, further up; but she probably comes down to swim because the falls make music that must be like her song. From the top of Nyangani you can see down into the Pongwe Gorge, and it is always filled with mists, with water vapour thrown up by the falls.'

'Like at Victoria Falls?'

'No, quite different: there it rises in a column, high; at Pongwe it just fills the valley. It's very strange and beautiful.'

'And here are Mtarazi Falls. You have to park here, and walk.' Peggy's and David's heads were close together over the map; Peggy's finger pointed things out and David scribbled them on a piece of paper. 'About half a mile, but there's a path. It's extraordinary; you walk along this little path and it is exactly like parts of the Highlands; dear little babbling rivers, big burns, and rocks and grass and then suddenly you come to the edge of the world. The rivers just fall over the side; it's the escarpment, but it feels like . . . the drop is vertical and if the weather is good you look out and down and you can see forever across the plain below you.' Peggy grinned suddenly, 'Don't tell Clare's mother, but when I go I feel like God, looking down over the world. It's the place of Christ's temptation, when the devil showed him all the kingdoms of the world.'

'There she goes again,' said Joyful, smiling collusively at Clare, as though the other two were overexcited but rather sweet children. 'You see she imposes white narratives even on our scenery. Mtarazi incidentally is the highest straight-drop waterfall in the world.'

'You won't be able to take in the verticality of it,' said Peggy. 'It's one of my favourite things in all the world. It makes me giddy, not from vertigo – I mean fear of heights, but from something . . . if Joyful wasn't getting at me I'd tell you that it was the view that Edgar had in mind when he describes the imaginary cliffs of Dover to his father.' And turning back to David she said, 'And this is the road to Nyangani itself.'

' "The highest mountain in Zimbabwe",' David interrupted, laughing at her, catching the words from her mouth before she could say them. 'Yes, we read about it; we were planning to climb it from the hotel – our guide book said about three or four hours.'

'About that. Do remember before you drive up there to report to the office at Rhodes Dam, because it would be a monumental bore to have to turn back.'

'Why do we have to report?' David asked.

Peggy opened her mouth to answer and Joyful said quickly, almost snappishly, 'It's a mountain in a very isolated area. No one wants to send out a rescue party for people who weren't up it in the first place; on the other hand, they hardly want to leave you there with a sprained ankle for weeks on end.'

Joyful did not like David, Clare realised, and felt warm towards her, as though they shared a small but delightful secret.

Peggy let the look of surprise which had sprung up at Joyful's tone fade from her face. She and David went back to the map.

Joyful turned to Clare, 'It is a very strange mountain. It isn't difficult to climb as such; a stiff walk – no more; but the weather changes very fast, mists come up, and it's very isolated and very near the border.' She paused as though considering something and then said, 'I don't know whether to tell you this, I dread to think what use you may make of it, but it's . . . haunted, if that's the word. It doesn't belong to you.' And then after a pause, 'Nor to me really. In the park you'll see the old ruins, if you want. Not like the cave paintings at Matopos, and not like Great Zimbabwe. The eastern highlands are different, no one knows much about them – less even than Great Zimbabwe. In a way you don't have to: it's not demanding like Great Zimbabwe, it is more . . . elemental, perhaps. I don't mean magic, I mean it comes out of the nature of the land, it's natural. The ruins there are about how to terrace land and drain it and keep your cattle safe at night; but they are a different people, a different history. And it's their ancestral mountain. Theirs and the boys who used the mountains to go to Mozambique. Mugabe went over, escorted by their big chief, from there. They went over the mountain passes and they came back into Zimbabwe through them, so it's their mountain too. But not yours.'

David and Peggy finished with their plans. She gave him the map and he folded it with the page of notes inside and thanked her sincerely. He was charming in gratitude, smiling, warm, boyish. She did not need to hate him. They were about to go in to supper and Joyful said, not just to Clare but to David as well,

'If you climb Mount Nyangani you'll find there's a whole list of rules, instructions, on a board at the bottom. You should, quite seriously, read them and stick to them, they're not there for fun. But I'll give you an extra rule: Do not mock, insult or abuse the mountain.'

She sounded quite relaxed about it, unportentous, almost amused and had already stood up to follow Peggy through to the dining room. David gave her back a look of such patronising contempt that Clare knew he would claim to find her sexy when they were back in their own room. He had always fancied women he despised. She felt frightened again.

Remembering the fright jolted her back into the present. Hester and she were still walking on the beach.

'Did Peggy tell you it was she who arranged for us to go and stay at Udu Dam? It was a real treat; some bits of the National Park system Zimbabwe sort of keeps for itself – not for tourists. You can stay in the hotels, but you can only book these little cottages from inside. For some they have a lottery each year. Peggy was kind and we were lucky.'

'Lucky?' said Hester, rather surprised.

'Oh,' Clare was surprised too. 'It didn't turn out very lucky, did it? Though we had planned to climb the mountain anyway. I meant we were lucky in her kindness.'

'She'll be pleased to hear that. She feels guilty about it.'

'No. No, she shouldn't. Tell her I said "lucky" quite without thinking about it. Tell her, Mummy.'

'I will. So then you left and went to this camp . . .'

'And if we had followed their advice properly we wouldn't have had the accident anyway.' It seemed important, suddenly, that Joyful should know, via Peggy, via her mother, along an attenuated but sturdy line of communication, that Clare knew that it was not Joyful's fault.

Joyful had tried to protect her. And now Joyful was protecting her again, here on this northern shore, because if Clare had not impulsively needed to send that message to Joyful she would very likely have fallen into Hester's neatly baited trap, and gone on to tell her about the days at Nyanga.

She grinned at Hester's slyness, and said, 'When we left, we thought we'd be back with the car in three days so she did not give me any messages for you. We parted so casually, naturally, and her final words were about how she'd packed some bottles of Zimbabwean wine and how she hoped it would be all right for David.'

She stopped. Hester sighed.

'You don't give much away, do you Clare?' she said. 'You never did, you know. You were always the most self-contained of all the children.'

'You taught me good manners and self-control.'

'Yes, I did.' There was a pause. 'Clare, is it true that you left Italy because you were in love with someone and it went wrong?'

'Which of them told you that? Yes, it's true.'

'I never thought of that. How odd.' Then after another pause, Hester said very gently, 'Can I help?'

Clare drew a deep breath. Then she said, 'No, thank you.'

Hester would not ask again.

By mutual agreement, the conversation was over. The two of them turned quite spontaneously and crossed the verge between grass and sand, slithered down the softness and through the tide line and joined the others on the beach.

There was a sudden relaxation among the grown-ups as they could see from both faces there had been no dangerous confrontation, and a rising complaint from the children who knew that, mysteriously, it was time to go home. Their protests were unavailing . . .

'And anyway,' said Louise, as a final clincher to an argument that had hardly started, 'we want to know how Dubs did, don't we?'

With rigid discipline Louise had not used, and would not let anyone else use, William's baby-name since the day he went to prep school.

'But,' said Hester, 'we will stop in the village and get everyone an ice-cream. Can you all remember to take your shoes off and shake them before we get back in the car? The sand here gets into everything.'

At the village shop they poured out of the three cars, and almost before Clare was conscious of her approach Alice was once more holding The Hand. Her head leaned against Clare's arm, and when they got back into the cars Clare lifted Alice on to her lap and let her curl up there stroking The Hand gently.

'Do hurry,' said Louise, glancing at her watch. 'They might be back by now.'

William had killed his stag and become a man. They got home to find them all just back from the hill and a wildly excited William, his face smeared in the blood of his first kill, dancing round two corpses hanging head down in the game larder.

'That one's mine; he's not as big as Uncle Tom's, but Duncan says he has better conformation.'

The chains that slung the animals from the ceiling were shiny galvanised steel; the dead beasts' coats were surprisingly rough, and they always seemed larger dead than free on the hill. Their eyes, still damp, were glazing over and a small amount of blood dripped on to the floor beneath them.

Will had passed through a strange initiation ritual and both Amanda and Alice were aware of it. They walked round his stag while he stood in the doorway preening himself.

'Only one shot,' said Louise, putting her finger into the small wound. 'Clever boy.'

She glowed with pride.

'He did it beautifully,' said Joseph, justified in his faith and love. 'We had a short stalk this morning. Tom was quick and efficient. Then after lunch Duncan said we'd drop over the shoulder above Loch Monnoch, you know the little one with the long scree down to it. There were a lot of beasts on the move beside the loch, but Duncan picked out a couple coming up the hillside, and Will and I went out with him. They came up very slowly, and there was an old sheep away on our left and you know what they're like, so we had to be careful not to shift it. Will was so good and did everything Duncan asked him, and was as patient as anything, weren't you?'

'And then Mummy, we wriggled along this tiny sort of dip in the grass and it was well wet . . .'

'Will.'

'Sorry, Mummy. It was jolly wet, and we had to keep our heads right down because they were coming up, you see. Daddy had to stay where he was, and just Duncan and I went on a little and he gave me the rifle and then they came, there were three of them, round this sort of pile of boulders, really quite near and Duncan was upset because the one he wanted me to shoot had sort of got behind the others. And he whispered – he can whisper dead quietly you know – he whispered that I could take the nearest one if I wanted, but I didn't. This one was mine and I knew Duncan wouldn't have let Daddy or anyone else take the near one, so we just waited and they shifted on a little more and then mine just turned and looked straight at me. I don't know if he saw me though, and Duncan just touched me to shoot, but I knew it anyway and I fired and he sort of jumped straight in the air and Duncan snatched the rifle and reloaded it, but he didn't need to shoot again. My stag just turned and started to run with the other two, but Duncan said we were all right and then he ran maybe twenty or thirty steps and then he just dropped over and was dead. And Daddy came out of hiding and then in a little bit the others came over the hill because they'd heard the shot, and Duncan cut his guts out for the eagles and Tom dipped his hand in and blooded me and I'm never going to wash it off.'

Louise was thrilled; they had seldom seen her so relaxed with pride and delight. She hugged William and Joseph and wanted photographs taken and Duncan to cut the antlers out.

Amanda and Alice prowled around the hanging deer, nervous, excited, half-touching. Clare watched, her mood sinking. Was this thrill inherited? Had William been born with it along with his soft fair hair; a genetic predisposition to find in death, death meted out by one's own hand, the moment of glory and triumph? Had she inherited it too? Is this how she had felt on her mountainside?

. . . he just turned and started to run, and then maybe he ran twenty or thirty steps and then he just dropped over and was dead . . .

. . . he just dropped over and was dead . . .

. . . he was dead.

She backed out of the game larder, crossed the gravelled sweep and went round the house on to the lawn. As soon as she was out of sight she stopped, leaned against the house and found she was shaking.

Across the lawn she saw Anni standing with her back to her, and looking across the Small Loch. After a few moments she turned, saw Clare and smiled. When Clare crossed the soft grass and joined her she saw Anni had been crying.

'Not for the stag, you know, for me. I don't know why I come. I don't approve of it and every year I come and I can't bitch about it because I don't have to come.' She looked at Clare and said, 'You didn't shoot him, you know. There wasn't a gun.'

'But I could have. I learned how to do it. You saw at practice.'

'Come the revolution,' said Anni, with a slightly strained grin, 'do you think they'll shoot us because of this?' and her hand flapped towards the group still gathered around the game larder, and then her arm swept wider across the house and the Small Loch and the hill beyond it, 'Because of all this? And Uncle William and those things? Or will they value us, let us be cadre leaders, because we can shoot so damn straight?'

'You'll be a cadre leader and it will be *á la lanterne* for me.'

'Do you know, I really did believe in the revolution. I believed and I couldn't keep the faith.'

'I don't think I ever had it, not really.'

'Faith is harder for you than me.'

'That's not enough. Not just . . . if more people like me had believed, it would have been easier for you; you might have pulled it off. Do you feel disillusioned?'

'No,' said Anni, 'if it had been illusions it would be good to be freed of them, good to be disillusioned. I feel dis-visioned. I had a vision and I lost it, or it was stolen, or I gave it away without thinking.' Clare had never heard this bleak Anni speaking before.

'When I was in Zimbabwe I met a cadre leader, you know; a real one. She was called Joyful.'

'They won,' but Anni began to grin properly.

'Now she's a witch; she works with magic, spells, traditional medicine.'

'Honestly?'

'Yes, honestly. She was wonderful.'

There was a moment's silence.

'Well,' said Anni, 'I'm still a vegetarian,' and her grin strengthened. 'I'll put in some broomstick training.'

'Granny?' said William after supper, while Joseph and Caro tried to organise them all into a game of charades, and Ceci tried to urge people to sing with her, and Ben, Anni and Felicity worked on the jigsaw puzzle. It was a confidential moment even though the room was filled with people.

'Granny, Daddy said you always cried when you killed a stag. Is that true?'

'Yes. Did you?'

'A bit. Don't tell Mummy, will you?'

'Not if you don't want me to.'

'Mummy,' called Ceci. 'Please come and play for us.'

'Us?' asked Hester, giving William's shoulder a tiny one-armed hug.

'Ben and me, but once we start . . .'

The house was filled with the sound of *Lieder*, with gentle music and then the familiar progression through hymns and childhood choruses to Gilbert and Sullivan and music-hall songs.

'Who still plays?' Ceci asked. 'I do.'

'Of course I don't,' said Felicity.

'What about you, Ben?'

'On my own, occasionally. Perhaps I'll take it up again.'

'You should. You were the best. And I like the clarinet. We have a string quartet. Not very good unfortunately. More of the sisters play the guitar actually.'

They all smiled at the thought of a convent full of twanging nuns.

Once they had all played musical instruments, a part of their childhood. That had come from James, unexpectedly, not Hester, although she played the piano well. James played the violin: the children had not been forced to start but once they had undertaken it, Hester had found them good teachers and made them practise hard. Once they had all played together: now Ceci was playing the cello with a group of women they hardly knew, Ben was playing his clarinet alone, and the rest of them had stopped altogether. Clare wondered briefly where her flute was, and then cut off the thought, aware that no synthetic hand would ever give her back that skill.

Despite the sadness she liked the music, liked to hear them all sing together. Because of the sweetness of the music, Clare thought she might have better dreams that night. But she dreamed of The Hand.

The Hand, designed to look like Clare's skin, chosen sensitively to match the very tone of her flesh, flexed its fingers and grasped the edge of its drawer. It pulled itself up and out. Delicately it explored Clare's room. But it knew it was not welcome there.

The bedroom doors in the girls' passage had latches, not smooth shiny handles. The Hand lifted the latch. The soft wind of the dreams in the house blew the door a little open. Enough.

The Hand made good its escape into the dark house.

Disconsolate, as angry and lonely as ever Mary Shelley's monster had been, The Hand roamed the dark house.

It passed down the small flight of steps and across the landing that led to the other wing of Skillen. In the soft dark of the summer midnight the mounted deer heads watched delighted as The Hand travelled by them: the memory of wholeness faded in the new knowledge that fragmentation has its own power. The stuffed birds, the great salmon in its glass cage were reduced by this new sight. The Hand delayed only seconds to exact the tribute that it was owed by these dead fragments. It paused, preening, by the great Chinese vase that had sat for a hundred years on the table at the top of the main staircase; behind it the heavy faded velvet curtain swayed in acknowledgement, and the dead stags' glass eyes glinted humbly before this modern monarch. But The Hand did not need these adorations and respects – it was hunting for love and acceptance. After a few moments of triumph it passed on.

In her dream it found Alice's room without difficulty, attracted by her dreams which were completely without words.

All night Clare dreamed that The Hand, which hated Clare and meant no good by her, squatted at the end of Alice's bed and adored, worshipped, venerated its new god. The human god which was flesh, not word.

14th August

OVERNIGHT, WITH A sudden, strange shift, the darkness and the wind swooped down. Even the near hills, just across the loch, did not climb out of the night towards the dawn, but sulked, hidden in driving rain. The house, which in the sunshine was spacious and welcoming, became closed and overcrowded.

The gale outside reverberated inside the house, too. While the darker dawn caused Hester to oversleep, the shaking of the wind woke Alice very early.

Alice always slept with a light on.

When Alice got really angry, or really sad, she would shut her eyes. With her eyes shut it was impossible to communicate with her at all. Felicity thought that being in the dark might recreate the anger and sadness; that night would become the unreachable, solitary place. Just as Joseph's children were forbidden to turn their lights on after bedtime, Alice was forbidden to turn hers off. So the late, fainter light of the morning did not affect her, but the almost imperceptible swaying of the house did as it did no one else.

She woke and, alone and peaceful, took the sheets of paper with the mazes on them out from under her pillow where she had hidden them and fell to work on the Aunts' Game.

The shapes welcomed her, the coloured patterns became orderly and, slightly after six o'clock, she realised that she had solved the problem. With delicate care she took a fresh sheet of paper, smoothed it over a book and coloured it in perfectly. None of the four colours slid over their appointed edges, each little box kept to its own boundary. It was finished and it was beautiful. She was puffed with pride. The grown-ups had played at this game, and she had succeeded where she knew they had not.

She wanted to show someone. She hopped out of bed, and ran

along the corridor to her parents' bedroom, her bare feet as silent to others as they were to herself. Her mother and father were sleeping in each other's arms. She watched them from the doorway, knowing that she could not disturb them, even though it frustrated her.

Her frustration and her pride made her bold. She knew what she wanted to do and she did it. She took her perfect sheet of paper back to her room and laid it carefully on her bedside table. She glided along the wide corridor and across the landing that led to the girls' passage. She paused a brief second beside the spindly table with the Chinese vase on it, and the dead stags' heads leered at her from the walls, their eyes glazed as William's stag's eyes had glazed in the game larder the evening before; the stuffed birds and the great salmon in its glass case stared at her, but she refused to be intimidated. She was the solver of the riddle, the heroine of the story. She ran up the small flight of stairs and counted the doors along the passage. She did not hear the accustomed creak of the loose board. With great delicacy she lifted the latch of Clare's room and went in.

The red eye of the battery charger winked at her encouragingly, and she looked swiftly round the room. Clare was asleep, sprawled on the bed, the stump of her arm hanging over the side, but Alice could not afford now the tenderness she had felt for her parents. Instinct told her that The Hand would have been hidden somewhere, and her quick eyes noticed that the top drawer of the chest of drawers was ajar. She pulled it out, felt inside for The Hand, grabbed it and slipped out again, victorious.

Now she urgently needed to reach the safety of her own room, where she could share with The Hand her triumphant success. But she was clumsy in her haste and passing across the landing bumped hard into the spindly table. The great chinese vase wobbled, tottered and crashed. The stags' heads on the walls were woken abruptly from their old dreams of rutting and roaring on hills now lost in rain. The crash reminded their high pricked ears of that sharp explosive noise: the last thing they had ever heard.

Alice could not hear the crash. But she had felt the table hit painfully out at her hipbone. She turned in time to see the vase wobble, and then fall, its shards falling apart, scattering across the wooden floor in the half-light. The vibrations scared her. By a mysterious process that she had never understood, china and glass breaking into tiny mosaic pieces always brought adults to the scene, usually cross adults, and in a moment of guilt and fear she dropped to her knees and crawled quickly behind the long velvet curtain that covered the window behind the small table.

The echoes of the smash fled down the corridors and brought Louise to her bedroom door; her immediate thought was that the children were up too early and up to no good. As she flung the door open she saw in the half-light of the curtained landing the shadow of Alice's foot whisking away into the window embrasure behind the heavy curtain, and she screamed.

Half the family were in the corridor before her scream had died away.

'A rat!' she panted, and then, seeing the fuss she had stirred up, added, 'I'm sorry. How silly of me; the crash startled me and I saw a rat.'

'Nonsense,' said Hester.

'A mouse perhaps,' said Joseph.

'No need to scream,' they both implied; a little mouse in a big house in the country, what on earth do you expect? Kerslake houses don't have rats in them. Even as she spoke, Hester remembered the rats in the biscuit tin in the curate's house, her first marital home. They were monstrous, evil things: she had taught herself to shout jokily whenever she entered the house, before she lifted Joseph out of his pram. The shout had been in order to scare the rats away; and the jokey tone had been in order not to scare Joseph. She had been humorous about it in public, and had summoned the rat-catcher, and bought tight-lidded jars for everything, and laughed about how the basement in the historic mansion of her childhood had been overrun with rats, and everyone had thought how good and sensible and brave she was. But for weeks her dreams had been filled with rats: rats nibbling Joseph's tiny peas-in-a-pod toes; rats gnawing on the soft bones of the baby she was then carrying. Part of her was impressed by her own calm; part of her struggled to rejoice that she could share the sufferings of the poor; and part of her was terrified, disgusted and ashamed.

She would have softened her scorn in sympathy with Louise if she had been given a chance, but Louise assumed a self-righteousness that repelled affectionate warmth.

'I rather doubt a mouse could have knocked that vase over,' Louise pointed out coldly. She had seen the shadow vanish behind the curtain and she knew that it had been too bulky for any mouse. She did not like the sneering tone of those around her, the sense of absolute solidarity that all of them would bring to even the suggestion of a rat in their beloved house.

She had a point. They all conceded she had a point. Draughts had not shaken the vase since before any of them were born. Delicate it might be, but also stable.

'Uncle William's going to have a shit-fit,' said Tom, rubbing his hand across his stubbly chin. 'It was worth a fortune. Well, a small one.'

'Don't use that sort of language,' Hester said shortly. 'It doesn't matter. What's done is done.' Rats. She shuddered. Her prayers had been interrupted and she felt envious of James, who appeared to be able to sleep through all this morning excitement.

'I'll talk to Duncan about it today,' she said, 'and let William know his house is infested. Oh blast.' Her children smiled as Skillen, which Hester was quite capable of claiming, of naming as 'mine' or more commonly 'ours', suddenly became her brother's, no concern of hers.

'It's not the end of the world,' she said firmly, while secretly she wished she had put her slippers on. She might be standing at this moment on the invisible footprints of the rat. 'We can live with a few vermin, can't we?'

Louise thought she deserved more sympathy. She knew that most of them were not convinced by the rat, and equally that a rat did not justify screaming before breakfast. She herself did not think a rat really justified screaming before breakfast and would have spoken sharply to either of her children if they had disturbed the household for so small a cause. She felt sheepish and therefore cross. Dismissed by Hester, she returned to her room a little sulkily.

Now the house was fully awake. In hiding behind the curtain Alice was paralysed. The wooden floors of the stairs and landing told her, by their shakings and movings that, as she had expected, people had arrived, but she could not tell what was going on. She curled up under the window, cuddling The Hand and watching the slight movements of the curtain with fear. When there was a lull in the storm of activity, she pushed The Hand as far into one corner as she could, and signed to it that she would return. Then, slyly, she drew back the heavy velvet folds and seeing the landing deserted, scampered for her room, hopped into her bed and lay there, her beautiful coloured diagram forgotten, pretending to sleep until Felicity came to get her up.

Clare's physical shock at not finding The Hand in its drawer was quickly adulterated by the furious conviction that this was a practical joke of Tom's. It was in appalling taste. Moreover the thought that he had been in her room while she slept, that he had watched her dreaming her dreams; that he might have seen the stump where her hand had once been and which she could not bear anyone to see; this filled her with a lethal anger.

'I'll kill you,' she said aloud, standing by the chest of drawers with the empty drawer open in her left hand.

A heavy silence shook her. She was the sort of person who killed people, whose anger exploded outwards and smote her enemies and hurled them into the pit. She was the sort of person who couldn't take a joke, who wasn't a good sport.

David and Tom's senses of humour might be different but her response was the same.

David had, of course, only been teasing on the mountainside when he had shouted into the swirling mist. Joyful, only half laughing, had told them there was an extra, unwritten rule:

Rule 15. Do not mock, insult or abuse the mountain.

But David, only to tease her of course, had said, 'You're letting this silly mountain spook you, my pet.' He had smiled at her, mocking and superior, and then he had laughed. He had thrown back his head and shouted at the mountain, shouted towards the invisible summit, shouted above the sweet singing, the siren song, 'Fuck you, you stupid bitch. You don't scare me.' He had thought it was funny.

She felt sick. This crude slice of memory dragged out other longer-forgotten echoes.

'Clare can't take a joke. Clare's a spoilsport. Clare's a bad sport.' The long fraternal windup towards tears and tantrums. 'Woofy, woofy,' they would taunt her. 'Snappy puppies get spanked.' Part of her had known, even from childhood, that there was no venom in this, and that if she could take it with Felicity's cool superiority, or join in with Anni's terrier-quick counterattacks, the boys would not mind, would indeed admire her and cease the persecution. Hester had a conviction that teasing was morally good for children, a necessary toughening up that did no one any harm. Hester, who was gentleness itself under her bossy manner, was still in thrall to certain aspects of the public school ethos. She would not protect even Clare from deft, verbal assault, so long as it was witty. The memories from childhood, the sense of increasing anger and impotence, joined her new memory of David on the mountain and it scared her.

She had to reclaim her justifiable anger with an act of will. She was about to charge down to the dining room demanding parental support and retribution, when she realised that it would mean going with only one hand. Why did that matter? She had only to go downstairs and open the dining room door and she would have taken an enormous step towards her own liberation. But she could not. She felt angrier. She pulled on her dressing gown, went along the girls' passage, down the three steps to the landing and leant over the banisters.

'Tom!' she yelled towards the dining room. 'Tom!'

Tom, shaved now and looking forward to his breakfast, came along the main corridor behind her.

'Yes, Ma'am,' he said, suddenly at her right shoulder.

She turned and he was too close to her, a man in a green jersey and cotton slacks looming over her. She gasped, stepped backwards, stumbled, reached instinctively with her right hand for the banister rail and banged her hideous stump hard against the newel post. Doubled over in pain, she shouted at him,

'What the fuck have you done with The Hand?'

Her anger, pain and terror, the word 'fuck' itself in his mother's house, confused Tom. Crouched below him, rocking herself, she looked like a madwoman; her question, in his innocence, sounded mad. He took an instinctive step backwards and stared at her, dumbfounded. Clare caught his appalled, distasteful look and dissolved into tears.

The landing was, once more, suddenly full of her family. Joseph said, 'For heaven's sake, not another rat. On balance, I prefer Lou's screams to Clare's language.'

William and Amanda scrambled across the hall below and gaped up at this new spectacle.

James, emerging from the library and the Eucharist, angry at the obscenity, at the wildness of noise, and at the disturbances of the morning, called for order. Caro rushed out of her room, clasping a baby, rather excited.

And then Hester came running up the staircase to take Clare in her arms.

Although everyone else had heard Clare's language and minded it on Hester's behalf, Hester herself had heard only the pain and the fear. She saw only the five-year-old, curled away from the world. The child who had needed her more than any of the rest of them ever had; the child she had been given, whom she had not chosen, and who was therefore especially precious.

'Darling,' she said, and her arms were round Clare. This had happened, Hester thought, because I didn't pray properly this morning. Lord help me to get this right. 'Clare, darling, pull yourself together. Come on now, you've frightened everybody.'

Clare leaned against her gulping, still childlike. Hester said, 'There there,' and 'There's a good girl,' and 'Now, whatever's the matter?'

I'm not a baby, Clare tried to tell herself. But it was good to be a baby. She could hear her own voice sounding like a little child,

'Tom's nicked my hand.'

It was almost impossible not to laugh; it was completely impossible to laugh.

'I have not,' said Tom, sounding very little older than Clare did.

She did not hear him. 'Mummy,' she wailed, 'Tom came into my room in the night and stole my hand.'

Hester looked up, 'Tom?'

'I didn't.'

'You did.'

'I didn't.'

Suddenly they are two adults again. They grin at each other. The moment of infancy vanished.

'I banged my wrist on the banister, and it hurt like hell,' Clare said shakily. 'Someone has taken my electric hand, and I thought it was Tom. And I yelled for him and he appeared like magic and it startled me. I'm sorry.'

'I really didn't,' said Tom. He wanted to be cross at being so unfairly accused, but had enough rueful self-knowledge to know that anyone else in the house would have come to the same conclusion.

'Who did?' said Hester. 'Because it's not very funny.'

There was silence.

'Clare, are you sure? Come on, we'll go and have a look for it. Everyone else can go and eat breakfast, if Anni has left us any.'

Clare and Hester walked together back to Clare's room. Hester hoped the hand would be there. It was exactly the sort of joke, she knew, that might appeal to any of the boys, and now it was not funny any more.

'Where did you put it last night?'

'In the drawer, I always do.'

'You've got tidier then,' said Hester, smiling.

The bedroom showed no other signs of improved tidiness.

Clare opened the drawer with confidence, and Hester peered into it. There was no space for confusion: the drawer was completely empty. Clare's hand was not there.

'I take it off,' Clare said, 'I take the batteries out and put them in the recharger. I've got two sets, but I always recharge them last thing at night. Then I put my hand in the drawer.'

Nothing much else was put in drawers; the clothes Clare had worn the day before were half on the chair and half on the floor. She had only been there for three days, Hester thought exasperated, and the place looked like a parish hall after a jumble sale.

Clare, seeing the room through her mother's eyes, did not feel the occasion was right to say that she never kept her room like this in her own house; that David would not have let her for one thing and she would not put her clothes at such risk; it was only here that she lapsed back into the habits of childhood.

The rooms in the girls' passage were all very plain; Hester sifted through the garments on the floor, looked under the bed, pulled open the other drawers, even the cupboard, but knew, as she had known from the moment she entered the room, that Clare's hand was not there.

'If one of the boys took it they meant it to be funny.'

'I know Mummy, but I don't like the thought of them in my room.'

'That's unlike you.'

'What?'

'To be so prissy.'

'Oh Mummy, it's not prissiness. Or not your sort.'

There was a pause, but now Hester was in her room, had penetrated her place of safety; now half the family at the top of the stairs had seen her handless arm, had formed their own disgust or pity; it was too late to wrap a kimono of secrecy around her deformity.

'Actually, I can't bear the thought of anyone seeing my arm like this.'

'Oh darling!' there was enormous compassion, but no indulgence. 'You're going to have to get used to it.'

'I don't see why.' She was indignant, hurt. 'Out there, in normal life, people don't come sneaking into your bedroom at dead of night, inspecting you, do they? It seems as simple a discretion as keeping your knickers on in public.'

Hester was irritated suddenly; Clare seemed obdurate, determined to keep her mother at arm's length. Hester, with her impeccable sense of justice, acknowledged Clare's right to her own privacy, but at this moment that only made her irritation more unbearable to her.

'Don't you believe Tom?'

'That's not the point. If I believe him, then someone else did it and I don't like it. You wouldn't let any of us laugh at the physically disabled, at Alice or something, would you? You'd tick off strangers in the street. You always do.'

Hester did. Over-developed civic responsibility frequently led

211

her to chastise others in public places, to tell children to pick up litter, teenagers to give up seats to old ladies. Once, years ago, Anni, Clare and Hester had been walking comfortably along a London street after a pleasant supper together, when sounds of mild female distress had emerged from a parked car.

'Don't,' a voice had said, 'no, don't. Please.' Nothing stronger than that.

Even while Anni and Clare had looked at each other with a shared hesitation, Hester had pulled open the door of the car and leaned in: 'Are you all right in there, or would you like to walk home with us?'

A young man had shot out of the car, angry and looking for someone to take his anger out on. If there had been a man he would probably have hit him.

'Mind your own business,' he had said ferociously.

Hester had not appeared to sense the menace. 'Oh, but I think it is my business, don't you?'

The woman in the car had been gently interrogated by Hester, had herself declared her own conviction in her safety and Hester had turned away smiling to find two excruciatingly embarrassed daughters. Now Clare found herself cross, the ancient embarrassment overlaid by a sudden resentment that her mother, who would take up a stranger's cause without even an appeal, was refusing to understand Clare's.

'That's odd,' said Hester, sorting and folding Clare's clothes and putting them into drawers while Clare looked on impotently. 'You're right. It is odd. I suppose I don't think of you as handicapped. Do you want me to?'

That was a body blow. Of course she did not want that, but . . . 'No, I want you to find which of my blasted siblings has stolen my artificial limb and request them to return it. I'm going out and I'm staying out and I won't ask any questions. I just bloody well want it back, in here, on the bed, before ten o'clock. Isn't that reasonable?'

'What about breakfast?'

'I don't want any breakfast.' She wanted to say, Sod bloody breakfast. The weight of Hester's immovable patience made that impossible. Hester was about the only person she had ever met who could manifest a physical look-at-me-I-did-not-flinch-at-the-word-bloody expression.

Clare ran down stairs, ignoring the babble from the dining room. She plunged her feet into a pair of wellington boots, and pulled a Barbour off a hook. The zip proved too complicated one-handed and she left it open, doing up the outer top button instead. She fled into the rain.

Surely she was being reasonable? A gust of wind dragged her hair into her eyes and she felt it further wetted by her tears, a rush of self-pity. People ought to be kinder to her.

They had been kind. She had been kindly treated and she knew it. Through hair and tears and rain she could feel the soft voices of the nurses saying leave her alone, leave her in peace, she's very ill. Post-traumatic amnesia is perfectly normal. They had been kind; their kind faces framed by white wimples. Peggy had been kindness itself. Joseph had crossed the equator to rescue her. Her family had defended and protected her and sought out for her the best treatment and she had a myeloelectric hand which was the envy of its own creators.

She turned below the boathouse and walked out along the narrow strip that separated the Small Loch from the Big Loch, and her boots sunk into the soft ground. Her footsteps marked her passing; like the footprint of the leopard along the path to the Victoria Falls. It had frightened her. What was the fear that drove her; that had driven her since she and David had gone to Zimbabwe?

They had flown to Harare, direct, from London. On the slow descent she had been filled suddenly with delight. Africa was laid out below her and the strange red hills in bright sunlight lifted themselves up towards the incoming plane; a new continent. Harare airport had seemed small, like a child's toy, and after the air conditioning of the plane the sun had struck hard down on her head. There had been people on the roof of the terminal waving and although they had not been waving at her she had felt welcomed and warmed by them and by the sun. The word Harare made a sound like laughter and she had laughed with it. A brief moment of hope before she had started to feel frightened, alien, adrift.

The wait, in what seemed little more than a shed, for the immigration processes to be completed deflated her. As they had shuffled and shifted forward she became surprisingly and shockingly aware of her whiteness; she had looked at her legs below the smart linen shorts which had seemed chic and appropriate in London and wished she had worn long trousers. She had not liked the smell of people. She had found the military presence unnerving; and peculiarly unnerving because every soldier was black. These things shamed her. She could not hear even the shape of the languages being spoken around her and she had not been prepared for the cross-examination which the word 'photographer' on her passport would stir up. She felt tired and grateful to David, who had taken over, reiterating with varying degrees of goodwill, and a certain complacent lordliness, that they were there on holiday, that Clare was not working, would not be working.

Yes, she had her camera, but that was for tourist shots only; no, she would not be taking any pictures at all of roads or bridges or military installations.

No, she did not have a work permit, because she was not going to work. She was a tourist. He was a tourist. They were tourists. They were on holiday.

No, she was not a journalist, she did not take 'those sorts of pictures', whatever-the-hell-that-means.

Clare had felt tired and crushed; she had been embarrassed, convinced she was holding up the queue. She had felt, and hated herself for feeling, that she was white and they were black and therefore she did not have the right to be antagonistic. At the same time she had been grateful to David and resented it, and resented his almost patriarchal goodwill. It had been very hot. She knew only that her legs were too white for this country, that she wanted a long bath, and that she was frightened. The things she knew, the skills she had laboriously acquired, the stories she could tell, would not work here.

The rain lashed her face again as she came out from under the slight shelter of the pine trees. The path forked, and she turned right up the Big Loch, away from the house. When she cleared the barricades of the trees and looked back, the house had vanished into the moving rain.

If she did not want to wear The Hand any more, as she had thought last night, why had she panicked when she had not been able to find it? She was angry with herself.

She walked faster. The wind ran in hard ripples, visible squalls, across the surface of the lake; the rain raced over her head and her legs were already soaking and chilled.

She did not know she was still crying.

The dark voices of the ancestors rode in this storm too. She had heard their voices singing to David from the rocks of Mount Nyangani; they had sung to her as well, inviting her, luring her, promising her. Joseph had come seven thousand miles to rescue her; but what rescue could he provide? From the home of the ancestors to her own ancestral home; and David, even after she had killed him, was still with her. Angry now because she had killed him.

She had been his puppet. The Hand was supposed to be her puppet, but it wasn't.

She walked and the walking did not relieve her tension.

The ancestors looked after their own; the dark gods who sang in the mists of Nyangani; the dead ancestors who had slain the great red deer on these hills and stuffed their heads and pinned them to the wall.

But those weren't her ancestors.

Joyful had said, 'They are not your ancestors. Don't try to put your reading on our stories. Go home and find your own, if that is what you want.'

Her ancestors had laughed as they died. Her parents had worshipped different gods; not Hester's sweet saints of selflessness and virtue, but the huge wild gods of danger and magic. Her parents had dedicated themselves to the gods of beauty and risk. They had lit their own pyre and laughed as they died.

After breakfast, a somewhat subdued affair during which everyone denied point-blank that they had touched Clare's hand, Hester asked Amanda if she would go upstairs and make sure all the landing curtains had been opened. Taking advantage of the moment, Bob told Alice to go up with her to brush her hair, and make her bed. He explained Amanda's chore, and at once Alice volunteered to do it.

'Alice says she'd like to,' said Bob with some pride. 'If Amanda doesn't mind.'

'Mind?' said Amanda. 'Of course, I don't mind.' She ducked her head away to dodge the repressive glance that she knew her mother would give her, and smiled gratefully at Alice.

Alice smiled and slipped off her chair, glanced round to make sure everyone was in the room and ran upstairs delightedly. It was the chance she had been waiting for. At the top of the staircase she swept back the heavy curtains and there was The Hand waiting for her in its corner. She snatched it up and carried it to her room. She balanced it neatly on the bedside table, wrist downwards, resting on her beautiful diagram, so the fingers reached upwards towards the lightbulb. Then, obedient to her father's commands she brushed her hair and pulled the cover over her bed with an easy competence. She was pleased with herself.

Alice loved The Hand. She had dreamed it in the night although she did not know or use the vocabulary of dreams. She loved The Hand and The Hand loved her. Alice did not play with dolls, because she still did not have enough vocabulary for the elaborate games of make believe which dolls enable, and she used the satin corner of a honeycomb blanket in the place of a teddy bear. Now she picked up The Hand, the wonderful toy which used the same language as she did, and engaged in her first imaginary conversation talking to it in Sign and receiving its responses.

The Hand, it told her, spoke only in Hand; Hand was its name for her language, the language of Sign. Like her it had no other language. Hand was for The Hand not a translation of another language but its very own. It was like her. She giggled. She had not understood a great deal of the conversation at breakfast although Bob and Felicity had endeavoured to fill her in: general conversation was generally beyond her, something that happened in her presence but without her.

Alice loved being at Skillen even though she was often confused and even frightened by the intensity of emotions and the constant incomprehensible talk. It was exciting, and she knew the immense love that they all had for her; Hester's laborious, and Anni's hilarious signing could both be frustrating, but Alice accepted their good intentions. Sometimes, though if she had been able to

216

articulate her thoughts it would not have been like this, sometimes she knew that Felicity and even Bob tried too hard. They wanted something from her all the time, they struggled with her, they . . . but they were diluted here; their concentrated energies dispersed, just as they were at church, and she found that a relief.

Now, alone but not lonely, she entered a new world, a world of imagination and power and love. Alice did not hear her own involuntary squeals as she played with The Hand, nor would they have been comprehensible to anyone else, but they were in fact spontaneous emissions of pure happiness.

She put The Hand down for a moment and showed it her diagram; it was very impressed. It told her that only people who could communicate in Sign could really do that sort of thing. It could do the puzzle and she could do the puzzle, but no one else could: this was another thing they had in common. The Hand was beautiful magic. Clare had said so. Magic.

Clare had also said that The Hand and the hearing aid were alike, but Clare was wrong. The hearing aid was horrible; through it came distracting noise, summons from another world; huge in her head, but without meaning, disruptive. The Hand was lovely. They could play together. She wanted it. It wanted her, it told her so.

But she knew The Hand was Clare's. Perhaps Clare loved it as she did. With a real unselfishness, she realised that Clare might be needing it, and after a while she picked it up again, cradling it like a baby, stroking it like a pet, embracing it like a lover, and carried it to Clare's room and put it neatly on the bed. She waved a farewell and was about to leave it there when suddenly a crafty thought occurred to her.

She took off her hearing aid, glancing guiltily around. She knew she was meant to wear it, knew the painful fights involved, but she loved The Hand and hated the hearing aid. She would swap with Clare, who thought the two were the same and would not mind.

But no one could love the hearing aid. There had been a fight when The Hand was missing and Clare could not eat her breakfast. Once Alice had the aid off the whole thing seemed easier; she left The Hand on the bed and hid the aid in the bottom drawer, under an old tartan blanket folded there against a chilly night and a thin-blooded guest. Perhaps she would never have to see the horrid thing again. Perhaps The Hand, who was so wise and clever, would deal with it for her. The Hand was her friend.

She danced out of Clare's room, and ran downstairs.

When Hester came up later to search Clare's room one more time, just to make sure the blasted thing was not lurking under some garment, although she knew it was not, she saw it lying there on the bed. She was angry with her sons, since she assumed that the prosthesis had been both removed and returned by one of them; angry mainly, she realised, that they had not had the courage to 'own up' at breakfast.

She was also deeply relieved that all was now well. She had no inclination to make further enquiries and very much hoped that Clare would feel the same way. She too then returned to her day, though with a sinking feeling that it would be hard to get through the next twenty-four hours in this household without some more drama.

'Spirit of Wisdom, who dances before the throne of the living God, dance now in me,' she prayed. It did not stop her feeling tired.

Over an hour later Clare came in from her walk, soaking wet, freezing cold and no happier. She did not want to see any of her family, and lurked in the drying room, where she hung whosoever's sopping jacket she had taken in the first place, until she could hear a silence in the hall and stairwell. She slipped up the stairs, and approached her room with no sense of homecoming, almost hoping that The Hand would not be there so that she could make a legitimate fuss. When she saw it, squatting malignly in the middle of her bed she was disappointed.

She was cold. When she reached out to pick it up her hand shook from cold, but the cold was part of the fear. She was frightened still, frightened by the anger inside her and frightened because her only claim to normality was to wear this thing which did not make her feel normal.

Perhaps she had killed David.

There had been lightning, and thunder, on the mountain, she remembered. She was frightened of lightning and thunder, because of the way her parents had died. There was the beginning of a new chronology to her life, because she could remember their dying.

Because of the way they had died, what she had wanted was to keep the rules, not break them; to stay on the path not to leave it; to be safe. To be safe. She had run away from the wild and dangerous love that Julia had offered her on the hill above Orvieto, because she wanted to keep the rules and be safe. Surely, of all people she would be among the last, already scared, already angry and distrustful of David, already frightened, in a thunderstorm, to murder someone.

She stripped off her wet clothes and pulled on her kimono for the second time that day. David had brought the kimono home for her from Japan; it was a blue-and-white print, cotton as soft as silk, with a scarlet obi. Why ever should she think she had killed him?

The bathwater was hot and she sank into it.

'You don't really hate me,' he had said. 'You think you do, but it's yourself that you hate. You've been very naughty. Shall I punish you?'

'Yes,' she had said, but it had always been a game. The rules for starting and stopping carefully laid down; just a game that amused David and turned her on.

She must not think about those things here; this was her mother's house where such things were not to be thought of, where sex was a natural development of love, an expression of the unity and affection between two people. The hot bathwater began to warm her; her belly muscles relaxed.

This house was safe. It had to be safe. She had not killed David. Of course she had not.

She wriggled further down into the bath; the water was silky and golden-brown. She watched her nipples soften and spread in the golden liquid.

Ben had had his nipple pierced; he had worn leather trousers, too tight in the crotch.

The surface of the water rippled as her stomach clenched again.

David had promised to keep her safe, but he had charged a high price. She had stopped loving him, she had been angry, but she had not killed him.

They why had she told the soldiers that she had killed him?

She had been delirious. She could not remember any of it anyway. Post-traumatic amnesia was perfectly normal.

Part of her wanted to stay in the warm water, safe and sleepy; but she was too frightened to be alone. She clambered out of the bath and went back to her room wrapped in a big towel. She got dressed and strapped The Hand back on; it seemed a small price to pay for the appearance of normality. She went downstairs to rejoin her family, resolving to be calm and behave normally.

The household, disrupted too early by Clare's tantrum, could not settle down. A sort of fractiousness took hold of them all, little spurts of ill temper.

'Anni, take your nose out of that book and come and play Monopoly,' Ben said.

'It'll only end in tears. I'm reading.'

'Don't be so antisocial.'

'You can talk – you always cheat anyway.'

'I do not. What's your riveting subject matter anyway?'

'The philosophical implications of Cantor's proof that there are different sizes of infinity.' Her voice held the same quizzical, self-mocking tone as she had used in the train with Clare, but now the context was different. She sounded only smug.

Since adolescence she had always been able to make Ben feel intellectually inadequate. 'Oh for Christ's sake,' he said, 'don't show off.'

Anni took herself and her book up to her room and did not come down even for lunch.

Felicity asked Tom about his computer: 'I want to update my word processing software.' She had no interest in the subject whatsoever and noted her own generosity in raising it.

'I suppose it would depend on your machine,' he said, a little surprised.

'I've got an Apple Macintosh.'

'I wouldn't know then. Out of my price range. OK for those who can afford it.'

'We're not exactly rolling in it, Tom. Teachers aren't well paid, as you ought to know.'

'Nor are estate managers.'

'You're hardly going to tell me you're impoverished.'

'I bet I get paid less than Bob does.'

'Well, you hunt twice a week. How do you afford that then?'

'Uncle William mounts me if you really want to know.'

'Oh, he does, does he?'

'Why shouldn't he? I ride well. Andrew doesn't give a fuck . . . about any of it. It's not fair.'

'Wish you were the son-and-heir, do you? Thomas, Lord Mereham.'

'You bitch.'

Felicity was affronted and looked nobly long-suffering.

Finally Tom and Joseph took themselves off for a walk.

'Coming Ben? Bob?'

Ben couldn't believe they really wanted him and so refused. Bob said he would stay with Alice so that Felicity could get a rest.

Louise said, 'I expect Amanda and William would like to go, wouldn't you?'

'No.' Joseph said with decision. 'We took Will yesterday; this'll be too far for them and they'll get cold.'

Louise looked ready to complain, but in a deftly masculine way Joseph and Tom disappeared.

'Bloody men,' said Caro, but without heat.

'Too right,' said Louise, also without heat, but with a chilly ferocity. Hester, Felicity, even Ceci, looked up surprised: their code, which allowed witty criticism, absolutely forbade whinge-ing. It was tough being a woman, tough and unfair and you were certainly allowed to get back at the men who would leave you to amuse half a dozen children on a wet day, but you had to be a good sport about it. Caro was a good sport, their mildly surprised looks implied and, therefore, Louise was not.

She hated their united arrogance, their complacent conviction that they knew and would always know exactly how one ought to behave. They weren't so bloody perfect themselves: they didn't behave properly by any etiquette except their own.

'I'll take them,' Ben offered, genuinely trying to help, to fill the loaded moment which was women's stuff he did not understand.

'Not me,' said Amanda. 'It's too wet and I'm going to help Lucy make the supper.'

'Go on,' said Louise. 'You can do that this afternoon. Good for you to get out. Say "thank you" to your uncle.'

'Please, Mummy.'

William said, 'Don't make her, Mum. Ben and I'd rather go alone.'

'Fine by me,' said Ben jovially.

'No!'

Whether the 'no' had been addressed to William or to Amanda or to Ben, Louise herself was not certain. She was already tense, but even so was as surprised as any one in the room by the explosive sharpness of her response. She looked at her son to justify herself. Serve Ben right, she thought into the silence, serve them all right. I wouldn't have dared say it, but someone should. Decent people didn't have to put up with Ben's sort of behaviour.

Ben went white. Whatever Louise's intention had really been, the silence that followed allowed everyone to hear her 'no' as Ben heard it, and their shock to confirm him in his hearing. The stillness lengthened; interrupted only by the flutter of Bob's hands trying to explain to Alice that nothing interesting was happening at all and she should pay attention to their book.

Ben stood up. He looked at Ceci. 'Perhaps,' he said in a voice none of them had ever heard him use, 'your religious attire is, despite everything about your unfortunate brother, sufficiently unsullied for you to teach the A-level facts of life to our sister-in-law. Could you please try to explain to her that I am neither a pederast, nor incestuous?'

He left the room. After a moment of total silence, Hester started to cry.

'For heaven's sake, Mummy,' said Ceci sharply, 'that won't help.'

Bob said, 'None the less it was an enviable exit line.'

Felicity said, 'Louise, how could you?'

Amanda said, 'What's a pederast?'

Louise said, 'I didn't mean it like that.'

'Oh, no? How did you mean it then?'

'Felicity,' said Hester, nearly as reproachfully as Felicity had said 'Louise'.

Clare got up. She was furious with Louise, but Felicity's liberal reproachfulness grated on her nerves just as badly. She had to get out of this room.

As she reached the door she intercepted a grateful smile from Hester. She had not been going off to comfort Ben, but knew that that was what her mother was thanking her for. Outside in the hall she leaned exhausted against the wall. For a brief moment she saw the whole scene and found it quite funny. Then she heard the darkness in Ben's voice and knew that it was not funny at all.

She had to remember what had happened to David, not just for herself but because of what all these open sores did to all these people who tried to outgrow each other and did not succeed.

The hall was badly lit, and on this dull day half-dark. She pushed herself off the wall and started towards the stairs. In the hall mirror, which was grainy with age, she saw a young woman, who looked just like her. 'What happened?' she asked the woman, whose right hand jerked at the question.

Behind the woman in the mirror there was a movement; the ghostly spirit of an old man appeared, tall and thin, coming round the end of the staircase. His shape was watery, indistinct in the flawed glass. She was startled. Shaken, it took her several seconds to realise that it was her father behind her, and his reflection, like hers, was distorted by the passing of time, and the slipping of mercury.

'Clare,' his voice was lovely, deep and gentle, as it always had been, not hollow, and grainy like the ghost in the mirror. 'I'm in the library. Come and have coffee with me.'

'I'll get it,' she said quickly. He had looked old in the mirror, old and spindly.

'Thank you.'

In the kitchen Lucy would have chatted. Clare was quick and efficient, though alarmed to see how quickly they were consuming her coffee. Her father had always preferred a cup and saucer to a mug. For him she decanted milk into a jug, as her mother would have done. He had probably forgotten about her hand, the only member of the family who would have happily accepted an offer from her to carry a coffee tray about the house. She chose a small round tray, reckoning if necessary that she could manage it one-handed.

'Biscuits?'

'In that red tin.'

The red tin was new, Clare thought resentfully, and then smiled at herself because she had not been here for ten years and it was ridiculous to freeze every biscuit tin for her comfort.

Her father was reading *Daniel Deronda*. His copy was a paperback, not new, the orange spine shot through with delicate white traceries from previous readings. Some things never changed; her father in an armchair in the library reading George Eliot because he was on holiday – Eliot or Milton or Ovid's *Metamorphoses*. At home he read differently; contemporary non-fiction, not so much theology as biography and history. On holiday he read for reassurance, for joy, but who other than James would be reassured, made joyful, by Latin poetry?

She poured the coffee. He took his cup from her with a smile, sipped it, put down and picked up his book again.

'Daddy,' she said boldly, 'I am not deceived. I've been set up.'

'Well,' said her father, unapologetic, 'I did want to talk to you.'

'I know,' she said defensively. 'Did Mummy tell you to?'

'What? No, this is all my own.' He smiled a little ruefully, 'Your mother doesn't really run my life as much as you all think.'

'I know that, I think we all do really. I'm sorry – what did you want to talk to me about?' She felt ready to shut him off, ready to run, but when she looked at him she realised he wasn't looking at her, but far away out of the window and into the rain driving across the water and covering the further hills up the loch towards the north in a blanket of invisibility. She hesitated.

'About your mother. Not Hester, I mean your other mother, my sister.'

Clare was taken aback. She could not remember that he had ever so much as mentioned her other parents to her. Neither Hester nor James talked much about her original parents. Hester had shown her photographs; pictures of herself as a baby, as a toddler, and in the pictures, somehow incidentally, were a tall thin girl, too young to be a mother, too flimsy to have carried a baby, and an immense solid bearded man. Both of them always appeared to be laughing. Her parents: her mother and father. She had no memories of them whatsoever, although she could remember with great accuracy the house in which they had lived, and the messy garden and the stables which doubled as the laboratory and into which she was never, under any circumstances, allowed to go.

'My mother?' she said now, and a sudden swoop of curiosity long suppressed swept through her. They had never told her about them because she had never asked, and both Hester and James, though from different motivations, would never have forced their knowledge upon her.

'My mother,' she said again, then catching a lost echo in what he had said before, added formally, as a gift, 'Your sister.'

She had been her father's sister in a real and concrete way, as she had never been Clare's mother. He owned her and she never could. She did not feel jealous, she felt loving towards him.

There was a long silence.

'She was wild,' he said, unexpectedly. 'Not wild in a bad sense, but confident, joyful. She could take risks; she wasn't . . .' he searched slowly for a word, 'she wasn't tame.' The word sounded odd; he noticed its oddness. And his own shyness.

'I don't think I'm explaining this properly. She was just seventeen when she married your father: she would have married him the year before, if my father had let her; but it wasn't childish romanticism, it was a risk, she knew it was a risk, and it seemed to her a risk worth taking. Not to the rest of us. He was more than twenty years older than she was. He was very strange. Perhaps I shouldn't say that to you. The thing is we all liked him, even your mother, I mean Hester, and he wasn't her sort of person. But he was . . . This is an odd thing for an elderly Anglican priest to say, but I suppose I thought he was a bit of a wizard, somehow magical.'

'An alchemist?' Clare said, tugging gently on a thread she had unpicked only two nights ago when the great stars had exploded in heaven and she had remembered his passing. James's face lit up, the doubt and hesitancy vanishing suddenly.

'Always wanting to turn base metals into gold. That's right.

There was gold everywhere for him, he made it. But your mother was not base metal, she was already gold. Refined gold, as magic as he was. He knew that, and it did not frighten him. It frightened lots of people; it frightened me.'

'Yes,' said Clare. 'Yes, I know. I knew someone like that once. It frightened me too.'

He nodded but he did not seem to hear her, locked in his own memories. 'They were both – well, when hippies happened I thought perhaps they had been premature hippies, but perhaps they were more like those Russian "holy fools". Except they weren't holy in any sense we use the word. On the contrary . . . I find it difficult to talk about her. I just want you to know about them; how they claimed each other, not stupidly or blindly, but judging it worth the risk. I don't think I'm romanticising this. It was very strange, she was so young and so clear. She knew the risks and thought him worth them. No. Felt him worth them.'

He reached out and patted Clare's hand and she watched him do it, and his tenderness and determination to talk about something difficult was so patent that she felt his love and did not notice that he had patted her right hand.

'Perhaps she was right. I'm the other way . . . I don't know where she got it from except that she was, as a little girl, so very much loved. We always wanted to tame her, to keep her safe, but your father, your real father, never wanted to tame her. They were a bit crazy, your parents. And a bit . . . dangerous. I mean, dangerous to people like me.'

'Daddy . . .' Clare said.

'I'm not very good at this, am I? I wanted you to know. I'm not good at talking about her, about your mother. When you came to us, we – Mummy and I – we thought you needed to be kept safe. We thought they had dragged you on a lonely wild journey that had been too risky for you. We thought we could make you safe, make you believe in safety, in being careful and keeping the rules.'

'Daddy, I . . . I saw them die. You don't need to warn me against breaking the rules, running any risks.'

'No,' he said. 'No, that's not what I meant. Quite definitely not. The opposite, in fact. It's hard for you having a mother who's a saint and a father who,' he smiled at her, inviting her to smile back, 'a father who, when all is said and done, probably does believe that we are saved by works. An old black mafia Anglo-Catholic who spots heresy lurking under every bush and thinks that it's better to be safe than sorry. I wanted you to remember that you had two other parents who weren't virtuous or saintly, but who were beautiful. Your mother once told me that there was no beauty without danger; she thought that people ought to break the rules and run the risks. Probably,' he paused and Clare knew instinctively and certainly that what he was about to say was something he had never said before and would not say again, 'Probably I loved her more than anyone else in my whole life; just because she was so beautiful.'

Clare said, 'All my life I've wanted to be safe; that's what I wanted. I didn't even know that was what I wanted.' She had to give him something of herself because he had given her so much, his secret love and his guilt at his disloyalty to Hester, given to her because he thought she needed them, because he loved her.

'That was why I was so frightened the other night. I have always wanted not to explode. I have hated my first parents for running those risks, I didn't think they had the right. Daddy, I clung to David long after it was good for me, or even maybe for him. I thought if I could be good, if I could behave, he would keep me safe. I could earn safety. Daddy, you don't know how boring he was.'

James gave her a slightly naughty grin, 'Yes I do.'

'No, not dull. Boring. He bored into me, like a drill and I let him and I wanted him to, and I tried and tried. I made him into God. When people ask me what happened I get frightened because I don't know; but also because I am afraid I killed God. Broke the rules and would be damned for ever. Does that sound crazy?'

'Ah. No, not crazy, simply wrong. I thought perhaps that was so. I want you to know that there is that other God, and one that Mummy and I, despite our best efforts, are quite unable to introduce you to. The dark God, you know, the wild, untamed, enormous God, who has no laws or dogmas. That was your other parents' God. It isn't mine, I don't like that God, I find him scary, but honesty obliges me to remind you that he does indeed exist. Or she, perhaps.'

They both, simultaneously, picked up their coffee and took a sip, tidy, domestic, tamed. They grinned over the edges of their cups recognising the other clearly.

'Daddy . . . I don't think I believe in any God,' Clare said.

'Don't worry about that. God believes in you, even if you don't believe in him.'

He had said that during her confirmation class, but she had not heard it then.

'I wanted to tell you something,' she said. 'When I was upset the other night I accused you of not telling me they had been laughing. I had forgotten that, but it wasn't just anger; it was true. The whole world went up in flames, in stars, like apocalypse. The big bang; and they were laughing. In each other's arms they were wrapped together, not thinking of me, that's why I was angry; but they probably knew, they must have known, that you and Mummy would keep me safe. They were laughing in that hell because it was beautiful and they thought it was well worth the risk.'

'Thank you,' he said almost formally.

She knelt down beside him in a swift graceful movement. She hugged him, wrapping her arms round his waist and laying her cheek on his chest. He raised one arm and patted her gently on the shoulder.

'Thank you, too,' she said.

He made her feel safe. She laughed at herself, though not unkindly.

Ben drove to Inverness. He knew perfectly well that someone in his family would follow him if he stayed in the house; that Hester would make sure that someone did find him, pet him and make him feel better. He did not want to feel better. He wanted the power of his anger at Louise. He did not want her to apologise, so that he would have to shoulder the guilt of failing to forgive her. Without even looking for a jacket, he left the house immediately by the front door. Then when the rain caught him, like a blow across the face, he got into the nearest car and sat there. It was Tom's big Renault. At Skillen they all always left the keys in the ignitions;

it saved looking for them, losing them, fighting about them. It also meant that anyone could drive any car, if need be, even if its owner had gone fishing on one of the high lochs, gone to Carnith in a different car, or was otherwise elsewhere. Ben knew it was also an arrogance, a way of saying: we own this place, no one would dare steal our things. So, on an impulse, without much thought and without any guilt, he turned the engine on and drove down the drive. The white gates were open and he swept through them. By the time he was out on the real road he knew he was going to Inverness, because he caught himself looking at the petrol register and wondering if he had enough money on him to refill the tank if necessary.

When he took the sharp bend just before the bridge at Carnith and joined the main road he knew he was driving too fast. He knew he was going to Inverness to find sex.

'You're addicted,' someone had once said to him.

'No, I just like it. You have cornflakes for breakfast every morning, but you're not addicted.'

The Bishop had said, 'Do you want help?'

'Whatever for?' he had said; the whole interview had filled him with anger. He had enjoyed the Bishop's obvious embarrassment, as he had enjoyed nothing all week.

'I'll go away if you like; you can have my resignation if you like. I'm sorry to have inconvenienced you, but I don't, in the sense that you mean it, want any help.'

'Your mother . . .' the Bishop had ventured.

'This has nothing to do with my mother.' He had tried to instil some semblance of civility into his voice. 'Father . . .' he had said without thinking, and then remembered that the Bishop hated to be called 'Father' and would hear it only as another instance of Anglo-Catholic affrontery. He could not help that.

He had said, 'Look, I've discovered something that I enjoy; I think it widens my imagination and expands my potential, and is a great deal cheaper than going skiing every winter, or breeding old roses or whatever other hobbies single clergymen develop, or you like to think they develop. I like to fuck like a bunny and the Church doesn't seem to have a context in which I can do that. Maybe the newspaper has solved a problem for us both. An end

229

at least to my own doublethink. But that's the Church's loss, not mine.'

He felt the car shake as he accelerated viciously. He made a conscious effort to slow down. There was more loss than he had anticipated. He thought about Sybil, his sacristan, his friend, who he had assumed had known about his sexuality; an intelligent middle-aged woman who enjoyed administering the lives of gay priests; and, when he had rung her, she had instantly invited him round and plied him with gin and supper, but she had looked at him with pity and when she said 'good-night' that evening he knew she had been saying 'goodbye'. He had let her down. And the kids in the youth group who sniggered, because they could not face putting together the warmth and friendliness. And the extraordinary silences when he arrived in rooms with his colleagues.

I don't want to be political about it, he thought, wrenching the car through the gears. I want it to be part of my life, not the whole of it. And now it would be the whole of it. What the hell was he going to do for the rest of his life? He liked being a parish priest. He liked the gentle rhythms of prayer, and the robust rhythms of social activism. He had thought other people, those whom it suited, could fight this battle and he could have a private life. Anni would laugh at me, he thought, slowing down for an elderly Landrover pulling out of a farm gate, and she'd be right. Nothing was private. Nothing ought to be. His clergy friends did not ring him up. He had let the side down by getting caught.

He had been almost surprised to find how little guilt he suffered. Shame but not guilt. He had dealt with the guilt years ago. He was more surprised to find that he wasn't angry either; there were two sets of rules, he played by one and the bishop played by another. He was angry with the people who avoided him, with the phone that did not ring; but he was not angry with the system. Tomorrow, he realised, was the Feast of the Assumption and he would go and hear, as so many times before, his father saying Mass in that distant depersonalised way that Ben no longer believed in but which he admired; and nothing would have changed. God did not mind him being gay. But he had to think about a job;

he had to do something. Right now it all seemed boring and impossible.

He deliberately thought about Inverness – the train station? the bus station? pubs on a weekday lunch time? the gents at John Lewis? He smiled. His mother admired John Lewis, she thought they maintained decent standards. He himself had been faintly, nostalgically, shocked when he had discovered the full range of facilities, besides haberdashery. Was there a John Lewis branch in Inverness? Fuck Louise. He had been careful to do and say nothing that would attract his family's pity and she had blown that clean into the sky. So had he, with his naked anger. Stupid cow. He wanted them all to see that nothing had happened, nothing that changed him. It wouldn't work. Something had happened.

He drove more carefully, and when after nearly two hours he realised he was approaching the city, he pulled the car into a lay-by, switched off the engine and carefully fished his ring out of his pocket and pushed it through the tiny holes. A nipple-ring under an elderly flannel shirt; he was amused. Of course something had happened or he would not both have taken it out and yet kept it, ready to hand, in his jeans pocket.

'Sorry, God,' he said aloud, and a little bit wryly, 'but it's neither of our faults.'

He sat in the car, watching the rain pour down the windscreen and smoked a cigarette. Then he drove into Inverness, parked the car in a multi-storey car park and walked out into the town.

From the hill above the house, Joseph and Tom saw the car turn out of the driveway and accelerate along the lochside.

'That's my car,' said Tom.

'Someone needs a getaway vehicle,' said Joseph, smiling.

Tom laughed and Joseph used his laughter as encouragement to say, 'It was true, wasn't it, what Felicity said?'

'Well, you know, who wouldn't? I wouldn't mind if bloody Andrew gave a damn about the place. It's true Uncle William mounts me, he does a lot for us actually; but it honestly is because he really cares about it all and wants someone to use it. I bet you

Andrew will sell Skillen, the minute he inherits. It just seems unfair. Not to me really, but to Uncle William. It makes me cross. But it's silly and I know it's silly, so I shouldn't let Felicity get to me.'

They walked hard; as they got up the hill the rain eased off, and they ate their sandwiches high up under the rock cliff of Scealillh. It was still grey and damp, but the distances seemed to be opening up for them.

'Where are they stalking tomorrow?'

'Damn, I forgot to ask.'

'Duncan will have our guts for garters.'

'Mummy's gun. They'll go up the north side.'

'Let's hope. They'll kill themselves laughing if it's you and me that shift the beasts.'

'We'd better tell Duncan, this evening. He'll cover for us.'

'Do you know what Mummy and Daddy are planning to do this winter?'

'How do you mean?' Tom looked surprised.

'Well, they'll have to leave the Vicarage, won't they, and they don't seem to have made many plans.'

'That's odd, isn't it? Are they OK?'

'For money, you mean? I think so. But Clare's costing them a bomb.'

'I thought David was loaded.'

'He was; well, cash rich. But if she killed him . . . I mean,' Joseph was embarrassed, 'I mean if his life insurance people decide she killed him; or decide he isn't dead, or something, she's stuck.'

'She didn't, Joseph.'

'Of course she didn't. But she did say it. I just wish she'd let us all in on what the hell did happen.'

'She's so damn secretive, she always has been. Don't you remember?'

'Sometimes, Tom, I think she's as crazy as her real parents were.'

'Do you remember them?'

'Not really, but enough.'

'Look, Joseph, if there's really a problem for Mummy, let me talk to Uncle William, will you?'

'That's what this is about, idiot.'

They understood each other very easily. The subject had been dealt with. They talked instead about their children's education; about the ungentlemanly whining of the afflicted Lloyd's names; about fiscal policy and an amusing case that Joseph had had recently; about the problems of Highland reafforestation; and about whether the bird that whirled up a hundred yards ahead of them was really a ptarmigan. They walked steadily, covering the ground, content with each other's company, wet and happy.

Back in the house though, there was no such contentment. In addition to everything else, Alice was behaving abominably.

Alice had fallen in love. She had found the companion that she sought. Because she did not live at the school like other children, she did not have the same opportunities for friendship. She had been lonely.

Sometimes at church she felt that acceptance and she loved Father Harris and Megan, the Sunday school lady, with a passion that gave her clues to this, her new love. But she only saw them when her parents chose; they might choose often, but still Church was not her own. The Hand was her own. No one knew that it came into her dreams at night.

She had been good, not to have hidden The Hand and kept it for herself. She had been kind to give it back to Clare: she knew that Clare did not love The Hand as she did. She saw it now hanging on the end of Clare's arm and she was jealous; but she had been good. And no one was nice to her because she had been good.

She had been bad. She had hidden her hearing aid. She felt guilty. She also felt bold. Yet no one seemed to have noticed; no one was cross with her because she had been bad.

Felicity and Bob had, in fact, both noticed that she was not wearing the aid, but both supposed that the other had given her permission not to – very occasionally, and for different motives, one or other of them would let her leave it off for a while. At home they would have consulted each other, but here, determined to appear united, and both shying away from a horrendous fight, they were each secretly relieved that the other had been too lazy to force the issue. But Alice could not know they had noticed, and their lack of attention made her angry.

Neither Amanda nor William happened to want to struggle with the impossible puzzle that Joseph had set them; the copies of it had been tidied up and put away. Alice, who knew she had been clever, wanted them to play so that she could show them that she had succeeded. They were depriving her of her planned moment of triumph. She tried her best to invite them to play, but they could not understand her and she was angry with them.

Because she was angry, she was unsettled, destructive. She was uncooperative and violent. At lunch she would not sit down, and when Bob finally physically picked her up and dumped her in her seat she shut her eyes and started to scream. The noise was intolerable to the grown-ups and confusing to the other children. Malcolm joined in; a wild cacophonous din. James stood up abruptly, silently, and left the room. Alice, peeking between supposedly closed lids, realised that attention had been taken away from her once again by the other child and she leapt off her seat, ran round the table to Malcolm's highchair and, without warning, bit him. She bit him hard, viciously hard, on his chubby knee just where it bent over.

The immediate result was silence. He was so shocked that his screams ceased as hers necessarily had for the bite. There was a moment of blessed peace, while everyone registered the new quiet without registering what had caused it. Then Malcolm's yelling resumed, though differently, now cries of real pain. Ceci, who was sitting next to him, realised what had happened and, suppressing a spontaneous laugh, scooped Alice up into her lap and held her there. Looking down she saw the tooth marks on Malcolm's leg: a red circle, which although it had not drawn blood had certainly bruised him. Alice struggled against Ceci's arms, kicking and trying to bite again. Ceci was calm; she pushed her chair back from the table and held on, trying only to restrain the hysterical child.

It was too late for calm; Caro was on her feet, outraged and distressed. Felicity and Bob the other side of the table both jumped up – Felicity embarrassed and guilty; Bob simply and purely angry. None of them had ever seen him angry. He came round the table and the rest of the room was frozen in the movement of his wrath. Ignoring Ceci as though she was not there, he scooped the child off her lap with one arm so that she hung still struggling over his forearm, her head dangling; and with his free hand he slapped her twice, with every bit of the ferocity she had used biting, and considerably more power and accuracy.

'Bob!'

Uncertain how many voices created this chorus, he was aware of Felicity's as the most shrill and ugly, rising over the general clamour and the underlying shock. It did not soothe him.

'Shut up the lot of you,' and he slapped Alice again.

Then turning her with a movement that seemed both brutal and efficient, so that she hung under his arm, he carried her out of the room. On the stairs she recovered from her stunned surprise and started to kick again: before they reached the landing he needed both arms to contain her, but he remained adamant. Alice's legs crashed against the banisters as Clare's hand had earlier, and it hurt her too.

He dumped her on her bed and she sprang off it, flung herself at him and tried to bite him. Her fingers grabbed, scratching at his face, and the simple pain of having his beard pulled made him gasp and push her harder than he would have intended. She fell back on the bed panting, but after a moment she wriggled sideways on to the floor the far side from his and, crawling on hands and feet like an animal, tried to get to the door. Bob stepped back fast, slammed the door and leaned against it. She wailed again, sitting up on the floor like a dog, and he recognised with pain that what he felt was disgust.

'Stop it!' he shouted at her impulsively, and then knew that he had to think how to Sign that. Compassion suddenly melted his anger. He sank down until he was squatting, almost at her level, and tried to make her look at him. She shut her eyes again, and did not stop screaming, but something in the pitch of her wails made him realise that the high wave of fury was subsiding, was turning to grief. He began to sense a victory; for a moment he felt almost exultant and was for the first time ashamed. Here they were on the floor like beasts and he was proud because he had dominated her. He sighed and held out his arms to her. He sat very quiet, very calm and suddenly very sad.

She would not open her eyes, she would not look at him or come to him, but after a long while, she flopped sideways, curled herself up in a little ball and lay there on the floor. He waited, and saw her thumb slip quietly into her mouth, submissive. Then he picked her up and carried her to the bed and put her on it.

He felt exhausted. The passionate tenderness she usually elicited from him had evaporated. He hardly thought of her, only of himself. He felt a gladness in him because he had no family. No wonder Felicity was always so tired. He knew absolutely why she would not risk another baby and why he had no right to expect her to.

'I'm not afraid of change,' he had said to Felicity when they discussed how and why so many marriages broke up under the strain of bringing up a handicapped child. 'I'm not afraid of change; I prefer to call it growth, it's healthy to grow.'

There was change. There was growth. But it did not have to be healthy. Cancers grew; attitudes changed and he was not the unconditionally loving, warm-hearted, liberal man he had been and had prided himself on being. He who had been a New Man before they were invented was now an old one: not regressed, but defeated. He had hit his child. He had hit his child in public and he believed he was right to have done so. Once he would not have done it. Once he would have done it and felt guilty. Now he had done it and would do it again and did not feel guilty, and would not feel guilty. Yet he loved her.

He lay down beside her, curling himself round her tightly furled body, and fell asleep.

Later Felicity came up to find them, driven by anxiety and exasperation; driven by relief that Bob had finally given way to temper; and driven by fear that if he too were to fall, as she had, into the bog of uncontrolled emotion there would be no safety. She smiled when she saw them asleep together, a smile sudden and warming, of affection and recognition.

Their sleep, the rare sweet sleep of father and daughter, released her. Very gently she laid the eiderdown over them, to keep them warm, and turned to leave. On the bedside table she saw Alice's diagram. Immediately she knew what it was that Alice had been trying to tell them all morning and she felt guilty. Looking, not just at the completed puzzle, but at the beautiful colouring-in she felt a great wave of pride. Pride in Alice first, and then in herself and in Bob. An enormous success to balance against the tiny failure of one wet and dreary morning. Alice would be all right. She knew it with a great certainty; and would be all right because she and Bob had done a good enough job. She placed the paper back on the table; if Alice did not see it when she woke up Felicity would find some way in which she could spring it on the rest of them as an impressive surprise. She understood quite clearly what her daughter had been up to.

She went downstairs. The drawing room was empty. She could hear noises in the kitchen, but felt no need to go and make herself useful. For the first time since they had arrived at Skillen she opened her work box and began again on her embroidery: a still life with bees and flowers. It suited her, this fine needlework: her thin, old-fashioned face lost its gauntness and became charming; even in jeans and an old shirt of Bob's she looked elegant.

She would, she thought, when she had finished this, make a patchwork for Alice, very bright colours on one side, a yellow sun with rays and gaudy floral prints, and on the other a dark sky with stars. Long diamond stars, or comets. And instead of background quilting she would sew in silver thread, catching the flashes across the dark cloth. Stylised stars, on a very dark blue sky, not black. Something to remind Alice of the Perseid shower; so that she could take that magic to bed with her and keep a hold on it. Now she picked out in silk against the matt wool background the edges of petals, glossy, brilliant. She sighed contentedly. She told herself she would face the fact that, when the quilt was finished, Alice would need it to take to residential school with her. It was not working, this staying at home; it could not be made to work. She, Felicity, could not make it work. It was not fair on Alice. She counted strands of silk floss, and tiny holes, and forgot the whole unhappy business, absorbed in her own work and smiling slightly, more from concentration than from pleasure.

Hester took James his coffee, forgiving him for leaving lunch. They sat in the library together, Hester at the desk writing letters and James in the armchair across the room. Occasionally they would look up and catch each other's eye. It was not the relationship that either of them would have dreamed of forty years ago, but it was peaceful and easy, based on a disciplined acceptance of difference. They were not alike, and the years had failed to make them more alike. But they were bound by a shared creed that they had absorbed into their different marrows and they recognised in each other a depth of commitment that had carried them to a place of gentle affection and would keep them there until one or other of them died.

Clare, exhausted by the day and by her family, also decided to take an afternoon nap; to join the babies, to be a baby. She went up to her room, listening to the quiet of the house.

She felt wary. She had promised her mother that once The Hand was returned she would ask no questions; but the sense of something being alive in her room at night, of someone coming in and looking at her in the darkness was still strong and so was her sense of The Hand's own malevolence. The half drawer at the top of the chest did not seem adequate protection; even while telling herself it was neurotic, she opened the lowest drawer and was pleased to see that there was a heavy tartan rug. Under it The Hand would be hidden and suppressed. She would be safe. Lifting the rug to bury The Hand, she saw Alice's hearing aid.

She did not consciously remember the dream of the night before. She did not know why the sight of the hearing aid made her panic; why she had again the sensation of being in a thick mist, a bright darkness.

When she and David had set out to climb Mount Nyangani she had felt physically dreadful for the first half-hour: it had not just been fear and anger. Perhaps it had been the altitude, but she had been breathless, wobbly, shaky. Her heart had pounded. She had wanted to stop, to turn back, to go down. At one point she had thought that she could not go on and she had not been able to say so because she had known that David would say she was sulking.

The path was well-marked, but rocky and steep; it went round a little kopje and then up beside a swift stream, a waterfall really. It was very clear; each time they paused, they could see further and further, an ever expanding distance. There were mountains behind mountains, navy blue in the longest distance, and furthest away of all there was a narrow gap between the horizon of hills and a low band of clouds, and she had thought that through that gap she would see eternity; and that eternity was not a place of safety, but of dissolution.

It had been bizarrely quiet. For some acoustic reason they could only hear the waterfall, noisy, busy, from some places, then the path would take a little turn and the sound would be cut off, as suddenly as if someone had pressed a switch. And although there were extraordinary flowers and caterpillars and tiger snails and wonderful butterflies – smaller than the ones at Matopos but more surprising, windblown, dancing – she had not been able to suppress her rising panic.

Standing in the silent room, she knew the same perilous foreboding. She dropped The Hand, uncaring, but its fall was cushioned by the rug, and she kicked the drawer shut with her foot. She threw herself on the bed and then that was not enough and she groped her way under the covers, shaking with fear, and, curled up like a baby, finally fell into an unrestful doze.

Images from her night dream repeated themselves, only now they were different. Alice had lured The Hand to her room last night. Now The Hand had seduced the hearing aid, had seduced Alice. The Hand and the hearing aid were entangled. The Hand and Alice were entangled. If she were involved too then it meant that The Hand was a part of her. She fled into sleep and hoped as she fell that she would hear the voice of Chirikudzi, rather than see or feel these newer confusions.

She woke up two hours later with a headache. She could hear the whole house moving, alert again. She did not feel rested; but she knew that if she failed to appear at tea-time someone would come and find her, and she could not bear anyone else to come into the room. She got up and with reluctance dug The Hand out of the lower drawer and struggled to put it on.

With even greater reluctance she turned her attention to Alice's aid. She did not know how it had come to be hidden under the rug in her chest of drawers. Hidden, it was; there could be no question of accident. If she took it down with her she would be betraying someone, and in such a moment of treachery it would be comforting to know who. Alice. Probably Alice.

The affinity she felt for Alice was deep, though untested. Even so, could it be right to assist Alice, to assist a five-year-old in hiding something that her mother was convinced was good for her? It was too risky; she did not know enough. Felicity was angry with her already.

Unwillingly, she picked it up. It was clumsier than The Hand and equally artificial. The box, the canvas body strap, the ear moulds; all the unmistakable marks of deafness. Yet it joined Alice to the hearing world as precisely as The Hand joined her to the world of limbedness. The Hand held the aid almost tenderly, although the wires trailed. She could not hide it for Alice; she could not hide it from Felicity. She went slowly down the staircase and into the drawing room.

An Edwardian idyll confronted her: the English family at tea. A great fat teapot and a large fruit cake on a polished table and a group of people relaxing about the room. Joseph and Tom had returned from their walk, looking pink and wholesome. Tom and Anni were playing tiddlywinks on the floor with Amanda and William; Alice was sitting on her mother's lap looking adorable and proud. Her finished puzzle was propped up, in pride of place beside the teapot where no one could miss it.

'Tea, Clare?' asked her mother, and, 'Nice nap?'

'Look what Alice has done,' said Anni, 'thus saving you all from watching me throwing up on a T-bone steak.'

Caro, by the tea table, picked up the pot to pour Clare a cup, but Clare did not immediately come towards her; almost shamefaced, trying to be discreet, she walked over to Bob and handed him the hearing aid.

'What?'

'Don't ask me,' she tried to smile normally. 'I found it upstairs.'

Bob looked surprised, though what he felt was guilty. He realised in a flash that he had not even thought about the aid. When he and Alice had woken up she had been in a sunny, restored mood. They had played, chatted and then he had seen the four-colour problem solved before his very eyes. He did not have to simulate enthusiasm: he was amused, delighted, proud.

He had brought his daughter down for tea and found a soothed Felicity and he had been happy. He had not thought about the hearing aid, and he knew that Felicity would have expected him to.

Almost as discreetly as Clare he reached out a hand for the aid, and at the same time searched for a quiet place to put it. Everything was peaceful now, he was not going to whistle up the wind of a new storm. He glanced across the room and noticed with relief that Felicity was chatting happily to Ceci and paying no attention to him or Clare.

The glance was his undoing. Waking with her father, forgiven, loved, warm within his embrace, Alice had known joy. They had got up together happily; and then they had found her picture and he had been as thrilled and proud of her as she could wish. She had assumed from his not mentioning it that he had accepted the disappearance of the hearing aid. She had not forgotten it and it had not occurred to her that he would. She thought of him with pleasure, that he was on her side, and, in this conviction of his love, she felt forgiving towards her mother. She was especially alert to him, sensitive to his presence and when he glanced at her it captured her attention and she looked up.

It was not that he had the hearing aid; it was that The Hand was giving it to him. The Hand had betrayed her. The Hand, whom she had trusted, was delivering the aid back to the enemy, who was not the enemy but her father and the man who loved her. The Hand, who was supposed to be her friend.

She did not hesitate for thought; as quick as a fish she wriggled off Felicity's lap, slipped across the room and before anyone was aware there was anything to be alarmed at she had grabbed the aid, with its ear moulds dangling between Clare and Bob, and thrown it hard at the wall. It hit with a thud, chipping a dent into the wallpaper, and fell back to the ground.

Felicity was on her feet as swiftly as Alice had moved. All the gentle pleasure of the afternoon only fortified her fury. She was angry at Bob for letting Alice get up and come down without going through this daily wrestling match upstairs and in privacy. She was angry with herself for not noticing: she had had Alice on her lap for fifteen minutes and had not noticed that she was not wearing the damn thing. She was angry with Alice for not accepting the necessity of wearing it, for not accepting her mother's love and knowledge and care. Above all, she was furious with Clare. She did not know how Clare came to have the aid and she did not think, she felt only that Clare – once again, as always, since the earliest days of her life – that Clare had arrived and spoiled her pleasures; that Clare had stolen from her even this afternoon of peace, as she had always stolen from her since she was five.

She did not know these things, but she knew her wrath.

She crossed the room ignoring everyone in it, flashed Bob a look which had all her ancient spite against Clare in it, although that was not her intention, and which hurt him. She seized her daughter, spun her round to face her, moved her face close up to Alice's and shouted very loudly.

'Put it on.' The emphatic mouth movements made her ugly. There was a moment's silence.

'I won't sign until you put it on.'

Alice was startled by the fury. She uttered a weird little squeaky scream. Felicity pulled her across the room by the arm, picked up the aid from the floor and held it out to her daughter.

'Put it *on*.'

She wrestled the child to the floor and started tugging at the straps of the body pack. Alice resisted. She resisted more from shock than from true obstinacy, but Felicity was not capable of knowing that. She seemed hysterically rough with the child and the room was stunned into silence.

Clare, recognising that her instinctive repulsion about returning the aid had been a sound one, felt also that once again she had disturbed the peace of her family, that everything was her fault, that their beautiful and orderly lives had been ruined by her, and although wisdom and a policy of non-interference dictated otherwise, it was almost without volition that she said,

'Let it go, Felicity, she hates it.'

'I don't care if she hates it,' Felicity was now trying to insert the ear moulds, a delicate operation, requiring both calm and co-operation and now there was neither. Alice shook her head, though whether from anger or discomfort was unclear.

'You don't understand.' Clare felt almost desperate; the fear and distaste on Alice's face seemed to match her own feelings exactly. She did not know whether the aid really was good for Alice and suddenly she did not think it mattered.

'And you do, Miss Know-it-all?'

It was the language of the nursery and ought to have made them laugh, but it did not. The whole family watched in silence, too aghast, and too fascinated, to interrupt.

'Yes I do,' said Clare, 'yes I do. I know how much I hate my hand, hate putting it on and taking it off and pretending that it's normal and wonderful and useful and also knowing that it is horrible and disgusting and doesn't work. I do know. Don't make her wear it, Felicity. Please.'

It was a true appeal, but Felicity could not attend to that; she was fighting for her own convictions, her own faith. She let Alice go, and the child, with the electronic box rather crookedly in position but the ear moulds dangling at the ends of their wires, slipped out of reach and sensibly retreated to Hester's arms. Hester sat down hugging her close, but watching her daughters.

'What do you think you know about it?'

'I don't know anything about it; I only know about the misery of wearing it.'

'You wear yours.'

'We talked about shame.' Clare tried to reach her sister, but she could not apologise because, in hiding the aid in her room, Alice had solicited her help. She had betrayed Alice by uncovering the aid in the first place and bringing it down and creating this public drama. Now she was called to a greater loyalty.

Felicity could not hear the appeal. She repeated,

'You wear yours. And make a monumental attention-seeking fuss about the bloody thing. Anyone would think that losing a hand was the worst thing that could happen to a human being.'

Clare said, almost without thought,

'OK. I'll stop wearing it when Alice stops wearing her hearing aid.'

It wasn't fair, and Clare knew it wasn't fair, but she clung doggedly to her sense of Alice's need which was outside the rules of fairness. She knew she could make the choice for herself, but Felicity had to make it for Alice. She searched Felicity's face, trying to make contact, to make reparation somehow, without betraying Alice's faith and trust. Felicity was still squatting on the floor, and her face was turned down and inwards.

'That's not fair,' Tom said suddenly, breaking the silence, joining in. It was always his rôle, as the baby of the family, to claim that things weren't fair.

Felicity, looking with abstracted concentration at a tiny patch of red-and-blue carpet, slightly worn, thought, damn this family, damn, damn, damn them all. She thought at the same time that she could not survive without them. Without looking up, she tried to get a sense of Bob and knew, absolutely and without anger, that he would support her in every way she might want and that equally absolutely he would agree with Clare.

She raised her head at last. She looked at Alice, curled up now on Hester's lap; she considered the daily fights, the constant assault on Alice's dignity. She remembered the gentler language, the dancing fingers of a woman at the deaf church who had, in conversation, not in challenge or criticism, told her that when she had been little she had hated her hearing aid, had found the booming and roaring of her aid both distracting and painful, but as a teenager she had become interested in the limited sounds it gave her.

She had never been made to wear it. But she had been the child of deaf parents – Sign had been the language of her home. It was different. She knew the conflict was not about what was good for Alice, but about what was good for her.

Anni said, carefully, in response to Tom, not to her sisters, 'They aren't parallel. It's not about fairness, it's about equality.' Anni was pursuing the difference in her own mind, an attempt at truth that had little to do with any fondness she might have for the individuals concerned. Hester listened and was appalled; she had never accepted before how like James her oldest daughter was.

'Equality. Clare's proposing to give up the signs, the appearance, of normality in exchange for Alice giving up the signs of handicap.'

'Don't say . . .'

'Yes, Bob, I will say handicap. "Hearing impairment" is an

244

insult to Alice; she isn't hearing impaired, she's deaf. They aren't the same thing. As long as she wears that aid she is handicapped and will be seen as handicapped. The minute she stops wearing it, she is simply a member of a minority cultural community – and then she isn't handicapped, she's discriminated against.'

Felicity felt her fierceness rising as it seldom rose in her own defence, as it so often rose for Alice and never herself. She even had time to thank Alice for honing in her the capacity for fierceness which she had neglected in her own childhood.

'It isn't about fairness, nor equality or . . . not exactly. There's just Clare, and she can decide. She's single now, she can decide for herself, no one else's business, except this family which makes everything their business. But with Alice, there's Alice and there's me . . . what do I do when what is good for Alice isn't good for me? What does clever feminist principle say about the conflict between self-fulfilment and the real goodness of putting your own needs into the cooking pot?

'I love her you know.'

She heard her own plaintiveness and took a deep breath. This was too important for self-pity.

'To give up on oralism is to give up on the child. No, to give up being the child's mother. Alice will go to boarding school next year. She ought to have gone already if Bob and I weren't so bloody determined that we could do it. Pride probably. Pride and love. How do you learn to say: this child's mother tongue isn't her mother's language?

'I want her to talk to me; to talk with me. I can't sign, not really. You all learn a few signs and that's lovely . . . we're all grateful, aren't we Bob? . . . but none of you know enough to know how bad mine is. It isn't my language. Alice's signing is already better than mine. If she needs to talk about things, she talks at school. I've tried – God knows I've tried – but they'll tell you, and its true, that the only hearing people who can really sign are the hearing children of deaf parents. She'd love not to wear the bloody aid; but the minute I let her I'm saying that I have given her away. It's for me that she wears it, and it doesn't seem too much to ask.'

Bob came over to her, he knelt on the carpet, there in front of all her family, and claimed her for his; he put his arms round her, holding her tight.

Alice began to wail, the weird birdlike noise of distress, learned and learned wrong in infancy; the sounds that carry no meaning except the meaning of attention.

Felicity, who had flopped against Bob, loving him simply and purely for a tiny second of time, got to her feet. 'You see,' she said wearily, 'now I have to explain to her in a language that isn't mine, and isn't hers yet either, that her mother is distressed because she has discovered that's she's too mean-spirited and selfish and possessive to do what is best for her child. Imagine trying to do that in French.'

She crossed the room ungently, took Alice very gently from Hester's lap, looked over her shoulder at them all and said,

'I don't think I can give her up, and I don't think I can face ever having another. She has taken even that away from me and still I love her.'

She stood Alice in front of her, facing her, and signed as best she could that they were talking about the hearing aid, but it was OK. No one angry now. All good. Love Alice. Love Alice lots. Love Mummy.'

Suddenly there was a blinding clarity, a knife-like cruelty and a burning generosity, all bound together.

'Clare,' she said, and her hands went on talking too, her face and attention still turned towards Alice. 'You're driving the wrong bargain. I'll make you a better offer. I'll surrender — no, I'll give Alice — to her own people, to her own community, when you give yourself back to yours. She will stop wearing her hearing aid when you stop fooling yourself and us. When you can stand in front of me and tell me, in any language you choose, what happened to David on your mountain.'

The line between spite and love, like the line between beauty and danger, was too narrow, was a tightrope they all had to walk on, dance or totter or fall.

Clare stood as though paralysed. Hester said, 'Darling.' It sounded futile, meaningless as Alice's squeaks, and no one knew to which of them it was addressed.

Felicity stopped signing and at last turned her face from her daughter. She looked at her father and said,

'I cannot live any more by your gospel of love. I cannot love enough. Sufficient grace is not enough. Your God's demands are unreasonable. Unacceptable. A God who wants that is not a big enough God. I can no longer bow down and worship false gods. You promised me a place of safety in love and order and discipline and it was a damn lie. There is no place of safety. I cannot love enough and there is nothing that can fill the gap for me. "Beware the false prophets who cry 'peace, peace' and there is no peace." There is no place of safety. Your God had duped me.'

James looked desolate, old and frail.

Hester quoted, ' "He never said, thou shalt not be tempested, travailed and sore; he said, thou shalt not be overcome." Felicity, I promise you, God is the place of safety, the rock beneath your feet, your fortress and your shield. The safe cocoon of love.'

Ceci, who never said anything, who distanced herself through silence and stony calm, stood up, four-square, her eyes blazing within the halo of her white wimple, and said:

'Bullshit.'

In the moment of shock, Clare looked for Ben to remind him with a glance that he had said that those members of the family who believed in God always swore in obscenities.

Before anyone had time to react, Ceci went on, the words forced out of some place as though, like Alice, this was no longer her language.

'People are always talking about God being safe. I don't get it. In the final count, it seems to me, God isn't safe, God is the only danger big enough.

'Unfortunately the world is full of Stanley and Perseus types. Sorry, Mummy, we were talking about them on the hill the day we saw the shooting stars. They muscle in everywhere, with their benevolence and clear-headedness and honest common sense. They do not dream at night and they know what is good for you. They want safety. If your labour goes on too long they'll knock you unconscious and give you a caesarian. If your life goes on too short they'll refuse to let you die, and wire you up to their machines until it suits them. If the Voice of God wakes you in the night suggesting you leave Ur of the Chaldees and follow your glorious destiny in the Wilderness, they'll give you therapy. They want to explain the beginnings of creation, and dictate the date of the Apocalypse. They plan to lay down grid lines of mathematical formulae to discipline the vast vacuity of chaos. Even Einstein, who was a genius, felt obliged to believe that "the old man didn't throw dice".

'There is no space left for the terrible beauty to be born.

'Yes, Anni, even your pretty little Mandelbrot sets, with their cute paisley patterns, only mark the boundaries of chaos. Out beyond that there is an enormous vacuum; a hideous caterwauling that is not measurable, or balanceable or safe or anything. That is God.'

There was a tiny pause; the rain beat on the windowpanes, but the room was appalled, motionless. Ceci went on:

'God doesn't say, be safe, be cosy, here's a woolly blanket, a tidy cocoon, a place of safety. God says, "If thine eye offend thee pluck it out. If thy right hand offend thee cut it off." '

She half grinned, 'and thine ear, too, I have no doubt. Hack them off, that's what God says. Bend and break the will, discipline and scourge the flesh, face blindly the unknown, the enormous, the terrifying. Love your life and you'll lose it. Risk it and – half blind, mangled, limbless, maimed – maybe, just, you'll totter into heaven; the place of both annihilation and total knowledge. The risk is absolute, you'll get nothing else out of it, not pleasure, not health, not affection, not comfort, and certainly not safety. Just beauty.'

She stopped, looked slightly embarrassed, and left the room. They heard her and her terrible creed tap their way up the staircase, and then far above them they all heard the bedroom door slam.

Stunned, the drawing room paused and then shifted. As though they had been given permission, everyone in the room moved and in their movement realised that they had been immobile. They were silent.

Hester sighed and stood up.

Joseph broke the silence to ask her if she wanted to take a whisky to her bath. She smiled at him.

Caro went over to where Alice was standing staring out of the window at the rain on the loch, touched her shoulder, mimed eating, said 'supper time' and held out her hand.

'Don't mime, sign,' said Felicity, but it was a ritual chant given from habit and without conviction, not an instruction.

Bob came over to Felicity and put his hand out towards her, but he was not greedy, he waited. There was no demand, no challenge and after a moment or two she reached towards his hand and held it with both of hers. Then she laid her head on his chest and started to cry, quite gently.

There was, however, both demand and challenge in the grin that Anni tossed at Clare. Demand and challenge and affection and mockery. For a moment she looked terribly like Hester and it made Clare grin back.

That night, for the first time, Clare dreamed of herself with only one hand. Not a nightmare, a simple ordinary dream in which she was driving David's big car to the bank to collect something for Hester. She looked at her right hand on the steering wheel and saw the stump; it did not seem to affect her ability to drive. She did not wear her prosthesis which had gone away outside the dream world. She did not take photographs or make love; none of the horrors and fears were dealt with. She proceeded through the dream action calmly and normally but with only one hand.

She woke chilled and startled. The room was grey, awash with pale pre-dawn light. The red eye of the battery recharger winked at her across the floor. She rolled on to her back and extracted both arms from under the blankets; held them up, profiled against the window. In that light there was nothing ugly about the stump; it was an absence, an absence of hand, not a presence of injured stump. She flexed her left fingers, tendrils of dark against the paler square of glass. She flexed her right fingers, which were dust and ashes somewhere in southern Africa, but she could feel them move, fainter than the physically present left hand's ones, but definitely there, a shadow against the light window, a soft distant sensation.

15th August

THE NIGHT WASHED their world. The misty rain from the day before had vanished altogether and the Small Loch bounced back a purity of blue sky and early morning sun.

Ceci and Hester had both been up early; even before Mass the breakfast table was decorated with white flowers for the Assumption. 'Not,' said Hester cheerfully, 'that there is exactly a wide range of choice. Cow parsley and daisies.'

'I never like lilies anyway,' said Ceci. 'Funeral, and expensive. In Carmel we always have roses.'

'I didn't think; there might still be some on the south wall; those small climbing ones.'

'Mummy, it doesn't matter.'

It didn't, Hester thought; this child who had always been the most touched by beauty, by flowers and music, who had, as a little child, cleaned her own shoes for the pleasure of their shining not for virtue, had stripped that off too.

'Is there anything you miss? I mean in Carmel,' Hester asked, and then felt guilty, as though she had been cheeky.

'Of course. I miss the children a lot; and I miss booze sometimes. And, this time, here, I realise I miss clothes, I mean I miss making that daily choice. Also I miss never being on my own. Obedience is my stumbling block.'

'It was when you were a child too, do you remember?'

'Oh yes; but not that sort of obedience; I can do what I'm told, but I find it almost impossible to think, to plan, to imagine with a common mind. I couldn't survive in any other order you know; it's only the eremitical tradition in Carmel that makes it possible.'

'You wouldn't become a solitary would you?' Hester felt a wave of panic.

Ceci laughed. 'No need,' she said. 'No need to make so much

fuss. I always have been a solitary, it's community that's the discipline.'

It was true, Hester realised, and she wondered why. Too much community when Ceci was a child, not enough space and time on her own?

'Why?' she asked her daughter.

'Mummy, if you're looking for causes, then you're looking for cures. It isn't anything I need curing of. It's me.' She turned back to the table.

Hester had a moment of clarity. Not about Ceci, but about Ben: all her guilt was because she was looking for causes; but there was no need. It was just him. At the same time she noticed her youngest daughter's deftness which somehow replaced tenderness; the children all had one big oxeye daisy in a sherry glass beside their places; each flower was turned so that it faced towards the breakfaster.

They looked comfortable together despite the contrast in their appearances. Hester in corduroy plus fours, ancient, soft and leather-padded at the knees, and a green flannel shirt that had once been Tom's and was rolled back at the cuffs several times to make it fit. Ceci was wearing her brown habit, with the black veil and white wimple; it gave her an ageless quality, emphasised by her huge eyes and curiously smooth skin.

It did occur to Ceci to wonder how her mother reconciled the idea of the flowers and the gentle celebrations of breakfast with the fact that she would, only an hour later, go out to stalk, but there were judgements that she did not have time to make. Not today, and her heart rose; today would make up for yesterday and what she had said would be forgotten; or else it would be remembered but lovingly. She was comfortable in her mother's love now; that love, which had oppressed her as a child, had oppressed her for as long as she had tried to find God through Hester, had become a pure and easy gift the day she had changed her obedience. She had never told Hester that: she let Hester think that she had become a Roman Catholic in order to follow her unexpected vocation, or because she accepted the principles of universality, and both were true: there was no kindness in telling Hester that she had needed to escape; that within the Church of

England she could never be out of her mother's influence. The freedom made her loving. She found that she was humming half bars from Bach.

Hester cocked her head, 'Is that the Magnificat in D?'

Ceci listened to her own hum. 'Yep,' and with a sudden abandonment she sang, and Hester sang with her, and James, coming down across the hall, heard them and poked his head round the dining room door and sang too.

'Let's waken the sluggards,' he said in a pause, grinning. 'Let them look to the ants and be wise.'

The three of them grinned and Ceci flung back her head and trumpeted,

> 'Then sings my soul, my saviour God to thee,
> How great thou art, my God, how great thou art.'

A chorus suddenly as rollicking and delightful as any they had sung round the piano, and they heard Ben's voice join them from outside and knew that meant he was coming to Mass and that pleased all three of them.

After Mass, Ben said, 'Can we come up the hill with you today Mummy?'

'We?'

'I'm not stalking, but it's a wonderful day. Anni and I thought, as you'll be using the aga-cat anyway, that we might get Clare out.'

'What a brilliant idea, darling,' said Hester; she was so pleased with him, because he had sung with her, and come to Mass, and thought about his sister, that for the first time that week she could look at him without feeling physically sick at the thought of the nipple-ring which presumably still lurked there under his green jersey.

'We haven't told her yet,' Ben grinned.

'Leave it to Anni.'

'She said "leave it to Mummy".'

Ceci laughed, 'The poor girl hasn't got a chance, has she?'

'Nope,' said Ben, laughing too.

252

Ceci felt the affection and goodwill between her mother and brother and discreetly left the room. There was a pause.

'Mummy . . .' Ben said tentatively.

'Ben, dear,' said Hester, at exactly the same moment. Then suddenly both knew that this was not the right moment. He was willing to talk to her, at least to try to talk to her. That would have to do for now. She would try not to ask for explanations, merely look at what he might do now. 'Not now, dear. Half a dozen grandchildren are about to descend the stairs for breakfast, I'm going stalking and it's the feast of the Assumption. That's quite enough for one morning.'

He understood her perfectly. 'It'll keep,' he said, smiling.

'Yes, but not for too long.' Then, so that he would know she trusted him, she added, 'Look after Clare, won't you? Don't let Anni bully her.'

Ben felt relieved and exasperated by her control. He remembered how much she loved him. He gave her a hug.

So, an hour and a half later, there Clare was, sitting sideways in the back of the ancient Land-rover, joggled against Anni and – when the lurches synchronised and their eyes caught – grinning at Ben. Hester rode in the front with Duncan, who was driving, and the low aga-cat was towed behind them. The hills with their soft complexity of colour were neatly framed by the square opening in the back of the Land-rover.

The Land-rover had no modern comforts, a fact that none of them regretted, and now they had turned off the road and on to the forestry track its normal lurchings grew wilder. Clare suffered a moment of fearful imbalance – convinced she would fall, fall lopsided, unbalanced, maimed; involuntarily her left hand grasped Anni's shoulder and her sister, without looking at her, reached down, grabbed one of the Barbour jackets and wedged it behind her back.

'Thanks,' she shouted, unnecessarily, as at the moment of speaking the vehicle was quiet and smooth. Hester glanced over her shoulder and smiled at her children with real pleasure. Infants again in the light of the loving gaze, all three of them ducked their heads self-consciously.

The back of the Land-rover was cluttered. There were, to start with, six legs: two of Ben's — in ancient grey flannel probably borrowed from Tom, and rough brownish-greenish ribbed socks below that: he had his boots on — greenish brown again but smooth, supple, well cared for leather — already laced and double-knotted just above his ankles. Then there were two of Anni's legs, her feet smaller than Ben's, and the difference in size emphasised because she was wearing only socks, but identical to his. Kerslake family standard-issue presumably — did Hester bring twenty-eight pairs of them neatly packed in a cardboard box with her when she packed for the holiday, along with the two whole hams and two weeks' worth of excellent malt whisky? The soft, slightly frayed hems of Anni's jeans nearly covered her socks. Clare's own legs, in beige corduroy, worn soft through use, looked to her preposterously dainty, bogusly feminine. She was irritated at her self-consciousness. Her socks were her own, thick cream cotton. Like Anni she hadn't put her boots on, but she was wearing trainers, untied. Her boots, which lay beside her feet, were the most serious-minded of them all: black leather Highland Water Board issue — Duncan had arranged their semi-legal purchase for her fifteen years before; the best walking boots she had ever encountered; David had envied them, not only for their exclusivity and the subtle claims that their ownership made, and so did passing DM wearers on the streets of London.

Apart from the six legs and the two loose pairs of boots, there was a lot of other gear on the dark green muddy floor. Hester's Barbour, a patched sleeveless leather jerkin that Ben had borrowed from the gun room, Anni's big black jersey; four lunch bags, two trout rods — one in a tan canvas case and one in a green waterproof one — Hester's ancient binocular case, Duncan's slightly newer telescope; a pair of waders, Hester's tweed cap, three woolly hats and a couple of spare socks. The shapes were precise, the colours a wonderful muted fugue, a tribute to good taste and old money: dark grey, green-brown, the colours of the hills around them. All the leathers, the straps on the rod-cases and the wickerwork basket, were old, soft, faded.

The sun, still barely clearing the eastern hills, bounced in and out of the back of the Land-rover tossing brightnesses and shadows. Clare's mind reached for her camera, choosing angles, focuses. Her smile stopped abruptly. There was no camera in the muddle on the floor; there was no hand to follow the subconscious impulse of her mind. The Hand that had replaced the hand that took the photographs did not even twitch. When they had turned off the macadamed road and taken to the forestry track she had leaned across herself and with her left hand discreetly turned off the switch in her supposed wrist. It was clamped now to the raised tailgate of the Land-rover. This made holding on over any bumps infinitely easier; it also made the taking of any photographs completely impossible.

What the hell was she doing here anyway? She felt a wave of lethal anger, and the fishing rods could not meet her need. One thing was missing from the equipment on the floor: the rifle. Duncan had it with him in the front of the Land-rover; he never let it out of his sight.

She knew that the gentle, civilised ritual of the day and the killing of the stag were inseparable and she did not need or want either of them. Her mother must be the only person left in the world who would find stalking a deer to the death an appropriate response to the feast of the Assumption; a celebration of eternal life. Clare's mind jerked mentally, the same jerk as her body had experienced when she had lain in the field that afternoon and fired at the target. She wanted to kill something.

She jerked again, dodging her own thoughts, her own anger. She should not be here; the shadow that hung over her was destructive; destructive to them all. Yesterday had been a nightmare; even the strange dreams of the night had been less hectic. She was a woman who had killed her lover. She was a woman who could not say with certainty that she had not killed her lover. Fiercely she wished that she had in fact had the courage to kill him and that, not in the darkness of her bed, but in the reality of this bright morning she could remember the thrill of killing him. Yet she would not shoot a stag; David was the proper prey to her hunting; she was squeamish before a pair of proud antlers. David had grunted when he rutted, but she had heard the roaring of the rutting stag. She did not want these thoughts; she did not know what she wanted.

She knew only that she did not want to be there. She felt a wave of anger towards Anni and Ben who were probably her favourite people in the world. They had bullied her out here, so craftily that she had not even detected the pressure; they and Hester had outmanoeuvred her, and exposed her to the wide skies and cool wind. She turned her head, lifted her left hand, ready to lean across Anni, tap Hester on the shoulder and ask to be let out, to be allowed to walk down, walk home. The Land-rover stopped. For a moment she thought it had done so at her whim. Then she realised that they had already pulled off the track. Duncan switched the engine off and there was a long moment of silence. The three of them in the back relaxed the muscles that had held them in place against the jolting. Ben and Anni both leaned forward, their elbows on their knees, looking for one moment remarkably alike.

Hester climbed down from the front seat and Clare could hear her, almost feel her, so near, as she walked along the side of the Land-rover to release the tailgate so they could get out. Those parts of Hester above the waist appeared suddenly across the open back cutting off the sunlight.

There was a pause.

'Come on, Mummy,' said Ben.

The pause went on.

Hester smiled at Clare, tenderly but meaningfully. Clare's hand was still fixed round the top of the tailgate. She blushed, deliberately relaxed and willed the hand to relax too. Nothing happened. The pause absorbed assorted emotions: Clare's frustrations, Hester's pity, Ben's irritation, Anni's – Anni's what? – curiosity perhaps, or disinterest. Clare remembered that she had turned The Hand off, deliberately, in order to make her life easier. Could it be feeling malicious glee if it was turned off, was without power? She was muddled and flustered. She could not find the subcutaneous – sub-plastic – button. She fumbled, increasingly awkward, increasingly cross. Duncan appeared round the other side of the Land-rover and stood watching her. Even after she had found and pressed the switch it took a measurable few seconds before she could persuade The Hand to let go of the metal strut.

'Relax,' Hester said firmly.

Ben twitched and looked away.

Suddenly it worked. For no apparent reason her arm lifted off the tailgate; Duncan undid the bolt on his side and Hester followed suit. The tailgate dropped noisily and they all moved, shifting, relaxing.

'Sorry,' said Clare, but she did not feel sorry, she felt ashamed and angry.

'Darling,' said Hester consolingly.

Ben, as though to apologise for his twitching, became dynamic and responsible, sorting out the stuff from the floor. Anni swung her legs over the now flat back of the Land-rover, pulled her boots on and began to lace them. Clare, still in her floppy trainers, climbed down and walked away from the others and stood with her back to them looking down over the loch. It was, now and always, achingly familiar and always changing; the light, shifting as though in the breeze, altered the whole aspect, the tone, the flavour, from moment to moment. Today it was bright and innocent, dancing, uncaring about her shame. Shame. She had so many things to be ashamed for and none of them, none of them, gave her that stomach-churning, sweaty embarrassment that The Hand could and did inflict on her.

She concentrated on the view: how softly the hill met the water the other side of the long narrow loch; how strongly the clump of trees which surrounded Skillen, the lodge itself, contrasted with the rest of the naked muted landscape; how strange that people should first have stripped away the natural trees from these folded hills, and then planted unnatural ones down beside the loch, in precisely the same place where they would not have grown naturally. From her high perch on the mountainside she could see the trees, but not the long low house; the southern end was hidden by the last folded spur of Ben Murdagh and the rest was wrapped in the trees, but she could see the white boathouse, the white game larder and the green lawn. Quite suddenly, as though she were the god of the mountain watching the antics of humanity, she saw Felicity and Alice walk across the lawn. They were too far away for details but it was obviously them and she waved.

Anni came up beside her. Her boots – which were in fact Louise's boots lent kindly for the day – laced, and her jeans tucked

257

into her socks. She had Hester's field glasses in her hands and raised them to watch Felicity and Alice far below them.

'Want a go?'

'No.' She heard her ungraciousness as though with her mother's ears and was sad at herself. 'Actually,' she said with an effort, 'it's too much hassle to focus them.' She raised The Hand with a little shrug.

'OK,' said Anni, sounding nonchalant. But she put her arm round Clare's shoulder. Her arm felt not heavy but solid, felt warm and sunny along her back.

Behind them, breaking the windy silence, they heard the confused noises of Duncan and Ben unloading the aga-cat.

Clare shifted her shoulders away from Anni's arm, and, feeling generous said, 'You could tie my boots for me.'

They walked back to the Land-rover together and she sat on its floor.

'It's the first time I've worn them since . . . since Africa.'

Anni accepted the gift without comment.

Putting on calf-length laced walking boots with three hands and no practice was not easy – they were both giggling by the time they got to the second pair of laces.

'Of course,' Anni said, 'your average parent does this daily.'

'We lack, dear sister, certain female accomplishments.'

'Thank God!'

'Annunciata Martha Kerslake, are you taking the name of God in vain?'

'Vanity of vanities. I am God.'

And both of them unconsciously looked round to make sure that Hester had not heard them. There was a tiny pause.

'Are you going to talk to us?' Anni asked almost casually.

'Probably,' Clare said.

Anni, with a flourish, tied the lace into a bow.

'Have you left me these boots in your will?'

Duncan was still busy getting them organised; he gave brisk instructions to Ben and appended a half-hearted 'please' to the ones he issued to Hester. He had a fierce joy for the day ahead. Whatever happened today it would be good stalking, because he had taught them to stalk. He knew they understood the love that he had for these hills. They weren't American tourists; they were people who would be gladder to see a ptarmigan couched in the flowing grass than they would to kill a royal stag too easily; they were people who, when he said 'do you see that stone, that big one over there?' would know where to look, would follow his lead and respond to his demands. He knew that Hester could shoot straight, not perhaps as straight as Louise or Tom but a fine shot, reliable and safe, and that Hester would walk as well as she could and keep her head down and say when she was exhausted. Donald had known Hester for the whole of his lifetime; she had been a young and beautiful woman when he had been a child, and now, at least one more time, he would take her out on his hills for her holiday treat and together they would find a deer for her to shoot and she would, as she always did, weep when the beast fell. His smile, though apparently general, was for her and she knew it.

Hester was amused by her own anomalies. She was a Labour-voting vicar's wife whose delight in killing had, despite her sixty-seven years, brought her up a steep hill to this wide view, to a day of tough walking, scrambling, crawling. She smiled now at Duncan, who still called her Lady Hester and whom she would not correct because it would destroy their friendship if she did. She smiled and knew her own joy and knew that it was a joy divided almost evenly between the joy of our Lady's Assumption into heaven, the sign of hope and the glory of the flesh, and the joy of the high clean wind and the long rifle nesting in its leather case. She could scarcely silence the song in her silent mouth, although she knew that Ben had ruined his career for a moment of foolishness that she could not begin to understand, and Anni lived a life that seemed bleaker than anything she could imagine, and Clare was locked in a world of nightmare and disintegration. Where did it come from, this praise? What she felt was only joy, was only glory,

> Then sings my soul, my saviour God to thee,
> how great thou art, how great thou art.

Why her? James laboured harder than she did, struggled with

issues of faith and morality and doctrine and ethics; and she who had seen, without knowing then what she had seen, a world aflame with bombs and death, had found in the shadows of death the vision of triumph that had sustained, sustained and amused, her for half a century.

Despite all the horrors of yesterday she could smile with a shared pleasure and a separate delight at Duncan, and assist him undoing the leashings of the aga-cat. The aga-cat was itself a dispensation from God. Out of the simple pleasure of knowing that it would not take too tiringly long, she said,

'Duncan, I'll walk up a bit; you can catch me up.'

'Want company, Mummy?' Anni asked.

She didn't. She wanted Anni and Clare to be together and she wanted Ben to help Duncan load the aga-cat. She wanted to walk a little way alone. She pulled on her jacket, and held out her hand for her binoculars. Anni shoved them back into their case and handed them to her mother; Hester slung them neatly round her neck and started up the hillside.

They followed not far behind her. Clare had never been in the aga-cat before and the sensation was peculiar: its engine was immensely powerful, she could feel it underneath her legs, but the body was so flimsy that it flexed itself with the contours of the land. Clare felt as though she were riding something alive; a great lizard, that humped itself over the rough hillside, swarming clumsily but steadily up almost vertical slopes and juddering its way over tussocks and rocks.

'Takes the rough with the smooth,' shouted Duncan, obviously proud of his toy. All their gear rode in it, and so did Clare, still delicate and unfit. After they had caught up with her, Hester climbed in; Anni was asked to get out at the steepest places and she and Ben walked up behind the machine, amused and tolerant.

It could take the rough with the smooth and so could she. Clare was perfectly aware that Ben and Anni had dragged her up the mountain, probably with Hester's connivance, to do her good. She ought to be grateful. She knew they loved her. The sick fear she felt was irrelevant; it was the pointless reaction of guilt. There was nothing to be afraid of.

Felicity had said, 'I'll make you a better offer. I'll surrender –

no, I'll give – Alice to her own people, to her own community, when you give yourself back to yours. She will stop wearing her hearing aid when you stop fooling yourself and us. When you can stand in front of me and tell me, in any language you choose, what happened to David on your mountain.'

Anni had said, 'Are you going to talk to us?' And she had answered, 'Probably.'

On the high plateau everything seemed clean and easy. When Duncan switched off the aga-cat motor there was a sudden silence and stillness, a hush until their ears caught up with quiet tones and movements. It was strange, the high flat place, covered with scree, stones swept flat by wind, and ground in places to gravel, almost to sand, with no signs of human habitation except the old bothy where, in Hester's father's and grandfather's day, the ponies had waited, protected from the wind, between carrying up the stalkers and carrying down the dead deer. Now it was only a pile of stones, little larger than the cairns that Duncan had erected to mark a path in case of a sudden mist. The view was wide, as wide as any they knew, except that from the side of Mount Nyangani Clare had seen as far as eternity; to the east, Cranach Head lifted itself above the nearer hills, and to the west they could see the sea, a sparkling line of light against the horizon.

'Look,' said Duncan: 'eagles.' And then, after a pause, 'not the lower ones, those are crows, hoodies; the two right up above the head.' Hester had her glasses out; Clare looked at the distant circling black shapes and wondered how any one could tell the difference, but she believed him absolutely; the two higher bird shapes were golden eagles. As children they had thought it lucky to see them. Perhaps it still was.

They had a discussion about where Duncan and Hester would go; so that the three of them could walk and not be in their way, and they arranged a time to meet.

'Or if you go down before we're back,' said Hester, 'leave a note in the aga-cat.'

Once there had been a muddle, once when they were ten and eleven Joseph and Ben had been left on the high hill.

'We won't walk far anyway,' said Anni decisively, 'and we'll stay this side. OK?'

Duncan and Hester walked off, Duncan already unbuckling the strap of his telescope. They would probably go southwards over the edge of the plateau and see what there was to see.

Clare, Ben and Anni watched them go.

'Of course,' said Ben, 'if we were up to our job we would whoop screaming and yelling across the hillside and shift every beast in Sutherland.'

'Hunt saboteurs,' agreed Anni. 'I don't know why, but I can never get away from resenting them. I know all about class privilege and animal rights and so on and so forth, but I still feel . . .'

'Don't start,' said Ben. 'We both know we ought to and we both know we aren't going to.'

'In Zimbabwe,' said Clare helpfully, 'I actually got convinced that the ivory ban wouldn't save elephants. Careful culling for reasonable profit was a better conservation policy.'

'This isn't careful culling, though,' said Ben.

'You were the one who said "don't start".'

They knew where they were going without discussion; an ancient, secret place for the three of them, a tiny sheltered fold of the hills where they dropped down steeply from the plateau, and from where, as they had discovered when children, you could see everything – Cranach Head, and a wide stretch of heather and way below Loch Gillad where they had all learned to fish, held in its cradle of hills, and beyond that the treetops of the narrow valley that fed the water down into the Big Loch above the house. They walked together, easily, not hurrying; the landscape changed abruptly from the strange flat hilltop into more expected highland scenery as they tipped over the edge and looked down on the world.

They came to their secret hollow and relaxed. When they had been young, before the aga-cat, it would take them most of the morning to climb up here. They would come not on stalking days, but on their own. Hester and James had let them, had encouraged them to roam. In Birmingham that freedom had not been possible. Their parents had never worried about broken legs or drowning, and at Skillen there were no other dangers. Not even farm machinery. 'Better drowned than duffers,' James had said. James had been brought up on a diet of children's adventure stories; Hester had been brought up by a Master of Foxhounds. Neither of them had anticipated the new urban terrors that beset their children: Skillen had been the magic place where those fears had gone away. Each morning, after breakfast, the kitchen table had been heaped with rolls and cheese and chocolate biscuits in silver paper wrappers, and apples. As soon as they were old enough to make their own picnic lunch they were old enough to eat it where they chose, so long as they could escape the burden of taking a smaller sibling with them.

Here they had played Kidnapped, and Escaping-from-Colditz, and John McNab; here they had spotted birds, identified wild flowers and muttered imprecations and curses on which ever members of their family were out of favour.

This particular bit of hill had been the place for the three of them. The patterns of intimacy within such a large family had always been complicated, shifting; but somewhere in their early teens the three of them had come to form a little grouping which had been strengthened when they had all been undergraduates in London together. There had always been other combinations too; the girls' place, where the four sisters had gone to escape the boys, had been up the other side of the river and the lochs, in the hills above the house. Joseph and Ben, later taking Tom with them, had gone off on their own to fish in one of the smallest of the high lochs towards Carnith. But at least once each summer holiday, and often more, from the time they had been nine or ten, Ben, Anni and Clare would make this particular climb to spend the day in this particular place. It was a fortress for them all, a place of safety.

Today, once again as it was in their three memories, it was sunny and warm in the hollow; the sky was blue, the eagles floated serenely round Cranach Head, and beyond that, low in the sky, five or six small white clouds broke the monotony of blue; something small and feathered broke the silence, not with a song but with a continuous chirping; they looked out and felt secure in the memory of childhood happiness. Clare knew perfectly well that Ben and Anni had plotted this, but she did not mind too much.

They did not shy away from the issue. 'We have,' said Ben, as though he felt it fair to make things clear, 'instituted ourselves as your inquisition.'

'Inquisition' had been their version of Truth and Dare; they had played it here before. Endlessly convicting each other of heresy. It was here, before they had left school, that Ben had told the two of them that he thought he was queer. The first women, the first members of his family. They had been impressed then by his courage, even though they had discussed the possibility between themselves years before.

'Who did the instituting?' Clare asked now, not aggressively, but with genuine curiosity. 'Are you Mummy's spies?'

The word was not kind, and Ben flinched from it, but they both knew what Clare meant.

'Not this time,' said Anni. 'We think perhaps Joseph was meant to do that in Mutare, when he went to get you. But you foiled him . . . her.'

'I think Daddy may be protecting you anyway,' Ben said with some bitterness. 'Like Mummy is protecting me.'

'Daddy is pretty furious with you, isn't he?'

'No,' said Ben, 'he's sad. I've proved a disappointment. I think Mummy is angrier. Or perhaps it's the other way round.'

'You'll have to talk to her,' said Anni. 'She can't bear it.'

'I'm not sure you're right. Actually, I tried this morning. What I have to be is ready to talk to her; I'm not sure she really wants to hear. I think it may be all right now.'

'Ben, why?' Clare asked.

'It's difficult to find a vocabulary to talk about sex to your son.'

'No, why did you do it?' Because if they were her inquisition she was allowed to ask too.

'I like sex,' said Ben. 'I like it best of all, when it comes to the crunch. I thought I could have sex and God, but if I have to choose I'll choose sex.' He grinned a small almost vulpine smile. 'I'll have to leave, I suppose, and God knows what I'll do – and I'll be sad about that, because I like the job, but I can't exactly regret it. I think I'm turning into a gay fundamentalist really: I don't want to replicate heterosexual joys any more – I want to develop our own; I want to . . . experiment, go to some limit, try out for real anything I can imagine. I don't know why, but it has taken a long time for me to get here and I don't want . . . I don't think I can just stop because I got caught.'

After a little pause he went on, 'That's why I couldn't tell Mummy, you know. She'd have welcomed a nice boyfriend, made him one of Us, incorporated him into her myth of family joy. She's such a fag-hag.'

'It's not altogether a myth, Ben,' Anni was not looking at him. 'Really it isn't. Here we all are, we come to drink at Mummy's fountain; we bitch about it, but we come. I don't know any one but us who still goes on a family holiday, let alone finds themselves sitting here on a mountain telling their siblings that they love sex more than they love God. We may all be a bit crazy, but it isn't just a myth. Or rather, as Mummy herself would say, myths are perfectly true in their own language.'

There was a silence, long enough for Clare to hear the small bird somewhere behind the rocks still cheeping.

'I'm sorry,' Anni said, 'I interrupted.'

'Well . . . you know when Ceci was baring her soul last night, I wanted to say, "that's what sex is for me." That, for me, is the place where the terrible beauty is born. It's the place, the language of risk and the place, the language of joy. No . . . all that is too pompous. It works, I like it. Of course the newspaper was a disaster. But I didn't choose it: it wasn't guilt or self-destruction, it was bad luck.'

'Yeh?'

'Oh piss off, Anni. Don't analyse me, you're as bad as the Bishop. How is anyone meant to know? Perhaps . . . oh, I don't know. I can't make the church, the Church of England anyway, work any more. I mean I like it and I like my job, but I can't make it work; it's not fun, it's not honest and it doesn't make sense . . . so maybe this was an easy way out. Saves me the effort of explaining to Mummy and Daddy why I was quitting. Saves me the effort of explaining to myself why I'm quitting actually, if I had quit, which I wouldn't have. But there isn't a place, a context anymore. Do you remember when we were kids, how much fun it was – the Walsingham National Pilgrimage, or any of the great high feasts, and everyone, well not Daddy of course, but so many of the clergy were gay and it wasn't a secret and no one bothered about it. But

265

now, it's all fuss and fuss and too much drink and not enough laughter. Everyone's embattled and defensive and mean-spirited and reactionary. The Catholics have retreated into a ghetto of their own; the evangelicals are seething with self-righteousness; and no one's having any fun, any joy, any glory. And where's the Gospel in all that?

'The gay bit hardly matters. So, maybe, feeling good about their generosity and nobility, Synod, or the bishops or whoever, will give some sort of grudging liberal permission for the poor old queers to have nice faithful loving relationships which look exactly like marriages without the children. But that isn't what I want – stable monotony. God, I loathe liberals, theological liberals I mean, and they're taking over.'

He laughed. Anni and Clare looked at him affectionately. Then they looked at each other and knew they were thinking the same thing. They laughed.

'It's not that funny,' said Ben, watching them quizzically.

They giggled.

'We want to see your nipple-ring.'

'Annunciata Kerslake!'

'Come on.'

'No. Absolutely not. No, you can't.'

'Please. Or we'll tickle you.'

Ben had always been extremely ticklish. When Joseph had first gone to secondary school and come back with an insufferable superiority, he had persuaded the three of them that there was a cure for being ticklish. All you had to do was let someone tickle you for fifteen minutes without stopping and then you would develop an immunity for ever. Ben, desperate for a cure, had let Joseph tie his hands and feet to the bed-end with their dressing-gown cords, and with his four little sisters watching Joseph had tackled this medical treatment with considerable relish. Ben's screams had brought Hester to the scene long before the first five minutes were up, and for years Joseph had insisted that if Ben had been able to keep quiet, it would have worked.

All three of them remembered, if not the actual event, then at least the repetition of its narration. They laughed now, and Ben blushed. Anni caught the blush and said,

266

'Want some more psychoanalysis?'

'Shut up.'

'Then show us your pierced flesh.'

'What will you give me?'

'My very best kept secret.'

'Is it worth it?'

'To you?' Anni considered the question. 'Yes, I should think so.'

Clare joined in. 'If you show us, I'll take my hand off and show you my scars.'

There was a pause; they were all aware that they were fooling around and at the same time they were tiptoeing on to dangerous ground.

'OK,' said Ben. 'You're on. But neither of you are ever to say that it was exhibitionism.'

They both knew at once that there was an element of that in it: he was proud of himself and wanted them to see.

'I had two done,' he said pulling off his jersey, 'so that you can put a chain between them, and so on and so forth, but one hole went septic and I had to take the ring out.' He unbuttoned his flannel shirt; the contrast between a nipple-ring and flannels and an elderly checked shirt gave them all an odd sensation.

Clare felt again the profound relief that David was dead and gone. She could imagine exactly what he would make of this: he would have despised Ben and found the whole thing profoundly titillating.

But it was not titillating at all. It was a small silver ring, slightly more solid than a hooped earring, and it had a rather pretty silver bobble to keep it in place. It went through the soft edge of Ben's areola at the very top of the nipple, just before it smoothed out into his chest. Nothing else had changed.

'Men's nipples are so weird,' Anni said, and with a delicate curiosity put out her finger and touched, not the nipple but the ring.

'It's pretty, Ben,' said Clare, but she was revolted. Her voice sounded like Joyce Grenfell's voice in the kindergarten teacher sketch. Ben started to re-button his shirt. She tried again, 'I don't know, somehow I feel that nipples belong to women; it's as though you were stealing something from us.' Her own nipples felt in need of protection suddenly, as though they would be pierced. She remembered how she had covered them in the train when Anni and she had talked about this, but there was still something she had to ask Ben, and it was now or never.

'Do you go in for that s/m stuff a lot?'

'Lay off, Clare.'

She ignored him, now was the moment for the beginning of her own confession. 'Because David and I did and I didn't like it. At all. Do you like it?'

'Yes,' he said, looking at her with sudden new eyes. 'Yes, I do.' Then, embarrassed, he disappeared into his jersey again. When he emerged he continued as though there had been no break,

'I should think it's different with straight people, because of the social power that men have.' She realised he had given it some thought; that they could, and would, talk about it more some other time.

He said, 'Now it's Anni's turn. And after that you'll have to come clean.'

Anni had prepared herself.

'I'm a virgin,' she said.

'Anni!'

They really were shocked, not in the sense of repelled but in the sense of surprised.

'I'm the only thirty-seven-year-old virgin in Britain,' she tried to laugh, but could not quite pull it off.

'Except for Ceci, of course.'

Ben meant this to be comforting somehow, but Anni grinned ruefully and said, 'She's not.'

'Anni!' and 'What?'

'She told me, but you mustn't tell her I told you.'

'But Anni, what about Morag?' Clare asked.

'Who's Morag?' Ben asked.

'A friend of mine,' Anni said, 'but, Clare, she was never my lover.'

'I'm sorry. I just assumed . . .'

'So did I, actually, for quite a long time, but she wasn't. She would have been, maybe; it was me. At the beginning the women's movement let me off sleeping with men, and then I thought, like you seem to have done, that I was a dyke. And then I realised that I wasn't and then, what with people thinking that, and me thinking that, I never quite found the opportunity, got around to it. And it's only quite recently that I've realised . . . and I've never told anyone . . . I was going to tell Ceci, because I thought it was something she had learned to deal with, I mean at least the curiosity and sense of loss bit, and then she told me . . .'

'Who?'

'Not telling. No one we know.'

'It was worth the nipple-ring,' Ben said, 'a real confession, a real secret.'

They were pleased with Anni for telling them, they were pleased with themselves because she had wanted to tell them.

Anni said, 'I have this theory about us. I mean all seven of us. When things develop, like people do, in highly complex ways, enormous differences in output can emerge from the minutest differences in input. This is what's called the "butterfly wing and the weather forecast problem". It's also perhaps a good image for children of the same parents, the same upbringings, almost the same ages. We all started in almost exactly the same place and we've ended up worlds apart. Our lives, so close and intimate once, have diverged, you see, and only recognising the chaotic nature of development can allow us to come together. Sensitivity to initial conditions, it's called, or non-linearity.'

They all laughed, because this was such an Anni-like thing to say, and at the same time it did indeed make them feel closer. On a wave of mutual approval and warmth Ben and Anni turned to Clare.

'Clare?'

'I don't know. Honestly, I don't know.'

'Tell us,' Anni said. They were leaning against the rock; it was very quiet, but not silent, the wind moving the grass.

'Tell us slowly, from the beginning.' She did not look at Clare, but at the eagles over Cranach Head.

'I don't know the beginning,' Clare said. 'I don't know where to begin.'

Once long ago there was a big bang. Fifteen billion years ago,

Anni said. A singularity, where the laws of physics break down; and before that big bang there was no before, except the everlasting deep chuckle of a God who had smashed nothingness into matter. Was that when the hydrogen that made her bones learned the triumph of violence? learned that risk is the other name for beauty? Was that her beginning?

Once long ago there was a big bang. Thirty years ago. On a crisp November evening when you could smell the coming frost hunting the swallows southwards. She had knelt on the broad window seat, chilly with excitement. Her first mother had advanced into the middle of the lawn and lit the fuse. She had retreated, stood beside her husband against the laboratory wall. When the pause ended all heaven broke loose; there were stars, and flames, new galaxies exploding into brightness; the window shattered, cold glass diamonds joining the hot fire ones. In a flash of sulphur lightning she saw them embrace, and explode. She had watched her parents explode in a cloud of stars. But she had also seen their fiery embrace, their wild smiles. They had found the display worth the risk. Was it then that she learned that beauty and danger walk hand in hand and cannot be separated? Was that her beginning?

Once long ago there had been a big bang. The promise of a big bang. Twelve years ago. Early in the morning of what was preparing to be a fiercely bright August day, high on a steep hillside in southern Umbria. She and Julia had stood looking down into the vast dead volcano; looking across at Orvieto perched high on its tufa plug, escaping gently from the morning mists; the civilised city that weighs down the ancient powers of fire and lava, holds them in, clamps them down. 'When we make love,' Julia had said, playfully, 'the volcano will wake up, and throw off that mingy little city, hurl it through the air as a firework display just for you and me.' She had smiled her slow smile and turned towards Clare, but Clare had been terrified; had fled down the hillside, escaped the bright morning, left the country, fled the promise of beauty, fled the dangerous joy. Was it then that she turned her back on risk and sought only safety? Had that turning been the moment of loss, not just of joy but of truth? Had that been her beginning?

'Clare,' Anni said patiently, but inexorably, still watching the distant circling of the birds around the shoulder of the dark mountain. 'Begin with that morning. Begin where you can remember.'

'No,' said Clare, 'I won't begin with that morning, I'll begin the day before. We left Peggy's, with Peggy's car, because she thought a four-wheel drive would be better.'

This was quite a safe place to start, the safest she had found. In this narrative they appeared securely as a young couple on holiday, thoughtfully visiting an old friend of her mother's.

'We'd been planning to go to a hotel, but we changed our plans. Peggy said that we ought not to do it that way, that if we were going to Nyanga we should stay in one of the lodges, on the dams; these little hermitage huts. We both looked a bit blank – I mean David and I aren't exactly the camping types, but Peggy insisted that these lodges weren't like that. And, as we discovered, she was entirely right, they're clean and lovely and well equipped. Well, Peggy is a bit like Mummy, you know, when she "lays one on you", it stays laid. And then Joyful began to talk about the mountains and the magic of them, and somehow we gave in and Peggy organised it all.

'We drove down from the escarpment, nearly as far as Birchenough Bridge and then climbed again, up to Mutare, which is a pretty town surrounded by big hills, very wide and spacious. It was a very hot day, not comfortable for driving. And in Mutare we went to the supermarket – I didn't like Zimbabwean supermarkets, they smell strange and musty, but we had to buy food and drink, although as a matter of fact Peggy and her household had equipped us pretty well. We had tea in this most unexpected café; it was like . . . it was just like a tea shoppe in a cathedral close, you know with lots of bits of craftwork for sale, all slightly badly made: macramé and doilies. It made us laugh.

'And then we drove north, climbing all the time, through this high rocky hillscape, and then higher still the land opened up.

'It was an extraordinary evening, the sun was setting gently; there were these sharp-profiled mountains, hard and harsh, and then in contrast the sky was soft, soft coloured and there were low clouds sort of nesting in shoulders and crevices of the hills,

271

and above us there were clouds of all sorts, all mixed in together blue grey and beige grey and very white fluffy ones, laid out in bands. We arrived in the park and signed in and they showed us to this lodge.

'It was lovely; a square thatched building beside a lake, with a lot of space and a log fire, and a huge window looking over the lake. After supper some amazing tiny frogs came out on the walls, little tree frogs with black backs and intricately patterned with red and white, but when they move their upper legs are luminous, bright, almost neon pink, translucent. One of them climbed up the windowpane, so that you could see it from underneath, and it was pale and had pink suckers on each toe. I took a whole bunch of pictures, tight close-ups, just for the pure pleasure of it. I got the mirror from the bathroom and tried to arrange it so that I could take their backs and their fronts at the same time – through the window, if you see what I mean. It was fiddly, because I'd get the mirror in place and then I had to run round, out the door to the other side and the frogs would have moved, or the mirror would turn out not to be in exactly the right place. Finally I got David to come and help; he held the mirror in the kitchen. It was fun. We were happy.

'Apart from the warthogs, those pictures were the last I'll ever take; the last I've got anyway. I ought to get them developed; they came back with the rest of my stuff. I don't know why I haven't done them, any of the ones that came back from Zimbabwe. They might be quite good, some of them anyway, and there must be other things on the same roll, now I think about it, that I took at Peggy's.'

She might, she realised with a sort of excitement, have pictures of Joyful. She probably had pictures of David; last pictures of David that she did not want. But she could stomach a picture of David for the unbelievably virulent and shocking pink of the frogs' little sucker feet and Joyful squatting on the veranda going over Chimurenga for ticks.

'Go on, Clare.'

'And then in the morning, I mean the next morning . . .'

In between there was also the night, the last night they had ever slept together; she remembered David pushing the beds together

272

to make a double out of the two singles provided. He had even turned the mattresses round, at right angles to the frames. She had not wanted him to; she had been hot and tired and still engaged with her frog pictures. David never let anything like that deter him.

'The next morning, David was in driving mood. In a hurry. Sometimes he was in such a hurry. I wanted to stay in bed, he wanted to eat up the whole world. And of course he was right; it was a wonderful day, and we went and swam under Nyagombe Falls, so early that we felt no one else in the world was awake. Actually the Zimbabweans are very good about tourism, about not exploiting natural resources, but it doesn't change the fact that all the other places we'd been – the Victoria Falls, and Matopos, and Great Zimababwe – are world tourist attractions, but Nyanga Park is different. There is a posh hotel, built around Rhodes' own country house, but these lodges are mostly for Zimbabweans, and there isn't any fuss, that was why Peggy arranged for us to get one. Anyway at Nyagombe Falls we felt we were the only human beings around. The water was powerful and cold.

'I wanted to stay, to swim and lie in the sun. David wanted to climb Nyangani, right then and there. We didn't have a fight about it because once David was in that mood there was nothing to do except give in with as much grace as possible.'

Because she could not face his anger, his scorn, his capacity to withdraw from her that left her cold inside. She could never do it. No matter how angry he made her, she could never go away, never escape into herself the way he could. In seven years she was the one, always, to apologise when they argued. It humiliated her. She would set her will against it; she would sit in whichever room in the flat he had left her and repeat almost dully to herself 'this time he can apologise, this time he can apologise. I've got nothing to apologise for, this time he can apologise.' He never did; and she always did, because if she didn't he might stop loving her and although she had long ago stopped loving him, still she needed him to love her, want her, desire her. That was why, although Ben had not asked her, that was why she consented to do things with him that she did not enjoy. She was glad he was dead. She pushed all her weight into that gladness because it would enable her to go on with the story.

'We had to report to the Parks Officer at Rhodes Dam. It was just after eleven o'clock then. It's in his book. I signed for both of us, because David was looking at the map. They checked it afterwards.'

This was as far as she had ever got, this painstaking detail. When she had told Joseph, told Peggy, told the police in Mutare, she always stopped there, with those neat signatures in the book. Her signing both their names and David across the room peering at the wall-mounted map. It was the final point of reality. Those two neat names in her handwriting. David Holland. Clare Kerslake. 11.05 2nd February. The Feast of Candlemass, of the Purification.

After that, she had said she could not remember, she could not remember anything else. But it was not true. It had been true at first, which is why she had stopped there, but she knew that she could remember more, and now, in these other highlands, she went on, very slowly, with a lot of effort, but helped by the careful listening of her brother and sister.

'In fact, we got delayed. We found I hadn't brought enough film, so we went back to our lodge; and then on the drive to the foot of the mountain we kept seeing things – kudu buck and strange birds, and a warthog family: two parents and their piglets. They were on the road and when we came round the corner . . . they stood for a moment and stared at us. The adults are spectacularly ugly, but the babies are little with yellow stripes, enchanting, just like piglets but furry. Suddenly they took fright and streamed away in a line, all five tails held high and waving like flags. They ran straight down the road in front of us for a couple of hundred yards. I leaned out of the car and took a picture of them on the new film. They were lovely. It was a last happy thing.

'We were getting later and perhaps driving too fast and then the car got stuck. We were driving along what looked like a perfectly dry bit of road, and suddenly at the bottom of the slope the car shook and stopped and when I climbed out to see what the trouble was I went over my ankles in yellow road-coloured mud. One back and one front wheel were sunk to the axle.

'I was a bit scared, because we had only seen one other car all day and the area is completely isolated, but David wasn't; he was superbly efficient. He shoved stuff under the wheels, but they kept sinking and we pushed and struggled. We did wonder what would happen if we couldn't get the car out and how long it would be before anyone passed by, because of course we weren't meant to be there. I mean, they would have thought that we'd gone straight to the mountain when we left the office, and they would have worried that we got lost on the mountain and not where we actually were. We laughed about it.

'Anyway, we did get out in the end. On one of those final slightly despairing efforts before you decide that you might as well start walking, there was a grinding sort of squidge noise and the car started moving. We were both a bit fraught by then. And also late. It was just before three when we got to the foot of the mountain.'

Rule no. 11. Do not attempt climb after 1430 hours, minimum time to beacon and return is 3 hours. It was the first one they broke.

'I wanted to wait; I thought we could just as easily climb the next day, but David insisted, said I was being silly, that we were both very fit and had no children with us and the weather was perfect and anyway no one would ever know.

'Then we realised that I'd left David's jacket in the lodge. David felt that it didn't matter, and given how sunny the day was he did have a point, but I felt the whole expedition was beginning to seem doomed. So we were annoyed with each other from the outset'

Rule no. 9. Ensure you have suitable protective clothing and necessities irrespective of prevailing conditions.

'So we set out. For some reason, the altitude perhaps, I felt dreadful for the first half-hour, breathless, wobbly, panting and shaky. I thought that I could not go on and I didn't want to say so because David would think I was sulking.

'I'll tell you something very peculiar: that bit about feeling ill, I remembered yesterday, quite clearly but without remembering any of the stuff either side of it. I mean, I remembered exactly what it was like and how dreadful I felt, and this great surging feeling of panic. But yesterday I remembered it in isolation, because very soon all that went away, and I felt good too; and it was stunningly beautiful.

'The path was well marked, but rocky and steep; it went round a little kopje and then up beside a swift stream, a waterfall really. It was very clear; each time we paused we could see further and further – further probably than I have ever seen before. There were mountains behind mountains, navy blue in the longest distance, and furthest away of all there was a narrow gap between the horizon of hills and a low band of clouds, and I had this sense that through that gap you could see eternity, I mean you could see for ever.

'Then after about an hour's hard walking we came to the top of that section, to a ridge, and we went over it into this almost flat hollow. The first of the three ascending crests of the mountain was on our right, with the others beyond it, all made of these vertical shivered split rocks. I heard a distant, very distant roll of thunder. It was miles way but . . . but I am frightened of thunder – you know I'm frightened of thunder, and David always thought it was silly.'

They knew she was frightened of thunder. When they had all been little, whenever there was thunder, almost as soon as the very first roll had died away Anni would be in her bed with her; her arms around her, hugging her tight and safe.

'I wanted not to be there, in that lush declivity, where it was totally silent, totally windless and we couldn't see out. It was very, very wet underfoot, the path vaguely following a stream, and there was long flowering grass and huge flat rocks. It was strange in that meadow, very hot and very still; it was hard to keep a sense of time and even harder to discipline oneself to stay on the path, although it was well marked with painted arrows and little yellow-painted cairns. We both kept having the feeling there must be other, better routes and also that if we left the hollow there would be a fabulous view.

'I was in a strange mood, a sort of anxiety state, partly because of the thunder –'

Rule no. 7. Do not attempt ascent if low cloud, mist or rain in vicinity.

' – and partly . . . well, the day before, Joyful, this friend of Peggy's, had been telling us that the mountain was haunted by ancestral spirits, and I found myself beginning to believe it.

'On this plateau, this meadow, there were really strange plants, very bright colours. Some things called protea, which are weird. I thought I'd take a picture of a clump of them and I got down really close and then I thought that if I could just twist a couple of stems round it would make a better composition and I tried to do that and one of the flowers broke off in my hand. And at that very moment there was another clap of thunder.'

Rule no. 14. No fires, plant picking or litter please.

'I know this sounds stupid, but it panicked me. I really did not want to go on with the climb. I became convinced I could hear someone on the mountain.'

She had heard Chirikudzi singing. She did not think she could tell Anni and Ben about that even here. As they walked across the meadow, the basin beneath the peaks, after she had picked the flower and heard the distant thunder, she had heard a low humming; not far away, but from no visible source, perhaps behind a rock or in a yet unseen chasm, a quiet humming, but wild, not unlike the freedom songs that Joyful had sung. She heard more very distant rolls of thunder. It was too strange in that meadow, very hot and very still. And, in the echo of the distant thunder she heard the soft singing.

'David,' she had said urgently, but her voice had come out in a whisper. 'David, what's that?'

'What's what?' his voice sounded too loud, vulgar.

'Shh. That singing.'

'There's no singing,' but he had lifted his head up and listened. 'There's no singing.' He had smiled, but he had not looked at her. He had heard the singing, she thought, he had heard it and known it was Chirikudzi the mermaid spirit calling to him. Chirikudzi stole people who crossed her path; she stole them away and they disappeared, they could not be found. Usually they were never found again, but sometimes they loved her and learned from her and if she let them return, after many many years, they knew the mysteries and could see visions and became great N'angas. Joyful had told her so. She had heard Chirikudzi singing and had known that she was not singing for her, but for David, that in this bright clear meadow with the sun high overhead and their shadows small and craven at their feet Chirikudzi would come and take David away and give him love and power and she, Clare, would be left alone on the mountain in the face of the hunting storm which would first darken the blue sky and then illuminate the darkness with flashes of lightning. Chirikudzi was singing.

'Singing?' David had said. 'Clare, I think you're cracking up. Don't be silly.'

She didn't believe him. He saw her disbelief and misunderstood it. He grinned.

Clare was crying; she felt the stinging in her eyes of impotence and anger and fear. Then David took her arm, 'Come on, darling, pull yourself together. I hope you're not getting sunstroke.'

'I want to go down.'

'Don't be silly, of course you don't,' but he looked worried, uncertain. The thunder had rolled again, and perhaps it had sounded nearer. He had glanced around as though for inspiration.

Then, 'Look, look there's the summit.'

Quite undeniably there, rising above them, still some distance away but clear and visible through the crevices and cuts of splintered rocks was the tall post marking the summit. Cheered up, he had smiled at her.

'I know it's bloody hot and a bit oppressive here, but if we start climbing we'll catch the breeze.' He turned away from her towards the climb.

She said, 'David, I don't want to climb any more. Please. I really want to go down. Please can we go down. Please.' She hated the whine in her voice. He was humiliating her, forcing her to beg and plead.

'Don't be ridiculous. I'm going up. If you don't want to, you can walk down on your own, or just sit there until I get back. Suit yourself.' And he turned away from her and started to walk on, all on his own.

Rule no. 1. No lone person to attempt ascent.

She did not believe he would do it. She stood still and waited for him to turn around, to recognise her real fear, but he went doggedly on, scrambling into the rocks that were made of vertical splinters, huge ragged rock faces. She was disordered, scared by the thunder and by the insistent singing, too scared to be able to endure his anger. She could not bear it, and after about five minutes she called to him to wait and scrambled after him. He paused, turned and smiled; once he had his own way he would forgive and forget with astonishing ease.

She took up the tale again. 'We plodded on and gradually the land opened out to the east, vast cliffs and rolling barrenness and pinnacled rocks, which was Mozambique. Then the route got rockier, not climbing, but scrambling at least. I could still hear, or thought I could hear the thunder, and I almost persuaded David that we should go down again and then through these broken fragmented piles of rock face we saw the summit marker, really not far away and I was convinced, and we had a happy scramble to the very top and sat there content on the summit of the world.

'It was magnificent. Gloriously clear and well below us we could see Pongwe Gorge filled to overflowing with dense white mist, a long strip of soft whiteness. David and I drank juice and ate biscuits and felt pleased with ourselves.'

She looked at Ben, suddenly curious, 'I wonder why I was so certain that the warthogs were the last pictures I took? Why didn't I take any pictures of us at the summit? It was the sort of thing we would do. I'd set the self-timer and we'd take pictures of ourselves together. We did it at the Victoria Falls, and at Rhodes' grave in Matopos. But I didn't, I'm absolutely sure that I didn't, and I wonder why.

'Anyway, west and south of us the mountain was almost vertical and way below us there were valleys laid out with their rivers green and smoky, we had a bird's-eye view like a geography diagram. Looking east and north the land remained much higher and more desolate and we could see other mountains, challenging the superiority of ours. It had not been a harsh climb; a good hard walk and a little scrambling, that's all. We almost wondered what the fuss was about. There was a cold, hard wind that felt fresh and lovely. Suddenly a cloud which had appeared from nowhere blotted out the sun and looking at the mountains on the Mozambique side it seemed horribly easy to believe in the MNR bandits, to believe in the dangers of the weather, little tiny wisps of cloud, like in baroque paintings, that you can't take very seriously, were flittering around the mountains obscuring them for moments. They looked pretty, tender, not at all sinister.

'We started to come down. We had reached the meadow that I described before; it was still hot, and somehow ominous. I looked back towards the mountain top – to remind me, I think, of the cool wind – and it had vanished. It was still quite clear and even bright in our hollow, but we could see nothing outside it.

'I said that we ought to go down as quickly as possible, but David insisted there was no problem, that there was no mist where we were and so it would be all right; that there was no hurry.'

Rule no. 8. If enveloped in mist whilst on the mountain make immediate descent via indicated track.

'Then the mist came down very suddenly. We were both alarmed by the mist. Then there was more thunder, louder, nearer. I kept thinking I could hear other people somewhere, but David thought I was being silly. I felt a kind of panic. I wanted to believe there was something in the world outside the hollow. But I also wanted to stay still, to do what we had been told.

'David was angry. I wanted to hold his hand and he thought that was idiotic. He thought I was childish to be frightened, and suddenly he shouted, like a school kid, he shouted at the mountain,

' "Fuck off you stupid bitch, you can't scare me" and he laughed.'

Rule no. 15. Do not mock, insult or abuse the mountain.

'He was laughing at me really. He did it because I was frightened of the mountain; and because I had told him that Joyful said we had to treat it with respect. He was in a strange mood; I think perhaps he was a bit scared himself, because he suddenly said he would leave the path and climb up the edge of the basin and look over to see how far the mist went.'

Rule no. 5. Follow the track indicated by yellow cairns and painted arrows to beacon and return by same route.

Rule no. 6. Do not leave track to explore as danger of quick-sands, concealed crevices and potholes.

Rule no. 7. Do not attempt ascent if low cloud, mist or rain in vicinity.

'There was more thunder. I think I asked him not to go. He

picked up a rock and threw it into the mist and when we heard it bounce a little way out he walked away from me into the fog and I could not see him.'

Rule no. 4. All members of parties to be within sight of each other at all times on the mountain.

'I shouted after him. I couldn't bear it. I wanted him to come back and he wouldn't. He called for me to come to him and I was crying.

'I went with him though, because of the thunder, because I did not want to be alone in the thunder. It wasn't far, and also like him I wanted to be able to see. I felt trapped in that sinister valley and all the butterflies had vanished. We walked less than ten yards and then the path had disappeared; the virulent yellow cairns all vanished. It was a strange sort of mist, unnatural, like something in a movie; there's perfect light wherever you actually are, everything seems extremely clear and precise: lichen on rock and rough grass; and then even a couple of yards away the world is cut off. There is nothing outside your little circle, nothing visible, but there are voices, the voices of thunder and the grass growing and then . . . we did not walk far. I was getting hysterical, stupid, I don't know why. David held my hand. Suddenly less than a yard away from us there was nothing; a shift of air, of mood, I don't know what and we were looking down a fissure at rocks like knives. I could hear voices, and thunder, and David's anger and this bottomless, knife-edged fissure. I couldn't understand what the voices were saying. I noticed a tiny jewel-red beetle on the back of my hand.

'I can quite clearly remember the jewel-red beetle; the thunder; the voices and the bottomless hole in the mountain that had opened to greet us.

'And then . . . I can't remember. Honestly I can't remember anything else.'

She was crying now, with the memory of the jewel-red beetle, the thunder, the voices and the bottomless hole in the mountain that had opened to greet them, welcoming them, there at their feet, the cliffs of fall.

She was crying with the effort of trying to remember, the strain of not being able to remember; crying for the fear, the enormous engulfing inescapable fear, the taste of which was in her mouth, now, still, as bright and blood flavoured as it had been then, as though she were about to throw up.

Anni and Ben did not help her. They sat silent, waiting beyond her tears and her terrors.

'I can't remember,' she said again, and she could hear the undertone of sulkiness in her own voice. She tried again to force the pathos so they would forgive her, love her.

'I can't remember.'

Still they said nothing.

She heard the little bird again as though nothing had happened, as though it did not care. She looked down at The Hand which kept its own secrets. She hated it. As though in response to her hatred, although perhaps really in response to the tensing of her left hand, which curled smoothly into a tight fist, The Hand's finger and thumb twitched together a little, slowly; a little jerk and then a pause.

She remembered that David had killed the chameleon.

Anni and Ben both shifted slightly as though they too were jerked by the power of her hatred. The bird kept up its silly cheeping, which suddenly became irritating to her, and she said,

'I've remembered something. I haven't remembered what happened next, but I have remembered why I wanted him to be dead. Why I wanted to kill him.'

She realised that she had never said that before, to anyone; that she had wanted to kill him. She had wanted him to be dead and he was dead. That was why she was afraid she had killed him.

'I told you that the car got stuck in this yellow mud. I forgot that we had a fight about it. We were on our way to the mountain and getting later and perhaps driving too fast and then the car got stuck. I told you that.

'David knew precisely what to do; he found a spade in the back of the car; he ordered me to gather grass and bush to wedge under the wheels. He made me drive and he was angry with me because he thought I revved too hard or not hard enough. Then he thought he could do it better than me, and he ordered me out of the car, and of course the moment he got behind the steering wheel, the car dragged itself out of the mud, reluctantly, slowly, but victoriously.'

She had been frightened and relieved and angry and shame-faced. She remembered all these emotions vividly. She had been suffocating with them all. Trying to breathe calmly, she walked a few paces along the road in front of the car, pretending to check for more mud. And she saw the chameleon.

'After we got the car out,' she said now, 'I walked a little way up the road checking for more mud, making sure it was solid. And I saw a chameleon. I didn't see it until my boot was almost crushing it.'

She looked down at her boots which, unlike The Hand, had been in Africa with her. She looked at their neat lacing. The once black paint on the eyelet rings, fixed into the leather to hold the laces, had chipped off in places so that here and there the rings shone with tiny stars. Everything had slowed down, so that she could notice the way even those minute scraps of clear metal could catch the sun and twinkle.

She spoke slowly, as though the words were heavy, as though she was having to drag them up from a pit that was filled with intolerable noise, each word a victory against the clamour.

'I almost crushed it; so abruptly did I stop the forward movement of my leg that I nearly over balanced. I can remember it absolutely. I had wanted so much to see one, someone had told me about them, and there it was.'

She had not seen it sooner because she had not been looking and because it was, as in every legend, so beautifully camouflaged. It did not deign to notice her, and it was yellowish with orange patches perfectly matched to the sandy yellow road. It walked as if wound up, a clockwork toy and not a very sophisticated one, each forward movement a jerk with a discernible pause between it and the next one. It had strange feet; as it picked them up they looked quite ordinary, narrow, appropriate, but as they jerked on to the ground with each step they split in two, spreading out to 180 degrees, making a perfect T, and each end of the crossbar had its own fringe of tiny claws. It had strange eyes too, with which it either looked at her or did not: each eyeball was enormous, like half a ping-pong ball, but covered in wrinkled skin in the middle of which floated, independent like a black dot on oil, a tiny bright pupil. When she touched it, its tail spiralled up in a crotchety movement not unlike an ancient and not very nice old lady. It was without grace. Joyful had told her that chameleons were ill-omened; taboo – hated and therefore untouched. They had caused the Fall; before the ancestors were established in their lands, before the spirits moved to their graves and the hearts of their N'angas, the Great Spirit had sent a chameleon with a vital message, but it had so creaked and dawdled upon its way that the message did not arrive in time and disaster struck like good rains; everything is immediately changed. It was a disaster so total and violent that no one now knew what had happened. Clare's chameleon looked evil, looked as though disaster would please it and make its tiny eyes shine brighter in their discoordinated wanderings about their little globes.

Joyful had also told her that the chameleon was called *Hamba Gahle* – the traditional parting words in Sindebele, which mean 'go slowly, gently', unhurried as the chameleon goes.

She had squatted down to look at it more closely, and became aware that David was standing behind her watching too.

'Come on,' he said, 'we'd better get a move on.'

She knew he was still wound up about the car and the growing lateness; so she had not even suggested photographing the chameleon to contrast with the wall frogs of the night before.

They got into the car, its engine still running, its passenger-side wing thick with the yellow mud; she realised that she had left him to put away the spade and sheets of sacking. She was looking at his face, trying to gauge how irritated he actually was, and she saw nothing of his intention on it. He had to swerve the car only slightly and the squashing of the creature on the soft road made less of a bump than the road surface itself.

'David!'

He did not answer her.

'David, for God's sake why? It's taboo, it's dangerous.'

She knew it was a stupid thing to say. He accelerated the car and she thought perhaps he was waiting for her to comment on her own stupidity; but he was watching the road, sensibly keeping to the middle of it, driving with skill and concentration. The insect bites on her ankles felt sweaty and very itchy. She wished with a simple clarity that they did not have to climb the mountain that afternoon. She wished he was dead.

'It was only a lizard,' he said.

'Then, when we got back into the car, David ran it over. He did it quite deliberately, coldly, and I was furious. I was so angry that I wished he were dead.'

'Wishing isn't doing,' said Ben.

'Why?' asked Anni. 'Why did you mind so much? I mean, I can see it was a shitty thing to do, but it's not that bad, is it? Why did it make you want to kill him?'

'Oh,' said Clare, surprised. 'No, it isn't, is it?' She paused, thoughtfully. 'I think I can tell you why. But it's a long story.'

'We've got all day,' said Ben, smiling.

'Do you remember the other night when we were watching the shooting stars and I ran away suddenly? I had to get away because they reminded me of how my parents died.'

'Mummy and Daddy always said it was an accident.'

'It was an accident. They blew themselves up with some fireworks they were making which went wrong. Mummy and Daddy never kept that from me; but the thing is, I was watching them, I saw it happen, and they were laughing.'

'Clare!'

'It's OK, Ben. The point is I remembered just how beautiful it had been; how beautiful and how exciting. I'd never remembered that before. Well, do you remember when I came back from Italy, the last time, in a bit of a state?'

'And you wouldn't tell me why . . . I bloody well do,' said Anni.

'I fell in love with someone,' she paused for a moment, but knew she would go on. 'She was wonderful. Julia, her name was.'

Clare could tell from the stillness in both her brother and sister that they were registering this, considering a brand new fact about her.

'I lost my nerve,' Clare said. 'It wasn't just because she was a woman, though I dare say that was part of it. Something I wasn't supposed to do, not in the book. I always wanted to keep the rules, to be normal, to be safe. But it wasn't just that. She was . . . she was crazy.'

'Insane?'

'No. Wild.' She could suddenly hear James's hesitancy in the study the day before, looking for a word to describe her first father; 'a wizard', he'd said, 'a wizard, somehow magical'. Now she said,

'She was magic. A witch.'

How could she describe Julia? The complete lack of discretion, the enormous and wild passion, the huge demands, the dangerous driving will. Perhaps she was insane; she certainly had an unerring sense for other people's vulnerability and an excessive need for extreme responses. She had demanded too much; she had wanted perfect concentration, a high romanticism that was intoxicating but dangerous. How could she describe her own desire? An obsessive kind of lust; she had feared that giving in to it would destroy her, would be too much pleasure for her to bear.

'I did love her,' she said now, and knew that it was absolutely true, 'but I lost my nerve. She wanted too much; she wasn't safe. I wasn't safe when I was around her. She was like Alice; you know the way that Alice can concentrate perfectly, shut everything else out. She played for stakes too high for me. She was a preposterous risk-taker.'

One night, about three in the morning when they had both been drunk, coming home from a party, they had come upon the Trevi Fountain, turned off for the night, and Julia had suddenly slipped over the low wall and waded in her shoes across the pool. She had bent down, gathered up handfuls of the small change thrown in by sentimental tourists, and tossed them in to the air so that they fell back splashing and sparkling; and then she had started to climb the fountain.

'Come back, you'll fall,' Clare had called to her; the marble had been wet and slippery.

'Not I,' she cried, 'I'm going to ride the horses.' And she had; she had climbed right up and sat side-saddle on one of the great white horses, laughing in the lamp light, her hair spilling out around her face, looking beautiful and untamed.

'Come up too. I love and adore you.'

Clare had been embarrassed, self-conscious in her laughter while Julia was free in hers. She had stood on the coping at the edge of the water and reached out, but she had not dared jump in.

'You need a broomstick, not a horse,' she had called.

'I can fly without,' Julia had shouted and stood up, balancing on the back of the prancing stallion, laughing, apparently ready to take to the air.

But as soon as she noticed that Clare was really frightened she had come down swiftly, paddled back across the water and, dripping and laughing, given Clare an enormous hug.

'It's true, I'm a witch,' she said, 'and not always a good one, but there is nothing to be scared of. Sleep with me, my gorgeous child, and I will teach you how to fly.'

Clare had never done so; she had put herself to a stubborn resistance that made a nonsense of the way they kissed, not because she did not want to but because she did not dare.

She told Ben and Anni now, 'I find it hard to describe how much I wanted her, and how much it frightened me. You might not guess from all this, but she was quite a bit older than I was. I felt she had enormous power, but she put risk and danger and beauty all together and I couldn't cope with that. Now I've remembered about my parents I sort of know why, but then I just fled.'

Again she paused.

'And . . . ?' said Ben.

'I came back to England. I felt defeated and I thought I did not want any of that stuff; I wanted to be safe. I was so frightened by myself, and then I met David and I thought he could do that, could make me safe. David and all the things that went with him; the money and the lifestyle and the authority that he had. I thought he would teach me how to behave properly so that the enormous magical power I knew I could have, like Julia, would go away and leave me alone. I thought he would discipline me.

'It worked, it almost worked. I didn't like it, but I was determined to make it work. I clung to him like a drowning person. He was only too willing to take it on. He wouldn't even let me be frightened of thunder.'

She tried to laugh. But Ben and Anni would not laugh with her.

'It wasn't all his fault, you know; I made him act the way that he did, I projected a lot of that on to him.'

'He was a bastard,' said Anni. 'When I first heard about the accident I wanted to send you a letter of congratulation so you'd know how delighted I was that you had finally got a good dose of common sense and pushed him off that mountain. But go on anyway.'

'I got more and more unhappy, and more and more convinced that it was all my fault. Less and less able to do anything. Then we went to Zimbabwe and everything was different. I just mean different. I didn't know how to behave properly, I didn't feel good there, all the stories I had known broke down and didn't make any sense. I felt as though I was cracking up. And I found I was scared of him, of David, as well as of myself and everything else. Then we went to Peggy's and I met Joyful and she was like Julia. I mean . . . I don't mean I fell in love with her, because it did not occur to me, but she was in touch with all that magic. Deeply in touch with it, and willing to share it. And I discovered that I needed it, I needed it dreadfully, and that was scary too.

'Joyful told me about chameleons and how they are deep magic; taboo and dangerous, but also, like all magic things, messengers from the gods. Then . . . so . . . so when David ran the chameleon over, just squashed it and said, 'it's only a lizard,' I thought he would kill everything that was magic, everything in me that was wild and untamed. And I knew I didn't have the strength to resist him. I just wanted him to be dead. I wanted to kill him before he killed me.'

'Oh Clare,' said Ben, with so much tenderness that the tears sprang to her eyes.

'But did you kill him? Did you push him?' Anni asked. 'There you were, you've told us, on the side of a crevasse, a bottomless pit, in a thick fog and with thunder in the air. You were frightened and angry. You wanted him to be dead. Did you push him?'

She asked, quite calmly and neutrally, 'Did you kill David?'

Clare took a deep breath. She saw the jewel-red beetle; she heard the thunder; the voices; she saw the bottomless hole in the mountain that had opened up to greet them. She heard the voices; the voice of Chirikudzi, the mermaid spirit, who sang for David and did not sing for her; she heard the darker voices of the ancestors, who were not and could never be her ancestors, growling in defence of their mountain; she heard the low hoarse mutters of the *banditos armados*, the MNR guerrillas. She looked at The

Hand. Without looking at Anni and without speaking, she pushed her cuff up slowly, up above the join, where her own skin met the plastic sheath that contained the machinery they chose to call her hand. She looked at it with great attention and care.

She hated The Hand, but she wore it because it silenced all the voices; because it was sensible and orderly and grown-up, but while she wore it she would never know whether she had killed David – Felicity had been horribly right to link the two together. She pressed the off-button, opened the small trap door and removed the batteries, which she dropped into the pocket of her jacket. And then pushing her sleeve up still further she unclipped the strap buckle. She took The Hand off.

It hurt to take it off. The concave ball at the top of The Hand was carefully made to fit the convex ball at the bottom of her arm, to fit and to fit tight. She used her left fingers to break the vacuum, and it made an odd sucking sound as though The Hand and her arm did not want to be separated, as though she were forcing their kissing lips apart. No one except hospital staff had ever seen her perform this somehow obscene task, but Ben had shown her his nipple-ring.

She knew that he and Anni were both watching her, and she could not expect them to do otherwise, but she did not look at them. The amputation wound was healed now, though still pink and puckered; it got very little air and no sunshine. The scars from the surgery were quite neat; they ran as small raised seams, like the seams of the lisle stockings she and Anni had had to wear at school, around and under the stump. It was not particularly ugly, it simply marked the beginning of an absence.

She put The Hand down beside her, balanced on the fingers, leaning against a stone and she looked at the place where her own hand had been. After she had dreamed of herself with only one hand last night she had woken chilled and startled. She had flexed her right fingers which were dust and ashes somewhere in southern Africa, but she could feel them move, fainter than the physically present left hand's ones, but definitely there, a shadow against the light window, a soft distant sensation. If she had killed David she had done it with the hand that was no longer there. Perhaps she had tried to cut it off herself. They had never known, never been

289

able to understand what had caused the injuries. But if she had tried she had failed. She had had to leave that final punishment to a doctor.

'I told Joseph,' she said, almost dreamily, 'I told Joseph that I did not want to leave my hand in Zimbabwe, but they had already thrown it out. The me that is here didn't kill David, but that hand may well have done. Either way, it has nothing to do with me now.'

'Clare,' said Anni, and now she spoke sternly, with great severity. As Joseph had done, she summoned Clare back from the dark place where the voices deluded her, even though the voices were now her own.

'Clare, did you kill David?'

She could hear Anni's voice, bright and golden, calling her not downwards now but upwards, up towards a place of light. The voices were silenced by Anni's clear calling which was not the darkness but the light. She looked up and saw the eagles still floating above Cranach Head. She had reached the point of knowledge and there was no need to search further. She withdrew her gaze from the birds and looked straight into Anni's concerned clear grey eyes and she said,

'I don't know, I can't remember.'

Then the awfulness of that struck her and she started to cry.

'I don't know,' she whispered, almost to herself, 'I don't know, I don't remember and I will have to live all my life not knowing, not knowing if I am the person who killed a man she was supposed to love because he failed to keep her safe. I wanted him to keep me safe; I wanted to be safe. I thought that if I loved him he would keep me safe. I thought that if I did everything he told me to he could keep me safe, and he couldn't. He wasn't a bastard, he wasn't. I made him into one because I was so frightened. I let him hurt me and maim me and limit me. I wanted to be an amputee. I loved him against the odds although he was not good for me and didn't really give a shit about me, but I would not let him say that. Felicity was right, there isn't any safety. My parents laughed when they exploded and they never thought of me. Now there is no safety anywhere, not even the safety of knowing who I am. I don't know if I killed him. I don't know how he died, and I never will.

'I can't remember. I do not know.'

There was a pause in the darkness, an audible silence, almost unendurable, between the moment when her mother applied the flame to the touchpaper and the moment when a firework came alive. The pause was built into the design and was deliberate: it was there simply to give the person with the taper a chance to run away; so much beauty was very dangerous, it could burn you up.

Was it then that she learned that beauty and danger walk hand in hand and cannot be separated? For anyone who loves their life will lose it, but anyone who is willing to throw it away will gain and keep it. Nothing will come of nothing. You have to go out and risk it all. She had refused to do so; she had wanted to stay in the place of safety which is death.

Her parents' best display was their last, on a crisp November evening when you could smell the coming frost hunting the swallows southwards. She had knelt on the broad window seat quivering with anticipation. Her mother had advanced into the middle of the lawn and lit the fuse. She had retreated, stood beside her husband, Clare's father, against the laboratory wall. When the pause ended all heaven broke loose: there were stars, and flames, new galaxies exploding into brightness; the window shattered, cold glass diamonds joining the hot fire ones. In a flash of sulphur lightning she had seen them embrace, and explode.

She had watched her parents explode in a cloud of stars. But she had also seen their fiery embrace, their wild smiles. The firework display had been worth the risk, but she had refused to see that. She had refused to accept what they had given her: the knowledge that risk must be desired, hunted, feared, embraced. She had refused to learn that beauty and danger walk hand in hand and cannot be separated. These were her ancestral spirits; these were the ancestors to whose voices she must listen if she wanted to be whole and well.

Now she would have to learn it here; here beyond the wild joy, here in the dark place. She would have to walk with dignity through her life and never know if she had killed her lover. She would have to live with that risk at dawn and at dusk; through every long day and in the darkness of her dreams at night. She would have to learn to live and love, while never knowing if she was dangerous to the beloved, if she was that sort of woman. It was terrifying.

She turned to Anni with her terror and found the strong arms of the virgin waiting for her. It was the Feast of the Assumption, the celebration of the hope of glory. Anni held her, held her tightly and murmured to her.

Anni told her that faith was a radical act because we choose what we will believe – the most basic axioms of mathematics, even say the commutative law of addition are acts of faith: they are no more provable than the existence of God – although you can adduce more positive examples perhaps, but numbers, like God, are infinite. So there is choice – there is nothing proven, and where there is choice there is obligation to choose, so that faith is a radical act, because it is an act of choosing.

Anni told her that it was definitely proven that infinities come in an infinite number of sizes. Anni told her that it is only on the boundaries of order and chaos that beauty can be created. Chaos is left to God and order to the world; it is on the boundary, where the two meet, that beauty happens and that is why God had to create *something*.

Clare wept and was comforted; and the comfort made her weep more.

Ben stood up suddenly and said, 'Enough.'

She looked up from the safe haven of Anni's arms and knew what he meant. It surprised her. When she started to speak there was a heavy inflexion of irony, but it died away before she had finished the first sentence.

'I confess to Almighty God, to Blessed Mary Ever-Virgin, to all the angels and saints and to you, Father, that I have sinned through my fault, my own fault, my own most grievous fault, in my thoughts and in my words, in what I have done and in what I left undone . . .

. . . for these and all my other sins which I cannot now remember, I am truly sorry, earnestly repent and ask of you advice, penance and absolution.'

Ben was still standing up: he raised his right hand and very slowly made the sign of the cross. Without any irony whatsoever he said. 'May the passion of our Lord Jesus Christ, the prayers of the Blessed Virgin Mary and of all the saints, whatsoever good you have done, or evil you have endured, be unto you for the remission of sins, the means of Grace and the joy of everlasting life. And by the authority granted to me I absolve you of all your sins, in the name of the Father and of the Son and of the Holy Spirit.'

'Amen.'

There was a moment of silence.

'Penance,' said Anni, 'You're supposed to give her a penance.'

'Yes,' said Ben, but he stayed silent.

'Tell her to drive David's Jaguar.'

All three of them laughed. Ben said, 'That's quite a good idea.'

He turned to Clare, 'And for your penance you must drive David's car over a hundred miles an hour and enjoy it. And . . .' he took a deep breath, 'you must start to take photographs again.'

'I can't.'

'You can.'

'Ben,' said Anni, appalled.

'Shut up, Anni,' her interference gave Ben courage. 'For your penance,' he said authoritatively, 'you must go back to Zimbabwe and take photographs of your mountain.'

Anni's slightly shocked face amused Clare; Anni did not think she would dare.

'All right,' said Clare. 'Can Anni come with me?'

Ben and Clare shared a sly grin, but Clare had committed herself. She was still frightened, but she had committed herself.

Nearer than they would have expected, a rifle shot rang out. All three of them heard with the experienced ears they would rather not have had, the slight but unmistakable thump sound immediately after the explosion. It was the bullet burying itself securely in the body of the stag.

They all jumped up and started to climb out of their hollow, towards their left where the shot had come from. Clare felt free and light, the hills danced in the sunshine and the eagles still circled round the high peak.

'Bet she's crying,' she said.

'Mummy?' said Ben, 'No takers. Of course she is.'

'You've forgotten your hand,' Anni said and her voice sounded a little shaky. She stopped and turned to go back for it.

'No,' said Clare, 'I don't need it any more. Leave it.'

Anni paused and looked at her. Then she said, 'Don't do that, it's a waste. Give it to Alice if you don't want it. She'll be giving you her hearing aid. Felicity is scrupulously honest.'

'Did Alice take it? Yesterday?'

'Yes.'

'How do you know? Why didn't you say?'

'I didn't know yesterday. I only just worked it out this minute.'

Clare grinned and childishly tapped her forehead with her index finger. 'Loony,' she said affectionately, and scrambled down the slope to pick up The Hand.

When she rejoined Anni, Anni said, 'That's not the sign for "crazy" you know.'

'I'll have to learn.'

They walked briskly up the slope towards Ben who had turned and was waiting for them.

That night Clare dreamed. The Hand was gone from the drawer, was doubtless propped up beside Alice's bed, and the room was peaceful, but she dreamed.

She dreamed she was a tight rope walker. She climbed the rope ladder slowly, carefully adjusting to its wrigglings. It was hard to climb with only one hand, and she had to use the crook of her right elbow to keep herself from slipping outwards. The wooden slats muttered to her all the way up.

The rungs her right foot stood on said, 'If you are afraid of falling, you will fall.'

The rungs her left foot pressed said, 'If you believe you cannot fall, you will fall.'

Eventually she arrived on the little platform at the top. She stripped off her track suit and was revealed in all her sequinned glory. The spot-lights swooped, refracting coloured prisms off the great mirrored ball that hung in the centre of the Big Top. She looked out and down. The audience was made up of her family, of Joyful and Peggy and Julia and David; their upturned eyes sparkling brighter than her costume.

Then the spot-light pinned her, and she heard its mocking tones. It said, 'Probably, in the end, you will fall anyway.'

And, in her dream, she listened politely and knew it was true. Then she went out sparkling, flashing, and danced on the void. That was the challenge, the moment of hope, to dance as near the edge of destruction as was possible, to be willing to fall and still not fall. And the audience cheered, because it was beautiful and because they knew that this time she might indeed fall and because they knew that was precisely why it was beautiful, and she had made it beautiful.

It was a good dream.

CHRISTOPHER BURNS
IN THE HOUSES OF THE WEST

On the banks of the Nile as Tutankhamun's tomb is being excavated, an oddly disparate English trio forms: Clive Oxtaby, an Egyptologist whose unorthodox mysticism makes him widely distrusted; his sister Lucinda, a young war widow; and Raymond Murchison, a resolutely rational official of the Antiquities Service who falls under Lucinda's spell. Drawn into Clive's obsessive quest for a key to the ancients' Other World, Raymond finds the lines begin to blur between genuine and fake, fact and supposition, magic and trickery.

'Absorbing . . . A thought-provoking, many-layered, satisfying read'
Leslie Wilson in The Independent on Sunday

'Everyone who has felt the fascination of ancient Egypt will want to read this book; others, having read it, are likely to find they have discovered a new and compelling interest . . . An impressive novel which rises to an exciting and moving climax . . . original and memorable'
Allan Massie in The Scotsman

'Burns uses archaeological facts sparingly and accurately . . . it holds the attention to the end'
T G H James in the Times Literary Supplement

'Offers a precise and deliberately claustrophobic study in obsession and duplicity'
David Profumo in the Daily Telegraph

sceptre